A Friend of the Family

A Friend of the Family

LISA JEWELL

MICHAEL JOSEPH
an imprint of
PENGUIN BOOKS

MICHAEL JOSEPH

Published by the Penguin Group

Penguin Books Ltd, 80 Strand, London WC2R ORL, England

Penguin Putnam Inc., 375 Hudson Street, New York, New York 10014, USA

Penguin Books Australia Ltd, 250 Camberwell Road, Camberwell, Victoria 3124, Australia

Penguin Books Canada Ltd, 10 Alcorn Avenue, Toronto, Ontario, Canada M4V 3B2

Penguin Books India (P) Ltd, 11 Community Centre,
Panchsheel Park, New Delhi – 110 017, India

Penguin Books (NZ) Ltd, Cnr Rosedale and Airborne Roads,
Albany, Auckland, New Zealand

Penguin Books (South Africa) (Pty) Ltd, 24 Sturdee Avenue,
Rosebank 2196, South Africa

Penguin Books Ltd, Registered Offices: 80 Strand, London WC2R ORL, England

www.penguin.com

First published 2003

1

Set in 13.5/16pt Monotype Garamond
Typeset by Rowland Phototypesetting Ltd, Bury St Edmunds, Suffolk
Printed in Great Britain by Clays Ltd, St Ives plc

A CIP catalogue record for this book is available from the British Library

ISBN 0-718-14556-9

For my sisters, Sacha and Tanya –
the greatest gifts my parents ever gave me.

Acknowledgements

Thank you to the crack squad of two: Sarah Bailey, my friend and unpaid editor, who once again sacrificed her time and energy to the pursuit of getting me through the early stages of writing this book – but at least this time she got a decent lunch and a couple of pints of shandy out of it. And Judith Murdoch, my lovely, talented and ever-supportive agent, who not only worked all the early knots out of this book but bought me lunch too! I am eternally grateful and incredibly lucky to have you both.

Thanks also to all on the Block for being such an amazing support network, to all at Penguin for being the best publishers in the world and to Jascha for being my husband and the best friend a girl could ask for.

'Boys do not grow up gradually. They move forward in spurts like the hands of clocks in railway stations.'

Cyril Connolly, *Enemies of Promise*, 1938

Wednesday Night at the Beulah Tavern

Bernie slid the microphone on to its stand and took a bow, smiling as the small crowd in the Beulah Tavern whistled and cheered.

Roger leapt on to the stage and leant into the mike.

'Ladies and gentlemen, a warm and wondrous thank you to our star turn tonight – the very beautiful lady with the very big *lungs*! The talented, the supreme, the incomparable Miss Bernie London. She'll be here again next Wednesday to sing the old songs and to give us a bit more winter cheer. So don't miss it!'

Bernie grinned again and headed straight for the bar, where Roger already had a gin and lemon waiting for her. She pulled her Silk Cut Ultras from her handbag and leant back against the bar, releasing a little of the tightness from the strappy sandals around her swollen feet. Bernie had been singing at the Tavern for nearly three years now, ever since Roger had taken over the licence, ripped out the twirly carpets, the tatty tapestry upholstery and reproduction Turners and turned the Tavern into 'Crystal Palace's Most Exciting Music Venue'. It was, Bernie was perfectly able to admit to herself, nothing of the sort – it was just a nice local pub that happened to feature live music a few times a week, mainly Irish bands with names like The Ceilidhs or old rock-and-roll singers in threadbare drapes with wilting white quiffs. Bernie sang what she liked to call Lounge Songs: 'Cry Me A River', 'The Way You Look Tonight', 'I Say A Little Prayer', 'Whatever Lola Wants'.

Roger, now back behind the bar, lit her cigarette, gave her a wink through large round spectacles and then moved away to serve someone else. Bernie settled herself on a bar stool. She loved this part of the evening – the fifteen minutes after her set when she sat alone with her gin and lemon and a fag and was just Bernie, a middle-aged woman in a black spangly dress and cubic-zirconium earrings who could sing well enough to get paid for it. A big-boned, bosomy woman with great legs, a little bit heavy around the waist now but with the thick, corn-coloured hair and sharp cheekbones of an older Geraldine James. She loved these fleeting moments of solitude when she wasn't her husband's wife or her sons' mother. Bernie always had the feeling that if her life was ever going to change it would change now, during one of these brief windows of possibility in her otherwise structured existence. When she'd finished her drink and smoked another cigarette she'd call Gerry and he'd walk round to meet her, then they'd wander home hand in hand and her real life would begin again. Bernie loved her real life, but she'd miss these moments if they were ever denied her.

She bent down to rub at her tender, stockinged feet. She really wasn't used to wearing heels any more, even though she'd practically lived in them when she was younger. Now they were just for Wednesday nights and special occasions. As she straightened up, a figure at the far side of the pub caught her eye. A young man, all in black. A nice-looking man? Bernie couldn't tell from this distance. He was very pale and Bernie caught the glimmer of silver in his lobes. She was sure she'd seen him here last week, too, sitting at the same table.

He smiled at her, then, the self-conscious smile of someone unaccustomed to smiling. For some reason, Bernie found herself smiling back. Bernie didn't usually have much time for the sort of men who hit on her in pubs. But there was something about this guy, the set of his shoulders, the shape of his head, the way he moved. Something reassuring. He picked up his drink and wend his way around the tables to join her at the bar. Bernie's fingertips went immediately to her earlobe, twisting the little chunk of zirconium.

'Great voice,' he said, sliding his drink next to hers on to the bar.

Close up, the man revealed himself to be anywhere between twenty-five and forty. His mouth was thin, his eyes heavy-lidded, and his hair was a jet-black flat-top, the likes of which Bernie hadn't seen since the fifties. He was wearing a scuffed black leather jacket, tight black jeans and a thin grey T-shirt with some kind of wash-faded graphics on it. He had a faded cobweb tattoo across his neck, a skull-and-crossbones ring on his middle finger, a flashy buckle on his belt and a missing tooth that Bernie didn't notice until he smiled at her and said, 'How long've you been singing, then?'

'Longer than you've been alive,' she said with a laugh, exhaling and stubbing out her cigarette. Bernie sensed that she should have felt uncomfortable, but she really didn't. There was something about this young lad – something familiar, compelling almost – that made him seem like the sort of person her fifteen-minute breathers were meant for.

'You all right, Bernie?' said Roger, suddenly appearing, owl-like, at her side.

'Yeah,' she said lightly, 'fine.'

'Let me buy you another drink,' said the man.

Bernie looked at her watch. Gerry would be expecting her phone call around now. But then again, knowing Gerry, he was probably so wrapped up in the candelabra he was polishing that he wouldn't have noticed the time. 'Yeah,' she said, 'why not. I'll have a gin and lemon, please.'

She eyed up the man's profile as he waited for Roger to serve him. His cheeks were slightly pock-marked and Bernie suddenly saw him as the spotty, awkward adolescent he'd once been. The black leather and the tattoo and the dyed hair were just a costume. He was no hard man, she thought, just a little boy, like her boys, like *all* boys. Bernie felt the familiar maternal throb in her chest.

'Saw you here last week,' she said, accepting her drink, 'all on your own then, too, you were. What's the matter with you – got no mates?'

The man laughed and offered Bernie a cigarette. 'Nah,' he said, 'not round here, anyway.'

'Just moved to the area?'

'Yup.'

'Where from?'

'Round and about.' He stopped to light her cigarette and then looked her straight in the eye. 'What about you? You a local?'

She nodded, wanting to tell him that she lived just around the corner on Beulah Hill, but stopping herself.

'Alone?'

She laughed. 'Not quite. With Gerry, my husband.'

'Kids?'

'Yeah. Three boys.' She paused. 'It's funny. I never really wanted a girl. Always felt more comfortable around men.'

He nodded. 'What sort of age are they, then, your boys?'

'Well,' she began, 'Tony's, the eldest. He's thirty-four. Sean's the middle. He's just turned thirty. And then there's Ned – the baby, he's . . . what is he? Twenty-six, twenty-seven? What year is it?'

'2001.'

She counted off on her fingers. 'Twenty-seven next month.' She smiled with relief. It didn't feel right, not knowing how old your son was. But then it had been a long time since they'd celebrated his birthday together.

'Proud of them all?'

Bernie thought of her boys – her beautiful boys. Of course she was proud of them. It was all she could do to stop herself exploding all over the place with pride.

Tony was a successful business man, ran his own

greeting-card company that he'd set up from scratch in a room in his flat when he was twenty-one. He employed twenty people now and had a lovely house in Anerley. Well, it was more of a flat, really – he hadn't been able to afford a house after the divorce – but it was very nice, overlooking a park with off-street parking and video cameras all over the place. She was a bit worried about him right now. He didn't seem to have got back on track after the divorce. Bernie couldn't put her finger on what was wrong; he just didn't seem quite himself.

And then there was little Ned – not so little any more, over six foot tall and as thin as a reed. He was the brains of the family, went to university, got a first in history of art, even worked at Sotheby's for a while. But then he and Carly split up – Bernie gulped at the thought; it still felt like a death – and he'd run off to Australia with some girl he'd met in a sports bar in Leicester Square and they hadn't seen him in nearly three years. *Three years*. He was working at an Internet café in Sydney, apparently, wasting his degree. But he'd be back one day, she was sure of that, back home where he belonged. And he'd make something of himself then. He had so much potential, that boy, it was just *oozing* out of him.

And then there was Sean. The jewel in her filial crown. Not that she'd ever admit it to anyone other than herself, of course; mothers aren't allowed to have favourites. He'd been a bit of a worry there for a while, her Sean, a bit wild, a bit troublesome. Middle children always are, she supposed. He hadn't really stuck at anything, had a different girlfriend every five minutes, each one better-looking than the last (he was her best-looking child, it had to be said). But then he'd written this book, a couple of years ago. He hadn't told anyone he was writing it – well, not his family, anyway – and all of a sudden some publisher had written him out a cheque for £50,000 and the next thing she knew he was in all the papers and everyone was talking about him, and it was *her boy*. Her little Seany! She still couldn't quite believe it. His book – *Half a Man*, it was called – was about a boy whose twin brother dies in a car crash and how he goes mad, after, and starts killing people. She didn't know where Sean got his ideas from, she really didn't. It wasn't from her, that was for sure – she had no imagination whatsoever – and as for Gerry . . . It was a good book, though. He'd biked her over an advance copy one Tuesday morning and she'd taken the day off work and read it in one sitting. A bit too much drug-taking for her liking, and an over-liberal use of the 'c' word, but a good book. The hardback had sold, what was it, something like 8,000 copies and the paperback had come out in the summer and was still in the top twenty now, thirty weeks later. Sean was something of a celebrity these days and oh God, was Bernie proud. She couldn't quite believe what she'd done. She'd produced a bestselling novelist! From within her own body. And she was prouder than any woman had a right to be.

Bernie never had any grand ambitions for her boys, never expected them to go to university, to make anything more out of life than she and Gerry had managed. A nice house, a happy family, a few quid in the bank. All she'd ever wanted for her boys was that they be good boys. And, if she could blow her own trumpet for a moment, she'd done a bloody good job on them. They were fine, fine boys, her boys, each and every one of them. Of course every mother thinks her sons are perfect, but hers really were. She honestly couldn't fault them.

Bernie turned to the black-haired man and smiled. 'Proud as punch,' she said with a laugh and a wink, 'but what mother isn't?'

'So. Are you a *happy family*, then?'

'What sort of question is that?'

'A very interesting one.'

Bernie smiled. 'Yeah,' she said, 'we're a very happy family. We've been lucky. They're good boys, my boys – very good boys.'

They fell silent for a moment. 'And what about you?' she said. 'Have you got any kids?'

'Yeah,' he said. 'Well, sort of. I've got a boy. He'd be about sixteen by now, I guess.'

'Lost contact?'

He scratched the back of his neck. 'Yeah. Long time ago. The mother didn't want to have anything to do with me.'

Bernie gulped and laid a hand on the man's arm. 'You poor thing.'

'Yeah,' he said. 'Well, you end up paying for your mistakes in life one way or another, don't you?'

'What's his name?'

'Charlie.'

'Nice name.'

'D'you think? I hate it. Sometimes wonder if I'd recognize him now. You know? If I saw him on the street or something. My own son.'

They fell silent again.

'Look,' he said, picking up his drink and draining it, 'I don't want to get in your face or anything. I just really wanted to tell you how great your voice is. You're very talented.'

'Bless you,' said Bernie, 'that's very kind and I appreciate it. Will I see you next week?'

The man's face suddenly softened. 'Yeah,' he said, 'deffo. I'll be here. My name's Gervase, by the way.'

Bernie grinned at him. 'You don't look like a Gervase,' she said.

'No,' he said, 'I don't, do I? I sometimes think that I was never supposed to have been a Gervase. You know, in a parallel reality and all that. D'you know what I mean?'

Bernie smiled and nodded.

'Thanks for the chat, Bernie. See you next week, yeah?'

'Yeah,' smiled Bernie, 'see you next week.'

He nodded at her, and smiled his awkward smile, before forcing his hands into the tight pockets of his jeans and sauntering out of the pub and into the chill of the January night.

Gerry Gets Technical

From: Gerald London [SMTP: grays@graysantiques.co.uk]
Sent: Sat, 17 Mar 2001 14:01
To: Ned London [SMTP: nedlondon@hotmail.com]
Subject: Surprise for your mum

Hello Ned . . . How are you? I'm just using this computer at work. Deandra's showing me how so I hope I don't mess it up. I was going through some old stuff at home last week and found some letters me and your mum wrote to each other when we were dating. Turns out our first date was on 26th May 1961, forty years ago. I took her to the Ritz for a cocktail and then we went to the cinema at Piccadilly. It cost me a week's wages. Also turns out that 26th May lands on a Saturday this year so I was thinking that instead of just celebrating our wedding anniversary like we always do, maybe I'd do something a bit special that she won't be expecting. I'm going to have a party for her at the Ritz – and book us a few rooms so we can stay over. Once in a lifetime, you know. I've spoken to your brothers about it and they're both keen. Anyway – I know money's tight for you and I can help you out a bit, with a couple of hundred maybe. Tony and Sean said they'll cough up for the rest. Just bung it on your credit card and we'll sort it out at this end. Hopefully you'll stay for a while, too – your mum would be the happiest woman in south London! And Monica's more than welcome if she can afford the fare. I've booked you a double room so it seems a shame to waste it! Anyway, I'd better get off. Write back soon (or call me at work) and let me know if you can make it or not – it wouldn't be the same without you, though – you know that?

Love to Monica. And love to you.

Your dad X

Dear Mon

Dear Mon,

By the time you get this letter I will be on a plane and on my way back to England. I'm really sorry to bugger off like this without saying goodbye properly, but, as you know, the past few weeks have been quite stressful for me and the more stressful things got the more we seemed to be arguing. Losing my job was just the last straw and I can't see any reason to be here any more. I haven't made the life for myself over here I was hoping for. I've just got stuck in a rut doing crap jobs and hanging out with the same people and as time goes by I miss my life back at home more and more. I miss my mum and dad. I miss my brothers. I miss just sitting on the sofa with Sean watching *The Simpsons* and I miss all my old friends. So much has happened since I've been here with you – Sean's had a book published, Tony's got divorced, and now Mum and Dad are having a big anniversary party back home. I don't want to miss it and I don't want to be away from my family any more. I miss England, too. I miss the weather and the TV and the people. I know I should have waited till you got home, talked to you face to face, but I've tried that before and you know how things always turn out – you go into mental meltdown, I try to make you feel better, we end up staying together.

Things started off so great for you and me, Mon. Meeting you was one of the most exciting things that ever happened to me and coming to Oz with you was the greatest adventure of my life, but it's over now. Finished. I've never really managed to make you happy, Monica – you know that and I know that. I think you'll agree with me when I say that our relationship really ended ages ago. I don't know what's kept us together for so long. I think it might be a combination of fear and habit. You were such a strong person when I first met you, Monica, but you've let me make you weak. I can't hold you up any more. You've got so much going for you – you're so funny and cool and clever. It's only your own insecurities that are holding you back – and me. You can make a go of things in Oz, I know you can. You've just got to get out of your shell and into the world, become the person I met in Leicester Square all those years ago.

I love you, Mon, I really do. You're one of the most amazing people I've ever known, but it's time for me to go home and it's time for you to get on with your life without me. I wish you happiness and success. I'll think of you for ever, Mon. Good luck.

Ned XX

PS: Enc: $250 for the next month's rent. I've also left you my football and my PlayStation, and the Fatboy Slim tickets are in my top left-hand drawer. There's some hash in the coffee jar next to the phone. I've sold my car to Spencer. And if you find my Titleist golfballs you can have them.

Unbridled Parental Joy at
Prodigal Homecoming

It was a perfectly miserable April morning when Ned finally came home. The city cowered glumly under a thick grey blanket of cloud and the air smelt of damp brickwork and diesel.

London, thought Ned, staring at the back end of a used-car depot through the misted-up window of a black cab. Look at it. Just look at it.

It's so beautiful . . .

The cab sped seamlessly through the empty streets of south London, stopping pointlessly at deserted traffic lights, gliding across roundabouts. Ned smiled as the Crystal Palace mast hove into view – a symbol of homecoming since the day he was born.

A few eerie, solitary figures moved through the mist that hung over Brockwell Park; early-morning dog-walkers and out-patients from the Marsden. A man in a red waterproof jacket practised t'ai chi under a just-budding horse-chestnut tree. Down Norwood Road, past West Norwood Cemetery and up on to Beulah Hill. And there it was: number 114. A two-storey Georgian villa, a bit like a child's drawing of a house. Steps up to a greying stone portico, large, stripped-oak front door, sash windows on either side. It was looking tattier than ever. Flaps of cream stucco peeled from the walls, last year's autumnal fall was still heaped in mulchy piles up against the front wall and rivulets of green mould streaked the paintwork.

The old bubble car that Tony had bought with his first pay-cheque when he was seventeen sat half-shrouded under a sun-bleached tarpaulin on the front lawn. In front of the bubble car sat Sean's Vespa, once the apple of his eye and the centre of his universe, now a mildewed and pitiful-looking creature, slouched defeatedly against an old set of Formica-topped drawers. Edwardian, Victorian and Georgian chimney stacks sat in a kind of Stonehenge arrangement on the other side, and between the detritus all manner of robust-looking weeds had taken root.

Ned had once brought a friend home from university who lived in the area too. He'd looked rather uncertain as Ned ascended the front steps, jangling his door keys. 'You live here?' he'd said. 'Uh-huh,' Ned had said. 'Shit – I always thought this place was a squat.' Which was, Ned could see with his newfound objectivity, exactly what it looked like.

He slung his rucksack over his shoulder and crept quietly up the path, kicking a sheet of old newspaper out of the way as he walked. His key in the lock sounded familiar, like it had been just hours since he'd last heard the sound. Even after all this time he still had the knack, turning the key at just the right angle and with just enough of a flick of the wrist, and then the front door swung slowly open.

Mayhem. Total and utter mayhem. He smiled wryly to himself and sidestepped a large stuffed rabbit, approximately the size of a Rottweiler, which for some strange reason was wearing Tony's Jim'll Fix It badge and had a packet of rolling tobacco on its lap. Walking into the Londons' house from the grey street outside was like leaping from monochrome to vivid Technicolor. The bleak exterior of the house masked an interior that made the word 'eclectic' seem a little puny in its powers of description.

Bernie and Gerry had a very *laissez-faire* attitude to interiors and made no effort whatsoever to exert any kind of control over their possessions. It wasn't that they had no taste. There were flashes of class, style and downright *Elle Decoration* in places. Gerry was an antique-silver dealer with a long-established stand at Grays in South Molton Street, and Bernie was a jewellery buyer for Alders in Clapham Junction. They knew nice stuff when they saw it. The problem was that they also managed to turn a blind eye to some truly grim stuff. Like the cut-crystal vase with a small ceramic cat sitting on the rim, a Christmas gift from Tony's ex-parents-in-law. It had pride of place on the mantelpiece, even though Bernie had hated it on sight and even though there was zero possibility of said ex-parents-in-law ever setting foot in their home again. Bernie had simply forgotten that she hated it. Ditto the carpet, which had been in the house when they'd bought it, thirty years ago, and was of the classic British 'swirl and square' design in violent hues of mustard and baby poo. The fireplace was still surrounded by the 'Brick-alike' false brickwork they'd put in when it was 'modern', in the seventies, and above it hung a rather nice late-Edwardian mirror that had fallen from its hook years earlier causing the glass to snap clean in two. Other people would have wailed about seven years' bad luck and rushed it to the mirror emergency ward to be fixed. Bernie and Gerry had simply tutted, sighed and re-hung it, and the fractured reflection it gave of the living room became yet another aspect of their home that you just got used to.

But what really set Ned's parents' house apart from other ill-furnished residences was the junk. Not just family detritus that had been hanging around waiting for a trip to Oxfam. Real, actual junk. Old chests of drawers, broken chairs, shop mannequins, boxes of rusting kitchen utensils, old Christmas cards, disembodied doll-parts, unidentifiable bits of oily machinery, mildewed curtains. And there were things that were just *in the wrong place*. A plastic swing-bin in the hallway. A pushchair in the living room. A shower curtain separating the downstairs toilet from the kitchen. A proper front door, replete with letterbox, knob and the number 15, hanging between the front and back rooms. A manky old hobby-horse with matted hair and a drawn-on moustache stood sentinel at the foot of the stairs.

Gerry was a skip-hound. He could not pass a skip without having a little rummage and coming away with at least one small trophy, be that an old telephone or a piece of skirting board. And Bernie was just as bad, bringing home whimsical odds and ends from the display storeroom at Alders, things that were going to get thrown away otherwise. She felt sad, she said, thinking that for a few weeks these bits of sculpted polystyrene and plywood had been spotlit and dazzling, enticing customers into the store, and were then discarded like pubescent child stars.

Ned walked from room to room for a while, absorbing the smells – French polish, tired carpeting, dog hair – and taking in the scenery – the junk, the cardboard boxes, the piles of magazines and abandoned embroidery – and thought to himself, This is me, all this clashing and clutter, this hoarding and piling. This is what made me and this is where I belong. And this was why he hadn't phoned ahead, why he hadn't told anyone he was coming home. Because he'd wanted to find home exactly as he'd left it three years ago and not as some fussed-over, tidied-up, bunting-festooned facsimile stuffed with aunts and uncles and neighbours and chicken-paste sandwiches and pork pies cut into quarters. Because he'd wanted to smell bed on his dad and see last night's dinner plates piled up in the kitchen.

He heard a scuffling, scrabbling noise coming from the other end of the hallway.

'Goldie!'

An ancient, threadbare golden retriever put his nose to the air, turned and made his way slowly but enthusiastically towards Ned, who dropped to his knees to greet him. Goldie was fifteen years old and looked like he too might have been found on a skip. He was wearing a scuffed Elizabethan collar; and just above his left eye was a shaved patch, zipped together with black plastic stitches, indicating yet another mishap. His eyes were thick and half-blind with cataracts. And he was opening and closing his mouth in an approximation of the bark he would never again be able to emit since a laryngectomy had left him mute four years ago. To compensate for his lack of vocal communication, he was wagging his tail so hard that he was almost back to front and his lips were stretched back into something that Ned had always sworn was a smile.

'Ooh yes, ooooh yes. Goldie boy, I'm home – I'm home!' Ned grabbed the ruff of fur that poked out from under the collar and scratched him good and hard, trying politely to ignore the fact that dear old Goldie hummed to high heaven.

He took off his boots and tiptoed quietly up the stairs, his socked feet instinctively missing the creaky bits and the ever-dangerous 'seventh step', which had remained unfixed since Gerry fell through it years ago when chasing Tony upstairs to give him a hiding.

He stopped at the top of the stairs to look at all the old framed photographs on the landing walls, yellowed and pinkish with age and sun. Ned, Tony and Sean on the beach at Margate, Bernie in a straw hat, Sean on a carousel at the local fair, Tony and Ned sitting on a step in nylon shorts with sunburnt noses, the three of them in their first Holy Communion outfits – snugly fitting white shorts, starchy white shirts and bow-ties. The family likeness was uncanny. All three of them with the same bog-standard brown hair, triangular noses, determined chins, blue eyes and sticky-outy ears. Ned, skinny like his dad; Tony and Sean, slightly sturdier like their mum. Ned smiled at the images, so much a part of him, and made his way to the end of the landing, to his parents' bedroom.

His parents' bedroom was, in some ways, the hub of the house. The bed was where they all used to congregate on weekend mornings, watching children's television and eating their cereal while Mum and Dad went through the papers and drank leaf tea that brewed in a pot on the bedside table.

The door was open – there was no such thing as a closed door in the Londons' house – and the sound of Bernie's snoring was now almost deafening. He pushed the door slowly and peaked around it to have a look at them. Their bed was a huge lace-festooned extravaganza of a thing that Bernie had bought from Biba in the seventies. It was four-poster and canopied with bits of twirly wrought iron all over the place. Bernie had attached things to the lace over the years – silk flowers, feathers, rosettes, tiny wire birds. Underneath this ornate marquee of a bed lay his parents. Ned felt a lump in his throat when he looked at them. His father was curled up on his side with his hands tucked under his cheek, like a small child. His head was the same shape as a rugby ball, covered from chin to crown in snowy-white, close-cropped hair with a couple of ruddy bare patches where his cheekbones were. His glasses and a Patrick O'Brian novel sat on his bedside table.

Ned's mother lay flat on her back, her ropey, honey-coloured hair spread out around her, her green polyester nightie rising and falling with each voluminous snore, a Virgin Atlantic eye-mask attached to her head with black elastic and her unlined cheeks gleaming with night-cream. Her glasses and a Maya Angelou book sat on her bedside table.

'Mum, Dad,' he whispered, loudly.

Dad twitched but remained firmly asleep.

'Mum, Dad, it's me. Wake up,' he whispered a bit louder, and approached the bed on tiptoe.

Mum grunted and turned on to her side and Dad twitched again.

Ned prodded his father, who woke up, dramatically and suddenly, opened his eyes, stared straight at Ned, muttered something incomprehensible and then turned over on to his other side and farted.

Ned sighed and decided to try again later. He headed towards his bedroom.

His was the only one of the boys' rooms that hadn't been overrun by general junk overflow. Because he'd never moved out. Even when he'd left three years ago, he hadn't actually been *leaving home*. He'd had every intention of being back within six months. He was aware that some might find it strange that at his age he would willingly choose to live in his parental home. But why shouldn't he? It was a great house, in a great location just twenty minutes on the 68 Express to the centre of town, his parents were the coolest parents in existence and he loved it here. Why fork out rent for some shitty flatshare or be lumbered with a ball-breaking mortgage?

No – he was giving himself until he was thirty before he even began to think about moving out.

He pushed open his bedroom door, his heart full of anticipation and warmth. He turned slightly to locate the light switch, flicked it downwards and then yelled out at the top of his voice when a man suddenly sat bolt upright in his bed. A very pale man with dyed black hair cut into an improbably geometric flat-top, wearing a selection of earrings and with a tattoo of a cobweb across his neck.

'Jesus Fucking *Christ*,' said Ned, clasping his heart with his hand.

'Urgh?' said the man in the bed.

'Jesus Fucking *Christ* – who the fuck are you?'

The man squinted at Ned for a moment, one hand reaching across to an ashtray on the bedside table for a half-smoked fag butt. He put it to his lips, lit it with a Zippo, inhaled and then clicked his fingers and smiled. 'Ned?' he said. His voice was deep and gravelly.

'Uh-huh,' said Ned, still stretched back against the bedroom door, his eyebrows somewhere near his hairline.

The man in the bed exhaled and then broke into a painful, hacking smoker's cough. He rested the fag back in the ashtray and pulled himself from the bed, still coughing. He was wearing black underpants and was very pale and unbelievably lean – solid muscle with just a hint of flesh stretched over the top, comparable, Ned thought, to the physique of a greyhound. There were more tattoos. A Confederate flag on his forearm, a line drawing of Marilyn on his upper arm and the words 'Live Fast Die Young' across his hairless chest.

'I've heard a lot about you.' He took Ned's limp hand and shook it. 'I'm Gervase,' he said and then wandered back to the bed and his smouldering cigarette. He started hacking even harder, then, producing all sorts of vivid sound-effects through his nostrils and throat.

'Yeah, but — who *are* you?'

'Didn't Bernie tell you?'

Ned didn't like the way he said 'Bernie' with so much familiarity. He shook his head numbly.

'I'm the lodger.'

'Lodger?'

'Yeah — you know — me pay money, me get room.'

'Yeah, but — this is *my* room.'

'That, Ned,' said Gervase, stubbing out his cigarette and pulling a fresh one from a packet of Chesterfields, 'is debatable.' And then he wandered towards the wash-basin in the corner of the bedroom, leant down over it and in one practised action hawked up the contents of his lungs.

Lose Weight Now – Ask Me How

It was the usual scenario: Millie, strong thighs clamped around a white stallion, thick chestnut hair flowing, never-ending beach, foamy waves crashing against the shore. Tony, slim, in white linen, lying in a hammock, watching her. There might have been a bird of some kind, a blue bird. He wasn't sure.

She dismounted her horse and approached, a half-smile playing on her lips, one eyebrow slightly cocked. There was sand dusted across her cheek. It glittered like ground diamonds. He reached out to brush it away and as he reached, she grabbed his wrist and slapped him, hard, across the face. And then, with the same hand she'd used to hit him, she delved into his trousers and held him. And it felt like he was being held by her throat, her warm, red throat. He couldn't explain it any other way. Her breath was on his cheek, her eyes were roaming his face, her hot hand throat-like on him, up and down. She leant in to his ear and as she moved him up and down she whispered, 'You are a god, Anthony. You are a *god*.'

And then he woke up. Just as he was about to come. Every night. Every fucking night. He wasn't sure

24

whether it was frustrating or pleasurable, hell or bliss, but at least he didn't make a mess on his sheets.

He pulled himself heavily from his bed and gave his body the customary mirror appraisal. A couple of years ago he'd look in the mirror and see a slightly stocky man with a burgeoning belly and ever so slightly budding breasts, a thirtysomething man who looked like he'd had a few curries in his time, the odd pint of lager, balanced out by sessions at the gym and the occasional game of football. What looked back at him now was a spherical, snowy-white blob with a belly large enough to house a five-year-old child and sad, slightly pendulous breasts that were bigger than Ness's (yes – she'd measured them).

He'd given up smoking a year ago and all he'd done since was eat. Going out with Ness didn't help. Ness was a *bon viveur*, a gourmand, a complete fucking pig. He'd never met a woman who ate as much as she managed to pack away. The bugger of it was that she had a fast metabolism and managed to stay rake thin, while Tony had the metabolism of a chronically depressed slug and now he was fat. Tony sighed, turned his back on the awful truth that was his thirty-four-year-old body and started getting ready for work.

He thought of Millie again as he showered. He thought of Millie pretty much all the time at the moment. But stranger than just thinking about her was that he imagined her *watching* him. Everything he did, everything he said, he envisaged Millie floating in a corner of the room, judging him, evaluating him, *rating* him. At home, in the office, in the car, she was there. If he did something clumsy, he'd blush. If he did something cool, he would puff up with pride. He held his stomach in when he was naked, he only sang songs he knew the words to in the shower, he didn't pick his nose, he didn't even fart when he was on his own these days. Well, certainly not loudly, anyway.

He'd only met her once, a week ago, in a bar on Charlotte Street. She'd arrived just as he and Ness were leaving. They'd met for less than five minutes. She was with her boyfriend. A nice bloke, but not good enough for her – she was way out of his league. He was a boy. She was a *woman*.

Tony had never really been a detail person when it came to women. He could never remember things like eye colour (Millie's were olive green, with gold bits in), or noticed wedding rings (Millie wore silver rings on three fingers of her right hand, none on her left). And he could never find words to describe things like hair (Millie had brown hair that was made up of about a hundred different shades of honey, mahogany, chestnut and red. It was thick and blunt and she grabbed it in her fist while she talked, as if she was showing it who was boss), or clothing (Millie wore a tight red sleeveless vest with low-slung jeans, half a centimetre of tanned belly showing). Her voice was throaty and coarse, she had laughter lines, her fingernails were cut short and square. Her skin was the sort of colour that suggested some kind of watered-down exotic ancestry; Latin American, perhaps, or Middle Eastern.

She held a Marlboro Light in the same hand as a bottle of Stella and she laughed like he'd never seen a woman laugh before. Big white teeth, three fillings, the back of her throat visible, pink and glossy in the overhead light.

Camilla, that was her actual name. 'Nobody calls me *Camilla*,' she'd said when her boyfriend introduced her. 'Makes me sound like I own a poncey handbag shop in Chelsea, or something. Call me Millie.'

Millie. Millie Millie Millie. *Millie.*

Tony's hand had subconsciously found its way to his crotch. He snatched it away impatiently. He didn't have time for a wank. He was going to be late. He got out of the shower, dried off and headed for his wardrobe, leafing sadly through all the clothes he was now unable to wear. Shirts that Tony had bought for their capaciousness years earlier, shirts he used to wear untucked and casual, now strained across his belly. And as his expanding girth forced his clothes to expand horizontally, so they diminished vertically so now all his trousers exposed at least a centimetre of sock.

Call me Millie. Millie Millie Millie.

She'd smiled at him as they left. It wasn't like a 'Thank God they're leaving now we can get back to our cosy evening' smile. It was a 'See you again soon, I hope' smile. It was a 'You interest me' smile. It was a smile that promised something, something substantial.

He'd had the foresight to make a plan. At the last minute, just as they were backing out of the door, he invited Millie and her boyfriend to his birthday dinner the following weekend. They said yes. It wasn't ideal. The boyfriend was a problem. So was that fact that Tony was fat and past his prime. But both these things were surmountable. The boyfriend could be dumped. Tony could lose weight. This was a long-term thing. As long as he had an opportunity to see her again, everything else would fall into place eventually. He knew it.

Tony hadn't really given much thought to where Ness fitted into his 'Millie' plans. In the short term it was probably quite good to have a girlfriend; it gave him the Women's Secret Seal of Approval. Having a girlfriend, especially a fairly cool one like Ness, said: 'I am not a sad, fat divorcee on my way to TV-dinner hell and an early heart attack. I am a guy who can function in a normal healthy relationship, who has regular sex and who women like to be with. I am Anthony London, successful businessman with healthy erectile function and fantastic interpersonal skills. I am good husband material on a stick.'

He dressed, breakfasted and did something to his hair with something called 'thickening serum', which appeared to do nothing of the sort, and then grabbed his briefcase and his laptop and left the flat. What a miserable day – so damp and overcast it felt like someone had thrown a tarpaulin over the world while he was asleep. He crossed the road towards his car, a bright-red MX5. A girl's car. He'd wanted an old Mercedes or Porsche – you could get something quite sexy with the six grand he'd had to spend – but for some reason he'd let Ness talk him into buying this thing. Power steering, she'd said. Good heating. Easy to convert. *Reliable.* And she was right. There was nothing wrong with it as such; it just wasn't very *him.* And to be quite honest, it was a bit of a squeeze – it was a Japanese car, designed for *small* Japanese people who ate seaweed, not hefty great English blokes who drank Guinness.

He stopped to pick something off his windscreen – a small green card.

Lose Weight Now! We're looking for 100
overweight people in this area.
Please call Wendy on 07978 245542.

He sighed, tossed it into the gutter and lowered himself into his tiny car, trying to ignore the likeness of the sensation to that of stuffing a duvet into a drawer, and headed for the office.

Fifteen minutes later he was on Clapham Pavement. Sidestepping a gaggle of scary schoolgirls in blue uni-forms as he got out of his car, he nearly collided with a laminated board hinged on to a metal stand, which most certainly had not been there yesterday.

For Millie's benefit, he turned to glare icily at the errant piece of street furniture and was confronted by a photograph of a very fat man in a voluminous T-shirt with at least twelve chins:

Overweight? Like to lose lbs? Lose weight fast the natural way.
First lesson free.

What? thought Tony. What is going on? Is there some kind of *conspiracy* at work here?

Bryan lost 31 lbs in just eight weeks.

Tony followed the wording to another photo of 'Bryan', this time wearing lurid floral surf-shorts, wading through the sea and proudly flexing his quads. No way, thought Tony, looking from one picture to the other. There is no way that that is the same bloke. He looked about ten years younger, for a start. But it *was* Bryan, he thought, looking closer, it really was. Bloody hell, he looked good. Tony passed his hand absent-mindedly across his belly and tried to visualize the taut muscles buried somewhere underneath the wobbly stuff.

Please take a leaflet.

Tony glanced around briefly to make sure no one was looking, grabbed a leaflet and jammed it into his coat pocket. Then he started walking, extra fast, for some reason, towards his office.

Sean's Older Woman

Sean was woken up at ten-thirty by the fat cat suddenly landing on the bed in the midst of some kind of mad-bastard attack, rolling around on his back and kicking himself in the chin with his back paws.

'Buffoon,' said Sean, rubbing his face into his hands. 'You're a buffoon of a cat.' Not his cat, though. Her cat. His Older Woman. Her flat, too.

He'd met her two months ago in a restaurant in Covent Garden, his older woman. He'd been having lunch with his agent and she'd been having lunch on her own. She was eating a big bowlful of rocket, which she'd forced haphazardly into her mouth with a fork while holding a newspaper in the other hand – the first time he set eyes on her she had rocket hanging from her lip and a splash of vinegar on her chin and was trying to shovel the stray fronds of greenery into her perfect mouth with a finger. He liked the fact that she shovelled. He liked the fact that she ate lunch on her own. And he liked the fact that every time he looked at her he felt like he was staring straight in the eye of his future.

She was older than his usual type. He'd imagined her to be his age, maybe a bit older. He'd been surprised when he found out that she was six years older than him. His last girlfriend had been twenty-two. The one before that, twenty. The oldest woman he'd ever been out with before her had been twenty-eight. He usually went for blondes. This woman was brunette. He usually went for conventional dressers. She was slightly bohemian in a vintage blouse and hoop earrings.

His agent had noticed that his mind wasn't on their conversation. 'What's up?' he'd said, looking beyond Sean to whatever it was that had been distracting him. And then he'd seen her and looked knowingly at Sean. 'Aha,' he'd said, 'I see. Why don't you send her over a glass of champagne?'

Sean had been appalled by the idea at first. It was corny and smooth. It was something that other men did. It wasn't his style. But then, he'd thought, neither was she. Sean's agent's advice had been perfectly judged, however, because she turned out to be exactly the sort of woman to appreciate being sent glasses of champagne by strange men – it appealed to her sense of adventure. His agent made a discreet exit and she came and joined him at his table. Up close she was better-looking than she was from a distance. She had an intelligent beauty, smooth olive skin, a natural perfume, an infectious laugh. He persuaded her to take the rest of the day off and they drank champagne together until the first evening diners arrived. Then they'd gone back to hers and he'd barely left her flat since. And who could blame him? Her place was stunning, a monster one-bedroom flat carved out of one of those huge stucco-fronted places in Paddington. Twelve-foot ceilings, wooden floorboards, shutters and big windows. And with a stylish interior that reflected her job as a lecturer in interior design at the London College of Art and Design. He glanced around her bedroom now, at the faded antique satin throws, the distressed velvet cushions, gilt-framed junk-shop paintings and ornate engraved mirrors. It was stylish but unpretentious, sumptuous but understated, simple but ornate. Sean wasn't generally one for interiors, for thinking about how things went together. He was more of a furniture person. Some furniture, that was all you needed, and maybe a lamp or two. But he loved this flat. It entertained him and enveloped him, made him feel like he was part of some magic enchanted world – just like her.

She'd set him up a little work area in her bedroom, by the window, found him a leather-topped desk and an old leather swivel chair. It pleased her greatly to think of him writing there, in her flat, looking through the window at her street while he searched for inspiration. Not in an 'Ooh, I've got a famous writer creating a masterpiece in my bedroom' kind of a way, but in a pleased-to-be-of-use way. She loved to feel useful. Nothing made her happier.

So how could he tell her that he hadn't written a word since the first day he set eyes on her? How could he tell her that her blotter and her lamp and her view of Sussex Gardens were doing nothing to inspire him, that when she left for work every morning he went back to sleep, or watched daytime TV?

33

His eye fell upon his sleeping laptop, the £1,200 laptop he'd bought for himself just seven months ago with some of the £50,000 his publishers had paid him sixteen months ago for his second novel, which was to be delivered in two months and which, according to his word-counter, currently consisted of a whopping 12,345 words.

Jesus, he thought, turning on to his other side, it was like a stalker, that bloody book. Every time he felt happy, every time he thought that his life was perfect, he'd remember 'the book' – this gargantuan task he had to complete, this impossible mountain he had to climb, and suddenly he'd remember how precarious this 'happiness' he'd achieved actually was. It all hinged on being 'successful' – and being successful wasn't like being a man, or being tall. It wasn't guaranteed for ever. Success could be taken away from you, just like that – or rather it could *slip away*. And where would Sean be without this 'success', without the aura that being 'successful' conferred upon him? He'd just be scruffy, irresponsible Sean again. And what would he have to offer his *older woman*, for God's sake? This amazing creature who he'd only just met, who'd never known him as Sean London, Office-Supplies Delivery Driver, who knew him only as Sean London, Guardian First Novel Award-Winning Author.

He dragged himself out of bed and decided that he wouldn't even try today. He decided that trying today would just make things worse. Besides, it was their two-month anniversary tomorrow night and Sean needed to go shopping, buy her something really special. Sean didn't usually hold with two-month-anniversary-type stuff, but then Sean had never felt this way about anyone before. He wanted to celebrate every moment he was with her, buy her gifts just for opening her eyes in the morning, for fiddling with an earring, for sneezing, for breathing, for existing. And surely, he reasoned, being a writer meant that affairs of the heart were paramount. How could he be expected to write about life if he didn't experience every aspect of it, daily, deeply, accurately, with every fibre of his being?

He got dressed, left the flat and walked down Bayswater Road towards Marble Arch. He then took the back roads towards Bond Street, walking through the redbrick streets of Mayfair.

How rich, he wondered as he walked, *how rich* would you actually need to be to afford to live here? In Catford, where he lived, in among the sprawling estates and tiny terraces, Sean felt proportionately loaded. The large five-figure sum sitting in his bank account, the cheques that arrived every few weeks from his agent – a thousand here, a thousand there, Polish rights, Catalan rights, Brazilian rights – the gadgets he'd bought, the new bed, the new bicycle, the big Smeg fridge in the kitchen, all paid for in cash, *these* things made him feel rich, unthinkably rich. In the context of where he lived, who he knew and where he came from, Sean was richer than he'd ever imagined he could possibly be. But here, in Mayfair, in among the gentlemen's clubs, foreign embassies and million-pound *pieds-à-terre* of anonymous international businessmen, he was a complete pauper. How, Sean wondered, was it possible for one person to accumulate *so much* wealth? Ironically, it was harder to contemplate the concept from his position of relative affluence than it had been when he'd had no money at all.

He zig-zagged through these elite streets, strolling past antique shops and gun shops and art galleries full of bland landscapes until he found himself where he wanted to be – on New Bond Street. Outside Tiffany's.

Sean had never been to Tiffany's before but decided the moment he walked through the door that he liked it, very much. He liked the way the doorman smiled at him as if he were a proper grown-up man, even though he still felt like a teenager. He liked the sleek, uncluttered layout, the symmetrical lines of the cabinets, the way the overhead lights caught every nuance of the metals and gems underneath.

He even liked the smell of it.

Once up close to the sparkling merchandise, he decided that he especially liked baguette-cut diamonds and platinum. Together. He also found, much to his surprise, that he really quite liked the accompanying price-tags, which were reassuringly expensive as opposed to complete rip-off. He liked the girl who served him, too. He liked the way her little hands darted in and out of the cabinets, hovering over rings while she watched his face to check she was in the right vicinity, plucking them out and handing them to him with a small smile that said that she was enjoying selling every bit as much as he was enjoying buying.

He liked the way they didn't call them rings, they

called them 'diamonds', and he liked the way the 'diamond' he chose was whisked away from him, like a newborn baby, and returned moments later snugly coddled in a shiny duck-egg carrier and presented to him like a prize.

He liked the way the doorman said 'Goodbye, sir', as if the duck-egg bag had conferred upon him membership of some exclusive club, and, more than anything, he liked the sensation of striding down Bond Street on a sunny April afternoon with Millie's engagement ring swinging back and forth in its carrier bag as he walked.

Sean was aware that he was rushing things. He'd known Millie for only two months, but getting engaged didn't mean that they'd have to get married or anything, not straight away at least. They could have a long engagement, get a place together, take their time, see how it went. Maybe in a year they could start talking weddings . . . or two. But in the meantime Sean wanted to feel like he'd made a commitment to Millie beyond just the next phone call or the next date. He wanted to make his feelings absolutely plain, so there could be no misunderstandings.

It was a horribly unromantic analogy to draw, but in Sean's mind buying an engagement ring for Millie was like putting down a deposit on an expensive and long-anticipated holiday or a brand-new and much-desired car. Like putting down a deposit on the house of your dreams. Or, in this particular case, like putting down a deposit on the sexiest, funniest, coolest and most beautiful woman in the world.

A Decent Breakfast

'There you go, angel.' Bernie slapped a plate of toast, beans and bacon in front of Ned and beamed at him. 'Bet it's been a while since you had a decent breakfast, eh?'

Ned thought back to his last breakfast, of home-made focaccia and sunshine-yellow eggs, huge chunks of terracotta chorizo and sour cream, sprinkled with freshly snipped coriander and eaten in his shorts on the terrace of a Bondi café, overlooking the sea.

'Too right,' he said, tucking in.

'Where's mine?' said Gerry, looking sniffily at Ned's breakfast over the top of his *Guardian*.

'Over there,' said Bernie, pointing at a jumbo box of Bran Flakes and turning back to beam at Ned again. 'D'you want ketchup with that?'

'Yes please.'

She passed him the plastic tomato that he'd brought home in his pram from the Wimpy when he was two and into which Bernie still religiously decanted ketchup all these years later.

'So,' said Bernie, folding her arms.

'What?'

'So?'

'What?'

'The deal. The story. The whole salami. Cough up.'

'Dunno,' he said, upending the plastic tomato and squirting ketchup all over his plate. 'Just wanted to come home.'

Bernie pursed her lips and threw him a look.

'I'd just had enough. That's all. Missed your cooking.' He grinned, trying the sweet-talk approach, but Bernie just pursed her lips tighter.

'Anyway,' he said defiantly, 'I'm not the one who should be explaining things. You two have got some real explaining to do. Tell me about that bloke. That bloke in my bedroom. Tell me about *Gervase*.' Ned folded his arms and eyed his mother from his lofty position at the peak of the moral high ground.

'You first,' said Bernie, '*then* we'll discuss Gervase.'

Ned sighed. 'It finished. With Monica.'

'What do you mean, it finished? What happened?'

Ned paused. He wanted to tell his mum and dad the truth, but that would mean admitting not only to ending the relationship with the girl he broke Carly's heart to be with, but also to ending it in the most cowardly fashion imaginable – Mum would never forgive him. 'She dumped me.'

'She *dumped* you?' his incredulous mother repeated in horror. 'But *why*?'

'I don't know. Anyway, it wasn't just that. It was time to come home,' he said quietly, his voice catching slightly. 'That's all.' Ned looked from his mother to his

39

father, cleared his throat, and stuck his fork into his bacon.

Monica was unlike anyone Ned had ever met before. She was like a bloke. She had muscles. And a strong jaw. And legs like sequoias. She played sports and drank beer and had her own drum kit. She shouted a lot and ate like a horse and made lascivious comments about women's breasts.

'Ned,' she'd hiss, elbowing him roughly in the ribs, 'look at that.' Her eyes would direct him to a girl in a lycra top or low-cut dress. 'Look at the tits on it. Incredible.'

She called people cunts and motherfuckers and got into fights. She could reach orgasm in thirty seconds flat and fell fast asleep on her back straight after sex, snoring like a warthog.

'I'm going to Australia,' she'd said five minutes into their first conversation, at the sports bar in Leicester Square.

'Oh,' Ned had said, 'right.'

'I'm going next month. In two weeks. So there's no point in chatting me up.'

'I'm not chatting you up.'

'Yes you are.'

'I'm not.'

'Yes, you fucking well are.'

'I'm not. I've got a girlfriend.'

'Oh right. Like that means anything.'

'It does, actually.'

'So – tell me about your "girlfriend".'

'Carly?'

'That's her name?'

'Uh-huh.'

'OK – tell me about Carly.'

'Carly's – Carly's . . .' Carly's my girlfriend – that's what he'd wanted to say. She's always been my girlfriend, since I was fourteen years old. Carly's warm and round and soft and knows how I like my tea and knows my shoe size and my parents love her like the daughter they never had. Carly has dimples on her knees and eats Wagon Wheels for breakfast. Carly lives up the road from me and Carly works as a pattern cutter for a company that make clothes for old ladies. Carly tickles my back for me and tells me when I need a haircut. She's allergic to peanuts and bees. Her breasts are large and slightly pendulous with quite big nipples and she's never had an orgasm just through sex. She's my best mate and I love her.

'Carly's great,' he'd said.

'Hmm,' said Monica, 'that was convincing. How long have you been going out?'

Ned had shrugged, slightly embarrassed to admit to the fact that he was old fashioned enough to have a teenage sweetheart. 'A few years,' he'd said.

But then he'd suddenly started to say something else, something he hadn't intended to say. Jesus Christ, he'd said, the freakiest thing happened last week, Carly took me out for dinner and she made a really big deal out of it and then, just after pudding, she asked me to marry her, she *proposed* to me – what the fuck was that all about? – and now I feel, Jesus, trapped, I suppose because I always kind of thought we'd get married one day but you know, not *now*, not *yet*, and now I don't know what the fuck to do, I mean I said I'd think about it and I've got to give her an answer soon and Jesus fucking Christ, am I freaked, I am just like completely, totally fucking FREAKED.

And Monica had nodded knowingly and lit a cigarette and before he knew what he was doing he was telling her everything. The going-nowhere life, the living with his parents, the jobs that came and went and failed to satisfy, the long-term relationship with someone who he knew so well it was almost like she was his sister, or something. And she'd blown smoke into his face and said, 'Come with me. Come to Australia – it'll be a right laugh.' And for a second Ned had sat suspended in time waiting for his mouth to open and say something sensible like, 'Don't be stupid. I can't go to Australia.' But the words hadn't come out and instead he'd looked into the eyes of this defiant, strong girl, this stranger with thick-set legs and stubby eyelashes, and he'd found himself saying, 'Yeah. OK then. Why not?'

He still couldn't quite believe he'd done it, even three years later, that he'd met a stranger in a bar and agreed to emigrate with her after less than an hour, that he'd been able to look into Carly's big grey eyes and tell her that he didn't want to marry her, that he'd met someone else and was leaving her and that he'd had the strength to walk away from her when she was almost doubled over with pain, like he'd just punched her. It was as if he'd been possessed by something, an external force. Because Ned just didn't do things like that – he didn't take risks.

But he'd done it – ended his relationship, cleared out his savings, got his visa, booked his flight and headed off to Australia with a complete stranger. It had been messier than that, of course. There'd been a couple more scenes with Carly, his mother's wrath to deal with, moments of uncertainty late at night. But he'd still gone through with it. And as he'd sat eating a rather tasty noodle soup on a Thai Air flight to Sydney two weeks later, with Monica knocking back rum and cokes at his side and a blanket of baby-soft white cloud beneath him, he'd felt serene and sure for the first time in his life.

The regrets hadn't hit him very fast. They'd taken a long while to percolate through the adrenaline. They'd treated it as a holiday at first, stretching out their savings, sitting on the beach, drinking beer at lunchtime. And even though Ned hadn't been even slightly convinced that things would work out with Monica, they had, and at some point they'd fallen in love with each other and things had started getting serious. They both got jobs, working together in the same bar, and then they got a room in a flatshare with three other Brits and became slightly obsessed with each other.

Sometimes they'd lie in bed all day in their tiny little bedroom with sun pouring through the windows just *staring* at each other. Staring at each other, for hours.

There had been moments when Ned had felt a bit silly, but Monica always had this way of making you feel like her way was the best way so if she thought that spending hours in bed staring at each other was a good way to conduct a relationship, that it *gave depth* to their emotions, then staring was what they'd do.

Ned had got fed up with the staring stuff before Monica and that was part of the problem. Ned, surprisingly, turned out to be much better at being in a foreign country, meeting new people and doing crap jobs than Monica was. He found, to his pleasure, that he made friends very easily and seemed to be liked by most people he met. Monica, on the other hand, scared the living daylights out of people, particularly women, and her brusque manner and quick temper put a lot of people off. Consequently she decided that she didn't like anyone and stopped going out, and Ned, fed up of the whole lying-in-bed-staring-at-each-other thing, started claiming back a bit of independence.

And that was when everything had started going wrong.

Mad Monica. That's what everyone had ended up calling her. Everyone who'd witnessed her psychotic behaviour, heard the tinkle of Ned's mobile phone every ten minutes as she sent him text messages, taken the hysterical phone calls and seen the unannounced arrivals when Ned was supposed to be having a night out without her. She'd hit two girls, too. Just walked straight up to them and punched them on the jaw, because she thought they were flirting with Ned. As the months had gone by she'd become weirder and weirder. She started pulling her hair out, a strand at a time, until she was left with little bald patches all over her scalp. And she stopped eating properly and did a lot of rocking back and forth.

Ned had tried to talk to her – it was obvious she was deeply unhappy. He'd tried to persuade her to go home. He'd phoned her parents and talked to them at great length about their troubled eldest daughter. But she refused to acknowledge that there was anything wrong. He even finished the relationship on at least three occasions, trying out the tough-love approach, figuring that it was *him* that was making her so unhappy. But she'd pretend she didn't understand and there she'd be the next day, outside his office, at the other side of the bar, on the beach, staring at him with those lashless eyes.

So, he'd left. Well – run away, to be more honest. He'd been wanting to come home for ages and then when Dad had sent him the e-mail about Mum's surprise party and offered to help pay his fare – well, it had only taken him about thirty seconds to make up his mind. He'd left Mon a note, tried to explain everything, but he knew that it hadn't really been enough. He owed her more than that.

He gulped and tried to swallow a piece of toast, but it got caught in his throat. He washed it down with lukewarm tea and cast his eyes downwards again, feeling hot with shame and guilt. But then he reminded himself: it wasn't his fault. He'd done his best. He'd tried, for three years. It wasn't his fault she'd gone mad. You know, you have a certain amount of responsibility within a relationship, obviously you do – but surely at a certain point, surely when the other person has just gone completely psycho, surely when you've tried everything you can possibly think of to make that person happy, surely when that person is no longer a person in any way that is recognizable, surely *then* it's not your responsibility any more? Is it?

And how strange it was, thought Ned, to have crossed the planet to live on the other side of the world among strangers and away from your family and to end up feeling that the only thing that was weird was the person you went with.

Dinner at Mickey's

'Hello?'

'Sean – it's your mum. I'm not disturbing you, am I?'

She *always* said that these days, as if he was some frantic, intense genius who worked through the night and was constantly in the midst of some unstoppable stream of consciousness.

'No,' he said, dropping the Tiffany's bag on the floor. 'Just got in.'

'Not at Millie's tonight, then?'

'No, she's got assessments and I need to put a wash through.'

'Good. Look. Are you free tonight?'

'Erm, yeah, yeah. I think so. Why?'

'Me and Tony and your dad are going down to Mickey's. For dinner. Will you come?'

'Course I'll come.'

'And Millie?'

'No, I told you. Millie's at home tonight.'

'Well, couldn't she catch a bus or something?'

Sean raised his eyebrows to the ceiling. What planet did mothers actually live on? 'Mum, she lives in Paddington.

She's hardly going to trek halfway across London for a plate of overcooked meat at Mickey's.'

'Oh Sean, love, I know you're trying to keep things cool and I don't want to put any pressure on you, but it's been nearly two months now. I bet you've met *her* parents, haven't you?'

'No, actually, I haven't . . .'

'And I'm sure Millie's probably dying to meet us by now – find out where you come from. Please, Sean. And besides – I've got a surprise for you. A big one. One that I think Millie will like, too.'

'Mum, she's not coming. OK?'

'We'll be good – promise. I'll even tidy up a bit. We won't embarrass you.'

'Look. I will bring her over soon. I promise. Just not tonight, that's all.'

'What about next week? Tony's birthday? She will be coming to that, won't she?'

'God, Mum, I don't know.'

'Oh come on, Sean – Tony said he invited her. She's got to come.'

'Look. I'll talk to her about it. We'll see.'

'Good, good. How's the writing going?'

Sean felt himself stiffen. 'Fine,' he said flatly, 'good.'

'Well, I won't keep you from it, Seany. See you tonight.'

'Yeah, Mum – I'll see you tonight.'

Sean sighed and put down the phone. He'd never before had any qualms about introducing a girl to his mum and dad – he was as proud as hell of his mum and dad and the strange bohemia into which he'd been born. But it was just that this thing with Millie . . . it was so perfect, so precious and he was scared to hold it up to any kind of scrutiny in case it just disappeared into the ether or came crashing down around him. But Sean was also realistic enough to know that their relationship couldn't exist in a vacuum indefinitely. So far their love had been blossoming under glass; eventually he would have to plant it out in the real world and see what happened – just not yet.

Tony was already in a funny old mood, before they even got there. He had an edgy, uncomfortable feeling, like his clothes were too tight, like there wasn't quite the right amount of oxygen in the atmosphere. Ness was sitting way too close to him and he jiggled around a bit in the back of the cab, hoping she'd get the message. But Ness was in a great mood. Ness was *always* in a great mood, particularly when they were going to see his parents. Both Ness's parents were dead and she'd embraced the London family resoundingly from the moment she met them. She and Bernie got on like best mates from the outset and even went out occasionally, on their own, which Tony couldn't help but feel a bit unnerved by. Ness and Bernie even looked vaguely similar, with their yellow hair, long legs and strong features. Except, of course, that Mum was ten times better-looking than Ness, even at fifty-five.

The front door of 114 opened before they'd even had a chance to ring the doorbell and Mum greeted them in a red velvet blouse with her hair in a top-knot and a glass of wine in her hand.

'Bernie!' Ness threw her arms around her and hugged her hard. 'You look beautiful – where did you get that blouse? It's *gorgeous*.'

'River Island!' Bernie exclaimed with pleasure. 'Reduced from £34.99 to twelve quid! It's nice, isn't it?' She gave a little dance to show off the bargain blouse.

'Now, close your eyes,' she said to Tony, closing the front door, 'no peeping.'

'Oh God. Do I have to?' Tony groaned.

'Come on, just do as you're told.'

Tony closed his eyes reluctantly and let his mum lead him through to the kitchen. Tony could smell the comforting aroma of dad's roll-ups and hear Goldie's overgrown toenails clacking against the wooden floor.

'OK – you can open them now.'

He parted his eyelids slowly and at first could make out only the blurred outline of someone standing by the kitchen table. And then his vision cleared and he saw a lanky bloke with a beard and shoulder-length hair grinning at him.

'All right?' said the skinny bloke.

Tony's face broke into a massive grin. 'Ned!'

They strode across the kitchen towards each other and shared a rib-crushing bear-hug. 'Jesus, Ned. What are you doing here? Are you here to stay? You know? Or are you . . . ?'

'I'm back for good. Back for ever.'

They pulled apart and regarded each other affectionately, their eyes searching for physical evidence of the three years that had passed since they'd last seen each other. And in Ned's case there was plenty of it. Creases had started to form at the corners of his eyes, his Adam's apple had begun to soften and there was definitely a little more beef underneath that baggy T-shirt. He'd left a boy and returned a man. Well, as much of a man as a skinny, bespectacled geek like Ned could ever hope to be.

'What the hell is going on with your hair?'

'What?' Ned pulled a hand through it.

'You look like you're wearing a fucking wig.'

'Oh, don't *you* start. I've already had Mum and Dad taking the piss. What d'you think of the beard, though, eh?' He ran a hand over it, thoughtfully. 'Cool, huh?'

'Surf's up,' Tony cackled, miming a surfer balancing on his board.

'You can talk,' said Ned, grabbing hold of Tony's belly and bouncing it up and down. 'Christ, you've got fat.'

Tony grinned at the insult – funnily enough it didn't hurt coming from Ned. And then he became aware of a figure hovering at his side. 'Oh God. Sorry,' he said, stepping out of the way. 'Ned, this is Ness, my girlfriend.' He watched Ned's face as he absorbed the reality of Ness, the unfashionable clothes, the slightly crooked teeth and the total and utter lack of similarity in any way to his ex-wife. 'Ness, this is Ned.'

'Nooo,' said Ness sarcastically, rolling her eyes at Tony and leaning in to kiss Ned on the cheek. 'How fantastic to finally meet you.'

'Great to meet you, too,' said Ned, 'you've come highly recommended.'

'Oh yeah?'

'Yeah – Mum hasn't stopped going on about you. She reckons you're Tony's saviour.'

Ness flushed pleasurably and Tony felt himself bristling with irritation. Saviour? What the hell was all that about?

A set of knuckles banged against the front door.

'Oh, that'll be Seany. OK now, quiet, everyone.' Bernie put a finger to her lips and went to answer it.

'Hello, angel,' they could hear her saying. '. . . Now close your eyes, Seany – I've got a surprise for you.'

'All my boys, all together, it's like being in heaven.' Bernie looked as if she were about to expire with pure joy as her eyes swivelled around the table from son to son.

'Mickey,' she said to the dark-haired man standing proprietarily by the cash desk, 'look – all my boys!'

'Aah,' said Mickey, snapping to attention and walking towards their table, 'so I see.'

Tony was never entirely sure whether Mickey genuinely liked his family or whether the bonhomie and familiarity were all part of some slick PR thing. The Londons had been coming to Mickey's since Tony was a baby. Mickey's had been the first Greek to open up in the area and for a while it was the most popular restaurant around. All the local young couples came here on Saturday nights to relive their Mediterranean holidays. When the boys were kids they'd been to Mickey's every Saturday night, sometimes just the family and sometimes with friends; they went there not just for the food but also for the 'entertainment' – musicians, dancers, plate-breaking. But nowadays they went only on special occasions: birthdays, promotions, engagements – and the return of youngest sons.

'So,' said Mickey, beaming beatifically at the family, his hand resting on the back of Tony's chair, 'where you bin hiding, Mr Ned? Why you leave your mother on her own for so long, eh? Your mother, she bin pining – pining pining pining.'

'You tell him, Mickey,' said Bernie good-naturedly. 'Three years, he's been gone – *three years.*'

Mickey tutted extravagantly and raised his hands to the ceiling. 'I tell you, if one of my boys did this – other side of the world, three years, no visits – Mrs Mickey, she would *die*, probably, die of a broken heart.' He clutched his hand to his chest to illustrate the breaking of Mrs Mickey's heart. Mickey was prone to melodrama, another trait that Tony had never been sure was genuine or part of an elaborately constructed persona. The whole family worked on the assumption that Mickey *loved* the Londons, but for all they knew he could be throwing darts at photos of them in his spare time and sticking pins into voodoo dolls. Tony didn't trust anyone who was in a position to make money out of him. Ever. They had too much to gain by being nice to you.

'What you bin doing out there in Aussieland for three years, Mr Ned? You bin surfing, huh?'

Ned grimaced and was about to answer when Mickey suddenly turned round to acknowledge a customer who'd just walked in. Another deeply loved customer, judging by the look of joy and delight that spread across his face.

'Hey, Mr Gervase!'

Tony turned in his seat. Gervase. Great. Fucking great. Couldn't this family do anything on their own these days without Skeletor turning up?

'All right, Mickey – how's it hanging?' The two men shook hands warmly and Gervase pulled off his leather jacket and took the empty seat between Bernie and Ness. 'Sorry, I'm late, Bern.' He kissed her on the cheek and she flushed with pleasure.

'Never you mind, love. We haven't even ordered yet.'

Tony caught Ned's eye. He was throwing him a 'What the fuck is this all about?' look. Tony shook his head slightly and sent him a 'This is just the way things are now and I don't like it any more than you do' look.

'All right, beautiful?' Gervase leant in to Ness and gave her a big smacker on the cheek.

Ness beamed and Tony stared at his menu, crossly. This was *their* restaurant. The Londons' restaurant. This was where *they* came, as a family.

Apparently Mum had met him at the pub, that place where she sang on Wednesday nights, and they'd 'got chatting' – whatever that meant. He'd given her some sob story about how his girlfriend had kicked him out and he was about to spend his last fifty quid taking a hotel room for the night and she'd said, 'Oh don't be daft, we've got a whole house *full* of rooms – why don't you come and stay at ours?' And he was still there, nearly two months later. Mum and Dad didn't even know what he did for a living. 'It's none of our business,' Mum would say. 'He's living in your fucking house, Mum – *our* house. He's in Ned's bedroom, for Christ's sake – of course it's your business.'

Mum would just purse her lips and sigh. 'I can't explain it, love,' she'd say. 'It just feels like the right thing to be doing. He's got nowhere else to go.' Dad had been a bit unsure at first. Had just shrugged and said 'Your mother seems to be quite fond of him' when Tony questioned the concept of letting a complete stranger live in their house. But now he seemed to be coming round to the bloke. He'd even given him occasional work, driving the van, doing deliveries.

Gervase was chatting to Gerry now about some delivery he'd done for him today, about some poncey woman in Lansdowne Square who'd made him take off his shoes before he was allowed in the house, and Ness and Bernie were in stitches, as if it was the funniest thing they'd ever heard. Tony turned to Ned again and they made more fucked-off faces at each other. Gerry hissed at them, 'Pack it in, you two', and they both covered their mouths with their hands and pretended to look chastened, kicking each other's ankles under the table and stifling giggles.

'Honestly,' muttered Gerry, 'like a pair of kids.'

Tony cast a glance at Sean to see if he was pissed off about the unwelcome interloper at the table, but he was absorbed in his menu, rubbing absent-mindedly at the top of his ear. In another world. As ever. Probably thinking about Millie, he mused. Probably imagining what he was going to do to her when he got home that night. Probably sitting there thinking, Christ aren't I just the luckiest bastard in all the world, with my bestselling novel and my toned stomach and my fantastically sexy girlfriend and . . . Oh, God. Tony checked himself. His napkin was screwed into a knot between his hands and he felt swamped by an altogether unsavoury set of emotions. Jealousy, he told himself. Not good. Unattractive. Pathetic. Especially when it's towards your little brother, who you love more than life itself . . .

Stop it.

Immediately.

Stop it.

He checked his breathing, straightened his cuffs and looked back at his brother. Sean. Little Seany. Seany who'd come along when Tony was four years old and had been the best surprise of his life. He remembered thinking that the new brother or sister was going to be some kind of green slimy monster, reasoned that it would have to be if it had spent nine months living in Mum's stomach. He'd been terrified at the prospect and then Dad had brought him to see Mum and the new baby at the hospital and he'd just been a little pink kid, a harmless little pink kid with huge ears and puffy eyes.

Sean, he thought, little Seany. My little brother . . .

'So, you and, er . . . *Millie*' – he tempered the tone of his voice in an attempt at nonchalance, but still felt convinced that he'd imbued her name with every last nuance of his desire for her – 'you still coming on Saturday?'

Sean looked at him blankly.

'My birthday.'

'Oh, yeah. Right. Well, *I* am. Not sure about Millie yet.'

'Oh,' Tony said, trying to hide the devastation in his voice, 'how come?'

Sean shrugged.

'He's ashamed of us,' Bernie butted in.

'Mum! I'm not. I told you . . .'

'He never used to wait this long to bring a girl home. It used to be the first place he brought them. Come in, meet my mum, meet my dad, make yourself at home. This one's obviously too good for the likes of us.' She winked to ensure that everyone knew she was joking, but Sean didn't notice.

'Mum! It's not that. It's just – she's different, this one. She's older. And more – *independent*. She's got a whole life thing going on. A big life. It just . . . I just want to take it easy, give her her space. That's all.'

'See,' said Bernie, triumphantly, a small smile playing on her lips, 'ashamed of us.'

'What's she like?' said Ned, his curiosity suddenly piqued.

'She's all right.'

'Wow,' said Ned facetiously, 'she sounds great.'

'No – I mean, she's great. She's funny, and she's clever and she's cool. Really cool. Tony's met her, ask him.'

Tony blanched. 'What?' he mumbled.

'What did you think of Millie?'

'God. I don't know. We only met for a few minutes. She seemed really nice.'

'Posh,' said Ness, inadvertently saving Tony from himself, 'she's very posh.'

'Posh, eh?' said Ned, grinning, 'how posh? Victoria Beckham posh? Or Tara Palmer-Pompom posh?'

'No, no,' said Ness, 'nothing like that. Not that blue-blood kind of posh. More sort of actressy. You know who she reminds me of, actually? That girl who used to go out with Neil Morrissey?'

'What – Amanda Holden?' said Bernie.

'No, that other one. With the dark hair. Rachel something . . .'

'Rachel Weissz?'

'Yeah! That's the one. She's like a slightly older version of her. She's stunning. And classy. Really classy.'

'Ooo-oooh,' said Ned, 'get you. You've gone up in the world a bit now, haven't you? Is that all it takes to get a classy girl, then? Just write a stupid book?'

'No,' said Sean, folding his arms and eyeing Ned playfully, 'it also helps if you're incredibly handsome, incredibly successful and hung like a woolly mammoth . . .'

And at that precise moment all Tony's feelings of fraternal affection became rancid green jealousy. He took a deep breath, unclenched his fists, turned his gaze to his menu and decided that tonight he quite fancied a kleftiko.

Death by Corkscrew

On his first morning back in England, Ned was awoken at eleven by the sound of Gervase clearing his sinuses in the hallway. Jesus Christ, he thought, will someone please take that man to the Ear Nose & Throat and get them to rip out his *adenoids*, for fuck's sake.

He heard the front door slam close and Gervase crunching down the front steps, and then he rolled over on to his side and cried out in pain as he felt something sharp digging into his hip bone. He felt around underneath himself and pulled out a corkscrew. Shit – he could have killed himself, could have punctured a vital organ and slowly bled to death during the night. That would have been nice for Mum and Dad, he thought, coming downstairs in the morning to find their prodigal son drained of blood and dead on the sofa. He hurled the corkscrew angrily across the room. This was all wrong – completely wrong. His first night at home after three long years away and he'd been made to sleep on the fucking sofa. Yes – his very own, actual *mother* had made her youngest son, her *baby*, sleep on the sofa while that mucus-headed weirdo got to sleep in *his* bed, in *his* room.

'Oh no, Ned, sweetie. It's not fair to kick him out right now, without notice. We'll clear out Tony's room for him tomorrow, love, then you can have your room back.'

'But what about tonight? Where am I going to sleep tonight?' Ned's voice had gone up about ten octaves and he'd felt himself rapidly reverting to childhood as his throat clenched and tears threatened.

'Hmm, well, Seany's room is out of bounds – your dad's got his old Norton in there. We could chuck a mattress on the floor in Tony's room . . . ?'

'No way. It stinks of piss in there. And the walls are all covered in old bogies.'

'Well then, you'll have to have the sofa.'

'The sofa! But, Mum – that's not fair. I've been travelling for, like, seventy-two hours. It won't do much for my jet lag.'

'I know, love, and I'm sorry, but there's nothing I can do – you could always come and sleep in our bed, like you did when you were little.'

'Mum!'

'Joke, Ned – joke.'

And Ned had smiled, not at the joke, but at the uncomfortable realization that some small, deep-seated, unformed part of him actually *wanted* to sleep in his parents' bed, wanted to snuggle down between them and hear them breathing all night long.

You sick, pathetic bastard, he thought to himself, no wonder your girlfriend went mad.

So he'd had a hideous night on the sofa, tossing and

turning, waking up every half an hour, despite the three Nytols his mother had given him to help him sleep. He'd had dozens of short, intense snatches of dreams, mainly to do with Monica. And then he'd finally fallen into a deep slumber some time after five in the morning.

He stumbled through the hallway and into the kitchen. His mum had left out his breakfast and a note that said, 'Didn't want to wake you – try not sleep until tonight. See you later. M x'

Ned nibbled half-heartedly on some toast and wandered aimlessly around the house for a while, trying to get his bearings, trying to feel normal. And failing. He was feeling unsettled and peculiar, caught between two places that had both at one time seemed like home but now felt like they'd been shifted off their axes by a degree or two. Everything seemed slightly off-kilter.

He'd known things had changed while he was away, obviously he did, but it was still bizarre seeing Tony without Jo. Tony and Jo had been together since Ned was a teenager. Jo was a fitness freak and made Tony do things like jogging and going to the gym. She was a workaholic like him and as a couple they'd oozed success, discipline and teamwork. But now Tony was – well, he was all middle-aged and fat. And sort of . . . *sad*-looking. His new girlfriend was great, though – Ness was completely different to Jo. Where Jo had been small and crisp with short dark hair, perfectly applied eye make-up and a mobile phone permanently attached to her ear, Ness was tall and rangy with wild blonde hair and a permanent megawatt smile. Where Jo had always ordered something like a bit of fish and salad and pushed it around her plate, Ness ordered big hunks of red meat and ate with gusto, knocking back glasses of red wine and talking with her mouth full. She was absolutely gorgeous in a pre-Raphaelite, Charlie Dimmock kind of way, with bright-green eyes and incredible legs. Mum obviously adored her and she even seemed to have some kind of bond with Gervase – but Tony had virtually ignored her. Tony had never exactly been a laugh a minute, but even by his own slightly morose standards he was a complete grouch last night. The divorce had obviously hit him really hard and maybe Ness was some kind of rebound relationship. But whatever it was that was bothering Tony, it was incredibly unsettling to see the rock of the family looking so . . . *lost*.

And then there was Sean. Fuck, it was all just mind-blowing. He was all *famous*-looking – Ned couldn't explain it any other way. Sean had always just looked like a bloke, a bloke with some clothes on and some hair and that was it really. But now he had this *sheen* about him. His teeth seemed extra white and his hair looked extra thick. And he was so much more confident. Sean had always been the sensitive one of the family, the one who took things the wrong way. He slacked round like Ned, wearing clothes he'd had for three years, doing half-arsed jobs, watching American TV on Sky One and eating Mum's food. Sean had never been in love before. Ever. Well, not since he was fifteen and Lindsay Morrow had broken his heart and humiliated him in front of the whole school. Ever since then he'd been Mr Cool as far as relationships went – girls came and went and Sean barely seemed to notice. But now he was all glossy and content and *in love*. Ned suddenly felt like Sean was an awful lot older than him and an awful lot more mature, and he couldn't quite imagine where he was going to fit into Sean's new life. The thought made him feel incredibly sad.

Mum and Dad, though – they were still the same, thank God. Still strong and happy, still the perfect couple and the people he respected and loved most in the whole world. Ned had tried to explain his mum and dad to people in Australia but had never managed to do them justice. They're the greatest coolest people in the world, he wanted to say, they really love each other and they really love their kids and they laugh together all the time. They still go out and drink and see friends and spend weekends together in hotels. They bicker but don't row, they notice each other all the time but give each other space to have their own lives too. They swear and fart and let us talk about how pissed we got last night or how stoned we were at the weekend without thinking that we're going to become drug-addicted, alcoholic drop-outs. They're what every couple should be like. They're my heroes.

The only unsettling thing about Mum and Dad last night had been the fact that they both looked ever so slightly older. Mum had more grey in her golden hair and Dad appeared to have shrunk. They were both nearing sixty; they were both getting old. The realization made Ned think about all the horrible things that could happen to your parents, things like cancer and heart attacks and senile dementia. The thought of Mum and Dad not being around for ever, or not being the way they were now, made Ned feel scared and vulnerable.

He looked at his watch again. Eleven-thirty. A whole lonely, empty day stretched ahead of him with nothing to do except worry about Mon and feel out of sorts. He needed to speak to someone, take his mind off things. He needed something else to think about.

Carly, he thought with relief, that's what he needed. Some Carly.

Ned's thoughts had turned more and more often to Carly as his relationship with Monica had degenerated. To soft Carly, who never lost her temper or did weird things. To sweet Carly, who was absolutely normal in every way. He wondered what she was doing and how she was and who she was seeing. He wondered if she ever missed him and how she'd react if he was to turn up on her doorstep one day. He tried to imagine it, tried to imagine her wide face and her big eyes and her silky brown hair tied back in a pony-tail. He fantasized about her scrunching her face up into a frown and folding her arms across her big, soft chest and pretending to be angry with him for a moment, before giving in and grinning and giving him a big, warm, *normal* Carly hug.

Maybe they'd be friends for a while or maybe they'd just leap straight into bed and have nice, *normal* sex, without any staring and instant orgasms and fancy stuff; just good old-fashioned Ned and Carly sex. But it didn't really matter what they did, in Ned's fantasy, because just being there with Carly would be enough, enough to make him feel normal again, and proper, and *home*.

He pulled out his old address book and leafed to the 'C' page. There they were, all Carly's numbers from over the years, written in different pens. At her parents', her bar job, her job at Dorothy Day Fashions, her flat on Gipsy Hill. All the stages of her life. And the numbers all so familiar, sequences he'd pressed into dial pads a thousand, two thousand times. He tried her at work first.

'Good morning, Dorothy Day Fashions.'

'Oh. Yeah, hi. Can I speak to Carly, please?'

'Carly who?'

'Carly Hilaris.'

He heard her rustling through some papers.

'Sorry – there's no one of that name here.'

'What! But, are you sure?'

'Yes, sorry.'

'Can you look again – she works in the cutting room.'

'Neeta,' he heard her calling to someone else, 'd'you remember a Carly, used to work in the cutting room?' She came back to him. 'She left about three years ago, apparently.'

Left? Dorothy Day Fashions? 'God. She left. Where did she go? Do you know?'

Ned heard more muffled conversation in the background.

'Mexico.'

'*Mexico?*'

'That's right. Lucky thing. She went backpacking or something.'

'*Backpacking?*' Ned was incredulous. Carly, backpacking? In Mexico? But Carly didn't even like going to Wales. Carly liked home. It was her favourite thing.

'Er, thank you, thank you very much.' He hung up and dragged his fingers through his hair. Carly was in Mexico. Or at least *had* been in Mexico. Maybe she was home now. He tried her home number with a growing sense of uncertainty. The answerphone clicked on and some girl called Nadia told him that she wasn't home but that he could leave a message, while Destiny's Child sang 'Survivor' very loudly in the background. Shit. He hadn't considered this possibility. It hadn't occurred to him that she wouldn't still be exactly where he'd left her.

He'd run out of options. He was stumped. Completely stumped. In his Bondi-based fantasies, he'd never really thought beyond meeting up with Carly. Crystal Palace mast, Mum, Dad, Goldie, dinner at Mickey's, Sean, Tony, own bed, *Carly*. And that was where it ended. Everything else, he'd assumed, would just sort of flow from there. Now he didn't know what to do.

He kicked off his shoes, pulled off his jeans and climbed back under the eiderdown on the sofa, thinking that so far this being-back-at-home thing was not turning out anything like he'd expected.

Skiving in the Park

'Hi – hi, who's that? Oh, Aliyah. Hi, it's Tony. Look, I'm feeling a bit, er . . . under the weather today so I think I'll work from home. Oh – it's going round is it? Oh right. Oh, OK. So anyway – if anything urgent comes up, you can contact me here. I don't think there was much on, was there? No. I didn't think so. I'll call in later, just to check everything's ticking over. Yeah. OK, thanks, Aliyah. And have a good day. Yeah, I will. Thanks. Bye.'

Tony took a deep breath and wiped the sweat from his brow. Yes, of course, it was utterly ridiculous to be so nervous about pulling a sickie on your own bloody company, but it was the first time he'd ever done it. In his life. It just wasn't in his nature to slack off. He was a grafter, always had been since he was a little kid and used to earn himself 5p for helping his dad polish antique silver. Tony liked to work. He liked going to work, being at work, working. He resented colds and coughs that kept him from doing his job. He hadn't even taken a holiday since he and Jo had split up. Couldn't see the point. But in a way he *was* sick today. Sick in the head. Sick of his life. Sick of himself.

Lovesick.

He considered his options now that he had a day to himself. He could go for a jog, maybe, or to the gym. He could take the car to be valeted. Maybe just go for a good long walk on Dulwich Common and have a quiet drink in a pub somewhere with the papers.

And then it occurred to him – Ned, he could spend the day with Ned.

Tony felt a bit bad about last night. He'd been so pissed off about Gervase turning up and so eaten up with jealousy every time he looked at Sean that he'd barely said a word to Ned. He'd had hardly any contact with Ned while he'd been away. He was too busy to send e-mails, and the time difference always seemed to work against him picking up the phone for a chat. And he really had missed him, particularly during the divorce. The whole family had enfolded him like a great big blanket but it hadn't felt quite complete without Ned.

A part of Tony had been angry when Ned left. The Londons were a family of five – that was their *shape*: hexagonal. It just didn't work quite so well as a square. And, if he was to be completely honest with himself, it wouldn't have been quite so bad if it had been Sean who'd gone away and misshapened their family, because Ned was the *bridge* between Tony and Sean. He was one of those sunshiny people who got on with everyone, and with Ned around the gulf be-tween the two eldest brothers hadn't really shown up. With three of them there was banter; with just the two of them there was the altogether tougher option of conversation.

Ned was grimacing when Tony turned up to collect him from Beulah Hill later that day.

'What's the matter?'

'My fucking back. Mum stuck me on the sofa last night – didn't want to kick her precious *Gervase* out of my room.'

Tony scowled. 'Fuck's sake.'

'Nice car,' said Ned.

'D'you think so?'

'Yeah,' he said running his hand over the paintwork, 'it's really cute.'

Cute? thought Tony. *Cute?* Well, that just about summed it up. That was exactly, *succinctly*, what was wrong with his red sports car. It was *cute*.

'Yeah, well – get in, then.'

They drove past the shops and restaurants of Westow Street in a companionable silence. Ned was drinking in the scenery, the plethora of restaurants completely out of proportion to the size of the area, the library with its intricate carved stonework, the tiny branch of Woolworth's, the huge pub up on the roundabout.

'It's all the same,' he said in wonder.

'You've only been gone three years. What did you expect?'

'God, I don't know – just new shops and stuff I suppose. Just things to be . . . *different.*'

'Ned, nothing ever really changes – haven't you learnt that yet?'

'Yes, it does,' said Ned, with a hint of sadness in his voice, 'everything bloody changes. And I really wish it wouldn't.'

Walking through Crystal Palace Park was always good for exacerbating an already melancholy mood. Tony had had a wander through most of London's big parks over the years – Regent's Park had its frou-frou rose gardens and its outdoor theatre, Hyde Park had its Serpentine and its horses, Battersea Park had its Buddha and its river views and Hampstead Heath had that whole countryside thing going on – but not one of them even began to compare to Crystal Place in terms of pure atmosphere.

Where the glittering glass palace had stood before it burnt to the ground seventy years earlier, the grassy terraces led down towards a panoramic swathe of steps, carved from pock-marked stone, from where you could see the whole of south London. If you stood at the top of the steps and looked around from left to right, the park looked like some tragic dumping ground for the world's greatest attractions. The mast rose Eiffel Tower-like from a hill to the left and at intervals between the steps stood headless statues and proud-looking sphinxes, staring stoically into the misty distance, unaware that the building they were guarding had disappeared from behind them for ever. Their beards and toes were sprayed with metallic tags and they always made Tony feel sad, like seeing a faithful dog lying at the feet of the corpse of an elderly owner.

When they were boys they'd come to the park in the

summer and explore the secret labyrinth of underground tunnels beneath the ruins of the palace, inventing ghosts to scare each other and tearing out afterwards into the sunshine, euphoric with relief. The park was mayhem in the summer but on a damp April day like today you could almost believe you had the place to yourself and let the idiosyncratic, ghostly atmosphere overwhelm you. Crystal Palace was awash with ley lines, if you believed that sort of thing, which Tony wasn't convinced he did. But there was something special, something *spiritual* in the air, that was for sure, something unlike anywhere else in London.

They took the steps slowly and in silence.

'It's good to see you, Tony,' said Ned.

'Yeah,' said Tony, 'likewise.'

'How've you been, you know, with the divorce and everything?'

Tony shrugged. 'Oh – fine – not bad at all really.'

They turned left, heading towards the cafeteria in the sports complex, dodging a flock of men in brightly coloured, skin-tight sportswear along the way.

'What happened exactly? With you and Jo?'

Tony laughed and stuffed his cold hands into his coat pockets. 'Shit. That's a big one.'

'Yeah, I know, but it was so weird hearing about it all from the other side of the world. It didn't feel quite real. It didn't make any sense. I mean, you and Jo, you were a real team – you were soul-mates.'

'Like you and Carly, you mean?' He raised an eyebrow at Ned.

'Yeah, but, that was different. We were kids when we met, we grew out of each other. But you and Jo – you were already adults when you met.'

Tony shook his head. 'No, we weren't adults. We were twenty-two.'

'Yes, but . . .'

'You're not an adult when you're twenty-two, not in this world, not these days. You look like one and sound like one, but you're still just a kid.'

'So is that what happened, then – did you grow out of each other?'

'Fundamentally, I suppose. But ultimately it all came down to one conversation – a conversation we should have had a lot earlier.'

Tony held the door of the cafeteria open for Ned and felt himself thawing under the warm air of a heater above it.

'Which one?'

'The baby conversation.'

'Ah – putting the pressure on, was she?'

'No, it was the other way round, actually. I was ready. She wasn't.'

'But what was the panic? Couldn't you just have waited a bit for her. She would have changed her mind eventually.'

'No point. It was a stupid fucking idea anyway. When I think about it now I realize I only wanted a kid because I was thirty-one, because we'd been married for years, because I thought I should be cracking on with it. You know: typical Tony. And when she said "no" it was like this great moment of realization. If I wasn't going to be doing the whole family thing, tying myself down with kids and working my bollocks off to pay for it all, then what the fuck was the point of being married, you know? Of going to bed with the same woman every night? And I guess Jo must have felt the same way too.'

'Why's that?'

'Because she left me for some bloke in her office two months later.'

'No way!' cried Ned. 'Not Jo. Jo wouldn't . . .'

'Yeah, she would. Of course she would. She always got what she wanted, Jo.'

'Shit – Mum didn't say *any*thing about that. She just said you'd come to the end of the road.'

'Yeah, well – I didn't tell Mum.'

'You're kidding – why not?'

'Don't know really. I didn't want Mum to think badly of her, I s'pose.'

'Yeah, but . . . why shouldn't she think badly of her? She fucked you over – she . . .'

'She did the right thing. Jo did the right thing. I was ready to cut loose and she was the only one of us who was brave enough to do anything about it. You know . . .'

Tony picked up a vinyl-topped tray and pushed it across the steel tracks in the café towards a display of sandwiches and baguettes. He selected a cheese-and-ham baguette, approximately a foot long. Then he picked up a scone with butter and cream and a can of Heineken. As he waited to pay at the cash desk, he slapped a twin pack of Ginger Nuts on to his tray, an impulse purchase.

He felt self-conscious as he watched Ned slipping a tuna sandwich and a bottle of mineral water on to the tray.

'Not hungry?' he said.

'Not really,' said Ned, grimacing. 'I'm feeling a bit dicky, actually, I think I might have picked up a bug on the plane, or something.'

'Not having a beer?'

'Nah. Thanks.'

It fell silent, save for the sound of Ned ripping the plastic seal off the front of his sandwich and the ring-pull going on Tony's beer.

'So,' said Ned, eventually, 'how are you now? I mean, how's your life?'

Tony shrugged. 'OK,' he said, 'work's busy.'

'The divorce, I mean, you say you're cool with it and everything, but how did it hit you? Really?'

'It didn't,' said Tony. 'Obviously it was a bit weird at first, moving out of the house, living alone, not seeing Jo every day. But now, it's fine.'

Ned threw him a look. 'Are you sure, Tone?'

'Positive. Single life agrees with me.'

'It's just that you don't seem very . . . You're not the same as . . . Are you sure you're happy? Because, you can talk to me if you're not. You know that, don't you?'

Tony smiled. 'I'm happy, Ned. Honest. Life's just different now, that's all. Not better, not worse, just different.'

Ned nodded and they fell silent again.

'I like Ness,' said Ned eventually, through a mouthful of food, 'she's really funny.'

'Yeah,' said Tony grimly, 'she's all right, isn't she?'

'Where did you meet her?'

'You know Trish? Rob's missus?'

'Yeah.'

'Friend of hers, from school.'

'Oh. Right. Are you going to marry her?'

Tony spluttered slightly and laughed. 'What?!'

'Well, why not? She's really pretty and really nice, and she obviously really loves you.'

Tony wiped his mouth on a napkin and grimaced at Ned. 'No, Ned. I am not going to marry Ness. We've only been going out for a year.'

'Well, are you going to live with her, then?'

'God, Ned, I don't know. I'm really not thinking like that at the moment. We're just, you know, hanging out. It's nothing serious.'

Ned nodded at him, knowingly. 'I prefer her to Jo,' he said in a small voice.

Tony looked at him in surprise. 'Really?'

'Yeah. She's more . . . *human*. More real. And she's got better legs.' He grinned at Tony and they laughed. 'But seriously, Tone, I think you've done really well for yourself there. She's brilliant.'

'What about you and whatsername?' Tony still felt vestiges of loyalty towards Carly when it came to Monica. 'What went wrong there, then?'

Ned shrugged and picked some cucumber out of his sandwich. 'Don't know really,' he said.

75

'What, she dump you? You dump her? What happened?'

Ned fell silent for a moment and contemplated a coffee ring on the table-top.

'Come on. You can tell me.'

Ned cleared his throat and leant in so close towards him that Tony could smell cucumber on his breath. 'Promise you won't say anything to Mum?'

'Uh-huh.'

'Well, she went fucking loop-the-loop. Completely, like, really, really scary.'

'How d'you mean?'

'Just lost the plot entirely. Started following me, hitting people, *pulling out her own hair*, you know, like actual big clumps of her own hair.'

'Christ. Shit. That's bad. So – what happened? Is she better now?'

Ned shrugged and picked at the plastic casing of his sandwich. 'No, not really.'

'Well, what did she say when you told her you were coming home?'

He shrugged again. 'Nothing much.'

'You did tell her, didn't you? You did tell her you were coming home?'

Ned shook his head and looked embarrassed. 'Well, I left her a note.'

Tony laughed. 'Oh shit, Ned – that's really low.'

'Yeah, I know, I *know*. But you don't know Monica. I mean, Monica's really – big.'

'What, you mean fat?'

'No – big. Like a bloke. Like a *big* bloke. And – I don't know – *anything* could have happened if I'd told her I was leaving. She could have beaten me up or cut off my dick or something.'

'You mean, you were *scared* of her?' Tony started to laugh.

'Terrified. I mean, *really* terrified. I saw her kill a kitten once.'

'What?!'

'Straight up. It was lying on the side of the road, half dead – it had been run over – and she just got hold of it, like that, and broke its neck. Calm as you like. She didn't even cry or anything.'

'Jesus.'

'Yeah, and then this other time she gave a little girl a Chinese burn – tiny little girl, you know, with ringlets and everything. Said she'd been giving her dirty looks.'

'Shit – she sounds psycho.'

'I know. And she hit me once. Well – twice, actually. Knocked me sideways – gave me a black eye. But the worst thing about Mon – the *scariest* thing – was the talking in her sleep. Groaning, wailing, screaming sometimes, too. She sounded like she was possessed by demons or something.'

Tony paused. 'Maybe she was. You know . . . it sounds like she's really quite ill, Ned.'

'Yeah,' Ned slumped a bit, the circus over, reality hitting home. 'Yeah. I think she is.'

'Poor girl.'

'I know – that was the thing. Underneath it all there

77

was this really nice girl, you know, this real sweetheart. It was as if she had so much love to give but no one had ever shown her what to do with it. And that was the bit I fell in love with, I suppose.'

Tony pushed away a token corner of his baguette which he could happily have eaten but felt self-conscious about as Ned had barely touched his sandwich. 'So, you just took off, did you? Did a midnight flit?'

Ned's face fell and he looked almost ashamed. 'That's about the long and short of it.' He gulped.

'Well, I can't say as I blame you really.'

'Yeah, well. I'm not in love with myself about it or anything. It's not the greatest thing I've ever done. But it wasn't just her, you know. It was everything. Hot Christmases, funny insects, everything being so far away. I just thought, shit, you know, Mum and Dad, what if something happened to one of them, what if one of them had a heart attack or something and I was two days away? They're getting on a bit now. I just suddenly really felt this need to be close at hand. And then there'll be nephews and nieces and things . . .'

'Not much chance of that.'

'Yeah there is. You and Ness – you've been together for a while. And Sean looks pretty serious about this Millie.'

Tony snorted derisively. 'Oh, come on – those two? They've only known each other for five minutes.'

'Yes, but you can tell just by looking at him, can't you? This is the real thing. I reckon Sean's going to go for this one.'

'Sean? Nah. Sean's not ready to settle down, no way.'

'Oh, he is.'

'No way.'

'Look – I've been away – I've got *objectivity*. And he's ready, mate, just you watch.'

Tony didn't like the way this conversation was heading. And besides, there was something that had been bothering him throughout this conversation with Ned, something he had to mention.

'Ned,' he said, 'will you please stop doing that – that *thing*?'

'What thing?'

'That making everything sound like a question thing? That turning up the ends of your sentences thing? You know, that sounding like an Aussie thing? Mate?'

Ned's face fell. 'Shit. Am I? Am I really? Am I doing it now?'

'Well, yes, of course you're doing it now, you div, you're asking me a question – you're supposed to sound like that. It's your normal sentences that're the problem.'

'Shit – look, give me a kick, will you, if I do it again?'

Tony smiled sweetly and kicked him under the table. Ned kicked him back. 'Bastard,' he said, with a grin.

'Come on, kid brother, let's go.'

Both brothers pulled on their overcoats, headed for the door and wondered silently to themselves just exactly what it was that the other one wasn't telling them.

Mon's Hair and Bernie's Soul

Ned got back from the park just as the sun was starting to set and came upon Gervase sitting in the kitchen, drinking a mug of tea and flicking through Dad's *Guardian.*

'Oh,' said Ned, 'hi.'

'Evening,' said Gervase, folding up the paper with a finality that suggested that he was angling for a chat. 'How's it hanging?'

How's it hanging? thought Ned. *How's it hanging?* What sort of a stupid dumb-ass question was that? Oh, it's hanging very pendulously to the right, thank you very much. He grunted and nodded and made his way to the sink to fill the kettle.

'There's some in the pot, mate,' Gervase indicated Bernie's teapot with a jerk of his head. It was wearing a cosy.

'I'm having coffee,' he said tersely.

Gervase nodded, in a 'Fair enough' way.

Ned dropped a couple of teaspoons of coffee into a mug – he was going to need a ton of caffeine to keep him going – and as he moved around the kitchen he felt uncomfortably aware of Gervase's eyes boring into the back of his head. This is ridiculous, he thought to himself, feeling uncomfortable in your own home, having some stranger watching you make yourself a cup of coffee.

'How's the jet lag?'

'Just starting to hit me. Big time.' He stirred his coffee and dropped the teaspoon in the sink and then, as he turned round to address Gervase, Ned noticed with a sense of unease that Goldie was lying at Gervase's feet. Not just at them, but *on* them, looking all contented and happy, like he usually did with Dad.

'What's it like, then?'

'What?'

'Jet lag. What's it feel like?'

'I don't know,' Ned shrugged, 'kind of heavy and spacey. Disconnected. And a sort of floaty-leg thing, like you're walking on a waltzer.'

'Oh,' Gervase nodded, 'right. Never been further than Aberdeen myself.'

'What – you've never been abroad?'

Gervase shook his head and lit up a cigarette. 'I'm not really from that sort of background.'

Ned could sense a conversation unfolding here and decided he couldn't face it. 'Right,' he said, cutting him off, 'I'm going to my room, see you later, yeah?'

'Yeah, mate,' said Gervase, 'see you around. Oh – hang on a sec. I forgot to say. A parcel turned up for you earlier. UPS. It's in the hallway.'

'Oh,' said Ned, 'right. Thanks.'

He wandered out into the hallway and saw a small box sitting on top of the 'throne', a red velvet chair with curly gilt bits, one of Mum's ex-display treasures. Who the hell would be sending him parcels? He'd only just got home. He picked up the box and shook it – it was incredibly light, almost as if there was nothing in it. He ripped the plastic pouch off the front and read the details. According to the UPS form, the sender was someone called Dilys Nickers who lived at 1345 Old Fish Drive in Sydney, Australia, and the contents were described as a 'gift'.

Ned immediately had a bad feeling and opened the package gingerly.

Inside the parcel was a small cardboard box.

With the word 'CUNT' written on it in red marker.

Ned slowly peeled the tape off the top of the box.

And there inside was a pile of shiny dark hair.

Human hair.

Ned stopped breathing. He touched the hair, tentatively. It was soft and silky. He picked up a strand and brought it to his nose.

Monica.

Ned immediately dropped the hair back into the box and sealed it closed. He picked up his mug and was just about to walk up the stairs when the phone rang and made him jump so hard that he dropped his mug; the mug snapped clean in half and brown liquid slowly seeped across the wooden floor.

'Fuck!'

'Whoa,' said Gervase, walking into the hallway, 'ner-vy.' He stretched over him to reach for the receiver. 'Hello, the London residence, how may I help you?'

Ned twitched slightly and leant down to pick up the pieces of mug, listening hawklike to the exchange currently taking place.

'No, she's out at the moment, she'll be back in about half an hour. Can I take a message?'

Ned breathed a sigh of relief and went into the kitchen to get some kitchen roll to mop up the coffee.

Gervase hung up and looked at him with concern. 'That was some reaction there, Ned. Is that a jet-lag thing, too?'

Ned grunted.

'You got something on your mind, Ned? You seem a bit *wired*, mate. If you don't mind me saying.'

'I'm fine,' he snapped.

'D'you want another coffee?'

'No. Thanks. I'm fine.' He wrapped the two halves of the mug in the damp kitchen towels, took them into the kitchen, threw them in the bin, picked up the UPS parcel and made his way upstairs to his room, where he collapsed on to his bed.

He opened the box again.

Fuck. It was still there. Mon's hair. Her lovely thick, shiny, long dark hair. The only really feminine thing about her. It was definitely hers, no doubt about it. It smelt of her shampoo — it smelt of *her*.

He stared at the hair for about five minutes, his mind in turmoil, his heart racing. An image of Monica standing in the bathroom with a pair of kitchen scissors and a hunk of hair in her hand went through his mind. Followed by an image of Sarah Miles in *Ryan's Daughter*. He slammed the box shut, re-sealed it and shoved it under his bed. He couldn't deal with this. He really couldn't deal with this at all.

He leapt to his feet and looked round his room. Gervase had officially moved out of it that morning but even though all his stuff had gone it still didn't feel right. There was a discomfiting, lingering smell in the room, stains on the carpet that hadn't been there before and Ned couldn't bring himself to even look at the sink in the corner since seeing Gervase hawking into it the previous morning.

Ned opened a window, rolled up his sleeves and decided to apply himself to something proactive to take his mind off the hair sitting in a box under his bed, and the insane, *bald* ex-girlfriend on the other side of the world. He swapped his mattress for the old saggy one in Sean's room even though it smelt a bit damp and was nowhere near as comfortable. He just couldn't stomach the prospect of sleeping on the same mattress that Gervase had been using. It wasn't that Gervase *smelt* or anything. It was mainly the thought of him wanking on it that had done it.

He got a bucket, a bottle of washing-up liquid, a load of J-cloths and a big sponge and cleaned his room thoroughly – skirting boards, window frames, handles, on top of things, under things, round the back of things. He poured bleach into his sink and let it soak for ten minutes before scrubbing it to the point of obsession. He hoovered his sofa, his curtains, every inch of carpet, even patches of carpet that hadn't seen daylight for more than two decades. He sprayed the room with something called Tranquillity room fragrance, hoping it might have a similar effect on him, opened the window and let the room air for half an hour. And then he retrieved his PC from Tony's room, plugged it in, re-established all the connections and, with his heart lodged firmly in his throat, went to his Hotmail account.

Jesus, he muttered to himself as he waited for his mail to appear, so slow, so slow. His inbox finally popped up and he scanned it quickly. Forwarded things from his mates in London who didn't even know he was home now. A bulletin from his temp agency in Sydney. Stuff from Amazon. But nothing else.

Nothing from Mon.

'Ned, mate,' there was a soft tapping at the door, 'all right if I come in?' It was Gervase.

Ned looked at him with something approaching relief. 'Yeah,' he said, 'sure.'

'Look,' he said rubbing his hands together, 'a suggestion. It's your Mum's night at the Beulah tonight and I reckon she'd be really made up if you came along.'

'What – to see her sing?'

'Yeah. She'd be chuffed silly.'

'Are you going?'

'Yeah. Highlight of my week. Never miss it.'

Ned looked at his computer screen and his watch and thought about the options. He could either a) stay in his room all night, checking his e-mail obsessively and going slowly insane; or he could b) go and have a pint or two, watch his mum sing and take his mind off things.

'OK,' he said, 'yeah. Why not? What time?'

'Leave at seven?'

'Cool.'

So he found himself half an hour later at the Beulah Tavern, on a wet Wednesday evening, watching his mum in a pink spangly top and black velvet trousers belting out a hairs-standing-up-on-the-back-of-the-neck version of 'Diamonds Are Forever'.

It was a strange sensation, watching his mum singing. He'd seen her singing before. She'd sung to all the boys when they were little and still appreciated it, and he'd seen her singing at cousins' weddings and things. But never in the pub around the corner. People hadn't come here specially to see her sing. They didn't *know* her. They'd come for a pint and she just happened to be here. Some people were ignoring her entirely, which upset Ned. A lot.

'Pisses you off, doesn't it? People not paying attention?'

Ned started. It was their first exchange since Bernie had got up to do her set. Ned nodded but didn't really know what to say.

'She's a real talent, your mum. A *real* talent.'

Ned nodded again. 'Yeah – she's not bad.'

'I was blown away by her, that first time I heard her sing. Totally. Blown away.' He folded his arms and leant back in his seat as if to say that his word was final. He stared intently at Bernie as she sang, then stood up when she finished, clapping and whistling as if he was in the back row at Wembley Arena. Ned looked at him in

86

surprise, and then looked around to see if anyone else thought he was as mad as he did, but no one seemed to have noticed.

Gervase sat down slowly, still clapping gently, then lit a cigarette.

'So,' he said, 'what about you then, Ned? Can you sing?'

Ned laughed. 'Er – no. Categorically not.'

'So, what's your USP, then?'

'My what?'

'Your USP: Unique Selling Point. Your mum can sing, your dad can restore things, Sean can write and Tony's an entrepreneur. What's your thing?'

His *thing*? Jesus. He didn't have a *thing*. He had a degree – that had always been his *thing*. But since making Mum and Dad cry with pride on graduation day, there'd been no more *things*. Just working in clothes shops, curating in galleries and running away to Australia with psychotic strangers. He shrugged. 'Fucking up, I suppose,' he muttered.

'Nah. You've done all right, haven't you? Got a degree? Had some adventures?'

'I guess so. But, you know, I'm twenty-seven now. I'm supposed to be taking things a bit more seriously.'

'So – what've you got in mind?'

'Nothing really.'

'Bernie says you were into art, used to work at Sotheby's or something. Couldn't you try getting back into that?'

'No. Not now. It was just a graduate thing anyway, it wasn't a proper job.'

'Thought about doing some work for your dad?'

Ned shrugged and grunted. 'Bit of a step backwards, isn't it? I mean – that's what I used to do when I was at uni.'

'Couldn't you think about it a bit more seriously now, though? A serious concept. Go into business with him?'

'What – like London & Sons, you mean?' Ned laughed.

'Yeah. Why not. Your dad would be made up.'

'No,' he said, taking a slurp of his lager, 'I don't think so. I couldn't do what my dad does. You've got to really love it. It's a skill. You know.'

'What about your brother?'

'Which one?'

'Tony. Couldn't he give you a job?'

Ned laughed. 'Tony? Are you kidding? I couldn't work for him.'

'Why not? He seems like a decent bloke.'

'Yeah. He is. But you know – he's my *big brother*. I've spent half my life being bossed around by him. No way. Anyway, he'd do my brain in. He's a real control freak.'

'Yeah,' said Gervase thoughtfully, 'yeah. He's a funny one, that Tony. I don't think he likes me very much.'

'Really? What makes you say that?' Ned shot back, not knowing what else to say.

'I'm not really sure. He's just being protective, I suppose, of his folks, his mum. I suppose he's wondering who the hell I am, what the fuck I'm doing there.'

Ned fiddled with his earlobe, noncommittally.

'But he shouldn't worry, you know, Ned. None of you boys should worry.'

'We're not worried.'

'Nah. Of course you're not. But, you know. Just, if you were. Everything's cool.'

'Yeah,' said Ned, trying to mask the concern in his voice. There was nothing more worrying than being told that there was nothing to worry about when you hadn't been worrying in the first place. 'Yeah. Of course it is.'

Ned shrugged again. And then something really strange happened. Gervase suddenly got a really concerned look in his eye, as if the thought of Ned ever worrying about him was breaking his heart. He rested his cigarette in the ashtray, and then, before Ned had a chance to complain, he grabbed his hand and began staring into his eyes, really deeply. The *really* strange thing, however, was that Ned quite liked it. It made him feel warm and safe, and his stomach felt like a big ball of melting chocolate. Ned wasn't sure how long the hand-grasping and staring went on for, but it didn't stop until Bernie's song was over and the sound of enthusiastic applause cut into his subconscious. Gervase slowly let go of Ned's hand and reached for his smouldering cigarette. He shook his head slowly.

'You need to sort it out, mate.'

'Sort what out?'

'You know.'

'No. I don't.'

Gervase sighed and leant in towards Ned. 'It's not going to go away if you ignore it. You can run, but you can't hide. You know that, don't you?'

Ned licked his lips. He didn't like the direction this

conversation was taking. 'What? What isn't going away?'

'Your little problem.'

Ned frowned.

'Your mess. The mess you left behind.'

Ned gulped. 'You mean – you mean in Australia?'

'Uh-huh. There's still a lot of pain there. You left a lot of pain. And I know it's not your fault, Ned. I know that. But you can't just run away and pretend that it hasn't happened. It'll catch up with you sooner or later, one way or another. Deal with it now or it'll only be more painful.'

'Monica?' said Ned, quietly. 'Are you talking about Monica?'

Gervase pulled away from him suddenly, as if someone had cut through a piece of thread that had been tying them together. He closed his eyes, took a deep breath and knocked back half his pint of lager.

'I don't fucking know, do I?'

'Oh.' Ned picked up his pint, too. His hands were shaking. And then Gervase suddenly banged his glass down on the table, stood up really quickly and stalked off to the toilet.

Ned breathed out a huge chilled lungful of air and tried to concentrate on his mum singing, but it was really hard. He wished there was someone sitting with him, a mate or something, so that he could just laugh and say, 'Blimey, what the fuck was all that about?' But as it was, he was stranded with his head full of the last thing he wanted there: Monica. Ned tried to recall exactly what Gervase had said. 'You've got to sort it out.' He shuddered. Because whether Gervase knew what he was talking about or not, he was right. It was a mess. But just because that mess was on the other side of the planet, didn't mean it had gone away.

The hair in the box under his bed was testament to that.

He downed some more beer and tried to put the thought of it to the back of his mind. Which was, he was aware, *all* he'd done since he got home and it wasn't a comfortable sensation. It was like spending the best part of a week holding in a really big fart.

'So – Ned. What kind of music are you into?' Gervase was back, smelling overpoweringly, but not unpleasantly, of the liquid soap they had in the toilets. Ned jumped a little in surprise, both at Gervase's sudden reappearance and the blunt tangency of the question. He exhaled. 'God. I dunno. Loads of stuff really. Chart dance music, you know, Fatboy Slim, Faithless, Moby . . .'

Gervase sneered at him. 'Cack. All of it. Music for fucking zombies.'

Ned was about to cut in with some kind of defence, but Gervase was on a roll. 'Rock and roll. That's the only real music.'

'What, like the old fifties stuff?'

'Yeah. Sort of. I mean I used to be into all that rockabilly, psychobilly thing, you know, King Kurt and all that. But, as I . . . *mature*, I find myself more drawn to the kings. The real stuff.'

'Like who?'

'Robert Gordon. Now there's a man. A real, bone

fide rock-and-roll singer who's still doing it, yeah? Doing it live. No Chuck Berry theatrics. No Elvis Vegas stuff, no rhinestones. Just a man, his band, his guitar and his voice. Pure unadulterated rock and roll. Do you like rock and roll, Ned?'

'Well, yeah – some of it.'

'Your mum – she likes rock and roll. Your dad, too.'

'Yeah. But all mums and dads like rock and roll, don't they? It's in their genes. They can all do it as well, you know, the dance. Every one of them can rock and roll.' Ned laughed. 'It's like they're these normal human beings. They watch telly and go to dinner and complain about you playing your music too loud and then someone puts on 'Great Balls of Fire' and all of a sudden they're up and out of their seats and dancing like fucking spastics. Doing all the twirls and everything. I mean – what the fuck are we going to embarrass *our* kids with at weddings when they're twelve?'

Gervase slapped his hands on to his legs, spilling a long finger of ash all over his jeans in the process. 'Exactly,' he said, 'spot on! There's no dance any more, is there? Our grandparents had the charleston, their grandparents had the waltz. Our parents had rock and roll and the twist. There was disco in the seventies. But what have we got? Sweet FA, that's what. It's a tragedy, Ned, a true tragedy. I mean dancing, it's tribal, right? It's an integral part of the way we express ourselves. You know? And now we express ourselves either by getting plastered at the office party and doing the Time Warp or by taking a load of poncey designer drugs and waving our arms in the air until eight in the morning.' He tutted, shook his head slowly from side to side and cleared his sinuses. 'It's a sad world, Ned, it really is. A sad, soulless, monochrome world.

'That's why I like coming here on a Wednesday night, seeing your mum sing. Look at her.' They paused and looked at her. 'If only everything in the world was like your mum, Ned. And I mean that with all the respect in the world, I really do. But your mum – she's so alive. It's like that house – your house – without your mum, it would just be a dump. And I mean *that* with all the respect, too. But it would. Your mum's got soul. *Real* soul . . .'

And then he turned to watch Bernie and his foot tapped up and down and the conversation, patently, was over. Ned looked at Gervase for a while, at the slightly beak-like profile, the pock-marked skin, the dyed black hair and sinewy, tattooed neck, and for a split second it was almost like he was looking at somebody from another planet. Or maybe just another era.

Ned felt a sudden surge of warmth towards this ageless, rootless man and settled back to enjoy the rest of his mother's set with a whole new appreciation for her talent and for her soul.

Romance in Catford

Sean pulled the ring out of its little navy box and held it up to the light. It really was the prettiest thing he'd ever seen. He slid it back into its crevasse, snapped the box closed and popped it in the table drawer.

Tonight was the big night. And not just because he was about to propose to his older woman. It was also the first time Millie had been to his flat. It wasn't deliberate, just that London law said that if you lived in a fantastically appointed, centrally located flat on the north side of the river the idea of going to Catford, for any reason whatsoever, was akin to having a toothache and going to India to visit a street dentist. There just never seemed to be a good enough reason to take her back to his, so he hadn't. But tonight, as chance would have it, Millie was having a late meeting in Camberwell; and once you'd crossed the river, well, sod it, you may as well get stuck in. So she'd suggested he cook her dinner here. Insisted, actually. She wanted to have a sniff around, she said, unearth all of his dark secrets. And, actually, it was perfect. He'd thought about a fancy restaurant, taking her to Nobu or the Dorchester, booking them into a swanky hotel room, but proposing here, in his flat, was much, much better. It was going to be fantastically un-corny.

He hadn't bothered to do much to his flat, just turned all the lights down really low and lit some candles so that you couldn't see what a state it was in and hoped that the aroma of garlic bread baking in the oven would draw attention away from it. He'd warned her in advance about the insalubrious nature of his home, so she had a fairly good idea of what to expect, and anyway, Millie didn't care about shit like that. Millie didn't care about anything that wasn't important – that was one of the things he loved most about her.

Sean never thought this day would come. He'd thought he'd spend the rest of his life working his way systematically through every girl in London between the ages of twenty and thirty with half a brain cell and a penchant for going out with commitment-phobic men. And then when he was too old to pull, he thought, he'd end up living here alone, for ever. And he'd been happy to think that, because he'd always preferred his own company to anyone else's. He never thought he'd want to marry anyone. He never thought he'd meet someone who'd turn his preconceptions about love on their head, who'd make him feel sociable, nurturing and strong. He'd always known that Tony would settle down and marry and he fully expected the same of Ned. They'd be the ones to replicate their parent's happy marriage, they'd provide the grandchildren and the stability. But now, well, it looked like there might be a last-minute contender coming up on the inside – him. Sean had fallen through a familial hole somewhere along the line and had always felt like he didn't quite fit in. But, since Tony got divorced, Ned buggered off to Australia and *Half a Man* came out, all that had changed. *He* was now the brightest star of the family. And now he was about to climb another rung on the ladder of parental approval. He was going to get married. And not to just anyone, but to this incredible, beautiful woman who was out of his league in every way.

He gave his arrabiata sauce a quick stir on the hob, chucked in a few more chilli flakes and put a pan of water on to boil. And then the doorbell went.

'Hi,' he said into the intercom.

'Hi. Uptown Girl here. Is that Downtown Boy?'

He smiled. 'Come up,' he said, 'eighteenth floor.'

'Blimey,' she said, 'sure I don't need special breathing equipment for that?'

He buzzed her in and waited for her outside the lift, subconsciously seeing it through her eyes. It wasn't bad, as towerblocks went. It was on a nice estate that was well looked after and mainly full of couples. He'd put his name down on the council waiting list when he was twenty. At the time he thought that he was never going to be in a position to afford to buy a place. And he was too antisocial to share a flat, anyway. And, yes, he should move out now, he knew that. He didn't need this place any more. He was taking up valuable space. You could get a family of three into his flat. And he would move out. Soon. It was just that he hadn't entirely got used to the having-money thing, he didn't *trust* it. It had taken him over a year just to feel comfortable buying things he didn't need, and even now he was able to spend his money only in bite-sized chunks. The idea of blowing the lot, in one fell swoop, just like that – well, it was terrifying. He'd be poor again. No more cabs, no more meals, just him, sitting in some beautiful flat he could never afford to leave.

The lift doors slid open and Millie strode out. She was wearing jeans with pointy-toed boots, a big suede coat with a furry trim and her hair was piled on top of her head. She was also, Sean was delighted to note, wearing red lipstick. She'd never worn red lipstick before and it was one of his favourite things.

'Hello, gorgeous,' she said, wrapping her arms around his neck and giving him a big kiss on the lips. 'I've just been chatted up.'

'Oh yeah,' said Sean, 'who by?'

'A ten-year-old boy wearing DKNY jeans. He said I was "hot". And that he liked my boots.'

'See – I told you you'd like it here.'

He unlocked his door and let her in. The sounds of Spiritualized wafted through the flat, along with the smell of garlic and fresh basil. The candles he'd lit around the place gave an almost romantic glow and then there was his secret weapon.

'Oh my God!' She pushed past him and headed straight to the back of the living room. 'This is amazing.' She'd spotted his secret weapon – the floor-to-ceiling plate-glass windows on three sides from which you could see pretty much every inch of London spread out below, like a glittering rug. 'Oh my God,' she said again, her hands pressed against the glass, her mouth open with amazement. 'Look – the Dome. The London Eye. And the river. Oh wow,' she moved to the south-facing window, 'look, it's the Crystal Palace mast.'

He joined her at the window, following her fingertip to the flashing head of the mast, and slipped his arm around her waist.

'You can see Crystal Palace from nearly everywhere,' he said proudly. 'Primrose Hill, Suicide Bridge, Alexandra Palace. Even from Ilford on a clear day. It's like the North Star.'

They stood for a while watching the blinking light on the horizon.

'God, I can see why you don't want to give this place up – it's absolutely amazing.'

'You haven't seen the toilet yet.'

'Why,' she said excitedly, 'what can you see from there?'

'Nothing,' he said, 'it's just really grim, that's all.'

She laughed. 'Look, I was brought up on a farm – I know all about grim toilets.'

Some farm, he thought to himself. She always referred to it as a farm but he knew it was an estate, with a management office and people employed to deal with things like dung and corpses and artificial insemination. The stable block was probably bigger than his parents' house and her father was a Sir.

'Aren't you going to give me the grand tour?'

He shrugged. 'This is it.'

'But where's the bedroom?'

'It's the dank, musty hovel just through there,' he indicated with his eyebrows. She pulled off her sheepskin coat and Sean pulled an ice-cold bottle of Louis Röederer from the freezer compartment of his Smeg where it had been chilling for the last hour.

Sean wasn't given to romantic gestures. None of the London boys were, really – it wasn't in their genes. Their father was a kind man, an affectionate man, a man in love with his wife, but Sean couldn't recall him ever buying Mum flowers or whisking her away for a surprise weekend. Gerry showed his love in other ways; nuzzling Bernie's neck while she was hoovering, talking proudly about her achievements with friends, doing the washing-up without comment and driving out to Croydon at two in the morning to collect his drunken wife from a nightclub after her monthly girls' night out. These had been the London boys' lessons in love.

Millie looked at the bottle in his hand with surprise.

'Well,' she said, 'you *are* a classy act.'

'What – *this*?' he said, waving the £45 bottle of champagne around airily. 'This is nothing. You wait to see what you get on our *three*-month anniversary.'

She smiled and sauntered around the corner into his bedroom. Sean carried the bottle and glasses on to the balcony. It was mid-April and Sean could just about distinguish the lazy, magical scent of a London summer encroaching. He could hear the *EastEnders* theme music coming through the balcony doors of the flat next door and the distant echo of children in the playground eighteen storeys below. Spring was very much in the air. Sean spent hours out there on his balcony in the summer, wrote most of his first book on it, when he used to write longhand. He'd miss this secret little corner of London when he finally got his act together and got out of here. He'd be hard-pushed to find another view like this, tons of cash or no. It was ironic that only the very poor and the very rich could afford a London panorama.

'Cool wallpaper,' Millie said facetiously, coming up behind him.

'Fucking shocking, isn't it? I keep meaning to do something about it, but you just sort of get used to bad wallpaper after a while, don't you?'

'Ah – so it wasn't your choice, then?'

'What?! How dare you! If I ever get round to buying my own place I will astound you with my natural sense of style and taste, I can assure you.'

'Oh, really?' She picked up a wine glass and held it up expectantly. 'So – are you going to open that, or what?'

He smiled at her and attempted to ease the cork from the bottle. 'Jesus,' he muttered as the cork refused to budge.

'Here, give it to me – I'm an expert.' She took the bottle from him and popped the cork easily. They both watched as it flew in an elegant arc across the London skyline, tracing the tops of towerblocks and cranes, caressing the curves of Blackheath Common and landing incongruously among the junk-filled paladins below.

Millie poured the champagne and passed Sean a glass.

'Cheers,' she said, 'here's to your flat. About bloody time too. And to meeting your family in three days' time,' she grimaced nervously.

'You don't have to come, you know. It's fine. I've given you a get-out clause. No one will mind.'

'No, no. I want to. I really want to. It's just a bit *daunting*, that's all.'

Sean looked at his older woman, then, standing on his Catford balcony in her Portobello jumper and inherited earrings, nervously clutching her champagne and looking up at him as if she were about to be introduced to the Royal family, and felt a huge, overwhelming surge of love for her that started in his stomach and went all the way to his tearducts.

'Aw, come here,' he said, holding his arms out to her. 'They're going to love you, you know that. They'll adore you.' She smiled warmly and stepped into his embrace and he hugged her tightly to him, inhaling her aroma. *Now*, said a little voice in his head. *Now, do it now.* There could never be a better moment; a mild April evening, London beneath them, the sun setting above and a whole bottle of chilled champagne left to drink.

He held her hands in his and looked at the ginger flecks in her olive eyes, the laugh lines that grew from the corners of her eyes, the little scar just above her top lip, the little imperfections he'd grown to love almost more than her perfection over the past eight weeks, and as he looked he found himself doing it, saying it, without even having to think about it:

'Millie – will you marry me?'

She looked at him in shock for a brief moment, a smile twitching at the corners of her mouth.

'What?!'

'I said,' he got down on his knee this time, 'Millie, I know we haven't known each other long, but we know each other well enough for me to know that I want to spend the rest of my life with you so I'd like to ask you – will you please marry me?'

He stared up at her, feeling slightly foolish but very excited, and waited for her to react. She stared at him blankly for a moment. And then she threw her head back and started to laugh.

'Are you winding me up?' she asked suspiciously. '*You* want to marry *me*?'

'Yup.'

She laughed out loud. 'But, *nobody* wants to marry me. That's the whole point of me. You can't possibly want to marry me.'

'Oh, but I do.'

'But I'm a spinster. I'm an old maid. I've never even *lived* with anyone. Are you sure about this?'

'Never been surer.'

'And I'm six years older than you. You do realize that?'

'Uh-huh.'

'And whatever happens in this world, I will *always* be six years older. In four years' time I'm going to be forty. And you'll only be thirty-four.'

'Yes.'

'I'm not going to miraculously turn into a twenty-three-year-old when you have your midlife crisis, you know?'

'Oh, Jesus Christ, Millie . . .' Sean smiled wryly and got to his feet.

'Ooh. Sorry, sorry, sorry. I'm just supposed to say "Yes" really enigmatically and gracefully, like I always knew you'd want to marry me, aren't I?'

'Well, yes, that's the . . .'

'Yes! Yes! Double yes! Yes, I'd love to marry you. If you're sure you know what you're doing and you've really thought about this and you don't mind hanging out with an old woman and . . .'

'Millie!'

'Sorry.'

'So that's a yes, then?'

'Yes! Oh God, yes, definitely!'

'Do you want your ring, then?'

'Oh my God! You got me a ring?' She brought her hands to her mouth and Sean could see tears shining in her eyes.

'Uh-huh.' He headed indoors to retrieve the ring from its drawer, his heart thumping with excitement.

She gasped in wonder when he presented her with the box. 'You're really serious aren't you?' She opened it, slowly and reverentially, and sucked in her breath when she caught sight of the diamond baguette. And then Sean slipped it on to her finger and she burst into tears.

'Oh God,' she snivelled through tears and laughter, 'I'm getting married.' She turned to face the world, cupped her hands around her mouth and shouted across the London skyline, 'I'm getting married!' And then she turned back to Sean and looked at him with tear-streaked eyes. 'I love you so much, Sean London. We are going to be so incredibly happy together. You know that, don't you?'

And Sean smiled because he did know that. 'Come on,' he said, wiping some tears away from under her eyes, 'let's go into my dank, musty hovel of a bedroom and have fantastic post-proposal, engaged-to-be-married sex.'

He didn't need to ask twice.

Just What He Always Wanted

'Happy birthday, Tony.' Ness handed him a huge and very heavy gift, wrapped in lurid green holographic paper topped with a fuchsia bow.

'Thanks.'

'Thirty-five,' she said, for about the hundredth time that evening, 'I can't believe you're thirty-five.'

He grimaced and began peeling away the holographic paper. Inside was a cardboard box. It had the words 'Organically Grown Pineapples' printed on it. 'Cool,' he said, 'pineapples.'

Ness threw him a withering smile. 'Come on,' she urged, 'open it.' She was almost quivering with excitement as Tony ripped the parcel tape off the box and pulled open the flaps.

Tony looked inside. It was some kind of electronic thing. It was black and clunky. He pulled it out and examined it.

Ness was looking at him, anticipation shining from her eyes. 'Don't you know what it is?'

Tony examined it further. 'Erm, some kind of time machine?'

'No! It's a Betamax video player! For you to watch all your old Betamax tapes on!'

'Aaah,' said Tony, realization dawning. 'Aaah! God, Ness, that's brilliant. That's so brilliant. Thank you.' And it really was brilliant. The Londons had owned a Betamax back in the seventies when nobody knew any better and Tony had recorded all his favourite programmes religiously for a couple of years, until the VHS had taken off and they got rid of it. But he'd kept his Betamax tapes for all these years; determined that one day he'd get himself a player and have a stride down memory lane. 'Where the hell did you get it from?'

'Well – it was a bit of a mare, actually. I started looking about six months ago and nearly got one at a car-boot sale, but it was completely knackered so I had a look on the Internet, but it all got a bit complicated. And then I got this one at the electric shop on Church Road. Just happened to be driving past, went in, there it was.'

'God, Ness, thank you,' he leant over to kiss her and she clamped her hands on to his cheeks and gave him a big smacker on the lips.

'You are very welcome indeed.' She grinned at him happily and Tony felt a creeping sense of unease in his gut. She'd gone to so much trouble, been so thoughtful, bought him the best kind of gift, the gift you really, really wanted but didn't know you wanted. A gift that showed that she listened to him, that she remembered things he said, that what was important to him was important to her.

A gift that showed she cared.

Way too much.

Tony felt a plume of guilt rising in his chest. 'Come

on,' he said, looking at his watch and putting the Beta-max back in the pineapple box, 'we'd better get moving. We're going to be late.'

The Loneliest Penguin

Mum had made it lovely in the living room – candles, a huge fire, Sinatra playing in the background. It was just the five of them right now: Mum, Dad, Ned, Ness and him. Hands darted in and out of bowls of nuts and Bombay mix, Dad threw pistachio shells on to the fire where they hissed and crackled, Mum sat radiant with joy at the prospect of having her whole brood together under her roof again.

Tony perched himself on the arm of a sofa and ignored the feel of Ness's arm as it fell across his lap and gripped his kneecap affectionately. He accepted a glass of red wine from his mother and took a large gulp, swilling it around his mouth, letting the lukewarm liquid reach into every crevice, numbing him.

The fire in the grate was throwing off far too much heat and Tony felt himself melting inside his fleece. He was just about to take it off when the doorbell rang. Jesus. It was them. He pulled his fleece back down, touched his hair, adjusted his posture, tried his hardest to look natural – which was nigh on impossible when every nerve in his body was jangling with anticipation.

He eyed the living-room door nonchalantly, drumming his fingertips casually against the side of his wine glass. And then there she was, standing in the doorway, just behind Sean. Everything else seemed to fade away, then – the introduction, the laughter, the sheer joyful volume of familial reunion. He was deaf to it all. All he was aware of was this beautiful perfect person standing uncertainly in the doorway, smiling at what was happening in front of her, looking as excited as everyone else in the room, even though she was a stranger.

'Everyone, this is Millie. Millie, this is everyone.'

'Sean, honestly, what sort of an introduction is that?' scolded Bernie, taking Millie by the hand and introducing her to everyone properly. Tony could barely breathe. She looked even better than he remembered, in an embroidered suede skirt, leather boots and a tight red sweater. Her hair was clipped back with a few mahogany strands hanging loose around her face. And she was wearing red lipstick.

'And you've met Tony and Ness, haven't you?'

'Yes. Of course. Hi again,' she beamed at them both, and then leant in towards Tony and grabbed his shoulder and kissed him on the cheek, properly, so that he could feel the ridges in her lips against his skin. 'Happy birthday!'

'Thank you,' he muttered, breathing in deeply. She smelt of fresh air and London rain.

He watched in awe as she leant in again to kiss Ness. Everything was still there, just as he remembered: the flecked eyes, the thick hair, the plump lips, the tawny skin, the blunt nails, the silver rings . . . But, hold on, one more silver ring than last time. A slender, silver ring, embracing a large diamond, third finger, left hand. The same finger on which he'd worn a band for eight years. An heirloom, he supposed dismissively, a grandmother's ring, something she wore on special occasions, probably the only finger it fit.

'Lovely to see you again, Ness,' she said, and the sound of her lips smacking against Ness's cheeks reverberated around Tony's head.

Sean leant in to hug him, then – a quick slap on the back, Happy Birthday, mate, a gift of some sort thrust into his hands – but all he was aware of was the fact that *she* was in the room. The woman he'd been fantasizing about for nearly two weeks. She was sitting over there, drinking wine, her legs crossed, in his parents' home. And she was going to be around all night.

Someone cracked a joke about the state of Goldie. 'Oh no,' said Millie, petting him furiously, 'I think he's lovely.' Goldie rolled over and offered up his horrible old belly, which Millie tickled obligingly, and Tony could never have imagined that the day would come when he would want, more than anything in the world, to be a senile, malodorous golden retriever.

'At least he's passed the age of the involuntary penile emergence,' said Sean, and everyone laughed.

Tony laughed too but stopped abruptly when he caught sight of his reflection in the glass doors of a cabinet and almost didn't recognize himself. And then he remembered – this was who he was now, a fat and very nearly middle-aged man, sweating lightly inside too many clothes, his cheeks flushed from the fire and the wine, his hair unkempt and woolly where he'd pulled his T-shirt over his head when he was getting ready.

His dad wandered around the room with a bottle of wine, a roll-up hanging from the corner of his mouth. 'Top up?' he said to Tony.

'Yeah, please.' He let his dad top his glass up to the rim and then took a big gulp.

'Tony?'

'What?' He snapped out of his reverie as he felt Ness banging his kneecap.

'Funny, isn't it?'

'What?'

'About the card?'

'What card?'

Ness rolled her eyes. 'Wakey wakey,' she teased, 'Millie was just saying that the first card she bought for Sean – it was one of yours.'

'No. Really? Which one?'

Millie sat forward on the sofa and readied herself to describe the card to him. 'It's this sort of shape,' she said, describing a thin rectangle, 'and it's got a cartoon drawing of a penguin on the front, a really *tiny* –' she indicated the tininess between thumb and index finger – 'little penguin with this sad little expression on his face and he's sitting all on his own on this glacier, nothing around for miles and it says . . .'

'"I'm feeling lonely",' Tony finished.

'Yes,' she said, 'that's right. But not because I was

111

lonely or anything. I just really liked the expression on the little penguin's face. It just – got me. Did you draw it, Tony?'

'No,' said Tony, wishing more than anything that he had. 'No. I commissioned it, though. It was by a woman, actually – a woman called . . . called . . .' he clicked his fingers, desperately trying to recall the name of the artist, 'Sybil? Something? Something French. "S" something . . .' He racked his brain so hard it hurt, wanting, *needing*, to give Millie the information she wanted, to give her anything, anything at all.

'Oh,' she said, watching him struggle, 'don't worry about it – it'll say on the back of the card. I'll look at it when we get back to Sean's.'

'You're staying at Sean's tonight?' he asked in surprise. He just couldn't quite imagine Millie walking through Sean's estate, taking that aluminium-lined, graffiti-ed lift up to his grotty little flat that always smelt of stale bedsheets.

'Yes,' she nodded and smiled, 'I was there on Wednesday as well, wasn't I, Sean?' she winked at him.

'You most certainly were, Millie,' he said, returning her wink.

'Shall we . . . ?' she wiggled her eyebrows at him.

'I don't know,' he said, 'd'you think . . . ?'

'It's up to you,' she said.

'Let's do it,' he said.

And they held hands and turned to face everyone and it looked as if their faces were about to split open with excitement and Sean squeezed Millie's hand and Millie beamed and he said, 'We've got something we'd like to tell you.'

'Oh yes,' Bernie sat bolt upright and gave them her undivided attention.

'Well,' said Sean, exchanging a nauseatingly complicitous look with Millie, 'on Wednesday night, I asked Millie if she'd marry me . . .'

Mum screamed and went rigid, her hands flying to her face to cover her mouth.

'. . . and she said yes. We're getting married!'

For a second the whole room fell into a suspended silence. Tony looked around nervously. It looked like a game of musical statues.

'See!' said Ned triumphantly, pointing a finger at Tony. 'Didn't I tell you – didn't I say?'

And then the room erupted. Everyone leapt to their feet to congratulate them and kiss them. Mum sent Gerry to the off-licence to get a bottle of champagne. Ness started crying. Ned went upstairs to get his camera. But not one person said, 'Hold on a second, you two hardly know each other – don't you think you're rushing into this a bit?' Not one person did the responsible thing. It was pathetic, this desperate thrill-seeking – Ooh, wonderful, someone's getting married, that lifts *my* dull little life out of the doldrums for a minute or two, who cares if they're making the greatest mistake of their life or not. Jesus.

Someone passed him a glass of champagne and he knocked back half of it, unthinkingly. 'Tony,' his mum chastised, 'wait for the toast! Honestly . . .'

Everyone was talking dates and proposals and rings and dresses, Ness was running her hand up and down his thigh, and Tony was left to stare at his reflection in the cabinet doors and wonder when exactly his life had turned out like this.

He'd been the catch. Him. Tony. *He*'d been the big brother, the good-looking one, the successful business-man. He'd been the one with the beautiful wife and the big house, the jeep and the bank account that never went into the red. Sean had just been his little brother, the scamp, the worry to his mother, the one who couldn't stick at anything.

But now Sean was 'the author' and being 'the author' meant that everything previously seen as negative about him had sort of fallen into place. Being 'the author' meant that a scruffy, lazy guy with smelly trainers who lived on a Catford council estate could persuade a woman like Millie to marry him. And being 'the author' meant that *he* was the catch of the family now, not Tony. Not any more. Jesus.

Tony waited glumly for the toast, raised his glass half-heartedly and knocked back some more cham-pagne. This wasn't right. There were constants in life, important constants, things to anchor you to the world – things like the fact that your mother would always love you, no matter what, and that one day you were going to die. And that you would always, whatever happened in life, be the big brother. But Tony didn't feel like the big brother any more. He felt like the slightly overweight, dull-witted younger brother who was never going to leave home and get married. He looked at Sean, glowing and triumphant, and at Ned, the beloved prodigal baby of the family. He looked at Ness again, his 'saviour', as she bonded with his mother and it occurred to him that his mother would probably choose Ness over him if she was ever called upon to do so. And then, as if to compound these pathetic feelings of insecurity about his previously unquestioned positioning within the family, a skeletal figure suddenly appeared in the doorway.

'Gervase! Come in love, come in. You're just in time. We've just had some wonderful news. Gerry, get Gervase a glass for his champagne. Tony, love, shift over a bit, let Gervase sit down.'

Tony shifted over and found himself clinging to the very edges of the gathering. He downed another mouthful of champagne and felt almost swamped by resentment.

He felt insignificant. He felt awkward. He felt as lonesome, dejected and detached from everyone as that little penguin on the front of Millie's card.

He didn't fit in any more. He wanted to start again.

He wanted another chance.

Ness didn't stay over that night. Tony really couldn't stomach the prospect. He just wanted to get into his own bed, on his own, think about Millie and feel sorry for himself. He didn't want Ness there, wrapping her never-ending legs around him, trying to cheer him up, being infernally upbeat – being his so-called fucking *saviour.* She whinged a bit but he feigned a splitting headache and an early start and ordered her a minicab and felt himself crumple with relief as he closed the door behind her. And, as he watched her from his living-room window, folding her long legs into the minicab, flirting with the driver, as he listened to her raucous laughter ringing around the mews even with the doors of the car closed, he felt suddenly angry with her. More than angry – completely, lividly furious. Ness, he suddenly felt, was the problem with everything. She was the symbol of the disintegration of his life and the abrupt end of his youth. If you were to draw a line through the middle of Tony's life to divide it into 'good times' and 'bad times' it would fall directly at the very point where Ness had come into it.

He was still thin when he and Jo split up, still up for it and positive about the future. And then Ness had come into his life and made him laugh. She'd been up for it, too – the two of them had gone out every night, drinking themselves into oblivion, laughing, eating, spending money. She'd taken his mind off any latent fears he might have had about his future as a single man and made him feel good about himself. And the sex had been a revelation after so long with the same woman. Ness's appetite for sex more than equalled her appetite for food and drink and she was up for everything. Tony had grown quite fond of her over the months, looked forward to seeing her more and more. And then, even though it wasn't supposed to have been anything serious, somehow, because all his friends were pairing off, they'd ended up as an item. Friends felt more comfortable spending time with Tony when he was part of a couple and they all loved Ness, thought she was *so* good for Tony. So she became part of the gang and part of his life. And no one had ever really asked him if he minded. They were so keen for the two of them to be together, for TonyAndNess to be a couple, that it just sort of happened. And he shouldn't have let it, he thought now, he shouldn't have let Ness knit herself so tightly into his life, because she'd blinded him to possibilities. The possibility of true love and a real future. He'd been living a compromise for ten years, thinking that that was all life could offer. He should have taken his chance when Jo had left, just like she did, taken the opportunity to find true love, to find what Sean had found, to find Millie, to love Millie, to marry Millie. Instead of just dreaming about her.

Marrying Jo hadn't been a mistake, Tony realized, and getting divorced hadn't been a mistake, but letting Ness love him had been one of the biggest mistakes of his life.

Millie's Curveball

'Thank God that's over,' said Sean in the cab on the way home from Mickey's, more to allow Millie the opportunity to tell him it had been a nightmare than because he was glad it was over. He'd had an excellent night. He always loved family nights out, especially now Ned was back. 'Thank you for going through that for me.'

'God, Sean,' Millie looked at him incredulously, 'don't be silly. It was a true pleasure. Your family are fantastic.'

He turned to look at her. 'Really?'

'Really. I've had a brilliant night. Your mum is amazing. And so beautiful. And your father's adorable.' Millie smiled and rolled into Sean's shoulders, nestling into his armpit. 'I'd like to get to know them. Your family. Get to know them properly. You know?'

Sean looked at her then and kissed the top of her head and loved her even more than he'd loved her that morning, more than he'd ever loved anyone in all of his life, and it was all he could do to stop himself from proposing to her all over again.

'I can't get over how different you three brothers all are, though.'

'What do you mean?'

'Well, you're all really similar in some ways; you've all got the same chins and ears and face shape. But Ned's all sort of hippiefied and sweet-natured and seems a lot younger than his age. And Tony's all strait-laced and grown-up and seems older than his age. I can't believe he's about the same age as me.'

'Yup. That's our Tone. Old before his time.'

'I think he's really sweet, though. Like a big teddy bear.'

'God, he'd slit his wrists if he heard you saying that. He's really self-conscious about his weight.'

'Why? He's not fat.'

'Yes he is. He's a complete bloater.'

'God – men are so *rude* about each other! He's not fat. He's just *cuddly*. All pink and fluffy in his fleece. I think he's quite good-looking, actually.'

Sean threw her a mock-horrified expression. 'D'you fancy him or something?'

'No, of course not! I don't fancy anyone in the whole galaxy except you, my love, as you well know. No – he's good-looking in that teddy-bear kind of a way. You know. I really like him. And I really like Ness, too.'

'Yeah, Ness is cool, isn't she?'

'Tony doesn't appreciate her, though, does he?'

Sean shrugged. 'No,' he said, 'probably not – not like I appreciate you, eh?'

Millie smiled at him and nuzzled closer into his shoulder. 'No one's ever appreciated me like you do.'

'I find that hard to believe.' Sean squeezed her tight

and breathed in deeply, savouring the taste of the moment and trying to halt time, because right then, sitting in the back seat of a Peugeot 406 with Millie on a Saturday night in April, Sean knew he was experiencing perfect and complete happiness.

There was a soft knocking at the bathroom door. 'Sean? Can I come in?'

'Just having a pee, Millie, I'll be out in a second.'

Sean jumped slightly when he heard the door opening behind him and felt Millie's hand brushing against his jumper.

'Millie!'

'Oh, don't be so silly,' she scoffed, 'we're bloody engaged. It's about time we admitted to the awful fact that we go to the loo, don't you think? Anyway, there's something I want to say and if I don't say it now . . .' She took a huge and audible deep breath. 'I'm sorry.'

'Sorry? What on earth for?' Sean's pee suddenly sounded extraordinarily loud so he tried to angle it down the side of the bowl.

'I think I'm about to throw you a curveball.'

Sean desperately wanted to turn round and look at her, but he was still, inexplicably, peeing.

'OK – hit me with it.' Sean was now also quite convinced that not only was this the longest pee he'd ever done, it was also quite possibly the smelliest.

'There's something I have to tell you. Something important. Something you're probably not expecting and something that's going to change everything. Big time.'

'Right.' Here it comes, he thought, she's going to dump me. While I'm pissing. *Actually* in the process of pissing.

'The thing is – and I still haven't decided whether this is a good thing or a bad thing, but I'm really hoping you'll think it's a good thing . . .'

A good thing, thought Sean, how could you possibly imagine that I might think that you dumping me while I'm pissing is a good thing?

'Sean – I'm pregnant.'

The last droplet of pee finally hit the bowl and sounded like a cluster bomb being dropped in the Atlantic.

Then the bathroom was silent.

Charming Sentiments from Overseas

'I am *stuffed*,' said Ned, flopping on to the sofa and switching on the TV, 'absolutely fucking stuffed.' It was the first time since he got home that he'd had any kind of appetite and he'd really gone for it at Mickey's that night. Houmous and tara with about four whole pitta breads, some deep-fried crispy things stuffed with minced lamb, one of Mum's stuffed vine leaves, the mixed grill, which was completely *massive*, ice-cream and liqueurs. Not to mention six bottles of Cypriot lager and all the champagne they'd had before they left the house. He pulled up his T-shirt and caressed his swollen belly tenderly.

Gerry came in carrying a large cardboard box full of green-tinged silver candlesticks and his cleaning kit. He laid out some newspaper, made himself a cigarette, put on his brushed-cotton gloves and started polishing, picking up his roll-up every now and then between cotton-covered fingertips and sucking on it contemplatively.

'Fancy giving me a hand?' he said to Ned after a few moments.

Ned glanced at him in a manner that suggested he was clearly insane.

'I'll give you a fiver.'

Ned thought about his rapidly diminishing bank account. 'Per thing?'

'You mad?' said Gerry. 'No – for doing half of it.'

'Half of it? You've got to be kidding. There's about twenty sticks in there.'

'OK, a tenner.'

'No way – three quid a stick. That's my final offer.'

'One.'

'Two-fifty.'

'One-fifty.'

'Two.'

'Done.'

'Cool.'

Ned wrenched himself from his seat and sauntered over to his father. He rifled through the candlesticks for a while, looking for ones without too much ornamentation and fuss, and then took them over to his position in front of the TV.

'So, tell me more about this big surprise for Mum,' said Ned.

'Shhh!' Gerry put his finger to his lips and looked at Ned sternly.

'It's all right – she's in the kitchen.'

'Well,' said Gerry, leaning towards Ned and whispering, 'I'm going to tell her I'm taking her out for a flash dinner, tell her to get all dolled up, drive past the Ritz, go all dewy-eyed, you know, remember our first date, that kind of thing. Tempt her in for a quick cocktail, and then – surprise, surprise – da-da!' He rubbed his hands together and winked at Ned.

'Who's going to be there?'

'You lot, obviously. The rest of the family. Family friends. About fifty of us. Champagne reception. Canapés. Things with caviar and quail's eggs. No expense spared.'

'Cool,' said Ned, 'and who's going to be staying the night?'

'Just us lot. Not forking out for the rest of them – you've got to be kidding. I've booked four rooms. And yours is a double, so you'd better hurry up and find yourself another girlfriend.' Gerry laughed at Ned and then pulled himself together as he heard Mum's footsteps coming up the hallway. 'Shhh,' he said again, 'she's coming.'

Bernie wandered back in with a crossword magazine and cup of coffee. It always amazed Ned that Mum was able to drink a cup of full-strength Colombian coffee at midnight and then go to bed half an hour later and fall into a deep, impenetrable slumber. Ned only had to look at a teabag after six to ensure that he'd be awake until the early hours, listening to his heart pounding like a locomotive in his chest. 'Aaah,' she cooed, stopping at the threshold to survey the scene in front of her, 'look at you both. Polishing away. Just like the old days.'

She fell into the sofa next to Ned, curled her feet up

under her, stroked her coffee cup affectionately and sighed pleasurably. 'Now *that*'s what I call a lovely evening. All my boys, good food, good wine, and a big fat helping of good news on top.'

Ned and Gerry grunted in response and carried on polishing and watching TV. Bernie reached for her Ultras and lit one up. She stared at her magazine for a while, but Ned could tell she wasn't concentrating. She was about to say something – she had that air about her.

'So,' she said finally, a couple of minutes later, 'what do you think?'

'Think of what, love?' said Gerry.

'About the news? Millie and Sean. What d'you think?'

'Lovely girl,' said Gerry, absent-mindedly, 'really lovely girl.'

'Ned,' she nudged him gently with her elbow, 'what about you?'

Ned shrugged. 'Yeah,' he said, 'I liked her.'

Bernie put the magazine down. Ned could hear her sucking in her breath, preparing to say what was really on her mind. 'You don't think . . . you don't think it's a bit soon, you know? They're rushing it a bit?'

Ned put down his candlestick. 'Well,' he said, 'I suppose it is a bit soon. But they really like each other, you can tell that just by looking.'

'Yes,' said Bernie pensively, 'but that's what worried me. I mean, when you first start going out with someone you're *supposed* to really like them. That's the whole point. You've got all these chemicals swirling around your body making sure that you really like that person. It's what happens after that that's the problem. I've always thought you shouldn't get engaged when you think the other person's perfect – that you should wait until you know they're not but you still love them anyway. I mean, don't get me wrong, I really liked Millie – I thought she was a lovely girl. But she and Sean, well, they're quite *different*, aren't they?'

'You mean she's the poshest fucking person you've ever met in your life?' said Ned, smirking.

'Well, yes, she is quite *posh*. But it's not that. She's just not his usual type, is she? And then there's the age gap – she'll be wanting babies soon. D'you think Seany's ready for babies? Gerry?'

Gerry glanced at her through a cloud of tobacco smoke. 'Course he is,' he said. 'Thirty years old – I had three of them when I was his age.'

'Yes, but boys these days. They don't grow up as fast. And Seany's always been a bit – irresponsible. You know . . .'

''Bout time he had a bit of responsibility, then, isn't it?' said Gerry.

Bernie sighed. 'Maybe he's just getting carried away by the romance of it – you know what he's like.'

Ned snorted derisively. 'Sean's not romantic,' he said.

'No – but you know what I mean. Maybe he's just a bit overwhelmed by the idea of marrying into that kind of *society*.'

Ned snorted again. 'Mum, you're basically saying that your son is a shallow, social-climbing dickhead who just wants to marry into the upper classes.'

Bernie looked momentarily flustered. 'No – that's not what I meant.'

'Other way round, if anything,' muttered Gerry. 'She's probably trying to piss off her old man by marrying into the proletariat.'

'Oh, I don't know – she's a bit old to be rebelling against her family, isn't she? Besides, Seany's hardly a prole these days, is he, Gerry? What with his book and everything.'

'Anyway,' said Ned, 'you two aren't really in a position to talk, are you? Nice Jewish boy marrying a good Catholic girl. And look at the disaster your marriage has been, eh?'

Bernie and Gerry smiled at each other. 'You're right, you're right,' said Bernie, 'but besides all of that, this getting-married-in-a-hurry thing. I don't know, it's not very Sean, is it?'

Ned nodded. He couldn't argue with that. But then again, writing a bestselling novel, earning a shedload of money and becoming the hottest young writer in town wasn't very Sean either.

'Maybe he's just growing up,' said Ned. 'You know – he *is* thirty; it's about time.'

'Yes,' said Bernie, picking at his fingernails, 'I suppose so.'

'I mean, look at Tony and Jo – they'd known each other for years when they got married, they seemed like they were perfect for each other. And it still went wrong.'

'Hmm,' said Bernie, nodding.

'And me and Carly – ten years we were together for and it didn't work out.'

'Yes. I know what you're saying, but there's just something worrying me about it. I just feel like Sean's not emotionally ready for this level of commitment. If it was you, say, or Tony, I'd feel more comfortable. But Sean – he's always been such a loner. He's always done everything for himself, never had to think about anyone else besides himself before. I just can't see him being ready to share his life with someone.'

'So you're saying that Sean should just spend the rest of his life on his own, then, are you?'

'No, I'm not saying that. I'm just saying that they should at least try living together for a while first before they do something as important as getting married. I'm just saying, I don't think Sean's ready yet. That's all.'

'Well, I do,' said Ned, feeling suddenly defensive of his older brother, 'I think he's ready. I think he's going to be a brilliant husband. And he's going to be a brilliant father one day, too.' He heard a familiar tinkle from his mobile phone, which was sitting in his jacket pocket in the hallway. A text message. Who the hell would be sending him text messages at this time of night? A shiver went down his spine and he wandered out of the living room to get it.

An innocuous little envelope icon flashed jauntily on the screen, trying to convince him that it was there as a symbol of something good and nice. Ned thought otherwise.

He pressed the OK button and the message opened up:

cuntcuntcuntcuntcunt
cuntcuntcuntcuntcunt
cuntcuntcuntcuntcunt
cuntcuntcuntcuntcunt
cuntcuntcuntcuntcunt
cuntcuntcuntcuntcunt

He sighed, switched off his phone and went back to the living room to polish candlesticks.

Pregnant?

'Pregnant?'

'Uh-huh.'

Sean tucked himself slowly back into his trousers and turned to face Millie. She was looking up at him like a small girl who wasn't sure whether the felt-tip-pen mural she'd painted directly on to the living-room wall was a good thing or a bad thing.

Sean felt something freeze inside him at that moment – and it was exactly the same part of him that should have melted.

'What do you mean, you're pregnant?'

Millie's face fell when she heard the annoyance in his voice. 'I'm really sorry, Sean.'

'How did it happen? I mean, we've always used condoms.'

'I don't know, Sean, I really don't know.'

Sean's mind fast-forwarded through every single sour-breathed early-morning nuzzle, every late-night, giggly, drunken fumble, every quickie on the sofa and leisurely Sunday-afternoon marathon session, until it settled on a point, two weeks ago, when Millie had stopped him reaching for the condoms. 'Not yet,' she'd said, 'put it on later. I just want to feel, you know . . .'

'No,' he'd teased, 'what?'

'You know.'

'No,' he'd laughed, 'I don't! Tell me – tell me what you want to feel.'

'*You*,' she'd said. 'I want to feel *you*. Properly. Inside *me*. OK?'

And it most certainly had been OK. Fantastic. Magnificent. Silken. Warm, soft and made for him. And a fine, fine development in their relationship, in Sean's opinion. After all, that was it, wasn't it? Once you'd reached the condom-on-at-the-last-minute stage, there was no going back. It was all part of the natural forward momentum of a healthy relationship – like leaving a toothbrush, like referring to each other as boyfriend and girlfriend, like saying 'I love you'. It was one of those no-turning-back-now rites of passage.

'Jesus,' he muttered, 'it's the condoms, isn't it, using them at the last minute. *Shit!* So stupid. So stupid.'

'Sean! It's got nothing to do with the way we use condoms. I'm seven weeks gone. It happened weeks ago.'

'*Seven weeks?* But we've only been going out for eight and a half!

'I know. I know.'

'But I don't understand. What were we doing?'

Millie raised her eyebrows at him. Sean felt another flash of annoyance. 'No – for God's sake – I mean, what night? Where had we been? What did we do differently?'

'Oh God, Sean. What does it matter? I'm pregnant.'

'It matters because . . . because . . . *I don't understand*! I've used condoms all my life and I've never got anyone pregnant before. Are you sure it's mine?'

'What?!'

Sean knew he'd overstepped the mark. He reached out to touch her arm. She flinched. 'Look. I'm sorry. I didn't mean that. But maybe if you'd slept with someone just before we met. You know . . .'

'Sean. You know I didn't. We've talked about this . . .'

He sighed. 'Let's go into the other room, eh? Talk about this properly.'

They moved into the living room and sat awkwardly at opposite ends of the sofa. Sean felt overcome by sadness as he glanced at the full cushion of space between them. This was, Sean thought sadly, their first row. He never thought that he and Millie would have a row. Ever. There hadn't been so much as a cross word between them in two months. But this – this was *worse* than a row. This was a cataclysm. Because no matter what anyone said or thought Sean didn't want a baby and the only fibre of hope he had to hang on to was that Millie didn't want one either.

'So,' Millie broke the silence.

'So,' Sean sighed and cupped his kneecaps.

'What do you think?'

'What do I think?' That note of irritation crept into Sean's voice again and he laughed hoarsely. 'I think it's a fucking nightmare.'

'Oh.'

They were both quiet again. Sean's jaw was clenched so tight his ears were aching.

He threw Millie a quick glance. 'What do *you* think?'

He heard Millie suck in her breath. 'I don't know. I'm confused.'

'Well, do you *want* it?'

'Sean.'

He turned to look at her. There were tears shining in her eyes.

'Why are you being like this?'

'Like what?'

'So . . . *cold*?'

'Well, you didn't expect me to be *pleased*, did you?'

'No. Yes. Well. I just thought you'd be more . . . *kind*. I thought you'd be kinder.'

'I am being *kind*.' He spat out the word as if he were confessing to a love of fluffy kittens. 'I'm just a bit shocked, that's all. I mean, we've only been together a couple of months. And now – a baby. It's just . . . it's . . .'

'I know. I'm shocked, too. But, Sean . . .'

Here it comes, he thought, here it comes. The five-word sentence that's going to destroy my life for ever.

'. . . I want to keep it.'

There it was. Sean grunted and slapped his palms down on to his thighs. 'I knew it,' he said. 'I *knew* it.'

'Sean, you're acting like I did this on purpose. Like I deliberately got pregnant to mess your life up.'

Sean grunted again. She was right. He *was* acting like she'd done something wrong, but he couldn't help himself. She was the one with the womb, she was the one with the power to decide, the power to change the course of his life irrevocably. He felt completely helpless.

'Well, *I* don't, Millie. *I* don't want a baby. I don't. I so, *so* don't.' Sean's ears buzzed with adrenaline. He waited for Millie to react. The silence lingered on.

Finally Millie turned towards him. 'I need to explain something to you. I'm thirty-six years old. And I always said that if I was going to have kids I wanted them late in life, because I was having too much fun being young. I thought that it was a waste of your youth, rearing children when you could be drinking tequila slammers in a bar full of beautiful men every night. So I never really thought about it. To be honest, I've never had a maternal urge in my life. And then I met you and I thought, Aha, now here's what you might call perfect timing, Mr Right, just when I should really be thinking about this baby malarkey. And I thought we could have a couple of years, you know, hang out, have some fun and then maybe force ourselves to try and make a baby. But, here's the thing, Sean – I'm pregnant now. Right now. And if this had happened to me ten years ago, shit, if this had happened to me *five* years ago, I know what I'd have done. I'd have got rid of it. But when you're thirty-six and engaged to be married then you're not really talking about a whole bunch of options. Are you?'

Sean breathed hot breath into his clenched fist. His mouth was dry with fear and stale champagne. He got to his feet and headed for the kitchen.

'Where are you going?'

Her voice already sounded different in his ears; shriller, more invasive. 'Getting some water.' He held his breath. 'Do you want some?'

'No.'

She was staring at her fingers when he walked back in. He sat down silently.

'Why does this feel like we're having a row, Sean?'

'I don't know,' he replied bluntly.

Millie suddenly got to her feet and spun around to face him. 'I'm really sorry, Sean,' she cried. 'I'm really sorry that you got me pregnant. And I'm really sorry that I love you enough to want to have your baby. I'm really, really fucking sorry, OK!'

Millie's sudden blast of uncharacteristic anger broke through Sean's defences. He got to his feet and gripped her wrists. 'Millie, Millie,' he soothed, 'I'm sorry. I'm sorry. I'm being a cunt. I'm really sorry. Come here. Come here.'

He wrapped his arms around her and she buried her face into his shoulder as she sobbed and Sean smelt her hair and tried desperately to remember what his life had felt like a mere fifteen minutes ago.

A baby.

Sean didn't want a baby. He wanted Millie. To himself. He wanted a baby *one day*. Definitely. More than one baby, in fact. A whole gaggle of babies. Lovely fat babies all over the place. But not now. He wanted his time with Millie first, wanted it to be just the two of them.

They'd only had two months.

*

They talked until two in the morning. Sean reassured her that everything would be fine, that the baby would be fine, that *they*'d be fine. Everything would be *just fine*. But after the conversation petered out and Millie's breathing became heavy and regular, Sean traced a finger across her shoulder and kissed her fingers where they rested against her cheek and then lay wide awake until five. And as he lay there, he stared at the muted lights in the windows of the flats opposite, flats where people were sleeping and content, where people had control over their lives, and he wished more than anything and for the first time in his life that he could be somebody else.

There's Good News and There's Bad News

Gervase came into Ned's bedroom on Monday morning and said, 'There's a girl called Carly on the phone for you.'

Ned had never got out of bed so quickly in his entire life. He hurtled down the hallway, threw himself on to Mum and Dad's bed and picked up the phone from Gerry's bedside table.

'Hello,' he said, breathlessly.

'Well, hi,' drawled someone ridiculously sexy-sounding.

'Carly?'

'Ned?'

'Yes.'

'God. Ned. It didn't sound like you.'

'Neither did you. Sound like you. God. Carly. How did you know I was home?'

'I bumped into Mac in Soho last night. He told me. Look, Ned, I'm at work right now so I can't really talk. But it would be really good to see you. Let's meet up. Yeah?'

They made a plan, they said goodbye and Ned hung up.

'Yes!' He punched his fist into the air and flopped

backwards against Mum and Dad's crumpled pillows. At last. The first good thing to have happened to him since he got home. Thank God. Him and Carly. Back on. Had to be. It was only nine o'clock – she'd only known he was back since last night and she'd phoned him first thing. She was keen. And they were meeting up next week. Fantastic.

He linked his fingers together behind his head and stared up at the ceiling for a while. A smile gambolled cross his face as he imagined the whole reunion scenario. He wondered how long it would take for things to settle down between them, how long it would be before they were back to normal. God, he really could not wait for things to go back to normal.

'Ned!' he heard Gervase calling up the stairs.

'What!'

'Parcel for you!'

And that was when it hit him. Life was far from getting back to normal. Life was a good long train ride away from normal.

Ned felt a chill run down his spine and he wrapped his parents' duvet around his shoulders, breathing in the aroma of their night-time bodies to comfort himself. He rolled himself into a duvet pancake and closed his eyes, counting slowly backwards to ten. And then he went downstairs.

There it was. Another box. Smaller than the last one. This one had been sent by airmail and, according to the green customs label, had been sent by someone called Tallulah d'Oignon of Chrispee Towers, Sydney.

Ned sighed. At least she hadn't lost her sense of humour.

He peeled the brown paper off the parcel and withdrew the small brown box, which was again emblazoned with the word 'CUNT' in red marker, this time written enthusiastically all over the box, like jaunty, X-rated wrapping paper. With a heavy heart he opened it. Inside there was a clear plastic pouch, like a spliff-holding sort of pouch. At first there didn't appear to be anything in it but then he held it up to the light and realized that it was full of tiny little dark hairs, about half a centimetre long. Little crescent-shaped hairs.

He tipped a couple on to the palm of his hand and peered at them. Eyelashes.

Mon's fucking eyelashes.

Oh Jesus. He tipped the lashes back into the pouch, put the pouch back into the box and closed it. 'Mon,' he muttered to himself, 'what the fuck are you playing at?' He pictured her there, in Sydney, hairless, lashless. Oh God. She was falling apart. He'd known it – he'd known that there was no way she'd have taken his leaving in her stride. She wouldn't just get drunk with her female friends, cry herself to sleep and lose loads of weight, like a normal girl.

He thought about phoning her. He really should. Kate and Jamie were there in the flat with her but she wasn't close to them. Ned was the only person who really knew her. He should phone her – talk to her.

But no – that was exactly what she wanted, he thought. If he called, she'd win, like she always won.

This was all a ploy, thought Ned, a ploy to make him worry. She was addicted to him worrying about her – and that was his fault. He'd allowed her to become dependent on him over the course of their three years together. Every time they got close to finishing, even when he *had* finished it, she'd haul him back in by going mental on him. He'd wanted to escape before when things were messy, but he'd never felt able to, always felt this huge tug of responsibility towards Monica. If he wasn't there to keep an eye on her then who else would? Ned ignored the nagging voice at the back of his mind saying, 'Who's looking after her, Ned? Who's making sure she's all right?' No, he thought, Monica wasn't stupid; she was, in fact, incredibly clever. She knew what she was doing. She was playing him. That wasn't even a full set of eyelashes and she'd been going on about getting her hair cut for ages.

He set his jaw and re-wrapped the box. He took it up to his bedroom and slid it under his bed with her hair and then he went back downstairs for some breakfast.

Gervase was eating a sandwich in the kitchen. A proper-looking sandwich cut into diagonals like your mum would make if you asked for one. He ate it off a plate with a folded piece of kitchen roll on it. Gervase was very proper, Ned had noticed. He used the pot with a cosy when he made tea, he answered the phone like an old lady and now this sandwich business. It was all so out of keeping with his appearance. And it was strangely endearing.

'Morning, Ned.'

'Morning.'

'How are you today?'

'All right. You?'

'Fan-tastic. As it goes.'

'Oh, really – why's that?'

'The sun is shining. I've got the day off. And my Robert Gordon tickets have just turned up in the post.'

'Robert who?'

'Gordon. Remember? That guy I was telling you about in the pub last week?'

'Oh yeah. The rock-and-roll guy. Yeah.'

'I've got a spare one, as it happens. Fancy coming along?'

'Er . . .'

'Friday week. It's up in Wood Green. But it's OK – my mate Bud's gonna drive.'

'You have a mate called Bud?'

'Yeah. Bud. He's a good bloke, Bud. So – what d'you reckon?'

Ned was about to go into frantic fabrication-of-convincing-sounding-excuse mode, when Gervase suddenly stood up, really fast, strode towards him and put his hands on to his shoulders. And then that chocolaty thing happened in Ned's stomach again and Gervase started staring at him.

'You haven't done anything about it, have you?' he said, his hands still gripping Ned's shoulders.

'What?'

'Your problem. The mess you left. It's still bugging you, yeah?'

'Jesus,' said Ned, 'what are you talking about?'

'I don't know what I'm talking about, Ned. Only you can know what I'm talking about. All I can do is tell you what I feel.'

'What are you?' said Ned, 'some kind of mind-reader?'

'No. I'm more of a vibe-reader, Ned. I can sense your pain.'

'My pain?'

'Yes, your pain. It's like an invisible coat you're wearing. But I can see it.'

'And what does it look like, this coat?'

'Well, it's not really like a coat. It's more like a cape, really.'

'Yes, yes. Whatever. What does it look like?'

'It looks – *scared*.'

'My cape looks scared?'

'Yeah. Scared and confused,' he loosened his grip on Ned's shoulder. 'D'you wanna talk about it?'

'My scared, confused cape?'

'Yeah.'

'No, not really.'

'Good. I'm not all that great on talking about stuff.'

'So why bring it up in the first place?'

'I don't know. I can't help it. I just see these things and they're kind of hard to ignore. D'you know what I mean?' He sat back down, stared out of the window for a second and then started eating the second half of his sandwich. 'There's a nice bit of ham in the fridge if you fancy one.' He gestured to the fridge with his head.

Ned looked at him in amazement. He really was the

most bizarre person he'd ever met. He was the sort of person you usually only met in some dodgy pub when you'd just had a spliff and ended up having a really surreal conversation with them. Except Gervase wasn't a hazy stoned memory from an unfamiliar pub – he was eating breakfast in Ned's kitchen.

'So,' said Gervase, 'this Carly. Who's she, then?'

'Don't you know?' he said facetiously, 'am I not wearing some invisible *hat*?'

'No. No hat. But you got out of bed pretty fucking sharpish. She's obviously someone *significant*.'

Ned felt himself starting to mellow and sat down and poured himself a cup of tea from the pot. 'Yeah. She is. She's my ex.'

'Aaah,' Gervase nodded.

'Yeah. We went out for ten years and then I dumped her to go off to Oz with Mon.'

'And you regret it?'

'Yeah. A lot. But I think it might still work out. You know?'

'Good. Good. I wish you luck, mate.'

'Thanks.'

There was silence as Ned stirred his tea.

'So,' he opened, 'what about you? Anyone special in your life?'

Gervase put down his sandwich and considered the question. 'Nah,' he said eventually, 'not really. There's girls, you know? But no one special.'

Ned nodded and examined the design on his teacup. 'Where are you from?'

'Nowhere in particular. Born in London somewhere. Moved around a bit. Ended up here.'

'Where were you living before you ended up here?'

Gervase cleared his sinuses very loudly and swilled the contents around the back of his throat. Ned tried to pretend that he hadn't.

'Vauxhall. With a bird.'

A bird. Ned liked that – it had been a long time since he'd heard a man refer to a woman as a bird. It reminded him of his childhood, in a Spangles-and-Pac-Man kind of a way.

'Yeah, I thought she was the one. She had everything, you know, everything that you'd want in a woman.'

Ned imagined that what Gervase wanted in a woman and what he wanted in a woman were two entirely different things.

'Intelligent. Clean. Nice flat. No kids. You know.'

Yup, thought Ned, entirely different things.

'Still. It was on the fourth floor.'

'What was?'

'Her flat. No lift.'

Ned nodded again and decided that he was banging his head against a brick wall. He stood up and poured himself a bowl of Shreddies.

'Anyway, no point dwelling in the past, Ned. Live for the day, that's what I always say. And that's exactly what I intend to do today. I'm going to get my hair cut, then I'm going up to Camden Town to get myself some new clobber, then I'm going to see some mates out east, have a few drinks, see a band. Lovely.' He wiped his mouth with the folded kitchen towel and put the plate in the dishwasher. 'Wanna come with me?'

'Eh?'

'Well, you're just hanging around here all day feeling bad about something or other. Why don't you hang out with me?'

As much as Ned would have liked to witness the secret artistry behind Gervase's extraordinary haircut and find out where he bought his manky old T-shirts, the thought of spending the whole day with him was too weird to contemplate. 'Er, no. Thanks, mate. I've, er, promised I'll do some stuff for Dad today.'

'OK, then. What about the Robert Gordon gig. Eh?'

'Er, yeah. Yeah. Why not?'

Ned had no idea where that had come from. It was a trick, obviously. Gervase had given him the more unpalatable of the two options first so that when he gave him the second he'd say yes in a knee-jerk response. Shit.

'Cool,' said Gervase, running his fingers across his flat-top. 'See you later.'

And then he sauntered out of the kitchen, his hands in his pockets, whistling 'The Wonder of You' and walking like the Fonz.

Hormones, Probably

The London College of Art and Design was housed in an imposing deco building on Woburn Place that Tony had probably walked past a hundred times in his life and never noticed. He found the interior-design department and wandered around aimlessly for a while, looking at displays of student projects in cabinets until he bumped into someone who looked older than him and asked them if they knew where he could find Millie. She'd popped out to get some lunch, according to the very helpful woman, but she'd be back in a few minutes. When he told the helpful woman that he was Millie's boyfriend's brother, her face lit up. 'Oh,' she said, beaming at him, 'you mean you're her *fiancé*'s brother.'

'Yes,' he muttered, 'that's right.'

'Oh well. Why don't you wait for her in her office, then?'

She showed him to the end of a corridor and left him in a room that had Millie's name on the door. Tony sat down for a moment on a very expensive-looking tubular-steel chair, but then stood up again almost immediately to have a look around. So, thought Tony, this was it – Millie's office. And what a very lovely office it was. Tony sat down in her chair for a moment, savouring the feeling of his buttocks caressing the indents made by hers in the upholstery. He leafed nonchalantly through her paperwork for a while – assessments, schedules, photographs of chairs and curtains, boring, boring, boring. And then his eye was caught by a small bejewelled picture frame. He picked it up and looked at it. It was a photograph of Millie and Sean, Sean at the forefront grinning like a goon, Millie just behind him with her arms wrapped around his neck and her cheek pressed against his, looking like a goddess. He let the frame drop back, glumly. 'Fiancé's brother,' he muttered to himself, 'for God's sake.'

'Tony!'

He jumped out of the chair.

'Millie!'

'Er – hi.'

She was wearing a knee-length red felt skirt, a black mohair jumper with beads all over it and tight, leather, zip-up boots. Her hair was clipped back and in a centre parting. And she was wearing glasses. The glasses did it for Tony, completely. Even more than the tight leather boots.

'Well,' she said, smiling slightly, 'this is a lovely surprise – what are you doing here?' She dropped a paper bag on to her desk and leant across to give him one of those big sincere kisses on the cheek, those kisses you could actually feel.

'I'm, um . . .' he grinned inanely, 'er . . . something I wanted to give you,' he flapped a big cardboard envelope around a bit. 'The post's been a bit useless round our way and I was passing, so . . .'

Millie smiled at him, a warm, relaxed smile that said that she didn't find his presence as unsettling as she actually should. 'So,' she put up a finger to slide her glasses up the narrow bridge of her nose, 'what is it?'

'What?'

'The thing. For me?' She pointed at the envelope.

'Oh. Oh! Of course. Yeah.' He handed her the package.

'Wow,' she turned it round a bit in her hands. 'Shall I – can I open it?'

'Oh God, yeah. Definitely.'

Tony watched her intently, not wanting to miss one tiny nuance. She slid the print out and looked at it – a hardboard-mounted illustration of a small, lonely penguin on a glacier. £250. And worth every penny. 'Ha! I don't believe it. Is this for me? Really?'

'Uh-huh.'

'Oh – that's so . . . so . . . kind, Tony. So unbelievably sweet of you. I can't believe you went to all this trouble. I don't know what to say. I . . . I . . .'

And then her face suddenly fell apart and she started crying.

'Shit, Millie. I'm sorry. I didn't mean to . . .'

Millie shook her head and lifted her glasses to wipe the tears from under her eyes. 'It's not you, Tony. It's not. It's . . . it's . . . oh God, how embarrassing. I can't believe I'm doing this.'

'Here,' said Tony, taking her elbow and guiding her

gently towards a velvet *chaise longue*, 'sit down.' He searched his pockets fruitlessly for the large white cotton handkerchief he'd never owned in his life. 'Are you OK? Can I get you anything?'

'Mmm,' she said, 'a new life, please.'

Tony looked at her in surprise. 'What?'

'Nothing,' she said, dropping her head into her hands, 'nothing.'

'Millie. Is everything all right?'

She nodded, shook her head, nodded again.

'Talk to me, Millie. Please. Tell me what's wrong.'

'I can't,' she said, 'I can't bloody talk to you.'

'Why not?'

'Because – because it's all top bloody secret and it's to do with your brother and blah-di-blah-di-blah.'

'Look,' said Tony, turning up his hands in a gesture of impartiality, 'I'm neutral. Honestly. You can trust me. Anything you say here will never go any further. Promise.'

'Especially swear you won't say anything to Sean.'

'I especially swear,' he said.

'I'm pregnant,' she said.

The whole world seemed to go concave, then, and all the blood rushed to Tony's head. 'What?' he said, letting his hand drop from his chest.

'I'm pregnant,' she said again, 'it still sounds really weird saying it. And I'd only just got used to saying I'm engaged. I'm not sure what's weirder, actually . . .'

'Pregnant?' said Tony again.

'Yes. Marvellous isn't it? Thirty-six years old, thought

149

I was going to end up alone and childless, and I managed to get engaged and pregnant within the space of two months. I should be an inspiration to Bridget Joneses the world over.'

'But – whose is it?' The minute the question left Tony's lips he wanted to suck it back in. Of course he knew whose baby it was. It was just . . . *Sean*. Urgh. It was distasteful, somehow, incontrovertible evidence that he and Millie had . . . and that Sean was capable of . . . And with a woman as magnificent as Millie. Or any woman at all, come to that. He felt slightly weak with nausea as the truth percolated through his system. He looked down at Millie's stomach and tried to imagine what was happening in there, his brother's cells and genes doubling and doubling and making a little Sean. In Millie. Oh God. How revolting.

'Well,' said Tony, searching for the polite response to such shocking news, 'that's really . . . God, that's great. *Congratulations*.' There it was, that word he'd been looking for.

'Thank you,' she sniffed.

'So, when's the baby due?'

'First of December.'

'That's Mum's birthday.'

'I know,' she said, 'coincidence, isn't it? I'm not supposed to have told anyone yet. Wanted to wait till I was three months gone. You know, be on the safe side. So promise you won't say anything, however much you want to.'

Tony's mind was reeling. Sean. A dad? It didn't seem

possible. It had been hard enough to reconcile himself to Sean being a prospective husband. 'So. Sean – is he excited?'

She shrugged. 'Yes,' she said, 'I think so. I mean, I think he's a bit shell-shocked, to be honest. It's not exactly what he had in mind. But he'll come round, eventually.'

Tony didn't like the sound of that. Sean's beautiful, magnificent, way-out-of-his-league fiancée was pregnant with his child. What was there to come round *to*, exactly?

'So,' said Tony, bracing himself to ask a sensitive question, 'why all the . . . ?' He trailed his fingertips down his cheeks to indicate her tears.

'Oh God. I don't know. Hormones, probably.'

'He does want you to have this baby, doesn't he?'

Millie shrugged and sniffed and started crying again. 'He says he does, but, I don't know – he seems a bit . . . a bit . . . nothing.'

'A bit nothing?'

'Look – I'd really rather not talk about it, Tony, if you don't mind.' She laid a hand against his and looked up at him beseechingly. 'It's making me feel all disloyal. You know what Sean's like – *intensely private* I believe is the correct term.'

'Do you want me to talk to him for you?'

'No! Absolutely not.'

'Look, Millie, whatever's going on, I'm sure that deep down Sean's really thrilled about all this.' He pointed at her belly. 'I mean, if it was me, I'd be over the moon,

I'd be so delighted. I just can't believe he could possibly feel negative about something so amazing.'

'Aw, Tony – you're really lovely, aren't you?' she said, laughing. 'You're such a lovely bloke.'

'I'm all right, I suppose,' he said, resisting the temptation to move a strand of hair off her cheek.

'Look,' she said, 'can you just forget that this conversation ever happened? I shouldn't have said anything to you. Ultimately it's going to be my decision. Mine and Sean's. I'm sure he'll come round in the end . . . But, thank you.'

'For what?'

'For turning up unannounced and letting me let off a little steam. I really needed it. Oh – and thank you for the penguin, too.' She gestured to the print on her desk. 'That was incredibly thoughtful of you.'

He shrugged it off.

'Have you had lunch?' she said.

'Er, no, actually, I haven't.'

'Would you like to share my panini? Emmenthal and ham?'

Tony glanced across at the sweaty paper bag still sitting on her desk-top.

'Is it a big one?' he said.

'Huge. Way too big just for me.'

'OK, then,' he said, even though he wasn't hungry and wasn't even particularly fond of Emmenthal. He watched her take the panini from the bag and pull it apart with her fingers. The same fingers he dreamt about every night, sliding into his linen trousers, cupping him, caressing him. He watched her tear the sandwich, spell-bound for a moment. Jesus Aitch Christ. She was incredible. She really was. She was quirky and strong and beautiful and funny and vulnerable and sexy. She was everything he'd ever wanted in a woman.

And she was engaged to his brother and pregnant with his child.

He chewed on a corner of lukewarm panini but when he tried to swallow it it got stuck in his throat.

Sean's Psychotic Parrot

On Friday night Sean and Millie went to their local trendy Italian for dinner. Sean had prosciutto and figs followed by papardelle with chicken livers. Millie had risotto of wild mushroom with an enormous rocket-and-Parmesan salad on the side and tagliatelle with smoked pork, cream and broad beans. They shared a huge panna cotta for pudding, but in reality Millie had seventy-five per cent of it. As well as the main meal she ate three slice of ciabatta with (thickly spread) unsalted butter and not only the biscotti that came balanced on the side of her own coffee saucer, but Sean's too. She claimed that she had an insatiable craving for carbohydrates and cupped her swollen belly while they waited for the bill to arrive.

Sean couldn't help feeling a bit concerned about this sudden doubling in the size of his girlfriend's appetite. Surely it wasn't normal for a woman, even a pregnant woman, to eat that much? 'So,' he said, tearing his eyes away from her distended belly and downing the last of the wine, 'where to now? Paradise Paul's?'

Paradise Paul's was a late-night, semi-legal, subterranean drinking establishment in Brewer Street, run by a wild-eyed, dyed-hair fiftysomething guy who was actually called Paradise Paul – he'd changed his name by deed poll when he was twenty-one. Apparently, when Millie first went to the bar as a pink-haired teenager in the eighties, Paradise Paul was a colourful, lively, eccentric character, but now he was somehow drained of colour, like a photograph that had been left out in the sun for too long. He never said anything that made any kind of sense and he smelt a bit of grimy shirt collars, but he did run a fantastically charismatic after-hours bar and Sean loved it there.

Sometimes they'd turn up after dinner and have a couple of beers and a surreal chat with Paradise Paul and then leave. Other times there'd be a dozen or so of Millie's seemingly never-ending circle of friends there and they'd stay until the early hours, drinking rum, whiskey and champagne, and, if Millie's friend Ruth was there, having a line of coke or two as well. It was a genuinely bohemian world full of unique characters and slightly odd encounters and, because Sean had never been there sober and certainly had only the haziest memories of actually leaving, he sometimes wondered if the bar really existed, so he'd been incredibly surprised to stumble upon it one lunchtime when he'd taken a back route to his agent's office. In the daylight hours, though, it was just a derelict-looking basement strewn with litter and without any kind of signage. This gave Sean an unsettling sensation, similar to the time he had bumped into his headmaster wearing a red shellsuit at the Whitgift shopping centre in Croydon.

Friday nights at Paradise Paul's were a ritual for Sean and Millie and without them Sean's insight into the human psyche would be informed entirely by his family, Robert Kilroy-Silk and the man in the local paper shop. It was an element of his life that he could feel developing layers of nostalgia even while it was happening – he could already hear the conversations that he and Millie would have in the future. Remember Paradise Paul's, they'd say to each other, what a time that was. And they'd both get a wistful, faraway look in their eyes and remember the magical days when they were still new to each other and the world was all shiny and perfect.

But looking at Millie across the table from him now, yawning dramatically behind her hand, grey shadows under her eyes and an untouched glass of wine in front of her, Sean had the distinct feeling that a night living it up at Paradise Paul's was most probably not on the cards.

Sean looked at his watch, absent-mindedly. It was eight-forty-five. He'd spent all week alone, sitting at Millie's window just waiting for her to get back and relieve his isolation. He couldn't face going home *now*, watching the telly, getting an early sodding night; and, as much as he knew he should be putting Millie's needs and feelings before his own now, he really didn't want to. She'd been knackered all week, said that all she wanted to do was 'sleep, sleep, sleep'. She'd got in at seven on Wednesday, poo-pooed Sean's suggestion of a night at the cinema, and crawled into bed at eight-thirty claiming that she'd never known such tiredness in her life. Sean's sympathy reserves were being rapidly drained. I mean, how knackering could it actually be, carrying a small cluster of cells around inside you? She hadn't even started showing yet, so why was she so fucking tired all the time?

As if reading his mind, Millie yawned again. 'I am sooo knackered. Do you mind if we just go home?'

A seven-year-old version of Sean pole-vaulted its way to the surface and pouted at her. 'What – *really?*'

'Yes, Sean, really. I'm all done in.'

He looked at her wan expression and baggy eyes and felt a huge surge of resentment. He forced a jolly smile. 'Well, I'm not,' he said. 'I'm oozing with excess energy.' He slapped his hands together to demonstrate his energy oozing. 'How about a quick one?'

'Oh, Sean . . .'

'Come on. It'll be fun. Just a quick one. Home by midnight. Promise.'

'Midnight?! I was planning on being in bed by ten.'

'Oh, Millie,' he wheedled, 'come on. I've been stuck indoors all week. I need a life fix.'

'Sean,' she said with a distinct note of exasperation in her voice, 'I am not going to Paradise Paul's – or anywhere else, for that matter. I'm completely exhaus-ted, the smell of cigarettes makes me want to hurl and I can't even have a drink. I'll be miserable.'

'Oh – so is that it, then? Do we just stay in for the next eight months?'

'Seven months.'

'Whatever – do we just stop going out?'

'No. Of course not. Just at the moment, while I'm this tired.'

'But why?' whined Sean, knowing that he was spraying verbal lighter fluid on to a conversational barbecue, but unable to stop himself. 'Why are you so tired? I don't understand.'

'Oh Jesus, Sean. I'm preg-nant,' she delivered the syllables slowly and separately. 'I am busy nurturing human life in here,' she pointed at her belly, 'in case you hadn't noticed.'

'Yes, but, why does that make you tired?' He was on the wide open road to self-destruction now but he was past caring.

'I don't know, Sean. I've got no idea. I've never been pregnant before. It's all a bloody mystery to me.'

He took a deep breath, rubbed his hand across his chin and prepared to launch the Exocet missile of a question he'd been wanting to ask her all week. 'Are you sure this tiredness isn't all in your head – you know, psychosomatic?'

Millie opened her mouth and started gawping at him like a pike. 'Sean,' she said, her voice chillingly steely, '*what* the fuck is your problem?'

'My problem,' said Sean, 'is that I want to go to Paradise Paul's on a Friday night with my girlfriend, have a few drinks, have a laugh and then come home and I can't because of this so-called tiredness that seems to have taken over your life.'

'Tell you what, Sean,' said Millie, pushing back her

chair and dropping her napkin on to the table-top, 'why don't *you* go to Paul's, eh? You go on your own and have a good time. But promise me one thing: don't bother coming home until you've grown up – you *child*.'

And then she pulled her jacket off the back of the chair, threw a £20 note at him and stalked from the restaurant.

Sean sat there for a while after she'd gone, assessing his emotions.

Relieved: a little bit, yes. He'd been wanting to question Millie's 'tiredness' all week, convinced it was all part of some female ploy to 'seem' pregnant and be made a fuss of.

Remorseful: a bit. He'd spoilt the evening and let Millie go home on her own. He'd been insensitive and selfish. But this was his life, too. He was allowed to question things, wasn't he? He didn't have to accept every change this pregnancy foisted upon his life. *He* still counted, even if the being growing inside his girl-friend had other ideas.

Confused: very much so. All his natural instincts told him that he should be changing, becoming a more selfless person. But he had this bloody great psychotic parrot sitting on his shoulder shouting, 'Self-preservation! Self-preservation!' at him morning, noon and night. He was very fond of his life and he was buggered if he was going to let something over which he had no control mess it all up for him.

Frustrated: extremely. Because ultimately there was

nothing he could do to stop this scary, uncontrollable process.

Sad: very. It had only been a week since Millie's curveball and already their relationship had changed beyond all recognition. If someone had told him a week ago that he and Millie would have a huge row in their favourite Italian restaurant which culminated in Millie storming off, and him letting her, he'd have laughed in their face. No way, he'd have said, not me and Millie. We get on so well. We never argue. And Friday's our favourite night . . .

Sean felt a seismic emotional shock run through his body at the thought of what they'd have been doing this time last week and clenched his jaw hard to hold back the tears that had suddenly appeared from nowhere.

He cleared his throat, picked up the bill and Millie's £20 note and thought about finding a newsagent, picking up a big bag of Haribos and some trashy magazines, walking back to Millie's, plying her with foot massages and scalp rubs, putting tonight behind them and making a fresh start.

But then the big, ugly parrot started squawking again – 'Self-preservation, Sean, self-preservation – don't let it win!' And five minutes later he found himself in the back of a black cab and on his way to Brewer Street.

Eating Cheese in the Moonlight

Tony thought it was part of his dream at first. He'd been having a particularly good one about Millie – no horses this time, just him and Millie lying together in a hammock, Millie tearing up bits of food for him and hand-feeding them to him while she massaged his groin with . . . her third hand? Well, with something, anyway. A large lizard had slunk up and grinned at them. It had a gold tooth and started making a strange noise, like a telephone ringing. They'd laughed at first, at this lizard and its strange phone-ringing noises, until it had become annoying. And then he'd reached out to shut the lizard's mouth and the lizard had kept dodging him, ducking and diving and grinning at him. And then Tony woke up and realized that his phone was ringing.

He looked at his radio alarm: 3.58 a.m.

Jesus.

He pulled the receiver towards him. 'Hello.'

'Doby,' came a strangulated voice, 'it's Mewell.'

'I'm sorry,' he said, 'I think you've got the wrong number.'

'No! No – it's me, Millie.'

'Millie!' he sat bolt upright and ran a hand through his hair. 'Are you OK? Is everything all right?'

'Yes. No. I . . . I . . .' she sniffed. 'Are you alone?'

Tony checked the pillow next to his, just to be sure. 'Yes. Alone. Totally. What's the matter?'

'I'm really sorry to wake you, Tony. I really am. I know it's late, but I'm in such a state and didn't know who else to talk to. I'll go if you want me to . . .'

'Nonono. Don't. Don't go. Talk to me. Tell me what's wrong.'

'I'm so sorry, Tony. I've just got myself so wound up. Too wound up to sleep. And I can't take a pill because of the baby. And . . . *shit*. I'm such a fucking mess.'

'What happened, Millie? What's the matter?'

'Me and Sean had a row. I stormed off and now he's buggered off somewhere and still isn't home.'

'A row? What about?'

'God – I don't know where to start. He's just . . . he's just . . . he's such a *child*, Tony.'

'Well, yes,' said Tony. 'Sean can be a bit childish.'

'It's this being-pregnant thing. He says he's happy about it but he just seems to be annoyed with me. Like, you know – You got yourself into this mess, don't expect me to make it any easier for you. You know, like I went out in the cold without a cardigan on and now I've got a cold and I've got no one to blame but myself.'

Tony tutted and shook his head. 'Christ,' he said, 'what a dick. I can't believe he's behaving like this. Do you want me to say something to him for you? Hmm? Have a word with him?'

'No! Absolutely not. He's my problem and I'll deal with it, Tony. But the thing is, you see, Sean came to me from nowhere, out of the blue – do you see? I've got no context to put him in. I don't really know anything about him. I mean, he's told me that he's never really had a serious relationship before, but then, neither have I, not really, and that doesn't mean that I'm incapable of sustaining one. And I just wondered, you know, maybe you could tell me things about him, things, I don't know, like, what were his ex-girlfriends like and why did the relationships end and what sort of things he's ever said about babies. All that sort of thing. But only if it doesn't make you feel horribly disloyal.'

'Disloyal?' said Tony. 'No. Not at all. I'll tell you anything you need to know.'

And he did. He told her about Sean's middle-child complex and how he always needed to be the centre of attention and panicked if he didn't think he was getting enough of anything, be it fish fingers or maternal love. He told her all about the blondes and the tears and the heartbreak. He told her how surprised the whole family were that Sean had found someone he loved enough to make a commitment to because it had looked like he might end up alone. He also told her how Sean had a touch of the misogynist about him, was impatient, selfish and short-sighted. How he'd never really developed emotionally and possibly wasn't equipped to deal with the complexities of a proper grown-up relationship.

'He's spoilt,' he said, finally, 'that's the problem with Sean. He's never had to work at anything. Got given a council flat. Had the girls lining up for him. And of course Mum and Dad have let him get away with murder for years, paid his bills, done his washing, taken him on holidays, never questioned what the hell he was doing with his life. And now that he's written this book and has got all this money and all this success, well, you know . . .'

Millie sniffed on the other end of the line. 'So you're saying that my fiancé is an emotional cripple?'

'No. Not a cripple. But he has a slight emotional *limp*, let's put it that way.'

'But babies, Tony, has he ever said anything to you about *babies*?'

Tony gave the question some serious thought. 'No,' he said eventually, 'I've never heard him say anything about babies, good or bad.'

'Oh,' said Millie, sounding slightly disappointed. 'But why would he ask me to marry him if he doesn't want babies? I mean, isn't that the whole point of getting married?'

'Well,' said Tony, 'I'd have thought so.'

'Oh God, Tony. I just – I don't understand him. I don't know what's going through his head.'

'Look,' said Tony, 'Sean's a complex guy. I don't think *anyone* really understands him. But you mustn't let him get away with it, OK? Don't let him think he can behave this way. He's a spoilt brat and he needs some discipline. He needs to realize that he's a grown man now, that he has responsibilities.'

'Oh, I've got no intention of letting him get away with anything, I can assure you. It's not in my nature.'

'Good on you.'

'And I'll tell you one thing for sure, whatever happens, I'm not letting him get in my bed tonight. No way.'

'Absolutely right,' said Tony, 'don't you let him any-where near you.'

There was a long pause before Millie said anything, and Tony listened to the sound of her snotty breathing down the phone and felt unbelievably close to her. There was something incredibly intimate about talking to someone on the phone in the middle of the night, in the dark, all naked and wrapped up in goosedown and cotton, like a baby.

'Anyway, Tony. That was all. I just needed a bit of *context*. You can get back to sleep now.'

'No – no. Honestly. I'm fine. I'm wide awake now.'

'God – I'm sorry. I really didn't mean to ruin your night's sleep . . .'

'Really, Millie, no need to be. I don't sleep all that well. I'd probably have woken up in ten minutes anyway. I usu-ally do. It's nice to have someone to talk to for a change. Actually,' he said, a thought suddenly occurring to him, 'hold on just one second. Don't go away. I'm just getting the other phone.' He put the phone down, pulled on his dressing-gown and padded across soft cream carpet towards his living room, where he retrieved the walkabout.

'Hi,' he said.

'Hi. What were we talking about?'

'Sean.'

'Oh yes. Sean. Don't want to talk about Sean any more. Bored of talking about Sean. He's a big, fat tosser and that's that.'

'So – what shall we talk about?'

'Hmm . . .' said Millie, in a kitteny, slinky kind of way

that made Tony imagine her naked on silk sheets with her hair all mussed up. 'Baby names?'

'Eh?'

'I like Nat for a boy. Or maybe Theo. And if it's a girl, I like Mathilda. I like Lois, too, but Lois London sounds kind of weird, doesn't it?'

'I suppose so.'

'What names do you like?'

'God,' he ran a hand over his hair, 'I've never really thought about it. David?'

'David?! You can't call a baby David. He'll end up being called Dave and having spots and greasy hair. What about girls' names?'

'Er . . . I don't know. Amanda?'

'Amanda! I used to *love* the name Amanda when I was little. *Amanda* . . .' she dragged out the syllables, 'Amanda London. Hmm, you know. I quite like it. It's got a sort of post-modern charm, hasn't it?'

'Hmm,' said Tony, wishing that they were talking about something about which he had an opinion of some sort. He wandered into the kitchen while Millie kept talking baby names, and absent-mindedly opened the fridge. A large hunk of vintage Cheddar winked at him and he pulled it out, got a knife out of a drawer and started shaving slivers off it, slipping them into his mouth and letting them melt on his tongue. He brought the hunk of cheese and a glass of orange juice into the living room and lay down on his sofa while they chatted. Through the glass set into the ceiling above him, he could see the sky starting to turn from black to an amber-tinged navy as the sun began its slow ascent somewhere over the horizon. The moon was big and fat overhead and Millie's voice was all husky honey in his ear as she recited baby names to him from a book: Albert, Amber, Anastasia, Archie, Astrid . . . Tony responded with 'hmm's, and 'no's, and 'quite nice's and stared at the moon while Millie chanted – Bathsheba, Bella, Boris, Bruce and Bryony. Baby names had never sounded so sexy.

'Are you eating something?' said Millie, suddenly.

'Nu-uh,' said Tony, trying to dislodge a wedge of pasty cheese from his tongue, 'just drinking some orange juice.'

'God – do you *do* that?'

'Do what?'

'Get stuff out of the fridge in the middle of the night?'

'Sometimes.'

'Ha. I always thought people only did that in American films. So – what else are you doing?'

'Nothing. Just lying here on my sofa. Drinking juice. Talking to you.'

'What does your house look like?'

'My house?'

'Uh-huh. Describe it to me.'

'Well. It's a duplex apartment, actually. In a gated mews development. It's a Barratt one, but really nice, you know. Architect-designed and everything . . .'

'Architect designed, eh? As opposed to a house that was designed by a dinner lady?'

'Ha ha ha.'

'Tell me about your sofa.'

'What?!'

'Look – I'm an interior designer. I need to know someone's sofa to really know *them*.'

'Well, what do you want to know?'

'Colour. Fabric. Dimensions. Upholstery.'

'Well. It's a kind of lemony cream. And it's a sort of *ridged* cottony fabric. It's a big three-seater with a low back and lots of cushions.'

'From?'

'Ikea.'

'*Ikea?*'

'Is that bad?'

'It's terrible, Tony, absolutely appalling. God – you live in a Barratt home and you have an Ikea sofa. You're not much like your parents, are you?'

'No, I guess not. I can't stand clutter.'

'So – how much of your furniture did you get from Ikea? Honestly? –'

'Er . . . all of it?'

'Oh, Tony.'

'Well – it's nice stuff and it all goes together.'

'It matches, you mean?'

'Yeah. It matches.'

'Tony, furniture is not supposed to *match*. It's supposed to *evolve* and inspire and communicate. It's supposed to tell people about *you* – about who you are.'

'Well, maybe it does. Maybe I'm a matching kind of a guy.'

'So – your pants and socks, do they . . . ?'

Tony laughed. 'On occasion,' he said, 'but never by design. But look,' he said as a rather exciting thought occurred to him, 'my flat. I've never really done anything to it and it's a really nice place. It's got a lot of potential. Would you ever consider a commission in the wilds of south London?'

'Where do you live?'

'Anerley.'

'Anerley – where the hell's that?!'

'Other side of Crystal Palace Park. Not far from my mum and dad.'

'Hmm, I'll think about it. I'd need to see some pictures, though, before I drag myself all the way out to Twin Peaks . . . Oh, hello, pud.'

'Sorry?'

'My cat's just walked into my room. Hello, beautiful . . .'

'You've got a cat?'

'I've got *four* cats, actually. I told you didn't I? Classic singleton. I've been preparing myself with all the essential accoutrements for my inevitable lonely destiny. Even had a gay best friend lined up until Sean came along with his engagement rings and his rubber-busting sperm.'

Tony laughed again. 'So,' he said, 'if single thirtysomething women have cats and gay best friends, what do single men have?'

'Very good question,' said Millie. 'Sports cars and female best friends, I suppose.'

'Shit,' said Tony, slapping his forehead, 'you got me. On both counts.'

'Yes, but it doesn't count, because you're not single.'

'Yes I am.'

'Er – then who is that very nice blonde woman with the amazing legs who goes everywhere with you?'

Oh yes. He'd forgotten about her.

Ness.

The very thought sent a chill running through him. He'd done everything he could to avoid Ness over the past couple of weeks. There'd been a lot of migraines and late nights at the office and family commitments. He should just finish it with Ness, Tony was aware of that. He should sit down with her like a grown-up and hold her hand and look her in the eye and say, 'Ness, you're a really great girl, and we've had some really good times, but . . .' and then deal with the consequences. But he just couldn't do it. He was, he supposed, subconsciously waiting for her to do something wrong so that he could pounce upon it as a perfectly acceptable excuse to dump her. But she never did. It was dawning upon Tony very slowly that Ness was actually perfect. She was the perfect girlfriend. But Ness had one big fault. A huge unsurmountable fault.

She wasn't Millie.

'Fuck,' said Millie.

'What?'

'The front door just went. He's back,' she whispered. 'I have to go now.'

'Oh,' said Tony, deflating. 'OK.'

'Thank you so much for the chat. It's been really lovely.'

'Don't mention it. It's been a pleasure.'

'You've really calmed me down. I don't know what I'd have done without you. Thank you.'

'Any time. Any time at all. Just promise me one thing.'

'Yes.'

'Don't let him get away with it. OK?'

'Oh trust me, Tony. He's not getting away with anything. Shit. He's coming. Sleep tight, Tony.'

'Yes – you too. Sleep tight.' But it was too late. She'd already hung up.

Tony switched off his phone and it felt a little like switching off a life-support machine. He tried to imagine what was happening in Millie's bedroom right now. Was Millie shouting at Sean, throwing pillows at him? Or was she crying again, was Sean comforting her? He wished it could be him. He'd smooth her hair and mop her tears and tell her that everything would be all right, that they'd be the best mum and dad in the world. And then he'd slip under the sheets with her and spoon her back and tell her stories all night long about how great their life was going to be.

He sighed and clutched the phone to his chest while he stared up through the glass again. He stared at the moon until it slipped out of view and was replaced by the early-morning sun and by the time he went to bed it was broad daylight and he'd eaten nearly half a pound of cheese.

Paradise Paul's without Millie in it, Sean soon realized, was just a poky, overcrowded basement bar full of braying, coked-up tossers. Paul barely gave him a second glance and Millie's friends seemed like unreachable strangers without her there to bond him to them. To compensate for his sense of distance from everyone, Sean drank roughly half a bottle of rum, had three very large lines of coke and didn't get back to Millie's until 4.30 a.m.

On the sofa in the living room were a spare duvet, three of the cats and a large handwritten note that said 'Your Bed'.

'Yeah, right,' he muttered to himself.

He petted the cats, picked up the note and tiptoed towards the bedroom. Millie was curled up on her side, her fourth and favourite cat pressed into the crook of her legs. The cat looked up superciliously when he heard Sean enter, and eyed him disdainfully as if to say, 'If you think you're coming anywhere near my beloved, slumbering mistress, you've got another think coming.'

He ignored the cat and trod softly towards the bed. Millie's hair was half over her face and her bare arm gleamed olive in the light from the hallway. He looked at her lovely mouth all pursed up like a little girl's and for a brief second he felt something like a paternal twinge as he imagined what it would be like if Millie had a little girl. Would she inherit her mother's snub nose, her good-enough-to-eat skin, that plump, stubborn little mouth? He imagined himself walking into a nursery after a night out, looking at his beautiful dusky-skinned daughter, adjusting her blanket, wondering what she was dreaming about. Yes, he thought, he could envisage that. He smiled fondly and reached out with one hand to brush the hair off Millie's smooth cheek.

'Fuck off.'

His hand retracted and he turned and left the room.

Duplicity City

'Tone, it's me.'

'Sean!' Tony wasn't used to receiving phone calls from his younger brother and especially not at ten o'clock on a Saturday morning.

'Look. I can't talk long. I'm on my mobile, just going down the shops to get some cranberry juice for Millie.'

'Oh. Right.'

'Look. I need to talk to you. Something's happened.'

Oh God, thought Tony, Duplicity City, here we come.

'Now this is top secret, right. You've got to promise not to tell anyone. Not Mum, not anyone.'

'OK.'

'Millie's pregnant.'

Tony mustered all his limited powers of artistic expression to sound surprised by the news.

'Yeah. It's a bit of a shock, really. Not planned or anything – well, obviously not planned. I mean we've only been together a few weeks. But the problem is, she wants to keep it.'

'Problem?' said Tony.

'Yeah. I mean, I understand why, I really do. She's thirty-six and she's at that age, you know. And I want to be really happy about it and be all New Man and understanding. But I can't.'

'Why?'

'I'm not ready. I'm not ready to share her. I'm not ready to give up my freedom. I'm not ready for her to change.'

'Change?'

'Yeah. You know, not drinking, not smoking, not wanting to go out. We had this great lifestyle and it was all new and fresh and now it's like living with bloody Geri Halliwell or something. All she wants to do is stay in and sleep and now I feel like a freak when I've had a few drinks. You know, there is nothing more self-conscious-making than hanging out with a sober person when you're bladdered and . . . well, I really pissed her off last night.'

'Christ – I'm not surprised, if that's your attitude. What happened?'

'Well, I wanted to go out after dinner and she said she was tired and wanted to go home. So I told her how that made me feel and she stormed off. Just like that. So I went out anyway . . .'

'What – you let her go home on her own?'

'Yeah. I know. I'm a cunt. But I was just feeling so . . . *powerless*. I know it sounds pathetic, but I just felt like if I'd gone home with her it would have been winning.'

'What would have been winning?'

'The baby. The baby would have won.'

'Sean, this isn't a competition, you know. That's your child she's carrying.'

'I know. I know it is. But I don't know *it*. It's not growing inside *me*, you see. It's *her* baby. You know, if it had been planned, if we'd been together a couple of years and deliberately stopped using contraception and then she'd got pregnant, that would be different. We'd have done it together. I could handle that. But this — this just feels like an alien has taken up residence inside my girlfriend. Like it's nothing to do with me. At all. Do you know what I mean?'

And in a funny way, Tony did know what he meant. But there was no chance he was going to say that to his brother. He was on Millie's side. All the way. 'Look, Sean,' he said, 'I know this is probably all a real shock to you and the last thing you expected. But you proposed to Millie — don't forget that. You made the ultimate commitment to her already and has it occurred to you that maybe *she*'s scared too? Eh? That maybe she's shocked. That maybe she'd have preferred to wait?'

'Well, she did say that she'd have been happier if it had happened in a couple of years.'

'Exactly. Look. You've got an incredible woman there. She's way too good for you and you know it. She's pregnant. You're the father. You're a grown man, so stop being a wanker, buy her some flowers and start dealing with it. Because if you really can't cope with it you'd be better off walking away now while she's still got some options.'

'What?'

'I mean — if you don't want her with your baby then leave her. At least that way she can decide to have an

175

abortion if that's what she wants, and get on with her life. But if you're just going to hang around making her miserable and making her feel guilty for something that isn't her fault then you're not doing her any favours. Either face up to it or walk away from it. OK?'

'Yeah,' said Sean, realization dawning in his voice, 'you're right. I know you are. It's just really hard. I mean, I think the world of Millie. I don't want to lose her. But I'm just so confused and even though I know what I *should* be doing I still find it really hard. Fuck, Tone . . .'

'I'm serious, Sean. You're just going to have to grow up. Make your decision, one way or the other.'

'Yeah. Yeah. Look. I'm just at the cash desk. I'm going to have to go now. But thanks, Tone. I'm really going to try and deal with this now.'

'You've got some serious thinking to do.'

'I have. I will. Thank you. Thanks for listening. And remember. Not a word to anyone. Yeah?'

'Yeah. Oh – just one thing. Just out of interest. Why did you call me? I'm not saying I'm not glad that you did. But you don't normally call me for advice.'

'Well, I don't normally need it, I suppose. And besides, you're my big brother – who else would I call?'

Tony put the phone down after Sean had hung up and stared at his feet for a while feeling guilty, duplicitous and exulted, all at the same time.

Purple Sofas, Mojitos and Leopardskin Mobile Cases

On Monday night at eight o'clock, Ned found himself in a very noisy, almost entirely purple wine bar just off Oxford Street. He was sure at first that he must have got the wrong address or the wrong place. It was full of curvy sofas, chrome lighting and the sort of people he'd spent his three years in Sydney trying to avoid. Men with gelled hair wearing shirts and ties that were the same colour. Girls in tight trousers and asymmetric lycra tops. People who looked like they worked in the lower echelons of media. Dim lighting. Loud music. Expensive cocktails. The antithesis in every way of everything that Carly liked. Carly liked pubs and caffs and places that served beer with funny names and at least four varieties of Walkers crisps. Places where you could get a seat and hear yourself think. Surely she was doing this all back to front, thought Ned. Surely you were supposed to start off with the loud purple-sofa places and work your way down to the old-man pubs as you approached your thirties.

He scoured the place for Carly, but she was nowhere to be seen so he ordered himself a vastly overpriced bottle of beer and tried to find somewhere to sit. He was about to perch himself on the corner of an enormous purple sofa when a slightly orange girl with a sheet of dyed blonde hair and wearing a fuchsia halter-neck threw him a 'My life would be perfect if you didn't exist' look and said, 'You can't sit there.'

'I'm sorry?'

'You. Can't. Sit. There.'

'Why not?'

'It's taken.' And then she turned away in a manner that suggested that she felt she'd already sacrificed enough of her precious life to dealing with him. It hadn't, patently, occurred to her that he might not follow her instructions.

And she was right, of course. Ned picked up his bottle of beer and slunk away, feeling like he had head-lice and yellow teeth.

Imagine, he thought as he tried to find a corner to hide in, if you were the sort of bloke who actually *fancied* girls like that, the sheet-of-blonde-hair girls, the you-bore-me girls, the high-maintenance, you-expect-me-to-get-on-a-*bus* girls. How soul-destroying to have to spend your life trying to please someone who was impossible to please just so you could go out with something pretty on your arm.

He fiddled with his hair while he waited. It was extraordinarily hot in here and his beard itched. And his hair, too, come to that. He had a sudden urge to comb his entire body.

His eye was caught then, by a cute-looking girl walking into the bar. She had blonde-ish wavy hair to her shoulders, rosy cheeks, a red coat, a rucksack and buckle-up shoes, like an enormous four-year-old. She stopped at the threshold and pulled off her stripy gloves, finger by finger, while her eyes scanned the room. And then her eyes fell upon Ned and she beamed at him. And then Ned realized. It was *Carly*! He put down his beer and headed towards her.

'Carly. Hi.'

'Ned.'

They hugged, Ned with his goatee and glasses, Carly with her red coat and rucksack, and Ned knew immediately that everything had changed. She smelt different, Ned noticed. She always used to smell of cherries and talcum powder. Now she smelt of some kind of proper but not unpleasant perfume.

'Look at you,' she said, holding his hands and eyeing him up and down. 'Love the beard.'

'Do you?' Ned ran his hand over the soft fluff and felt a flutter of pleasure at the first compliment his goatee had received since he got home.

'Yeah, suits you. Makes you look more . . . interesting.'

'Are you saying that I used to look dull?'

'Deadly, sweetie.'

Sweetie? Carly didn't say things like *sweetie*.

'And you,' he said, gesturing at her blonde-ish hair and trendy coat, 'you look brilliant.'

She grinned and bobbed up and down. 'Thank you.'

They walked to the bar. 'What d'you want,' said Ned, 'a beer?'

'No,' she replied absent-mindedly, picking up the

cocktail menu and perusing it, 'I'll have a ... a ... mojito.'

'Really?' he said, his voice so full of concern it was as if she'd just asked for a pint of skunk's milk.

'Yeah.'

By the time the twenty limes that Carly's drink seemed to require had been quartered and pounded, a table had come free at the back of the bar and they carried their drinks over and sat down.

'So,' said Carly, resting her face on glamorous hands with long, manicured nails and flashing a rather meaty cleavage at him. 'It's really great to see you.'

And Ned thought, This is *so* weird, so unbelievably weird. This was Carly – definitely, he was sure about that – but, at the same time, it *wasn't*. This was Carly Deluxe. Carly with make-up on and shiny fingernails and a cleavage and self-confidence oozing out of her like liquid gold. She was a little bit *scary*.

'So, anyway – *you*!' He suddenly sounded like a game-show host. 'Let's talk about you. I mean, new job, new hair, new everything. Seems like everything's going really well for you. Tell me everything.'

Carly smiled and fiddled with the zip of her rucksack while she talked.

She'd gone travelling after Ned left, cashed in her savings, rented out her flat and gone away for a year, had *the* most amazing time. The Amazon – *amazing*. The Aztec Palaces – *incredible*. *Stunning* apartment in the Bahamas where she looked after a millionaire's shih-tzu. San Francisco – *the* best city in the world, without a doubt. *So awful* having to come home, could have stayed away for ever. Made so many new friends, had so many experiences. And the *boys*. Boys, boys, boys. Blond ones with tattoos and Bermuda shorts. Dark swarthy ones with Vespas and speedboats. American ones, Danish ones, Australian ones. Should have done it years earlier. Built up her self-confidence *no end*, all that flirting and chasing. But that's what being young's all about, after all. I mean, if you can't do it when you're young, when can you do it, eh? *Soooo* depressing coming home, the weather, grey skies, dirty old London town and all those miserable pasty faces. Urgh.

Still, she had to get back to real life some time. Did a bit of temping, moved in with Mum and Dad, sold the flat, made a fortune, a *mint*, bought this stunning one-bed flat in Brixton. Of course, Brixton is so cool now, loads of really brilliant bars and restaurants – it's really trendy. Her flat's already gone up thirty per cent in value in just eighteen months. Soooo – she was temping for this really cool company on Eastcastle Street, just over there, and she and the boss, this really, really cool woman called Marty – forty-three, but looks about thirty – well, they just *clicked*. It was weird, really, like they'd known each other for ever. And Marty just turned round one day and said, 'I've let the senior pattern-cutter go – the job's yours.' And it's soooo great. Loads of money, loads of free samples, really nice clothes – she has no idea how she stuck it among all that Crimplene at Dorothy Day for soooo long. And it's so great now that she's a size 12, because the samples all fit – they even use her as a house model sometimes. So, she's got this great job and this great flat and this great figure and then Marty introduces her to her cousin Drew. And Drew is soooo gorgeous – blue, blue eyes, dark, dark hair, loaded – and whisks her off her feet. Meals, holidays – oh, they've been to Majorca, Mauritius and Zanzibar already and they've only been going out for ten months. He's *wonder*-ful. And Carly's life is *perfect*. Just perfect. Like a big fat fucking fairy tale.

Ned nodded and smiled grimly, nearly paralysed with boredom and bitterness. 'Great,' he said, grinding his teeth together so hard they almost gave off sparks, 'that's really great. I'm so glad everything's worked out so well for you.'

'Yeah,' said Carly, 'I've been really lucky. Life's *so good* right now. What about you?'

'Well, you know, I haven't really been back all that long.'

'What are you doing? Are you working?'

'Yeah. Yeah. Well – sort of. I've been doing some stuff for my dad.'

'Oh,' said Carly, looking like an air hostess during severe turbulence, 'right. That's good.'

'Well, no, it's not really. I'm intending to do something about it.' And as he said it his jaw set hard because although he'd been gently toying with the idea since he'd got back, he was now absolutely, 100 per cent determined. A job. Yes. Definitely. He was going to get one of those. And a good one, too. With a good salary. Yes.

'Still at home?'

'Uh-huh. Yeah.'

'Is that just . . . temporary, or . . . ?'

'Yeah,' he said abruptly. 'Yeah. I'll be, er . . . looking for somewhere as soon as I get myself together, sorted, you know . . .'

Carly nodded and they fell silent. Ned contemplated his empty beer bottle and realized that this was possibly the first time there'd been a silence between them. And he knew why. Because there was now a gulf between them that had never had the chance to develop when they'd been together. Carly had moved on. And on. And on. She'd moved so far away from him that she was now just a blot on the landscape.

He gulped and felt sad, scared and very alone. Because Carly wasn't the only one who'd left him behind during these last three years. His other friends had, too. They'd started cohabiting, getting mortgages – some of them even had people working for them now. That was the weirdest thing of all in some ways – or the most unexpected, at least. His friends had *staff*, hired and fired, chaired meetings, ran departments, were the subjects of bitching sessions in the pub after work. And it had all happened so quickly. It felt like he'd only been gone for about five minutes, but in those five minutes Mac had lost forty per cent of his hair, Sarah had dumped Colin, slept with Mac, and moved in with John – whoever the hell John was. Mike had been made area manager, Rob had proposed to Sam and Michelle had got married within six weeks of meeting someone called Tizer, had two miscarriages, got divorced two years later and had aged about ten years.

And Carly – Carly had transmogrified entirely into this glamorous, slightly bizarre *blonde* person to whom he could think of nothing to say.

'Do you want another drink?'

'Mmm,' she nodded and knocked back the dregs of her mojito, 'thanks.'

When Ned got back with more drinks Carly was on the phone. Her mobile had a leopardprint casing. Ned shuddered.

'OK, sweetie,' she was saying. 'Yeah. No. Not sure what time I'll be home. Oh. Right. OK. No, that's fine, midnight's fine,' she laughed, 'more than fine. Really fine. OK – completely fantastically fine. Oh, you! OK. Yes. Love you too,' she said then sighed annoyingly and turned off her phone. She was still smiling when she looked up at Ned. 'So,' she said, picking up her drink and holding it out towards his beer. 'Here's to life and destiny and moving on. Cheers.'

They clinked glasses. 'It's so weird,' she continued, 'just think – if you hadn't met Monica in that bar, then you'd never have left and I'd never have left Dorothy Day and gone travelling and met Marty and moved to Brixton and met Drew and everything would have been so different. It's a funny old world, isn't it?!'

She looked utterly thrilled by how funny the old world was and Ned gulped. Just think, he thought, if I'd never met Monica in that bar, I'd never have ended up living in Sydney with the unhappiest woman in the world and come home three years later to find that all my friends have left me behind and that my beloved ex-girlfriend and former best friend is a blonde, leopardskin-mobile-cover kind of a girl with a boyfriend called Drew and a taste for trendy South American cocktails . . . Where was the real Carly, he thought? What had happened to that round, apple-cheeked girl who only wore make-up to parties and never shaved her armpits in the winter?

They got through the evening together in time-honoured tradition – by getting pissed. Ned capitulated to Carly eventually and started drinking mojitos too. He liked them. They tasted like old-fashioned lemonade and got him good and pissed in record time. His tongue unstuck after a couple and, though he and Carly never quite recovered their old rapport, they did find things to talk about – mutual friends, mainly. Ned filled her in on all the gossip and she filled him in on hers. By ten o'clock they were actually laughing together and, although it was nothing like it used to be, if Ned had closed his eyes and pretended he was having a drink with someone else entirely – with a girl he used to go to school with who he'd bumped into unexpectedly on a bus, say – he'd have to concede that he was having a perfectly enjoyable evening. At eleven o'clock, or thereabouts, they put on their coats and gloves and headed out into the damp night air.

'So,' said Ned, forcing his hands into his coat pockets.

'So,' said Carly, twirling her scarf a little tighter around her neck.

'I'm going to get the bus.'

'Number 3?'

'Yup. Good old number 3. What about you?'

'Oh, I'll get the Tube. It's quicker.'

'Oh. Right. Are you sure?'

'Uh-huh. Yeah,' she cast her eyes downwards. 'I've, er, arranged to meet Drew at my flat at midnight. I don't want to be late.'

'Right. No. Of course.'

'So, thank you for a lovely evening.'

'And you. And you. It's been really nice.'

'Yeah. It has. OK, then,' she stretched on to her tiptoes to kiss him then, just a brief, warm brush of her cheek against his, too quick for Ned to respond or reciprocate in any way. 'Bye. I'll phone you.'

'Yes. Do. That'd be great.'

And then she smiled at him, a tight, inscrutable kind of smile, waved at him stiffly and walked away. Which was really silly, actually, as the Tube and the bus stop were in the same direction. But it would have been too embarrassing, Ned felt, to start walking behind her, so he turned 180 degrees and started walking in the opposite direction anyway. And as he walked he felt something really weird happening to him. It started as an ache in his gut, turned into a stabbing pain in the back of his throat and then a tingling in his eyes. Tears. He had tears in his eyes. He swallowed hard, trying to force them back in. And then he heard something.

'Ned!'

He turned around. Carly was standing on the corner

of Great Portland Street with her hands cupped around her mouth.

'What?'

'I . . . I . . .'

'What?'

And then she let her hands drop from her face and tucked them into her pockets. 'Nothing,' she shouted. 'Nothing. Just – welcome home.'

Ned shrugged and shouted, 'Thanks.'

And then Carly turned away again and disappeared around the corner.

When he got home, there was another parcel from Monica waiting for him.

He didn't even bother opening it.

www.morningsicknessremedies.com

'Oh. Hello. Is Millie there, please?'

'Speaking.'

'Millie. It's Tony. You sound dreadful. Are you OK?'

'No. I'm awful.'

'What? What's the matter?'

'Oh, just the onset of the truly delightful morning-sickness phase of my pregnancy.'

'Oh dear,' said Tony, 'have you been sick?'

'No. Not yet. Just spent the whole time feeling like I'm about to. I've gone from eating like a bulimic horse to not being able to eat anything at all. Everything I swallow just makes me feel worse.'

'Shit. Is there anything you can take for it? Medicine or anything?'

'Unfortunately not. They tried that with thalidomide but it didn't really work out. No – it's just another wonderful aspect of pregnancy that you don't realize until it's too late. I mean, you know you'll have to stop drinking and smoking and taking recreational drugs. But nobody tells you about all the other things you're suddenly not allowed to ingest. Like mayonnaise, for God's sake. And soft cheese and runny eggs and sushi and rare meat and *shellfish*. Shellfish, for fuck's sake. Imagine it, Tony – no prawns for *seven months*. It's tragic. And then there's the whole pharmaceutical thing. No Nurofen, no paracetamol, no Rennies, no cold remedies or cough mixture – I'm not even allowed a bloody throat lozenge, for God's sake. Just got to grit my teeth and take it like a man.'

'Bloody hell,' said Tony, who popped half of Super-drug at the merest suggestion of pain or discomfort, 'Isn't there *anything* you can take at all?'

'Nope. I tell you, it's so ironic. We go to so much trouble making sure that our unborn children aren't tainted by anything even slightly chemical or unhealthy, bring them into the world all perfect and wholesome so they can spend the rest of their lives shoving as much crap into their gullets as they can fit in. I don't know why we bother. Maybe we should just get them on the hard stuff from the outset.'

Tony laughed nervously.

'God – listen to me,' she said, 'I sound deranged. You're probably going to get the social services on me.'

'No,' said Tony, 'but you don't sound very mellow.'

'I'm sorry,' she said, 'it's just, I'm so tired and so ill and so fed up. And these fucking mood swings – they're so tedious.'

'Why don't you go home, Millie. Get some sleep.'

'Hmm. I don't know. I've got a lecture in half an hour. I was going to struggle through that and then see how I felt.'

'Maybe Sean could come and pick you up?' Tony ventured tentatively and, he thought, rather cunningly.

'Hmph,' said Millie. 'In what? On the back of his pushbike? Anyway – he's the last person I feel like seeing at the moment.'

'Really? You didn't sort things out on Saturday, then?'

'Er, no. Not exactly. He was all super lovely for a while that morning. All schnuzzly and going to the shops for me and bringing me tea and I was being all ice queen . . .'

'Did he apologize?'

'Uh-huh. Said he was a selfish bastard, didn't deserve me, started discussing baby names, talking about the wedding, being all, you know, *gorgeous*. But I could just tell by looking at him that he was finding it really difficult to muster up any enthusiasm, that he was acting the role of happy father-to-be. And then on Monday, when I started feeling ill and didn't want to go to the cinema with him, he got all shitty again. You know, he went off to his flat yesterday morning to do his washing and stuff and usually he'd come back in the evening. But he wasn't there when I got home so I phoned him at his flat and he was all off-hand and "Oh, sorry, I didn't realize you were expecting me to come back." Said he'd started writing and had got really into it. Which is fine, you know, obviously I understand that that's his job. But it's just that he's managed to get so absorbed and so far away from me and what's happening that he actually forgot all about us. Me. Everything. And . . . urgh . . .'

'What? Are you OK?'

'Urgh. Sorry. Just another engulfing wave of nausea. Look. I'm sorry. I didn't mean to rant on at you like that. I mean, that's all I ever seem to do these days – chew your poor little ear off. And I know he's your brother. I'm probably putting you in such an awkward position . . .'

'No, no, no,' said Tony, 'not at all.'

'. . . But there's no one else for me talk to, you know? I mean, my hormones are up in the air and Sean's being awful and I really need to offload.'

'It's fine, Millie, honestly. I really don't mind.'

Millie sighed deeply. 'Anyway. Look. I'd better go. I've got to prepare for this lecture.'

'Oh. Right,' said Tony, who'd just started to get into the swing of the whole slagging-off-his-brother thing. Well, anyway – I just wanted to check up on you. Make sure you're OK.'

'Thanks, Tony. You're a real sweetheart. I don't know what I'd do without you.'

'Any time. Anything you want. You know where I am.'

'Absolutely, Tony.'

'Well, bye, then.'

'Bye, Tony. Lots of love.'

'And to you.'

Tony put down the phone and smiled, feeling all warm inside. And then he turned to his computer, dialled up his Internet connection and typed 'remedies for morning sickness' into the query box. He clicked on to a website called www.morningsicknessremedies.com

and thought to himself, not for the first time, what a truly amazing thing the Internet was. He speed-read the advice on the site. Plenty of naps. Cool rooms. No spicy food. Blah, blah, blah. And then he found his way into a chatroom, full of women called Kimberley and Teena from places like Minocqua, WI, and Columbus, OH.

'I am 9 wks pregnant,' said Ilena from Berkeley, CA,

and suffering from morning sickness all day every day. Last week my husband went to the health-food store and was recommended Newton Homeopathic Morning Sickness Drops. I put 6 drops on my tongue when the symptoms got real bad and about an hour later the symptoms faded away. However, I was a little concerned when I read that the ingredients included 15% Alcohol. So I will only take this remedy when absolutely necessary.

Oh, per-lease, thought Tony. Six drops. *Six drops*, fifteen per cent alcohol. You'd be ingesting more booze if you stuck your tongue in a glass of shandy, for God's sake. No wonder parenting was such a stressful thing these days, with people getting their knickers in a knot about a microscopic drop of alcohol. He could just picture Ilena from Berkeley, too. All neurotic skin and bone, everything folded and ironed, husband not allowed to use foul language, shoes off at the front door, sex with the lights off. Jeez. He made a note of Newton Homeopathic Morning Sickness Drops in his diary anyway, despite the risk it posed to the welfare of Millie's unborn child, and scrolled down to someone a bit more sensible-sounding.

'Ginger cookies,' said Jackie L. from Cherry Hill, NJ.

'Suck a lemon,' said Tannita from Hawaii.

'Eat a Graham cracker when you wake up,' said Sherri from Milwaukee.

Tony scribbled things down as he read. Ginger tea. Vitamin B6. Essential oil of lemon. Peppermint tea. Apple cider vinegar and honey. Fresh ginger. Lemon peel.

And then at one o'clock, instead of sending Anne-Marie down to the sandwich shop next door to get him his usual egg-and-bacon baguette, he wandered down the road to the nearest health-food store and spent the best part of an hour painstakingly searching the aisles for all the items on his list, like a potential suitor asked to complete an impossible task before he would be considered worthy of the hand of a beautiful medieval princess.

Sean's Diatribe

Sean looked at the time on his laptop: 17.35. He stretched his hands behind his head and felt all his muscles singing out in exquisite pain. He'd been hunched over his computer since eleven o'clock this morning. He hadn't stopped for lunch and had only got out of his seat twice, to pee. He scrolled back through his document and smiled to himself. Thirty-five pages of text. Thirty-five big, fat lovely pages. He moved the cursor to 'tools' and clicked on 'word count':

Pages	35
Words	8,485
Characters (no spaces)	38,401
Characters (with spaces)	46,544
Paragraphs	153
Lines	680

One of the most beautiful sets of statistics Sean had ever laid eyes on. Finally. He'd cracked it. He'd broken through the brick wall he'd been headbutting for the past three months. Stuff was making its way out of his head on to his keyboard at last. Good stuff. Stuff that felt like it was going somewhere.

He'd got back to his flat yesterday lunchtime, ostensibly to do some washing, but mainly, and in reality, to give himself some space from Millie. He'd taken Tony's advice on Saturday, tried his best to be positive about things, to reassure Millie, make a fuss of her. But then on Sunday night they'd been watching some TV drama with loads of children in it and there'd been an uneasy silence between the two of them as the TV kids ran around on the screen, as if they'd both stopped breathing. What they'd both been thinking had been obvious: that'll be us soon, we'll be like those people on the telly with the unmanageable children and the mess and the toys and arguments. He'd gone to bed that night and barely slept a wink as all his good intentions about getting into the dad groove had fled his consciousness. He couldn't do it, he thought, just couldn't.

On Monday night he'd tentatively suggested a trip to the cinema, thought maybe Millie would like to see *Bridget Jones's Diary*, thought he was being considerate and unselfish. But she reacted like he'd suggested a night out in a crack den. So he'd decided that he needed some time to himself, packed his toothbrush and his shaving foam this morning and come home.

The sun had been shining when he got back, so he'd taken a notepad out on to the balcony, just like when he started *Half a Man*. He'd just been planning to do some warming-up exercises, really, play around a bit, make some notes, *do something*. And suddenly it had come to him. A whole new story. New characters. New plot. Everything. He'd spent so many weeks cogitating and mulling over the same old turgid, dead material; and, because the first book had started out pretty much as it had ended up, it had never occurred to him to let go of his original concept. *Half a Man* had been a work of pure fiction. A page-turning suspense novel about people and situations that had come entirely from the pungent paddy fields of his own imagination. This second book, he'd now decided, was going to be different. It was going to be autobiographical.

It was going to be about a man whose girlfriend gets pregnant just after they meet and insists on having the baby even though the man isn't ready yet. It was going to be a paean to men the world over in thrall to the power of woman's ability to reproduce and hence make the most important decisions in the world. Women carped on about men making decisions that started wars and led to death and destruction, but whose decision was it to bring the Uzi-toting little bastards into the world in the first place, eh? Yes, that's right: women. One unilateral decision led inexorably to the other. Obviously, there were still women in the world who didn't have choices, who couldn't abort or defer or avoid, who were left with no choice but to procreate. But Western women, the very women who complained the most about male oppression, about equal rights, about 'fairness', were also the most strident in their right to decide whether or not to bring a child into a relationship and into the world. The only decision left for a man to make was whether to stick around or not. Great. Stick around while some-one else decides what path your life is going to take for the next sixteen years, or bugger off, he branded a bastard and spend the rest of your life haunted by the thought of a child who barely knows you. Some choice.

Sean was a great believer in fate. His approach to life was to sit back, crack a beer, relax and see what turned up and he'd found that this *laissez-faire* attitude to his own destiny generally brought home the existential bacon. It brought him girls and experiences and fun and now it had brought him success, money and true love too. Sean didn't view the less idyllic chapters of his life as the results of 'mistakes'. He didn't believe in mistakes. He believed in a preordained path, and so far every point on this path had felt right. Every bad relationship had felt right, every shitty job he'd done had felt right – because *he*'d chosen them.

But this – this baby thing. Someone else was messing with his life path, with the natural timing of things, and it didn't feel right. Millie had taken away his power to let his life unfold in a leisurely fashion and be account-able only to himself and he'd never felt so out of control in his life.

So he was going to regain a little control through this book. Give the men's perspective. Men were supposed to be so accepting these days. All those pictures in the papers all the time of smug celebrity geezers with their kids strapped to their chests, like a pale imitation of a pregnant woman. Men were supposed to share the whole experience these days, go to antenatal classes, read books, *empathize*. Funny how you weren't expected to empathize with your woman when she was menstruating, weren't expected to know all the ins and outs, how all the strange bits of white cotton, straps, wings and strings actually *worked*. Women just dealt with it by themselves and all you were expected to do as a man was to keep your head down and avoid saying anything stupid. You could take an active interest if you so desired but no one was going to call you an insensitive Neanderthal if you chose not to.

And ditto other *girls'* things – vibrators, sisters, girls' nights, crying at adverts, complicated shoes, discharge, secretions, hair removal and breast surgery. As a man you knew these things existed and that they occasionally impinged, sometimes in a positive fashion, sometimes not, upon your life, but you weren't expected to *participate*. No woman would complain if you had no idea how to work her vibrator or refused to sit and hold her hand while she had her bikini line waxed. But pregnancy and childbirth . . . you were expected to be there, every step of the way, to soothe, understand, sympathize – *participate*.

Men of his father's generation had it easy. A bit of chivalrous lifting and carrying for your wife while she was pregnant and a few pints of stout in the pub with your male relatives while she popped it out. You arrived in the maternity ward full of beer and cigar smoke and were handed a clean pink baby, as opposed to something with yellow gunk and bits of placenta all over it. And then your life went back to normal.

'We're pregnant,' said modern men. And that was the problem. They weren't bloody pregnant. Their partners were. Being pregnant was something that happened to women and women alone, and along with all the physical discomfort came the most amazing experience a human being could ever go through, the miracle of nurturing life within their own bodies, of making that incomparable connection to another human being, an experience that men would never truly be able to conceive of, however many antenatal classes they went to. Women had the monopoly on the whole experience – they made the decisions, they experienced the miracle, they made the ultimate connection. Men could only ever be pathetic hand-holding, back-rubbing voyeurs whose only real contribution to the miracle of life had been the successful launch of one solitary, determined spermatozoon.

It wasn't until the child was born, weaned and walking that the father could even begin to share equal billing with the mother. At some point in a child's development a father could start to have an influence and at that point Sean might be ready to compromise his lifestyle. But right now this was Millie's pregnancy. Her body was being squatted by a stranger whom Sean had never asked to meet and who was seriously hampering their relationship. Millie had chosen to pursue this path – it was her decision – and, while Sean was happy to administer foot massages, back rubs and spaghetti Bolognese by the bucketload, he wasn't prepared to let Millie's condition take precedence over his own existence.

And this book – writing this book – it felt so good.

It was good to be back at home, to be sitting at *his* table, looking out of *his* window and writing about *his* feelings. He felt like a man again – and even better than that, he felt like a *writer* again.

He stood up, stretched up on to his tiptoes and cartwheeled his arms. He turned up the volume on the Café del Mar compilation he'd been listening to and went and stood on his balcony for a while. The sky was an intense turquoise and there literally wasn't a cloud in sight. It was crisp and fresh but the tentative spring sunrays warmed the skin on his forehead and cheekbones. Summer was definitely on its way – Sean could feel it and smell it.

He gazed around his city and for a few seconds he enjoyed the usual sense of anticipation at the onset of his favourite time of year. He envisaged deckchairs in Green Park, coffee at pavement cafés, cabs with open windows, cold lager in beer gardens and softball in his mum and dad's garden. But he soon felt himself deflate when the fatal flaw in these fantasies occurred to him: they all involved him and Millie – as a couple. They were all about being young and in love in London in the summer. But there wasn't going to be a carefree summer of love for him and Millie. There was going to be a summer of maternity-wear and hospital visits, no sex and no drinking. His first summer with the woman of his dreams was going to be spent waiting pensively for his life to change overnight. It was going to be about Millie and her pregnancy.

Fuck.

He wanted to sit out on Millie's candlelit patio drinking beer at midnight while they stared at the stars, he wanted to share a spliff with her on his balcony, wearing short-sleeved tops, listening to really loud music and looking down on their amazing, thrilling city while it oozed with potential for good times and nights out, places to drink, people to meet, drugs to take, experiences to have. He wanted it all, the whole magical summer-in-the-city thing, and he wanted it with Millie.

The baby was due in December. By next summer the baby would be six, seven months old and they'd be parents. They'd be tied down. Their freedom would be gone, wrenched from them, not to be returned until they were middle-aged.

Jesus.

It was so unfair.

Sean kicked the wall of the balcony in frustration.

Fucking life.

Fucking babies.

Fucking condoms.

Fucking Millie.

Fucking hell.

Sean looked down at something at his feet, something glinting in the sunshine. It looked like a piece of gold leaf at first. And then he noticed that it was foil torn from the neck of a bottle of champagne. From the bottle of Louis Röederer he'd opened the night he'd proposed to Millie, to be precise. He fingered it sadly, smoothing out its wrinkles, and thought back to that night, only two weeks ago. Millie had been a different person then, an eccentric, warm-hearted bundle of energy, an incredible, unpredictable, free-spirited woman. She'd made him laugh, made him excited, made him feel nervous like she was a beautiful, brightly coloured kite on which he had only the most tenuous of holds. Sean had been in awe of her, terrified that she might just float away from him if he loosened his grip.

She'd been everything then, absolutely everything.

And now – well, now she was just pregnant.

Sean rolled the little sliver of gold foil into a ball between his thumb and index finger, balanced it on the wall of the balcony and flicked it sadly off the wall and into the distance.

And then he went indoors and wrote a whole chapter about how it felt to miss out on summer because your girlfriend was pregnant.

Millie's Enchanted Kingdom

It was a bright afternoon as Tony exited his cab in Gloucester Terrace, and the sun bounced off the stuccoed houses that lined the road. Tony had driven through these roads of giant, imposing white houses so many times in his life but it had never occurred to him before that real people actually *lived* in them.

Millie's house was one of the smartest on the terrace – it was freshly painted and had shiny knobs and knockers and swagged curtains hung in the windows. Tony suddenly felt very suburban in the face of such overt sophistication. He looked down at his shoes and wished that they were hand-made Italian calfskin jobs rather than slightly scuffed £69.99 loafers from Jones the Bootmaker.

Millie answered the door wearing a loose cotton embroidered top with a slit at the neck that reminded Tony of one his mum used to wear in the seventies. Her hair was down and shaggy, like the first time he saw her, and she was wearing skinny thong sandals revealing small, dark feet with chipped nail polish and the beginnings of a bunion. 'Tony,' she said. 'What are you doing here?'

There was a note of unease in her voice and Tony flinched slightly. He'd blown it. He was too much. Too stalky. Too intense. He shouldn't have come.

'I, er, got you some stuff.' He held aloft the Holland & Barrett carrier bag and adopted the body language of a man about to be on his way.

'Stuff?' said Millie, taking the bag from him and peering into it. 'What kind of stuff?'

'Things for morning sickness.' He pulled out a packet of biscuits. 'Ginger snaps. Ginger's supposed to be really good for it, apparently. And lemon –' he pulled out a fan of lemon-flavoured lollipops – 'or you can use the essential oil; just put it on a tissue and sniff it. Or there's this homeopathic stuff in here somewhere –' he ferreted through the bag, searching for the tiny bottle – 'but you need to be very careful with that, apparently – it contains fifteen per cent alcohol.' He grinned at her and was gratified to see a small smile crack her deadpan face. 'I mean, I don't know how much good all this stuff will actually do, but I thought it would be worth a bash. You know.' He put his hands into his pockets and threw her another cheesy grin.

She looked at him and then back at the bag of goodies.

'Anyway,' he said, 'you look exhausted. So I'll get going. Leave you to get some rest . . .'

'No,' said Millie, tucking her unruly hair behind her ear, 'don't go. I mean, you've been to all this trouble. The least I can do is offer you a cup of coffee. Or maybe . . .' she pulled a packet out of the bag, 'a nice cup of organic lemon-and-ginger tea.' She smiled. 'If you've got time, that is.'

Tony looked at his watch and then looked at her. She looked more relaxed now. He'd redeemed himself. 'Er, yeah,' he said, 'sure. I don't need to get back just yet.'

'Cool,' Millie smiled and held the door open for him. Tony's heart lifted as he crossed the threshold – he felt like he'd been granted admission to some enchanted kingdom.

'Sorry,' said Millie as she let him into her flat, 'it's a bit of a mess. I only ever bother to tidy up when I'm expecting visitors.'

Tony looked around the not even vaguely messy flat in awe. The ceilings were high and the windows were floor to ceiling, with painted shutters. The walls didn't look like normal walls – they looked like they came from inside some ancient Italian palace. The room was a treasure trove of beautiful objects; coloured crystal chandeliers, antique French furniture, stained-wood floors, an embroidered silk shawl, Victorian tasselled lamps, a dramatic *chaise longue* in raspberry velvet, Afghan fur rugs, abstract paintings, framed sepia photographs, a brown suede pouffe. Millie had mixed together objects, art and furnishings from every continent and every period in history in every conceivable hue of pink, brown, gold, cream and ebony. But it all worked beautifully, because every item in her flat had been chosen with something that Tony suddenly and overwhelmingly realized he didn't possess – taste.

'Here are my boys,' she was saying, pointing at four slumbering cats draped artfully over her threadbare velvet sofa in complementary coats of cream, grey and champagne. Even her cats were tasteful.

'This is Dorian – because he's grey. This is Eric – because he's cream. Cream – Eric Clapton – get it? This is Barry – because he's white. And this is Brando because he's a big fat handsome bastard. He's my favourite. Or I'm his. I'm not sure which. Anyway. Tea? Coffee?'

'Coffee, please,' said Tony. 'White. One sugar.' He strolled around the living room while she made coffee and felt like he was in a dream, or squashed between the pages of *Elle Decoration*. 'This place is beautiful,' he called to Millie, picking up an exquisite and entirely useless piece of twisted turquoise glass and holding it up to the light.

'Not too feminine for you?'

'No – not at all. I mean, most of it is stuff I probably wouldn't have chosen for myself. But the way you've put it all together – it really works.'

'Thank you,' she said, putting a pair of mugs on the coffee table and folding herself into an overstuffed armchair. 'So. Tony. How did you know where I live?'

Tony stared slightly. 'Oh,' he said lightly, 'the college gave me your address.'

'The *college*?' she looked alarmed.

'Yes,' stuttered Tony, nervously, 'I was going to drop this stuff off for you there, but I phoned and they said you were off sick. The woman I spoke to said she didn't have a phone number for you, just an address.'

'Jesus,' she muttered, 'I can't believe they just hand out addresses willy-nilly over the phone to just anyone . . .'

Tony sucked in his breath in an attempt to make himself very, very small indeed. 'Sorry,' he whispered.

'No, no, no,' Millie put her hand to her chest and looked at Tony, 'I didn't mean it like that. *You*'re not just anyone, of course. But you could have been. You know?'

Tony nodded thoughtfully. 'Look, Millie,' he said, 'I really hope you don't think I'm plaguing you or anything. It's just, I'm really worried about you. You're pregnant and my brother's letting you down and I feel somehow . . . responsible. Do you see what I mean? And if you'd rather I just butted out . . . ?'

'No,' said Millie. 'No. Not at all. I really don't want you to butt out. I need you. I mean, I know that sounds strange, but you're my only link to Sean right now. My only insight into him. And I can't tell you how much I appreciate everything you've done for me. I'm so confused about everything and it's very reassuring to know that somebody's thinking about me.'

Tony smiled. 'Good,' he said, 'that makes me very happy.'

It fell silent. Tony sipped his coffee. Millie sipped her ginger-and-lemon tea.

'Does Sean know?' said Tony eventually. 'Does he know that we talk?'

Millie shook her head, a small, barely perceptible movement. 'No,' she said. 'He doesn't.'

Tony nodded tersely and wondered what that meant.

'So,' he said, 'how's everything going?'

'Awful,' she said, 'my life's a farce. I haven't seen the father of my child since Tuesday morning.'

'What?!'

'He's camped out in Catford permanently now – says he works better there.' She raised her eyebrows at him in a manner that suggested she thought there was more than a splatter of bullshit about this claim.

'You mean, you haven't seen him at all?'

'Nope.'

'And will you see him tonight?'

She shrugged. 'I doubt it.'

'Fuck. What's going on?'

She shrugged again. 'I'm pregnant. He's creating. The two are mutually incompatible, apparently.'

For the first time in his life Tony wished he had no responsibilities, wished he could just switch off his mobile phone, open a bottle of wine and spend the afternoon here with Millie talking about how shit his brother was. How could he go back to his office now and pretend to be interested in copyright law, when he could be sitting here, enveloped in the cocoon of Millie's warmth? He wanted to curl up with her, like one of her cats. He wanted to stroke her hair, caress her feet, *snuggle* with her. God, how pathetic – but he did. He wanted life to be one long Sunday afternoon with Millie and him on her sofa. He wanted to be absorbed into her world, totally, to the exclusion of everything else in his life – his job, his family, his friends. Just him, Millie and the baby . . . How could Sean not want to be here? It made no sense to Tony, whatsoever.

Tony shook his head in disbelief. 'Christ. He should be here. He should be with you. I mean, you're carrying his baby, for Christ's sake.'

'I know that and you know that, but Sean, it seems, has no concept of parental responsibility. I can't even be bothered to think about it any more, you know? I'm just so tired and I'd really rather conserve what little energy I have for this little blob in here.' She caressed her belly affectionately.

'How is the little blob?' said Tony, brightening at the concept of new life.

'Well, apart from the fact that it's making me puke my guts up every hour and making me cry twice a day, it's an absolute delight.' She smiled wryly and patted her belly again.

They ran out of conversation again, then, and Tony found himself wondering if maybe he'd imagined the other night when they talked so easily on the phone in the early hours. And then he remembered his other reason for popping round. 'Ooh,' he said, grabbing his briefcase and pulling it towards him. 'I nearly forgot. I brought you some pictures. Of my place. Thought you might like to have a look at them before deciding whether you wanted the job or not.'

'Rooms! Excellent,' said Millie, putting down her tea and clapping her hands together enthusiastically. 'Let's have a look, then.' He passed her the pictures and for the next hour they talked interiors. Millie sipped her ginger-and-lemon tea and talked Tony through her ideas: curved lines, blues, taupes, red highlights, nautical with a hint of New England beach house, great marine salvage yard in Rotherhithe, seagrass carpeting instead of his 'foul' laminate-woodstrip flooring.

Some of it sounded great, some of it sounded interesting and some of it sounded downright dodgy. But Tony didn't care – he was mesmerized watching Millie's heavily ringed hands as they deftly sketched shapes and lines, as they swooped down on to her enormous mug of tea and gripped it, as she ran them through her thick hair. Tony found it vaguely thrilling to be discussing the size of his bed with her, the colour of his bedclothes. In fact, he found the whole experience of sitting in Millie's living room on a Thursday afternoon so thrilling that he completely forgot that he was the managing director of his own company and was supposed to have been in a meeting at three o'clock, and got a genuine shock when his mobile phone rang at quarter to and Anne-Marie was on the other end wondering which meeting room he wanted her to set up in.

'Shit,' he said, as he put his phone away, 'I've got to go.'

'Well,' Millie said, retracting her ballpoint pen, 'what do you think? Do I get the job?'

'What,' said Tony in surprise, 'you'll do it?'

'Yes. Why not. But I won't be able to start for a while – probably not until the summer holidays.'

'Summer holidays – when do they start?'

'June.'

He nodded. 'June's fine. June's great. Definitely.'

'Excellent! Put it here!' she offered him her hand to shake and he took it eagerly. It was warm and dry and firm and he didn't want to let go of it. Ever.

'It's a deal.'

Millie smiled and opened the front door for him.

She reached up to kiss him on the cheek. Her lips connected with his skin, like they always did, but this time she hooked an arm around his neck and drew him to her. Tony found himself with his nose in her hair and suddenly lost control of his arms. He tentatively found a place for his left hand in the centre of her back and gave her a quick squeeze.

'And thank you so much for all the ginger and lemon. I already feel a bit better, actually. That really was incredibly sweet and lovely of you.'

'You're welcome.'

'You really are such a wonderful man, Tony. Are you sure you and your brother are related?'

'No – I think there's every chance that the babies got switched in the hospital.'

Millie smiled, and then frowned. 'God, Tony. I could really do without all this. You know?'

'I know,' said Tony, pausing slightly, unsure whether to say what he was about to say or not. 'Millie,' he began tentatively, 'whatever happens, right, you know you can walk away. There are people who will hold you up, support you – you wouldn't be left alone. Do you see what I'm saying?'

Millie crinkled her nose up and squinted at him.

Taking the piss. Tony didn't mind. 'I don't think it's going to get to that stage, Tony, but I do hear what you're saying. Thank you.' She squeezed his arm again. 'I'll call you,' she said, 'arrange to come over and see your place. Maybe next week?'

'Next week would be great.'

A cab was approaching so Tony leapt down the front steps and on to the street to hail it. He turned round to see if Millie was still at the door, but it was just closing behind her.

He fell into the back of the taxi and watched through the back window as Millie's enchanted kingdom receded into the background.

A wonderful man.

Millie thought that he was A Wonderful Man.

And currently thought that his little brother was a complete waste of space. How the hell had his lazy, self-centred, slacker of a brother ever managed to get his hands on such a classy woman? What was it about him that had appealed to a woman like Millie in the first place? OK, so he'd written a book, but that didn't change him fundamentally as a person and Millie was patently not some shallow little celeb-chasing girl who got a kick out of going out with a published author. There was obviously something else to her attraction to Sean. His looks? Possibly – he was a nice-looking bloke, but there were better-looking guys out there if that's all she was interested in.

Maybe it was a maternal thing – maybe his boyish incompetence brought out her mothering instincts. Or maybe it was just one of those completely inexplicable attractions that you encountered every now and then in life – a bizarre chemical collision between two people who had nothing in common except some pheromone that happened to correspond with the other person's pheromone at some fleeting moment in time. That seemed more likely, and would explain Sean's sudden cooling off at the prospect of making such a lasting commitment to Millie. Marriage was one thing; a marriage could be arranged at the height of the chemical collision and unarranged when said pheromones had departed the scene. Divorce was a friend of the whirlwind wedding. The prospect of something as irreversible as a baby, on the other hand, could cause pheromones to flee immediately, screaming and waving their hands around in horror. There obviously wasn't enough substance to Sean's feelings for Millie to sustain a real life together. So he was doing what Sean always did: he was backing off. Backing off and waiting for the girl to get so upset and so angry and so hurt that they told him to fuck off. But he couldn't get away with that approach this time. This time there were babies and engagement rings involved. This time he was going to have to grow up and deal with it.

Tony ran a hand over his belly and looked down at his high-street shoes. He really was going to have to sort himself out if he wanted to stand a chance in hell of attracting Millie. Not seeing so much of Ness lately had helped – he wasn't drinking so much and his clothes all felt a little bit looser. But if he wanted Millie to look at

213

him as anything other than Sean's much nicer older brother he had a hell of a lot more work to do.

He rummaged through the pockets of his coat and found what he was looking for – the Natural Weightloss programme leaflet he'd picked up weeks ago.

He pulled out his mobile, phoned the number on the leaflet and made an appointment for a consultation the following week.

Big Quiffs and Little Cars

It had been a long week for Ned. As well as his disastrous night out with Carly, he'd had the pleasure of receiving eighteen delightful text messages from Monica, an envelope full of her toenail clippings, a package containing wax strips with her pubes attached and then the *pièce de résistance* this morning. A small vial of her blood. It was only tiny – she'd siphoned it off into one of those miniature plastic bottles of soy sauce you get in sushi boxes. But the fact was that the more parcels and text messages she sent him the less concerned he felt. He found them quite comforting now – they meant she wasn't dead, that she wasn't in a plane on her way to London and that she wasn't getting any worse. The scale of the gruesomeness of the 'body parts' had diminished rather than gathered momentum; there'd been no severed digits or bits of flesh. And when the toenail clippings had arrived on Tuesday, Ned had actually breathed a sigh of relief. Toenails weren't disturbing – they were just grim. Now she was just being annoying instead of scary.

The blood was a bit more of a hark back to the days of hair and eyelashes, but it wasn't hard to extract that much blood from yourself – it might not even be blood; she might have got it from a joke shop or something.

No – unless Mon suddenly upped the ante and started sending him thumbs and eyeballs, he wasn't going to let it get to him. He had enough to worry about without worrying about Monica and her stupid little games.

Like tonight, for example.

He was sitting in the living room at the moment, watching *The Simpsons* on Sky One, eating Jaffa Cakes out of some kind of new-fangled metal-tin affair and waiting for Gervase to get back from work. He was waiting for Gervase because tonight he, Ned London, was going out with him. Bizarre. He'd scoured his mind, searching for the perfect excuse to get out of it, but had been unable to come up with anything. The fact that they lived in the same house meant that in order to concoct a believable excuse he'd actually have to have somewhere else to go; and, sad to say, he didn't. The ritual Friday night out with friends seemed to have fallen off almost as quickly as Mac's hair after Ned left the country.

'No one really goes out any more,' Simon had said, sadly. 'Everyone's just sort of coupled off. It's all *Friends* and *Frasier* and home-delivery Thai on a Friday night now. Unless it's someone's birthday – we still go out on people's birthdays.'

But he'd made a few phone calls last night, anyway, hoping for a last-minute reprieve in the form of an alternative social engagement, and found that everyone else was doing things like staying in because they were knackered (pathetic), working late at the office (tragic) and having dinner with their parents (verging on the sick). Even Simon, the only other single guy left in their circle, had other plans for the night: competing in a ten-pin bowling tournament in Streatham. He'd said that Ned was welcome to come along and give him some moral support, but when Ned had sat down and weighed up the options, going to see some greasy old rock and roller in Wood Green with Gervase just about had the edge over spending the night watching his mate chucking big shiny balls down a runway.

When Gervase got home he went straight upstairs to get ready. When he came back down half an hour later he was wearing far too much aftershave and a battered leather jacket with fringing and studs all over it. He was also wearing a violently purple shirt, open pretty much to the navel, and very pointy-toed boots with a slight heel. Ned had never seen Gervase 'dressed up' before and was caught momentarily somewhere between laughing out loud and a quiet sense of awe. He looked utterly ridiculous and kind of cool, all at the same time.

At the same moment that Gervase entered the room, a horn went in the street and Gervase clapped his hands together. 'OK. That's Bud. Let's rock.'

Ned ran to the kitchen, pulled a four pack of Kronenburg from the fridge, grabbed his jacket and followed Gervase outside. Parked on the street was a bright-yellow, souped-up Robin Reliant, with red flames painted down the side. At the wheel was a man wearing a red leather jacket who had a gigantic peroxide quiff that nearly filled the whole car.

Ned gulped.

'All right,' said Gervase, as the quiff guy got out of the Reliant and shook his hand. Standing, the quiff guy turned out to be about five foot two and so thin that Calista Flockhart would probably have refused to stand next to him in case he made her look fat. He had intensely blue eyes and a sharp, rodenty face with two pointy little yellow rat-teeth.

'Bud, this is Ned – he's my landlady's son.'

'All right, Ned,' said Bud, giving his hand a squeeze. 'All right.'

'Nice motor you've got there.' He indicated his parents' driveway with a jerk of his head. Ned looked round at his father's ancient Transit van and his mother's even more ancient Vauxhall Cavalier, and looked back at Bud. 'Which one?'

'The little Isetta.'

'The what?'

'The bubble car. Lovely. What is it – '68? '69?'

Ned turned and looked at the sad little car that was now so much a part of the furniture outside their house that he barely noticed it any more. 'I've got no idea,' he said, 'Tony got it for his seventeenth birthday.'

'Lovely. Really lovely little car.' Bud stared at the mouldy old car longingly and nodded his head appreciatively.

'Bud likes little cars,' said Gervase.

'Oh,' said Ned, 'right.' And then he turned to get into

Bud's little Reliant. There was a small bench in the back that looked better suited to a lunch box than a six-foot man, and he realized that simply stepping into the car and sitting down was not going to be feasible. Some kind of strategy was called for. He tried getting in with his right foot first and then employed a kind of 180-degree twist to the rest of his body, but that didn't work. He tried lowering himself in arse-first, which at least meant that eighty per cent of him was now in the car, but he couldn't find anywhere to put his left leg or his head. He slid his bum along the little bench and managed to accommodate his left leg, but his head was still folded flat against his chest. Gervase and Bud chatted on the pavement while Ned performed his tribute to Houdini and Ned was tempted to say, 'Tell you what, Gervase, you're at least four inches shorter than me – why don't *you* get in the back', but realized that this contravened lift-giving etiquette, which of course stated that the driver's best mate/girlfriend/wife got the passenger seat and strangers got the back – regardless of shape or size.

With a few more adjustments, Ned managed to lift his head an inch or two off his chest, but then Gervase flattened the passenger seat, which effectively cut off a whole side of the back of the car, so Ned was left with no choice but to curl himself up into a sub-foetal ball, with his arms wrapped around his knees and his bottom bones digging into the poorly upholstered bench.

'You all right in the back there?' asked the more suitably proportioned Bud.

'Yeah,' said Ned, 'fine.'

The car made a milk-float-type noise as Bud turned the key and then they were off.

It was the longest drive of Ned's life. The car never really felt like it got going – it was like spending the entire journey in first gear – and every pit and pebble on the road sent painful jolts up his spine through his bum bones. Halfway through the journey he started feeling like he was going to faint, so he twisted around and hooked his legs over the back of the seat so that they hung in the cargo area of the boot.

Bud and Gervase talked about music in the front, chain-smoking, drinking Ned's lagers and breaking into tune every now and then. Gervase did most of the talking, accompanied by Bud saying 'Damn right', 'That rocks' and 'Fuck, man' every now and then, and laughing as if someone was tickling his feet with a feather. Ned had very little idea what most of their conversation was about and didn't really care. All he was concerned with was the impending end of the journey and getting out of this sardine can on three wheels.

By the time they finally pitched up in Wood Green, it was dark and Ned thought he might actually be dead. Bud and Gervase swung casually from the car looking fresh as daisies and Ned slowly unfurled himself from the torture device, every bone and muscle in his body complaining loudly as he did so. The first thing he did when he got out of the car was to check his wallet to see how much cash he had. He didn't care how much it cost, he was getting a cab home.

Bud and Gervase started to get more and more animated the nearer they got to the doors of the Old White Horse. They started singing again and Bud started doing Buddy Holly-style air guitar, his big meringue of a quiff bouncing up and down like an overexcited poodle. Ned followed them dismally into the pub and waited at the back while Gervase and Bud queued up for drinks at the packed bar. He looked round him while he waited. To his right was an enormous whale of a man wearing a bomber jacket designed for someone half his size. His head was shaved completely bald save for a solitary ginger tuft at the front, which he'd teased into a tiny quiff that looked like a bunny's tail. To his left stood a rock-like man in head-to-toe black leather, with bumpy skin and jet-black hair. His fringe had been coiled into a grease-slicked ringlet that sat on his forehead and tickled the end of his nose.

The girls of this new and undiscovered world seemed to come in two main varieties. There was the peroxide-ponytailed and leather-jacketed type with, on the whole, a slightly hatched-faced appearance, not complemented by enormous black beetles for eyebrows. The alternative was the more feminine, pin-curled and vintage-clothed variety with dirndl skirts and stiletto heels.

Ned fingered his bum-fluff beard and looked down at his Nikes and felt hugely, enormously out of place.

Where did all these people come from? Ned never saw people like this walking down Beulah Hill, on the Tube, in airports, on the television. Where did they all live? What did they do when they weren't going to Robert Gordon gigs in Wood Green? What did they all do for a living? Did they have families? Children? Did they flatten their quiffs and mothball their leather jackets when they got home?

Ned remembered Tony going through a brief phase of being a rockabilly when he was a teenager. He'd Brylcreemed his hair into a quiff and worn faded checked shirts from Flip and brothel creepers from Robot. But it had just been a phase – it had passed, and by the time Tony was nineteen he was a fledgling yuppie, buying himself suits from Cecil Gee. But these people, they weren't teenagers going through a phase – they were living it, breathing it, doing it, *believing* it.

'There you go, mate.' Gervase emerged from the throng at the bar clutching two plastic pints of beer. Bud followed behind with an orange juice and lemonade with a straw in it, looking like a slightly over-coiffed schoolboy. Ned downed his plastic lager in about ten gulps while he stood and chatted with Bud and Gervase.

'So. Bud,' he said, hoping to gain a little insight into the ageing-rockers scene, 'what do you do?'

'Civil servant.'

'Yeah?'

'Yeah. I'm chief executive in charge of paperclips. And vice president of retractable pencils.'

'He works for the Town Planning Office in Croydon,' said Gervase, helpfully. 'Office-supplies manager.'

Bud nodded enthusiastically. 'Been there twelve years,' he said proudly. As they chatted it transpired that Bud lived in a three-bedroom house in Shirley with his wife and their three kids (one of whom was a teenager). Any money he had left over after paying the mortgage and bills went on his car and his clothes and he was, Ned realized as they talked, truly, unapologetically happy with his lot.

''Tell you what,' he said, 'if I was to win the Lottery, I'd keep, say, fifty, sixty grand. Just enough to pay off the mortgage, pay for a couple of decent holidays. Then I'd give the rest away. Wouldn't want it. It might *ruin* everything. You know?'

Ned nodded, not knowing, but wishing more than anything that he did. He couldn't even begin to imagine the sort of happiness that could potentially be 'ruined' by three million quid.

His parents had it, though, he thought. They'd attained Bud-like levels of contentment. Both of them loved everything about their lives. They loved their big messy house, their jobs, their kids, *each other*. And his brothers were on their way to existential nirvana, too. They both had job-satisfaction, self-confidence, great girlfriends. Even Gervase seemed content with his lot, in his own strange way. And now that all Ned's friends were coupling off and climbing the career ladder – where did that leave him? Twenty-seven, no career, no flat, no girlfriend.

What was wrong with him? If runty little Bud with his rat-teeth and strange taste in cars could find true happiness, then why couldn't he? Ned was better-looking than Bud, he was taller, younger, better educated, less *weird*, yet Bud had everything and Ned had nothing – except his ex-girlfriend's toenail clippings.

Ned sighed and looked down into the bottom of his

empty plastic pint. And then he thought about Monday night and his meeting with Carly. Oh yes – what a truly depressing experience that had been. Jesus. He really was all alone now. He couldn't turn to anyone else to make him feel better about things. There was no soft cushion of Carly, no ever-available circle of friends – even his family didn't seem to get together as frequently as they used to. How do you start again at twenty-seven, he wondered to himself? How do you make a fresh start? Maybe you couldn't. Jesus, what a horrible thought. He'd blown it. He was never going to have what Bud and Sean and Tony had. He'd turn into a reclusive weirdo. He'd end up looking forward to watching Simon playing in his ten-pin bowling tournaments in Streatham on a Friday night. Jesus – he'd probably end up being best friends with Gervase. He might even get his hair cut into a quiff and . . . Oh God. Why the hell had he ever gone to Australia? Why hadn't he just stayed here like a normal human being and got on with his life?

Ned marched to the bar and ordered another round of drinks. He was starting to feel quite panicky and maudlin. He needed to get drunk. Very drunk. Ugly drunk. He necked his pint while he was still at the bar and ordered another one and by the time they finally moved through to the stable block at the back, where the gig was being held, Ned was feeling decidedly unsteady.

Bud disappeared after a few minutes to talk to some mates and Ned and Gervase stood in amiable silence at the back of the hall watching the support band. There was something strangely soothing about the atmosphere in here, about standing with Gervase among all these odd people, watching a band, feeling pissed. Ned turned to look at Gervase in profile, at his flashy purple shirt, razor-sharp hair and pointy boots, and felt a sudden overwhelming urge to hug him. Gervase turned to look at him.

'You all right?'

'Uh-huh.' Ned turned away abruptly and looked at the band.

He really wanted to talk to Gervase. He was getting that chocolaty feeling in his stomach again and he had so much on his mind. He hesitated for a moment before turning back to Gervase. 'Am I . . .' he began, 'am I wearing a cape tonight?'

Gervase smiled and looked him up and down. 'Yeah.'

'Well, how come you didn't say anything?'

'Thought I'd give you a break. I could tell I was getting on your nerves.'

'What does it look like?'

Gervase turned and squinted at him. 'Scared and pathetic.'

Ned nodded keenly. That was exactly how he was feeling.

'Wanna talk about it?' said Gervase, grimacing as he took the final drag on a cigarette and dropped it to the floor.

'I thought you said you didn't like talking about stuff?'

'I didn't say I didn't like it – I said I wasn't any good

at it. Subtle difference, Ned. But I can listen. I'm good at listening. Wanna tell me what you're so scared of?'

Ned looked at him thoughtfully and then nodded. 'But you've got to promise me you won't say anything to anyone else. To Mum or Dad or my brothers. Promise?'

Gervase gave him his Scout's honour. 'The very soul of discretion,' he said, 'that's what I am.'

And then, with his mouth an inch away from Gervase's ear to be heard over the live music, Ned told him everything. He told him about Carly and their disastrous night out, how much he missed her and how scared he was that he was missing the boat, that everyone was leaving him behind. He told him about Monica and how he'd done a runner and was now being plagued by rude text messages and unsavoury parts of her person. He told him how even though it made him really angry he still couldn't stop feeling guilty and worrying about her, how she was in his thoughts all the time, how it was like even though she was on the other side of the planet he still couldn't escape her. And as Ned talked he could feel all his deepest fears dissolving into a big warm mulch, like he'd been emotionally constipated and Gervase's ear was a pint of prune juice. He'd never felt like this before, he'd never had this sense of total and utter honesty and, more importantly, of being truly listened to. It was like there was some kind of invisible telegraph wire between his mouth and Gervase's ear and his thoughts were being transmitted directly into Gervase's head without the awkwardness of having to translate them into cumbersome words first. He felt like his mouth and Gervase's ear were all alone in the room, hermetically sealed in a warm, pink bubble. It was like being on E but a hundred times better.

'Well,' said Gervase thoughtfully, when Ned had finally finished speaking. 'Well, well, well.' He pulled a Chesterfield out of his top pocket and lit it. 'You feeling a bit better now?'

'Er – yeah,' said Ned, 'definitely.'

'Good,' said Gervase, patting his shoulder, 'good.'

Ned waited for a moment, expecting Gervase to say something, to comment on the litany of human patheticness he'd just regaled him with. But he didn't say a word. Just stood there, smoking his fag, watching the band.

Ned felt himself deflate a little. But then Gervase turned round and looked at him. 'Monica,' he said, 'she's not your responsibility, all right?'

'Yes, but she *feels* like my responsibility. All the time. For three years and even now. I can't get rid of her.'

'What you want to do, Ned, is *delegate*. Pass the baton. Yeah?'

'No. What do you mean?'

'I mean – you wanna hand responsibility over to someone else. Her family, for example. Give them a ring. Tell them you're worried. Tell them what she's been doing. Then *they* can worry about her instead of *you*. You've done your bit, Ned. It's time to pass the buck.'

Ned nodded enthusiastically. Of course, he thought, her parents. He had their address in his book at home. That was the thing to do. Definitely.

'And I'll tell you another thing, Ned. You want to try and be a bit more *philosophical* about things.'

'What – think about them more?'

'No, Ned. Think about them *less*. Everything in life happens for a reason, Ned. I know it's a cliché, but it's true. There's a pattern to life and if you just stop worrying and stressing, if you just relax a little bit, then you can see it.'

'What?'

'The pattern, Ned – the fucking pattern. And you'll see that, if you're a good man, everything'll work out in the end. Just let go, man. Stop trying to control everything, let go, see where life takes you. You're a good man, Ned. Good things will come to you. Chill.'

Ned nodded mutely. And then the support band finished their set and Gervase went to the bar to get another round and Ned stood there swaying slightly in among this sea of sweaty, boozy, slightly bizarre humanity, feeling completely shell-shocked. *Chill*, he thought, *see where life takes me*. But wasn't that exactly what he'd been doing all his life? Wasn't that the Story of Ned? All he'd done for the past twenty-odd years was chill – and look where life had brought him: Wood fucking Green.

'All right?'

Ned looked around and then down at Bud.

'Yeah.'

'You enjoying it?'

'Yeah,' said Ned. 'It's different. But, yeah.'

Bud grinned at him. 'So,' he said, 'how long've you known Gervase, then?'

Ned shrugged. 'A couple of weeks.'

Bud looked a bit surprised. 'Oh,' he said, 'right.'

'You?' said Ned, expecting Bud to say that they'd know each since they were kids.

'Same.'

'What – you mean you've only just met him?'

'Yeah. Met him at a record fair in Addington. Got talking about music. Funny – I got the impression you'd known him longer. That he was some kind of family friend, you know?'

'No,' said Ned, 'he met my mum in a pub three months ago and she rented him a room. I've only known him since I got back from Australia. Funny – I thought you'd known him for a while, too. You seem to have such a strong rapport.'

Bud nodded. 'Yeah! That's it! That's spot on,' he said, 'we're on the same wavelength.' He waggled his fingers out from his forehead to demonstrate the wavelength. 'It's incredible, man. I feel like I've known him for ever.' Bud pulled himself up, then, and smoothed his quiff, obviously feeling he'd been a bit too forthcoming about his feelings for another man. 'He's a good bloke, though, that one. Diamond. Solid gold.' He cleared his throat and turned back to watch the roadies loading equipment on to the stage, and Ned stood there wondering more than ever who the hell Gervase was and why he suddenly felt like he loved him.

Horse Shit on Beulah Hill

Ned ended up drinking somewhere in the region of eight pints that night. There might have been more, he couldn't remember. He'd been so pissed that he'd managed to get into Bud's car really easily at the end of the night and didn't recall feeling any discomfort whatsoever. All he could remember was being dropped off on Beulah Hill at some unspecific time of the night, falling backwards out of the car and landing straight in a pile of what had at first appeared to be mud but soon identified itself as horse shit. *Horse shit.* On Beulah Hill. In the middle of the night. For fuck's sake.

He'd had a shower when he got in. He couldn't remember much about that either but he had a very uneasy feeling that Gervase might have helped him get undressed. He'd woken up this morning completely naked with very strange hair where it had dried against his pillow in the night.

He'd also woken up with one of the worst hangovers he could remember since his university days. It had been so long since he'd had a hangover like this that he'd actually been under the impression that he didn't *get* hangovers any more. He thought he was hardened to it, that he could take his alcohol like a real man. But what he realized, as he contemplated the extent of his unwellness that morning, was that these days he simply didn't drink as much as he'd drunk as a student. And he also didn't drink things with Pernod in them. He'd subconsciously developed a cut-off point over the years – five pints usually did it these days – then he'd switch to water or go home. But he'd felt so morose last night, so alone and out of his depth, that he'd lost sight of his usual boundaries. And actually, as bad as he was feeling now, he was glad in a way that he'd lost control. He'd had a top, top night.

He had another shower, attempted to do something with his bizarre hair, got dressed and headed downstairs towards the kitchen. It was just gone twelve and the house appeared to be empty. He poked around in the fridge, hoping for a sighting of a packet of bacon and maybe an egg or two, found nothing suitable so gave up and decided that he'd go into Crystal Palace later for a fry up. He took a cup of coffee into the living room and did a double take.

Ness was sitting in front of the TV, watching *Football Focus* and wearing a very short skirt.

'Ness!'

'Hello, Ned.' She turned round and smiled at him, giving him a quick once up and down. 'Rough night?'

Ned looked at her and for some reason felt an enormous blush exploding all over his body. She had her shoes off with one unfeasibly long leg tucked up underneath her. Her hair was all wild and unkempt and, even though she wasn't classically pretty, there was something unbelievably sexy about her – the way she looked at him as if he was a badly behaved schoolboy and she was the hot young biology teacher. Her eyes were green and twinkly. She looked like she'd be fantastic in bed, a really good laugh and a good listener, all wrapped up in one.

'Er, yeah. You could say that.' He looked around the room and behind him. 'Is Tony here?'

'No. Just little old me.'

'Sorry, I didn't realize you were here – I'd have offered to make you a coffee otherwise.'

'S'all right,' she said, pointing at a mug in front of her, 'Bernie already made me one.'

'Where *is* Mum?'

'Upstairs, getting ready.'

'You two going out somewhere?'

'Uh-huh – it's the traditional day-after-pay-day shopping extravaganza. We're off to Bromley.'

'What, you do this every month?'

'Yup. We both get paid on the same day every month, so we hit the town and burn holes in our credit cards.'

'Cool,' said Ned, who was the only member of his family apart from his dad who'd never really understood the appeal of retail therapy. Spending money just stressed him out. Probably because he never had any.

'So – what were you up to last night, then?'

'I was out with Gervase, actually.'

'Really?' She smiled at him in surprise. 'And what sort of places does the mysterious Gervase go to?' Ned felt his blush ratchet itself up a few notches under her interested gaze. She really was completely fucking gorgeous. She was wearing a sort of woollen cardigan thing with, apparently, nothing underneath it at all. Her breasts, from what he could ascertain without gawping, appeared to be of the small but perfectly formed variety and there was definitely more than a hint of perky nipple there.

'Er, sorry?' he blustered.

'You and Gervase – where did you go?'

He told her about Robert Gordon and Bud and driving all the way to Wood Green in his Robin Reliant. He told her about the eight pints and the horse shit and showering in the middle of the night and she laughed out loud like it was the funniest thing she'd ever heard in her life. The more she laughed the more Ned embellished the story until eventually he became so animated that he completely forgot he had a hangover.

'God,' she said, wiping tears away from under her eyes, 'that's so funny. Where the hell did the horse shit come from?'

'I have absolutely no idea. Maybe it fell out of an aeroplane. You know. With horses on it . . .'

She burst into hysterical laughter again and Ned smiled contentedly.

'You two sound like you're having fun,' said Mum, walking into the living room with her coat on.

'Bernie,' said Ness getting to her feet and displaying the full vertiginous extent of her legs, 'Ned fell into horse shit last night – out there.' She pointed through the window at Beulah Hall, snorting with laughter. 'Where d'you reckon it came from?'

Bernie looked out of the window in bemusement. 'What – out on the road?'

'Yes.'

'I've got no idea,' she said, starting to laugh. 'But trust Ned to find it, eh?'

She ruffled his hair and he shrugged her off.

'OK,' she picked up her handbag, 'let's hit the shops.'

Ness pulled on a fawn-coloured coat that was the exact same shade as her hair and made her way to the broken mirror over the fireplace. Ned watched her as she examined her teeth and teased her hair, twisting it up suddenly into a top-knot and sticking something into it that made it stay there. She pulled some bits free so that they framed her face, adjusted her cardigan and her skirt with a wiggle and then picked up her handbag. Funny, thought Ned, but in a strange kind of way Ness seemed to *belong* here. She fitted the surroundings, with her unruly hair and slightly mismatched clothes. She had the same warmth as this house, the same sense of cosiness and welcome.

'What are your plans for the day, then?' said Bernie, pulling her car keys out of her bag.

'Dunno really. Going to get some breakfast up the road. Might get my hair cut . . .'

'Oh, don't get your hair cut,' said Ness unexpectedly. 'You've got lovely hair.'

Ned blushed and put a hand up to his hair. 'Do you think so?'

'Yes. It's gorgeous. It's funny, 'cause I don't usually

like long hair on men, but yours really suits you. Don't get it cut.'

'Er, OK,' stammered Ned, 'I won't.'

'You might want to think about losing the fungus, though,' she said, suddenly lunging at his chin and rubbing her fingers across his beard. Ned was too shell-shocked to say anything.

'Well, have a good day. And watch out for the horse shit.' She grinned at him and left the room and Ned sat there feeling slightly dazed. He was all buzzy and sweaty and nervous. He fancied his brother's girlfriend. He really did. God almighty – was it even *legal* to fancy your brother's girlfriend?

His mum's car horn sounded in the driveway and Ned went to the window. Ness was standing in the road waving at him and pointing at the pavement. Ned wondered what she was doing until she pinched her nose with her fingertips and waved away some imaginary smell. Then she tossed her head back and laughed and got into the passenger seat of Mum's car. Ned watched the car reversing out of the driveway and on to Beulah Hill. He watched Ness sliding on her seatbelt, chatting with Mum, adjusting her hair with her fingertips, laughing. God. She was great. She had all that confidence and up-frontness he'd loved about Monica when he first met her, but without the dark side. You could tell that she had sunshine running through her soul – she didn't appear to have a negative or cynical bone in her body. He wondered how old she was. He'd assumed she must be Tony's age because she was going out with him, but actually, in the daylight and out of context, she looked quite young – maybe late twenties. Maybe around his age . . .

Shit. He felt himself flushing red again. He was shocked at himself. He'd never fancied any of his brothers' girlfriends in the past, not even the ravishing beauties Sean used to bring home. He'd always assumed that there was some sort of gene that actively prevented you from taking a sexual interest in someone a member of your family was involved with, that it was only strange people on the *Jerry Springer* show who wanted to have sex with people their relatives had already shagged.

How did it work, he wondered, fancying your brother's girlfriend? And what happened if Tony and Ness split up – would he be allowed to go out with her then, or was that completely beyond the pale? God, what was he *thinking*?

He got to his feet and searched the house for Goldie. He eventually found him in the laundry room on a pile of clean sheets and dragged him to his feet.

'Come on, mate. We're going for a walk.'

Goldie wheezed and whistled and finally creaked himself upright, placidly allowing Ned to clip him to his lead.

Ned walked all the way into the village, relishing the fine drizzle that sprayed his skin and dampened his clothes. He walked incredibly fast, almost as if he was trying to sweat out his unclean feelings about Ness. He walked so fast, with his head so full of strange, alien thoughts, that for the first time since he got back from

Oz he completely forgot about Monica. She could have been riding piggy-back on his shoulders with a crop in her hand shouting, 'Gee-up, pony-boy', and he wouldn't have noticed. His thoughts were all over the place, veering from imagining how he'd break the news to Mum that he was going out with Ness, to shaking hands with Tony and Tony saying, 'Fair-dos, the best man won', to him packing a bag and leaving Beulah Hill for ever, his family standing on the doorstep with stony-faces and folded arms, to having sex with Ness, to Ness having sex with Tony, to having babies with Ness, to whether his dick was the same size as Tony's, to whether he'd be as good as him in bed.

He tied Goldie up outside the caff and wolfed down a full English breakfast and a mug of stewed tea, staring through the misted-up window at the street outside while he thought about the fact that Tony had a flash flat, a sports car and his own business versus the fact that Ned had nice hair, a flat stomach and a degree. He wondered what sort of flat Ness had and whether he'd like living in Beckenham or not. He even found himself thinking about train routes and how long it would take to get into town from Beckenham Junction and whether he could live without the number 68 bus.

He wiped his plate clean with a piece of toast, left the caff, untied Goldie and started the walk home.

And when he got home he went straight to the bathroom and shaved off his beard.

A Terrifying Proposal

Because Ness was going shopping with Bernie in Bromley on Saturday, and because they were having dinner at Rob and Trisha's that night, Tony said he'd pick her up from Beulah Hill at seven.

Mum's car wasn't in the drive when he got there so he assumed that they were still lost in retail nirvana somewhere and let himself in with his keys.

He headed straight for the fridge, like he always did when he came home, and had a poke about. Packets of ham, pots of cream, fresh fruit, five different types of cheese, leftover cake. Yummy. He resisted the temptation to make himself an enormous cheese-and-mayonnaise sandwich with the thick-sliced loaf sitting in the breadbin and just nibbled on a handful of grapes instead.

He picked up Dad's *Guardian* and had a quick wander around the house, another thing he always did. Jesus, he had no idea how they lived like this. And it got worse the older they got. He worried about them, actually – they were still young now, still had all their faculties; but what would happen to them when they were older, when Ned wasn't at home any more to keep an eye on them? Their house was quirky now, eccentric – things got piled up and hoarded, washing-up got ignored, hoovering was a monthly event, if the carpet was lucky. But it was still warm, homely and relatively clean. That might not always be the case. There was a fine line between clutter and squalor. What would happen when it got unsavoury and unhygienic – what would happen to Mum and Dad then? God, they'd end up like those loons you saw on documentaries who had rats the size of cocker spaniels living in their mattresses and their neighbours would call the council on them. Jesus, they'd become a *health hazard*.

Tony put these niggling little concerns to the back of his mind and headed into the living room. Where he found Gervase stretched out on the sofa, fully clothed, slack-jawed and snoring voluminously with Goldie lying across his legs, drooling.

Delightful, thought Tony, just absolutely delightful.

'Goldie!' he snapped, striding into the room. 'Get down off there!' He tapped the dog on the haunches with the *Guardian* until he finally heaved his stinking old carcass off the furniture and flopped on to the floor.

Gervase stirred slightly and made a disturbing snorty noise.

'Tony,' he said, raising himself up on to his elbow and reaching for his fags. 'Sorry, mate. Didn't hear you coming in. I was out for the count.' He snorted, wiped his nose with the back of his hand and lit a cigarette.

'Yes,' said Tony, 'I noticed.'

'Wasn't intending to fall asleep like that. Last thing I

remember I was watching the racing,' he indicated the TV, which was now showing *Stars In Their Eyes*. 'Bit of a heavy night last night.' He swung round on the sofa, reached for the remote and switched off the TV. 'Fucking hate that cunt,' he said by way of explanation. 'So. Come to see your mum, have you? I think she's out shopping.'

'Yes. I know. She's out with Ness. I've come to pick her up.'

'That's nice,' said Gervase, inhaling and smoothing the top of his flat-top with the palm of his hand. 'Taking her somewhere nice?'

'Who?'

'Ness.'

'No. Not really. Just to a friend's for dinner.'

'Well – that's nice, isn't it? Dinner at a friend's? I'd like that.'

Tony started, thinking for a moment that Gervase was trying to get himself an invite, and then relaxed when he realized that he wasn't.

'So. Tony. How are you?'

'Good. I'm good.'

There was a brief silence during which Tony felt the pull of social convention forcing him to ask Gervase how he was.

'You?'

'Me? I'm fantastic. Specially now I've had a bit of a nap. You're looking trim.' Gervase eyed him up and down.

'Really?' Tony patted his belly. 'Do you think so?'

Gervase squinted at him. 'Yeah. Definitely. Especially round here –' he squeezed his own cheeks – 'around the chops. You been on a diet?'

Buoyed by this unexpected compliment, Tony relaxed a little and flopped into the armchair opposite Gervase. 'No. Not a diet exactly. Just been watching what I eat. You know.'

Gervase nodded at him encouragingly.

'But I am, er . . .' Tony paused, wondering why he was about to say this to Gervase, but saying it anyway, 'I'm joining a slimming club, actually.'

'Oh yeah?'

'Yeah. First class on Monday.'

'Yeah? I've heard they work, those slimming clubs. Good on yer.' Gervase threw him one of his stiff, awkward smiles and Tony felt disproportionately pleased.

'But don't tell Mum, will you?' he said. 'She'll get all worried. You know – mums. And don't tell Ned. He'll just take the piss.'

'Course not. Your secret's safe with me. Everyone's secrets are safe with me . . .'

'What d'you mean?'

'Nothing, mate, nothing. Just that I'm a very discreet man. I am the very *soul* of discretion.'

They fell silent for a moment. Tony examined his fingernails and then looked up to find Gervase *staring* at him intently, with a really concerned expression on his face.

'You OK, Tony?'

'Yeah. I'm fine,' he replied, tersely.

And then Gervase suddenly got off the sofa, his cigarette hanging out of his mouth, strode towards Tony and put his hands on the crown of his head. Tony wanted to react in some way, to protest, but there was something about Gervase's touch that made him go all liquid and ineffectual. It was like Gervase was sucking all the negativity out of him and leaving him with just the few odds and ends of nice stuff he still had floating around somewhere in there.

He heard Gervase suck his breath in. 'Jesus Christ, Tony, you've got to stop it!'

'Stop what?'

'This madness. It's not going to work.'

'What – the slimming club?'

'No. Not the slimming club. The slimming club's a great idea, Tone. Honest. No – you've got to stop this obsession. Knock it on the head.'

Tony flinched.

'Keep your dreams real, mate. The only person who's going to get hurt otherwise is you, you know?'

'What are you talking about?'

'I don't know what I'm talking about. All I know is I'm right. What I'm saying is right. It's up to you to work out what the fuck I'm going on about. OK?'

'OK.' Tony felt mesmerized, unable to respond or react in any way.

'Look around you, mate. Look at what's real. You've got it all. Yeah?'

'Yeah.'

'You've got more than most. You don't need anything else.'

And then Gervase suddenly pulled his hands off Tony's head, and started slapping it instead. 'Fuck – sorry, mate – dropped a bit of ash in there. It's all right, though – it's not smouldering or anything.' He patted Tony on the back and went back to the sofa. Tony ran his fingers through his hair vigorously and shuddered.

Before he had a chance to question Gervase about the bizarre thing that had just happened there was a commotion at the front door and the sound of high-pitched female excitement. Mum and Ness.

'Hello, boys,' said Mum, bundling into the room with about ten carrier bags and a red-wine flush about her cheeks. 'Hello, love,' she leant down to kiss the crown of Tony's head. She took a big sniff of his hair. 'Oh, Tony – you haven't started smoking again, have you, love?'

'No,' he muttered, 'I haven't.'

Ness rolled in after Mum, with approximately twice as many carrier bags as her and an even deeper red-wine flush. She flung her arms around his neck and gave him a big smacker on the lips. 'Hello, gorgeous.'

She smelt of garlic and wine and he resisted the temptation to sneer at her. 'Hi,' he mumbled.

'Coffee, anyone?' said Mum.

'Yes, please,' said Ness. 'Sorry we're late. Bernie dragged me into All Bar One and forced me to drink wine.'

243

'Oh yes, like it took much persuasion,' said Bernie, laughing and disappearing into the hallway.

'So I guess I'll be driving tonight, then?' said Tony, somewhat unnecessarily as he'd already offered to drive that morning.

'No one asked you to drive, Tony,' said Ness, kicking off her shoes and sitting next to Gervase. 'I said I'd be happy to pay for cabs. Hello, you,' she said, leaning in to kiss Gervase. 'I hope you're in a better mood than old grumpy chops over there.'

'I'm always in a good mood when I see you, gorgeous. Mwah.'

'Aww,' said Ness, grinning and giving him a quick hug.

Oh, for God's sake. Tony couldn't stand this. Bloody Gervase. What was that just then with his head touching and the stupid bloody warnings? And Ness, pissed again and all buddy-buddy with Mum. And all over Gervase, too. Look at her. What was it with that bloke, extracting confidences from him, taking over his parents' house, flirting with his girlfriend?

He watched them with annoyance, giggling together, Gervase's eyes straying to Ness's long, shapely legs every few seconds, and for some inexplicable reason Tony suddenly felt consumed with jealousy.

'Come on,' he said, standing up abruptly, 'let's go.'

'What?' said Ness, looking at her watch. 'But we don't need to be there for another half an hour.'

Tony took a deep breath. 'I don't care. I'll drive slowly. Let's just get out of here.'

Ness exchanged a look with Gervase and got to her feet. 'Yis, *sah*,' she said, standing to attention. 'But let me get changed first – I want to wear my new skirt.'

Tony sighed and sat down. 'OK. But get a move on.'

Ness grabbed one of her myriad carrier bags and headed upstairs to the bathroom. Gervase stared at Tony, thoughtfully.

'What?' said Tony.

'She's a good girl, your Ness. You should be a bit nicer to her. You'll lose her if you're not careful.'

'Jesus *Christ*!' said Tony, finally losing the plot and feeling all his insides rushing to his head with anger. 'What *is* it with you, eh? Haven't you got your own life to think about? Eh? Your own family to plague? I mean, what was that shit just now, with the . . . the *head* and everything?' He grabbed his hair in exasperation. 'And what the hell is it with you and Ness, eh? Always all over her, all that "gorgeous" business. And don't think I haven't seen the way you look at her legs, mate. I mean – just . . . *what*?! What is it with you? *Who the hell are you?!*'

'Tony!' said Mum, coming into the living room, clutching two mugs of coffee. 'What on earth is going on in here?'

'Nothing,' said Tony, giving up the whole playing-the-big-scary-man thing and landing petulantly in his arm-chair. 'Nothing. Just . . . just. Nothing.'

'I think Tony was just wondering what I'm all about, actually, Bern. And who can blame him? It's a question I ask myself. Often.'

'OK,' said Ness, walking into the room wearing

a skirt that was even shorter than the skirt she'd been wearing before, which was some achievement. 'Let's go.'

'Are you actually going out in that?' said Tony, staring at her legs in amazement.

'Yes. And?'

'And – well – it's a bit *short*, isn't it?'

'Oh come on, Tony. Look at those legs,' said Bernie, 'they're incredible. Ness should be showing them off.'

'Ten years ago, maybe,' he muttered under his breath.

'Oh, Jesus, Tony,' Ness raised her eyebrows to the ceiling, 'you really are in a spanky mood tonight, aren't you? OK,' she said turning to Bernie and Gervase, 'I'm going to get this miserable old sod out of here. See you both soon. Come on, you old bugger.' She gestured at Tony and he rose from his armchair with a grumble.

They drove to Rob and Trisha's in near silence. Tony knew he'd been a complete git and his head was full of apologies but he couldn't seem to transfer them to his mouth. He hated the way Ness did this to him. It didn't matter what he said or what he was feeling or how ridiculous he was being, she just ignored it. She was like human Tefal – he just glided straight over her. If only she'd get angry. If only she'd get hurt. If only she'd said, 'God Tony, I don't deserve to be treated like this, I'm out of here.' But she didn't – she just ruffled his hair and called him a bugger and made him feel like a normal human being.

Which was probably why they were still going out. Any normal woman would have walked out ages ago. But not Ness. Ness just went on and on and on loving him. She had an infinite supply of love. And not just for him. For anyone. His parents, cab drivers, animals tied up outside supermarkets, people on the television, *Gervase*. She was a big, oozing love machine. And oh God, he could do without it right now, do without *her*.

He didn't want a big, oozing love machine. He wanted a woman who wouldn't put up with his shit, who would force him to behave like a proper, decent person. He wanted a bad-tempered, honey-skinned, pregnant woman with a flat full of beautiful things. If he was with Millie, he thought, he'd stay slim, he'd wear nice clothes, and no matter what sort of mood he was in, or how bad a day he'd had, he'd make sure he was happy for Millie when he got home. If he was with Millie, he'd be different. Everything about him would be different. Everything about him would be *better*. Just being in her presence made him feel like someone completely new.

Being in Ness's presence made him feel like the biggest old cunt known to man.

'Tony,' said Ness, breaking the silence, 'I know this probably isn't the best time to bring this up. I know you're in a bad mood, but, let's face it, if I waited until you were in a good mood to talk to you about anything, we'd never talk to each other again. But I've been thinking. You know how we haven't been seeing much of each other lately? And you've been really busy at work? Well, I really miss you. God knows why, but I do. And I was thinking, we've been together for nearly a year now and maybe it's time we thought about, maybe, you know, *moving in together*?'

Tony absorbed the question, slowly and carefully, digesting it like a huge piece of really chewy meat. Right, he thought, don't panic. Just don't panic. Just nod, slowly, nod, look like you're thinking about it and don't say anything.

'So – what do you think? I mean, I'm sick of living out of a bag. And we wouldn't have to make such an effort to see each other. We'd just sort of, *be* there. It would make life much easier . . .'

Tony nodded slowly again, resisting the temptation to fling open the door and throw himself bodily from his moving car. 'Hmm,' he managed to mumble, 'let me think about it.'

Ness smiled at him and squeezed his thigh. 'You think about it. You take your time.'

Tony smiled grimly and wished that he was dead.

Passing the Baton

Ned folded Monica's hair into a brown envelope and sealed it shut. Then he pulled off a sheet of Mum's posh letter paper and wrote the following message:

Monday 30 April

Dear Mr and Mrs Riley,
Hi – this is Ned here, Monica's boyfriend. Well, ex-boyfriend, to be more accurate. Things didn't really work out for me and Mon, unfortunately. As you know, Monica had a lot of problems adjusting to life in Australia and well, life generally, really, and it took its toll on our relationship. So I ended our relationship a few weeks ago and came home to England. I still feel really guilty and really bad. Monica's an unstable person and I'm really worried about her. She hasn't got much of a support network in Oz – she's got friends, but no one who's really prepared to take her on wholeheartedly and she can be a bit of a handful, as you know.

But now I'm even more worried. Ever since I got home Mon's been sending me parcels. Really strange parcels. Her hair, her eyebrows, other (non-fleshy) bits of her body. And plaguing me with unbelievably crude text messages. It doesn't seem to be stopping and even though part of me really wants to phone her and talk to her and try and sort this out, I know that that will just make things worse. She's really dependent on me and me phoning her will just be giving her a fix of what she craves – my attention.

So, I thought maybe it would be better if you dealt with it. She really respects both of you, I know that and it would give her a real shock if she knew that you were aware of the way she's been behaving. To be honest, I still think the best thing for her would be for her to come home, spend a bit of time back at home with her family.

Anyway. You don't need me to tell you what to do. She's your daughter and your responsibility. You'll do the right thing.

I really hope everything works out for Monica. She's a great girl and I love her very much.

I've enclosed her hair. I thought it would be better off with you than sitting under my bed.

Yours,

Ned London

Ned folded the letter into an envelope and slipped it in a Jiffy bag with the hair. He sealed the Jiffy bag and slipped it into his rucksack. And then he put on his jacket, left the house and dropped the envelope in the first letterbox he passed. He breathed a sigh of relief as the envelope dropped through the dark hole and into the blackness below.

She was gone.

Mon was gone. She and her anger and her neuroses and her paranoia belonged to somebody else now. To the people who'd created her. And, for the first time since he'd set eyes on her in Leicester Square all those years ago, Ned was free.

He swung his rucksack back on to his shoulder and headed for the number 68 bus stop. There was more than a hint of a spring in his step as he walked. He felt unburdened. He felt euphoric.

He was heading into town, to an appointment with a recruitment agency that Tony had recommended. He was heading towards his bright, new, Monica-free future. It was time to get his life back on track.

Typing Tests and Origami

'So,' said the girl in the ruffly, low-cut blouse, who was called Emma and looked roughly thirteen years old, 'tell me about your experiences.'

Ned shuffled in his seat. Experiences. Well, he thought, that could mean a lot of things. I could, for example, tell you about my night out on Friday with a bunch of fortysomething rockabillies when I got so pissed that I fell out of the back of a Robin Reliant and landed in a pile of horse shit.

Or I could tell you about living with a chain-smoking, phlegm-producing, tattooed stranger who can see my innermost fears and feels like the only person in the whole world who really understands me.

I could tell you about the fact that this morning I opened a parcel which contained my ex-girlfriend's used tampon. That was nice.

Or I could tell you about the night I went out with my even exer-girlfriend and found out that she was in love with some guy called *Drew* who takes her to Zanzibar on holiday.

Or how about fancying my brother's girlfriend so much that I've started wanking about three times a day and fantasizing about living in Beckenham. *Hmm, are those enough experiences for you?* he wanted to say? *Will that do?*

'Er,' he scratched his head, realized that that was unprofessional-looking and turned it into a hair-smoothing motion. 'Well, I worked for Sotheby's for a few months when I graduated.'

Emma and her bosoms nodded thoughtfully.

Ned felt his eyes start to water slightly as he tried to think of something impressive to say. 'And then I pursued a career in retail.'

'Uh-huh. What sort of retail?'

'Well.' He opened the vaults of his mind and tried to retrieve the relevant information. 'Music. Erm, food. Clothing. Art. Furniture. Oh, yes, and, er, antiques. I've spent quite a lot of time working in, er, antiques.'

Emma raised an eyebrow at him and then looked down at his CV. 'So I see,' she said, 'and that would be for G. London, Esq.'

'Yes. That's right. My dad.'

She smiled at him encouragingly. 'And then you went to Australia, I see.'

'Yes. In '98.'

'And what sort of things did you do in Australia?'

'Well, er *retail*. Mainly.'

She smiled at him and nodded.

'Sports equipment. Art. Food. Some bar work. And I was working at an Internet café for a few months before I left.'

'And what sort of positions did you hold within these various retailers?'

Jesus, he thought. This is a nightmare. A total nightmare. He'd thought his CV would have been sufficient. It was all there, he thought, every last pathetic detail of his retarded career. Why did she have to ask him all these questions? He flipped frantically through every facet of his career in retail trying to find the one occasion when he'd risen above the ranks of 'bloke who stayed for six months and left before things got too serious'.

'Oh, consultant, mainly,' he said, nodding furiously, 'I prefer to be at grass-roots level. I like that personal one-to-one connection with the customer. Well – *liked*, I liked it. Obviously, now I've had my time away, I'm looking for something a bit more, er . . . *substantial*. You know.' He rubbed his newly shorn chin and squinted at her.

'Yes, absolutely,' she said, 'I can see that you'd want to move on. And what sort of career progression did you have in mind?'

'Well, *ideally* I'd like to move out of retail, into something a bit more . . .' *Grown-up*, he wanted to say. *A proper man's job with vast wads of cash and secretaries and business trips. Please.* 'Something a bit more . . . Well, let's put it this way – it's not my life's ambition to be a retail manager. Not that there's anything wrong with being a retail manager. But you know, all those keys, working Saturdays, it's just . . .' He stopped himself and took a deep breath. 'I'd like more of an office type of job. Thing.'

'OK.' She scribbled something down on a piece of paper. 'And what sort of experience do you have that might be relevant to an office environment?'

'Well, I'm computer-literate.'

'Any IT experience?'

'Yes. I know my way around a computer.'

'Would you consider IT-support work?'

IT support – weren't they the smug guys without girlfriends who hated anyone who didn't know as much about computers as they did? The guys who got paid to tell terrified secretaries to reboot their computers whenever anything went wrong? Er, *no*, thought Ned. No thank you.

'Yeah,' he said, trying to look positive, 'I'd consider it, definitely.'

'Great. And how's your typing?'

'Well, I can type. I've not been taught, or anything, but I can go quite fast.'

She smiled with what appeared to be genuine delight. 'Wonderful! Let's get you to do a little test, then, shall we?'

'A test?!'

'Yes. Nothing to be worried about. It only takes a couple of minutes.'

Ned gulped. Why were they making him take a test? He didn't want to *be* a secretary – he wanted to *have* a secretary.

Emma stood up and beamed at him and led him through the posh offices to a small, somewhat foreboding-looking room containing a desk, a chair and a solitary PC. Ned felt his throat constrict and started to panic. This was like being asked to sit an 'A' level that he hadn't revised for. A test. Shit. Besides the exams for his degree, he couldn't remember the last time he'd taken a test – probably his driving test when he was seventeen, and that had been the single most terrifying experience of his life. In fact, when Ned thought about it he realized that not having to take tests any more was probably the single greatest thing about getting older.

Emma used the mouse to open up a program called 'Trish's Typing Test', which was conducted by an animated woman in horn-rimmed glasses with drawn-on dimples and a pudding-bowl haircut. 'Hi,' she said in an electro-American accent, 'my name is Trish. Welcome to my test. Please take some time to make yourself comfortable.'

'OK,' said Emma, 'I'll leave you to it. Just follow the on-screen instructions. And don't worry if you mess it up. Just start the program again. OK?' She flashed him her teeth and he flashed his back at her.

After she left the room he studied the screen and flexed his fingers. OK, he thought, typing test, no problem, I can do a typing test. Trish smiled at him unnervingly and brought him up some text, telling him in a really annoyingly patronizing tone of voice to relax, take it easy and not correct any errors as he went. A little clock started to tick away the seconds and Ned felt his gut clench up in utter terror. He took a deep breath and started typing.

Halfway through, he cursed and wiped a slick of sweat off his top lip. This was hideous, he thought, absolutely hideous. His hands had gone all stiff and unyielding. His brain stopped interacting with them entirely at one point and he just sat there, suspended, with his fingers hovering uselessly over the keyboard awaiting instruction from mission control. He tried to memorize whole sentences so that he wouldn't have to keep looking at the text box and could just keep his eyes on the keyboard, but was unable to retain more than three words at any given time.

After five minutes, this was what was on his screen:

Today teh world of secnt is being rediscoverd. The tail-blazers and pioneer expolrers were the young. They ere the first to realsie that out sense of smell can be ducated to be as receptive to pelasures and and expereinces as our other senses. They have learend to surround themselves with scent on a scale that the Western worlkd has not known for hundreds, pergaps thouasnds of years. They use scents with the same freedom as did the people of aome ancient natoins long before the birth of Christ. But they have an afdvantage over those earlier people's. Living in the altter part of the 20th century, they are able to enjoy scented products in a verity never before known

Five minutes – to type 120 words. That was . . . that was . . . shit. He couldn't work it out, but it was bloody pathetic. He took a deep breath, gave Trish a stern, don't-fuck-with-me look and started again. This time it took him five minutes and twenty seconds. His third attempt took him six minutes and eleven seconds and he was just about to launch into a fourth attempt when Emma walked back into the room.

'So,' she said, looking at him as if she had every faith in his typing ability, 'how did you get on?'

Ned scratched his head. 'Erm, not too well, I don't think.'

Emma sat down and remained stoically unfazed by his paltry scores, totting them up with a positive air that suggested that she believed Ned might secretly be a typing wunderkind.

'Well,' she said, scribbling something down and smiling at him, 'it's about, roughly, going on your first test, at least, about twenty-five words per minute. And I know how off-putting these tests can be. So, shall we say thirty-five words per minute?'

'Yes,' said Ned, wanting to fall to his knees, bury his head in her lap and never let her go. 'Yes. That would be great.'

'Good.' She got to her feet. 'Right. Let's go back to my office and see if we can't sort you out with something.'

Two hours later Ned found himself sitting in the reception area of a record company just off Soho Square. Emma had managed to find him 'something' all right; but, as much as Ned had been keen as hell to find himself some sort of gainful employment, to leap on to the career ladder and get going with the rest of his life, he hadn't been quite prepared for it to start today. He wasn't mentally ready to start the rest of his life just yet. He wanted another day just hanging around doing nothing. Or maybe two.

He would have dressed differently if he'd thought he'd be starting work today, worn different underpants, probably, different shoes. Still, he thought, £8.50 an hour. He couldn't grumble about that. And it was only for the week. Maybe they'd run out of work for him again come Friday and he'd get a long weekend.

'Ned London?' A man of about forty with a Hoxton Fin, dressed in head to toe Diesel, walked into reception with an air of complete and utter indifference. Ned suspected that greeting temps in reception was one of the things he hated most in the whole world. 'You're from the agency, right?'

'Yes. From the agency. Hi,' Ned got to his feet and put out his hand.

'Hi. OK. It's already lunchtime. There's fuck loads to do. You're going to have to get your arse into gear. This way.'

Jesus, thought Ned, following him through corridors coated in gold discs and posters, what's *his* problem? It's not my fault it's nearly lunchtime. It's not my fault he wasn't organized enough to get someone in *this morning*.

All Emma had told him about this job was that he'd be working in the PR department, helping them out with a 'very important project'. Ned imagined a huge, open-plan office full of beautiful music-business girls all answering phones and talking to journalists at *Q* and the *NME*. He imagined being handed a list of journalists and having to phone them all and talk about some hot new band and try and set up interviews and arrange photo shoots.

'OK,' said Hoxton Fin man, who hadn't even introduced himself yet, 'this is where you'll be working this week.' He opened the door to what looked like some kind of store cupboard and switched on a light – to reveal what was undeniably a store cupboard. 'Right. We've got three big releases coming out at the end of June. One album, two singles. Press packs have to be on journalists' desks by Monday at the latest otherwise we're fucked. OK? So . . .' He led Ned to a corner of the storeroom, slit open a cardboard box with a scalpel and pulled out a piece of dark-blue card with the company logo printed on it. 'Start by constructing the folders.' He folded the piece of card deftly into a folder. 'They're in all these boxes here. There should be a thousand. Let someone know *immediately* if it looks like you're going to run out. Then you need to collate the press information.' He ripped open another cardboard box and pulled out a large Kodak box full of photographs of some twelve-year-old boy wearing hair gel and jewellery. 'Biography on the bottom, press release on top of that, then a photo, a CD and a business card. You need to staple the business card on to this flap here. OK?' He slammed the folder shut and looked at Ned accusingly, as if he was expecting him to say that no, it wasn't OK, the photo should go in the middle.

Ned shrugged and nodded. 'OK,' he said.

'Right. Good. Once you've worked your way through that lot, come and find *me*.' He pointed to himself in case Ned was in any doubt as to who he was referring to. 'I'm in the room over the corridor. OK? Photocopier is in there, too, if you run out of press releases. Coffee machine around the corner to your left. Toilets on the landing where we just came from. OK?'

260

'OK.'

'Right, then.' Hoxton Fin looked at Ned awkwardly as if he'd just noticed that he was a sentient being, shoved his hands into the pockets of his trendy trousers and left the room.

Ned looked around disconsolately. It was horrible in here. There weren't even any windows. And it was a really lovely day out, the sort of tentative spring day that made you want to open all the windows and feel the sun on your skin. And he was stuck in this room full of cardboard boxes assembling a thousand press packs for some tight-rectumed dickhead with a haircut he was ten years too old for. Great. Did people who worked in temp agencies have any idea, he wondered, what it was actually like at the places they sent you to? There they were in their lovely plush offices being all smiley and nice. They lulled you into a sense of belonging and security and then sent you out into the world to work in strange hostile places full of unfriendly people, to be the lowest of all possible life forms: a temp.

He pulled a card folder out of the box, studied it for a while and folded it up into the required shape. Shit – it wasn't even difficult. It was piss-easy. He wasn't even going to have the challenge of mastering some origami-type paper-folding skill while he was here. He dropped to his haunches and let his head fall between his knees. So, here he was. The first day of Ned London's big new grown-up life and he was stuck in a stockroom, folding things up, just like when he worked at Benetton in 1995.

He stood up and tried to think positive. Think of

your CV, he thought, think of having Electrogram Records on there. You never know who you'll bump into at the coffee machine. Someone might take a shine to you and offer you a proper job, with a desk. And windows. You never know. It's a start, he thought to himself, it's shite, but at least it's a start.

He went to the coffee machine and got himself a hot chocolate and then he came back and folded another folder, wondering where the hell this particularly miserable chapter of his life was going to lead him. His mind wandered as he folded some more and he started imagining the life that had petrified him so greatly in Wood Green on Friday night, the life of watching Simon ten-pin bowling and having his hair cut with Gervase. Now he could add sitting alone in a windowless room folding bits of card all day long to his unsavoury little vision of the future.

He sighed, sniffed and folded another folder.

Fifteen Stone and Three Pounds

'OK, Tony. If I could just ask you to take off your shoes and pop yourself on to the scales.'

Tony crouched down to unlace his shoes and pondered the idea of using the opportunity afforded to him by his 'starting blocks' pose to sprint out of the door and keep running until he got home.

He slipped off his shoes and slowly climbed up on to the scales. This was it. He hadn't weighed himself since the last time he went to the gym, about eighteen months ago. He'd been just over twelve and a half stone then. In his mind he'd gone up to about fifteen stone since he met Ness, but after Gervase's comments on Saturday he was feeling hopeful for something around the fourteen to fourteen-and-a-half mark.

He took a deep breath and brought his second foot on to the scales. Jan slid weights across a metal bar until the bar balanced itself out.

And there it was – the grim truth, staring him mean-spiritedly in the face.

Fifteen stone and three pounds.

Fifteen stone and three pounds.

Tony felt blood rushing to his head with the shock

of it. That meant that he must have been over fifteen and a half before he started losing weight. My God – he was absolutely *enormous*.

'So,' said Jan, oblivious to Tony's trauma. 'Ninety-seven kilos.' She jotted down the hideous sum on a form she was filling out. 'And what's your ideal weight?'

'Well,' he said, dismounting the scales with a heavy heart, 'I was about twelve and a half stone a year ago. I'd quite like to get back to that.'

'OK,' she scribbled that down, too. 'That sounds like a perfectly healthy and realistic goal. Given your height and build.'

'I've lost a few pounds already,' he said, trying to inject something positive into what was turning out to be a miserable experience, 'just by cutting back on the booze, not eating out so often, that kind of thing.'

'Well done!' She gave him an encouraging smile. 'Now, if you'd like to put your shoes back on and fill out some forms.'

Tony filled out the forms quickly – he'd filled out similar things so many times in his life now. No diabetes. No allergies. No heart condition (well, not that he knew about, anyway). No serious operations. Blah, blah, blah.

'Right, Tony. The meeting's about to start. Are you ready to join us?'

'Er, yeah. Sure.'

'And don't be nervous about being a man, Tony. We get quite a few boys in the group now – ever since we put Bryan on our posters. We've got one at the moment, actually.'

Tony smiled at her nervously.

'And after the meeting, maybe you could stay behind for a couple of minutes. Just for a chat. I always like to have a little chat on the first week. Find out a bit more about what makes you tick. And you can find out a bit more about us. OK?'

'Yeah,' said Tony, 'no problem.'

Jan pushed open a door and there it was. The group. Oh God. About twelve of them. All fat. All chatting like they'd known each other for ever. A particularly gruesome man in a red sweatshirt looked up and smiled at him joyfully. 'Hallelujah,' he said, in an extremely loud voice that suggested he was a man who always said everything in an extremely loud voice. 'A bloke,' he boomed. 'Praise be to Allah. Save me. Save me from all these insufferable women.'

The insufferable women all looked at the red-sweatshirt bloke as if they were used to him being overbearing and obnoxious.

Red sweatshirt patted the empty seat next to him. 'Come and sit here,' he said, 'us chaps have got to stick together.'

Tony looked at Jan imploringly as if to say, 'Please don't make me sit next to the horrible, overbearing man, Auntie Jan, *please*.' But Auntie Jan just beamed at him and put a hand on his shoulder. 'Everyone, this is Tony. Tony's our new member this week so let's all make him feel welcome, shall we.' And then she pointed him in the direction of the empty seat next to red sweatshirt. Tony grimaced and walked through the group towards the seat.

'Kelvin,' said the man, extending a meaty hand, 'nice to meet you, Tony.'

'Yeah, you too.' Tony shook his hand and then Kelvin leant in really close to his ear.

'Bunch of hippos. Look at 'em. Poor things.'

Tony looked round the group of overweight women, and then back at the even more overweight Kelvin.

'Tell you what I like about hippos, though,' he said, wheezing slightly, 'they're ever so blumming grateful.'

Tony looked at him with alarm. 'Aren't you here to lose weight?' he said.

'No. Of course not. I'm here for the lovely laydeez.'

'And have you . . . have you *been out* with anyone yet?'

Kelvin shrugged his enormous shoulders up and down. 'No. Not yet. I've been working on the luscious Tonia, though.' He indicated a very glamorous blonde with incredibly long fingernails.

Tony lapsed into silence and wondered if maybe he should do the decent thing and tell Kelvin that Tonia was actually quite a babe and that he didn't stand a chance in hell, but then Jan began to talk and the session started.

In all honesty, Tony found the whole experience quite riveting, in a trashy-TV kind of a way. As he wasn't yet participating in the programme, he could treat the session as a form of light entertainment. He was fascinated to hear about Tonia's experience at a hen night the previous weekend when they'd gone to a TFI Friday and she'd been *that* close to eating everything on the menu – because TFI was her absolute favourite – and how it had only been the thought of Jan and the group and how much faith they had in her that had reined her back in. He was moved by the fact that Arabella had managed to get through the week in which her elderly mother had died without breaking her diet – even at the funeral, with all those canapés. Jenny had had a terrible time, apparently. Eaten pretty much a whole leg of lamb, slice by slice, with bread and butter, over the course of the week. Tony sympathized with her hugely – he'd have done exactly the same thing if he'd had a leg of lamb lying around the place. Jan reassured her that a bad week didn't make a bad person, that everyone lapsed occasionally and that maybe next time she had a joint of meat left over from the Sunday lunch she should put it straight down for the dog.

The group were incredibly supportive of each other and no one judged anyone for anything. With the exception of the dreadful Kelvin, they were a truly delightful and heart-warming group of people. Tony had been expecting a bunch of freaks and was pleasantly surprised by how comfortable he felt here, in among all these people with healthy appetites and a penchant for overdoing it. And, although they reflected the parts of himself he disliked, he didn't dislike *them*. It was strangely soothing and reassuring to know that he wasn't alone, to know that he wasn't the only person in the world who would work his way systematically through a quarter of a sheep if left to his own devices.

After the meeting, which lasted about half an hour, he and Jan retired to her little office and had what she referred to as a 'nice little chat', during which she asked him about his private life, about whether or not he lived alone, who he'd be able to call on for support, his general eating patterns, what sort of exercise he got. Then she gave him some photocopied guidelines and recipes and told him how much she was looking forward to seeing him the following week and Tony had to resist the urge to hug her and tell her she was fantastic – because she was. This was more than just a job to Jan; this was a labour of love. She did this because it made her happy.

Tony flicked through the notes and the recipes and felt a distinct fluttering of excitement. He felt evangelized, energized, enthused. He could do this, he thought as he put on his coat and headed for the exit, he could shift this weight. He could rediscover the old Tony. He could be slim and youthful again. He could, he knew it. This was just what he needed. He'd known there must have been a reason for him picking up that leaflet all those weeks ago. He'd found his destiny. His whole life might be a mess but this was something, in fact, the *only* thing over which he could actually exert any control.

He still had Ness's proposal hanging over his head and yes, it sounded simple, didn't it? Just to give her a call and say, 'Well, I've given it some thought and, well, *no*, I don't want to move in with you.' It *sounded* simple but life *wasn't* simple. It wasn't simple because for some inexplicable reason he and Ness had ended up having a really nice weekend together. Not for any particular reason, just one of those nice, drifty, carefree weekends.

Dinner at Rob and Trisha's had been surprisingly convivial and then they'd woken up yesterday morning and it had been all sunny and spring-like so they'd had some particularly pleasant sex and driven over to Dulwich for a pub lunch (Tony had a toasted sandwich instead of the full Sunday roast he'd usually have ordered). Then they'd gone for a long walk on the common and Ness had just been . . . well, *Ness*, he supposed. But for some reason she hadn't got on his nerves and Tony had allowed himself to enjoy her company for once. It was one of those strange and unfathomable things. But pleasant as it was it didn't make things intrinsically any *different*. He still didn't want to move in with her. He still didn't want to end up with her. He still wanted to be with Millie. In fact, he'd spent a large portion of the weekend imagining Millie watching him and thinking how much fun it looked to be his girlfriend.

But he wasn't ready to finish it either. Relationships, in Tony's experience, got a sort of stench about them when their time was up. It was impossible to pinpoint the precise moment that a relationship went on the turn, but if you tried to end a relationship before it was over in that stinky sort of way, it always went wrong and you usually ended up getting back together and splitting up again further down the line, a pattern that at its worst could go on repeating itself ad infinitum. No, Tony was sure of this, you had to wait until a relationship was a stinking rotten carcass before bailing out; that way everyone concerned could just walk away from it without any desire to turn around and have another look.

His relationship with Jo had gone stinky a few months before she left him. They'd both known it and both politely ignored it, until Jo had done the decent thing and fallen in love with someone else. But his relationship with Ness hadn't reached the rotten-carcass stage just yet.

It could be argued that Tony was being unfair to Ness by stringing her along. She was twenty-nine, nearly thirty. She was looking for stability, a future and children and every day that she spent with Tony was a day lost in the pursuit of her own happiness. But really, it was her own fault. Tony had never given her any indication that he wanted to settle down with her. He was rude to her, thoughtless and inconsiderate. He didn't tell her that he loved her, buy her gifts or talk to her about babies and weddings. She was an intelligent woman and it was her informed choice to hang around with him while her youth faded away. Maybe she was subconsciously waiting for the stench, too, Tony pondered. Maybe he was on some invisible countdown, maybe suggesting that they move in together had actually been some kind of masked ultimatum. Maybe she was going to finish it if he said no. Which was exactly why he couldn't say no. Because he wasn't ready for it to finish. He wasn't ready for empty weekends and going to weddings and work dos on his own. He wasn't ready to be perceived as single, by Millie or by anyone else. It wasn't time. Not yet.

A few of the people from the group were milling around on the pavement outside the centre. Kelvin, who was busy sweet-talking Tonia, looked up as he saw Tony leave the building. 'We're all off to the pub. Fancy a drink?' he said.

Tony looked at his watch.

'Go on,' said Tonia, eyeing him desperately.

'OK,' he said, thinking that he could be a hero just for one night, by helping Tonia to extricate herself from the foul Kelvin's attentions. 'Just a quick one.'

They went to a stripped-pine-and-blackboard wine bar called Bubbles – Tony didn't think that there were any wine bars with names like Bubbles still in existence, thought they'd all disappeared with the economic crash of the early nineties. It reminded him of being in his twenties, of the business starting to take off, of marrying Jo, being young and being richer than his wildest dreams. It reminded him of wearing Hugo Boss suits and going for dinner with Jo every night to trendy restaurants full of men in Hugo Boss suits and being served microscopic portions of food. It reminded him of how good life used to be and of how much he'd lost.

After a few minutes, Tony became aware that Tonia was flirting with him, and, although he could see that she was an extremely attractive and utterly charming woman, the awareness made no impact on him at all. He sipped his wine and asked Tonia automated questions about herself – she was thirty-three, lived in Balham, worked in theatre, liked ethnic food, didn't like dieting, etc., etc. – and felt a terrible despondency engulf him. How had he ended up here? How had his golden life become so tarnished?

But then he reminded himself that this was just the first step back towards the sunshine and the good times. That was why he was here. Because the only person in the whole world who could offer him the glitter he craved so much was sitting alone in a beautiful Paddington flat being dragged into the gutter by his selfish younger brother. Because the two of them together could take on the world and make everything golden again. And because there was no way that she'd love him until he loved himself and he couldn't love himself like this. He had to be thin. It was the only way.

He took another sip of his wine and politely asked Tonia if she'd been on holiday lately.

Nachos with Ned

At seven o'clock on Tuesday night, Sean's mouse hovered over 'word count'. He held his breath and clicked it:

Pages	123
Words	28,981
Characters (no spaces)	130,544
Characters (with spaces)	159,300
Paragraphs	724
Lines	2,445

Nearly 30,000 words. That was nearly a third of a book, could even be half a book if he didn't overcomplicate things. Fuck. He was going to make it. He was going to get this book finished. He'd received a diffident little e-mail from his agent yesterday morning, asking him about his MS and when he might expect it. If Sean had received that e-mail a week ago it would have sent him into a paroxysm of terror and he'd have started hyperventilating. As it was, he'd smiled to himself and calmly penned a reply informing his agent that, although he might not quite make the deadline, everything was progressing very nicely and he should get it to him by July. He'd been working flat out, hadn't seen Millie for a week, hadn't seen *anyone* in a week. He'd been working late into the night, going to bed when it was nearly morning, getting up late and starting the process all over again. He hadn't even watched TV.

Millie, obviously, wasn't pleased with this turn of events, but that was tough shit, quite frankly. He'd already put his career on hold for her, put his whole *life* on hold for her. He'd explained to her exactly what he was going through, that he'd got into a groove and that if he took himself out of the space he was in right now, everything might come to a grinding halt again. She'd said that of course she understood, in a tone of voice that suggested that she really didn't. 'When can I expect to see you again?' she'd said in her clipped, polished English. 'I don't know,' he'd said, 'when it feels like I've reached a natural break.' He could almost hear the subtext in her voice: 'But I'm pregnant, what in the whole world could possibly be more important than the miracle of life?'

But right now this *was* more important. It was more important than babies and relationships and eating three proper meals a day. It was more important than anything. And he, of course, had his own subtext. It wasn't just the book, it wasn't just making deadline – it was being away from her. It was doing him good. Rediscovering his old routines and habits, drinking PG Tips instead of English breakfast, going to bed whenever the fuck he wanted, not having to consider anyone else's preferences. He had no idea if he'd be feeling this way if she wasn't pregnant, but he suspected not. Un-pregnant Millie had been unpredictable and exciting – he'd wanted to hang around with her and take on board her preferences because he never knew where he might end up and there was always some form of pay-off, be it a great night out, a surreal encounter or the discovery of something new and exciting. Pregnant Millie was just a drag, to be quite honest. There was no longer any promise of the unexpected. He found it really hard to relate to her while she was in this condition. It was like she'd found Jesus or something.

He still thought about what Tony had said to him and he knew that he was right. He did need to make decisions. He did need to think about the future, but the problem was that he didn't have room in his head to think about it at the moment. He still loved Millie; of course he did. But he didn't really know what he felt about weddings and babies and the future. Every time he tried to free up some mental disk space to ponder the situation his head would crash and he'd start thinking about his book instead. Millie, her flat and her cats all felt like a distant, lost world, like something from his past.

He looked at the time on the computer screen again. Ten past seven. He re-read the last bit of text he'd written and realized with some surprise that he'd reached a 'natural break'. He could easily jump on a train, make his way over to Paddington, spend the evening with

Millie. But he didn't want to. Not in the slightest. But he did have this sudden need to get out of the flat and talk to another human being.

He gave his predicament a moment or two of thought and then picked up the phone and called Ned.

Forty minutes later Sean was installed on the sofa at Beulah Hill watching *Buffy the Vampire Slayer* with a beer in one hand and the remote control in the other. Mum was in the kitchen delightedly rustling up a big plate of nachos for her boys, Ned was stretched out full-length on the other sofa reading *heat* magazine and picking his nose, and Goldie was lying in front of the TV with his front paws in the air, snoring contentedly. Sean breathed a sigh of relief. This was nice, he thought, this was right. He was back where he belonged.

He'd managed to sidestep all the questions from Mum about him and Millie. No, they hadn't set a date; no, it probably wasn't going to be a summer wedding; no, he had no idea whether it was going to be religious or civil. He and Millie were having a long engagement, he'd said, and Mum had smiled and looked more than satisfied with that. 'That's good,' she'd said. 'There's no point in rushing into anything, is there?'

He still had no idea when he was going to tell his family that Millie was actually pregnant. Luckily, she was being cautious about it, wanted to wait until she was twelve weeks gone, until she was 'safe'. She'd told her sister and a few close friends, and Sean had told Tony, but apart from that no one in the whole world knew about it and Sean liked it like that. Other people knowing wasn't going to make Millie any more pregnant than she already was but it would make it harder for him to pretend that it wasn't happening.

'How's the book going?' said Ned, putting down his copy of *heat*.

'Brilliant!' said Sean, appreciating Ned's unwitting diversion of his thoughts away from the more problematic areas of his life. 'Yeah – it was a bit shaky to start off with, but now it's going really well.'

'What's it about?'

'Well, it's about this bloke who falls in love with this woman . . .'

'What – you're writing a *romance*?' Ned looked appalled.

'No, no, no – he falls in love with this woman, right, thinks she's the one for him. And then she gets pregnant.' He looked at Ned, waiting for his reaction.

'Right. And then what?'

'Well, she gets pregnant and wants to keep it and it's about the guy's perspective on the situation.'

'Oh,' said Ned, sounding slightly confused. 'Right. What's the twist?'

'It hasn't got a twist. It's just, you know, women have all this power over men, make all these decisions about babies and everything and men just have to go along with it. And it's not just babies, you know, it's everything. All those TV adverts they have on all the time with some 'stupid' man being shown how to put up bookshelves or fit the car radio or buy the car insurance or scrub out the fucking bath properly by their superior wives. It just pisses me off. There's this attitude in this country – and it's not just perpetuated by women, it's men too – that men are these big, dumb, useless creatures who get everything wrong – like we're one rung above fucking *Goldie* on the evolutionary ladder. And women are these celestial beings of wisdom and insight and emotional fucking intelligence. It's so fucking patronizing.'

'So what does he do, then, this bloke with the pregnant girlfriend?'

Sean shrugged. 'Dunno,' he said, 'I haven't decided yet.'

'Is he going to *kill* her?' said Ned, his face lighting up at the prospect.

'No.'

'Is he going to kill all pregnant women, then? You know, like a serial abortionist or something?'

'No. It's not like the first book. No one's going to get killed.'

'Oh,' said Ned, looking slightly disappointed. 'Never mind.'

Neither of them spoke for a moment and Sean did some flicking around the channels while the adverts were on.

'Where d'you get your ideas from?' said Ned suddenly.

'What ideas?'

'You know. Like *Half a Man* – where d'you get all that stuff about twins from?'

Sean threw him a look. Being separated from Ned when he went to Australia had been the inspiration for the idea. Sean had been so shell-shocked by Ned's sudden departure and disappearance from his life that it had got him thinking: imagine what it would be like if one of your siblings actually *died* – how would a person ever get over such a loss? Your siblings were the only people in your life who'd been there from the beginning and knew what your childhood had been like from the same perspective as you. One day you're having physical fights on a regular basis, the next you're sitting in a pub together drinking and enjoying each other's company, and the next one of you disappears to the other side of the planet, possibly for ever. Sean couldn't imagine a greater loss than that of a brother or sister and had extrapolated the idea into a book about identical twins.

'You,' he said, watching Ned's reaction, 'you going to Australia. Made me think what it would be like if you died. Or Tony,' he added.

Ned's face lit up. 'You mean, I inspired your book?'

'Uh-huh.'

'Fuck!' He smiled embarrassedly and looked pleased. 'That's so cool! So why didn't you dedicate it to me, you bastard?'

Bernie walked in with nachos and beer and laid them out in front of the boys. They launched themselves at the dish like a pair of starving urchins and Sean wondered to himself why he didn't do this more often. He'd got out of the habit when Ned went away. As much as he loved Mum and Dad and loved being in this house it just seemed slightly sad hanging out here without his brother around. In fact, when he thought about it, he owed his book and his success to Ned in more ways than one. If Ned hadn't gone away to Australia Sean would probably never have started writing the book in the first place.

'Did you hear that, Mum?' Ned said to Bernie. 'I inspired Sean's book.'

'Oh really – you're a serial killer, then, are you?'

'No – me going to Australia. Made him think about what it would be like if I died.'

Sean glanced across at Ned's excited face and felt his stomach curl itself up like a cat. His little brother. The only person in the world who ever really 'got' him, who didn't make him feel like an oddball. And the only person who Sean had ever really felt comfortable hanging around with. Until Millie, that is. He'd neglected him these few weeks since he got back. He'd been so wrapped up in Millie and engagements and pregnancies, not to mention his work, that he'd barely spared a moment for Ned. But that was going to change, he decided, everything was going to change. Whatever happened with him and Millie, whether they stayed together or not, got married or not, or had a baby together or not, things were going to change. He'd allowed her to absorb him totally into her world, draw him in with her quirky furnishings, trendy drinking clubs and unpredictability. But he didn't belong in her world – this was where he belonged and these were the people he belonged with. His family.

He sighed contentedly and stuffed another handful of sour-cream-drenched nachos into his mouth.

*

At ten o'clock he pulled on his jacket, kissed his mum goodbye, gave Ned a rough but tender hug and wheeled his pushbike out on to Beulah Hill. It was a clear, cool night brightly lit by an almost full moon. He'd just mounted his bike when a silhouetted figure smoking a cigarette appeared around the corner.

'All right, Sean? How's it hanging?'

'Oh. Hi, Gervase,' said Sean, feeling suddenly shy. He'd never really been alone with Gervase before, and felt slightly awkward. 'I'm good, thanks.'

'Been to see your mum?'

'Yeah. And Ned.'

Gervase nodded approvingly. 'That's good,' he said, 'he's been missing you.'

'Has he? Why? What did he say?'

'Hasn't actually *said* anything,' said Gervase, 'just a feeling I got. You're very close you two, aren't you?'

Sean shrugged and nodded. 'Yeah. I guess so.'

'That's nice,' said Gervase, taking a deep drag on his cigarette. 'Nice to have a brother like that – nice to have that sort of relationship.'

'Yeah,' Sean said, nodding and feeling strangely compelled to keep talking even though he was balanced precariously on his bike and really wanted to get home and do some more work.

It was silent for a moment, Sean wobbling back and forth on his bike, Gervase bouncing up and down slightly on his heels.

'Read your book the other day,' said Gervase suddenly.

'Oh yeah?' said Sean, feeling slightly surprised – Gervase didn't look the reading type.

'Yeah. I'm not much of a reader myself, but I thought, you know, living in your house and everything, seemed to give it more purpose.' He left a silence, that silence that Sean always hated – he thought people did it on purpose, to wind him up.

'Well,' said Sean, eventually, 'what did you think?'

'Fantastic,' said Gervase, rubbing his hands together. 'Read it in one day – a real page-turner.'

'Thanks,' said Sean, feeling strangely moved by this declaration.

'Don't know how you do it, you writers. Where you get all that inspiration from. And all that discipline.'

'Yeah,' admitted Sean, unconsciously dismounting his bike and leaning it against the garden wall. 'It's tough sometimes. I had a nightmare with this second one.'

'Oh yeah – bit of the old writer's block?'

'Yeah. Just couldn't write a word. I don't know if it was my circumstances or my brain chemistry, but it just didn't happen – for ages.'

Gervase sucked his breath between his teeth. 'Shit, that must be really scary.'

'It is. You just feel so impotent. Like your book's this beautiful, beautiful woman and she's lying there in bed, naked, legs open, waiting for you, and you just can't get it up. Sometimes you try to get it up for hours, other times you just give up and put your pants back on immediately.'

Gervase laughed at Sean's analogy. 'Shame you can't get some kind of Viagra for writers, isn't it?'

Sean nodded and laughed. 'Yeah.'

'So what unblocked you, then? What was your "Viagra"?'

Sean hesitated. He opened his mouth, about to say something, and then checked himself and shrugged. 'Not sure really,' he said. 'Just a bit of a change of lifestyle.'

And then something really weird happened. Gervase suddenly grabbed Sean's arms and started looking really deep into his eyes. As he did so, Sean felt himself go all soft and pliable and got this strange swirling sensation in his stomach, like someone had just given him a really nice compliment.

'What?' he said, looking at Gervase in alarm.

'You're in denial,' he said, sliding his hands down Sean's arms and grabbing his hands.

'About what?'

'I don't know. But you're just kidding yourself. Putting on an act. Building walls around yourself.'

'What are you talking about?'

'I told you – I don't know. I'm just telling you what I see. And what I see is a very scared man who's trying to pretend not to care about someone. And whoever it is – you care. You know you care. And if you don't let the other person know that you care . . .'

Sean stopped breathing and stared into Gervase's eyes.

'. . . you may as well give up living. You're teetering on the precipice of hell, mate – you're going to ruin your whole life. Look into yourself. Look at your family.

This isn't you. Drop the act. Demolish the walls. Be a man.'

And then he suddenly dropped Sean's hands, took a step back and cleared his sinuses. 'Anyway,' he said, 'I'd better let you get on. Nice talking to you, Sean. And, er . . . hopefully see you around here a bit more often now, eh? Maybe you'll come and see your mum singing at the Tavern some night?'

'Er . . . yeah,' said Sean, scratching his head and feeling slightly dizzy.

'Cool,' said Gervase. 'Maybe tomorrow?'

'Yeah,' said Sean, 'maybe.'

And then Gervase dropped his cigarette to the floor, ground it down with the heel of his shoe and crunched across the gravel towards the front door of number 114.

Sean stood for a while, letting the experience sink in, trying to make some sense of what had just happened.

Mad, he thought, staring into the bright circle of the moon and shaking his head, obviously as mad as a hare. But as he turned his bike around, pointing it in the direction of Catford, he couldn't shake this feeling that Gervase had something on him. That had been such an intense experience, like he and Gervase had *conjugated* somehow. It hadn't just been a mad person ranting at a sane person – it had been some kind of *fusion*.

Drop the act, he thought as he slowly remounted his bike, be a man.

What act? he thought. He wasn't acting. He was being, existing, getting on with his life the best way he knew how. Be a man. That's what Tony had said to him.

And Millie, too. But he *was* a man – this was what it was all about, wasn't it? Being successful, keeping some sort of control over your own destiny, being your own person. He'd been Millie's lapdog since they met, followed her round everywhere, done things her way, let his work slide, made all the effort. He'd even bought her a fucking engagement ring.

It was only now that he was starting to feel like a man again.

He cycled fast over Westwood Hill towards Forest Hill, purging Gervase's comments from his consciousness with every revolution of the pedals.

Rileys' Response

There was a letter waiting for Ned when he got back from folding cardboard on Wednesday night. The handwriting was unfamiliar but the letter had an English postmark, so Ned knew it wasn't from Monica. He sat down on the stairs and petted Goldie's head absent-mindedly while he read it:

Tuesday 1 May

Dear Ned,

Your parcel and letter arrived this morning. As you can imagine, we were both horrified by the contents, but we wanted to thank you so much for thinking to send it to us. You're right. Monica isn't your responsibility any more. We both know how hard you tried to make her happy and we also know how hard she made it for you. We phoned her today and she's very down. She says she can't see the point of anything. She couldn't explain why she's been plaguing you in such an odd manner. But we think you're probably right. She just wanted some attention. So we've booked our flights and are going to spend some time with her in Sydney, see if we can persuade her to come home for a while. It's an overdue visit. You're such a strong boy with such a big heart and I think we always depended on the fact that you were with her and that you would look after her. I feel we've neglected her horribly.

So thank you, Ned, for all your care and support over the years. We know you'd never have hurt Monica deliberately. And we can assure you that you won't be receiving any more macabre parcels or obscene text messages.

We wish you all the luck in the world in whatever you end up doing.

Yours gratefully,

Ann and Geoffrey Riley

Ned read the letter twice, a small smile spreading across his face, before folding it up, slipping it back into its envelope and heading towards the kitchen and a nice cold beer.

Dinner at Tony's

'God, I love Nigella Lawson,' said Ness, pulling some kind of greenery apart with her hands and throwing it into a pot before twisting around, grabbing an enormous glass of white wine and taking a huge slurp from it. She broke a large hunk of cooking chocolate off a slab and slipped it into her mouth. 'Chocolate?' she said, looking inquiringly at Tony.

He shook his head. 'No thanks.' It was bad enough that Ness was in his kitchen making excruciatingly fattening food that he wasn't going to be able to avoid eating, let alone her tempting him with huge and entirely unnecessary lumps of chocolate, too.

He looked at the clock over the cooker. Six-twenty. They were due in forty minutes, 'they' being Sean and Millie. Yes, Sean and Millie were coming for dinner. It was all Ness's fault. Well – it was his bowel's fault, actually. He'd been on the toilet last night and the phone had rung at the precise moment that it was least possible to answer it, so he'd called out to Ness to pick it up. And it had been Millie, of course. *Typical.* Hours and hours he spent not sitting on the toilet, able to answer the phone. Hours and hours when answering the phone would be the easiest thing in the whole world. How long did he actually spend on the toilet anyway – five minutes a day? Half an hour max. And Millie had somehow managed to choose that small window of inopportunity to make the call he'd been waiting for patiently for five long days.

'That was Millie on the phone,' Ness had said when he emerged from the bathroom a few minutes later. 'Said she'd been talking to you about a makeover for your flat – I didn't know you were thinking about making over your flat; what a brilliant idea! Anyway, she said you'd invited her over to have a look and I thought, well, seems a shame for her to come all the way over here just to wander around a bit. So I invited her for dinner. And Sean, too, obviously. She sounded really pleased!'

He'd phoned Millie at work this morning to check that she really was 'really pleased' – Ness was the sort of person who assumed that everyone was pleased about everything all the time – and apparently she was. She'd been hoping to engineer a visit to her recalcitrant boyfriend into the long trip down south and this made it seem less like she was door-stepping him and more like a nice social thing.

He walked out of the kitchen and looked around his flat. Shit – it looked awful. He should have bought some flowers, something to make it look a little less *sterile* in here. He bounced around for a while, rearranging cushions, moving chairs and tables around, opening curtains, shutting curtains, hiding objects that suddenly, with the prospect of being looked at by Millie, seemed vulgar and ugly, before glancing at his watch and realizing that it was quarter to seven and he was still in his work clothes.

He sprinted upstairs to the bathroom, showered in three minutes flat and then had a hideous ten minutes of trying and failing to find something nice to wear. Having lost a few pounds, he'd foolishly thought he might be able to rediscover some old favourites in the back of his cupboard and wasted precious minutes pulling too-small trousers on and off and poncing around in front of the mirror before admitting defeat and putting on his trusty chinos and a blue fleece. His hair appeared to have very little interest in looking nice but he didn't have time to worry about that any more. It was seven o'clock. And then the intercom buzzed.

He took the stairs two at a time. 'I've got it,' he called to Ness in the kitchen. And then he stopped for just a moment and stared at the little video screen. There she was. There was Millie. She was standing just behind Sean, adjusting her hair and looking stony-faced. The street lighting and the fuzzy black-and-white monitor made her look like a tragic, beautiful 1920s movie star. Tony took a deep breath, touched his hair, hit the intercom button and let them in.

Tony had had no intention of getting drunk that night, but by eight o'clock he'd had the best part of a bottle of wine. He was actually drinking faster than Ness, which was something of an achievement, and he was most certainly the drunkest person at the table. Sean was sipping slowly at a beer, claiming that he had to take it easy because he couldn't write with a hangover. Millie, of course, was going to make one glass of wine last all night, and Ness was packing it away as usual, but had such a high resistance to alcohol that she never appeared that drunk, no matter how much she drank. Tony, on the other hand, hadn't really had a proper drink for the best part of a fortnight, had had absolutely nothing to eat all day, and was rushing headlong towards pathetic drunkenness on a grand scale. He glanced across at Millie, who was fresh-faced and sober, and wished that he could reverse the process somehow, but it was too late. He was pissed.

Ness stood up to clear away the starter plates and Millie immediately leapt to her feet to help her. Tony got up and changed the music. He pulled out the Macy Gray CD they'd been listening to and replaced it with *White Ladder* by David Gray.

'See your musical tastes are as cutting edge as ever, Tone,' said Sean in a really snide way that made Tony's hackles rise. Tony bought about three new CDs a year and they were always the same three CDs that the rest of the British population had bought. Tony didn't keep up with music, never really had, not since he was a teenager. He had a tenuous knowledge of the likes of Steps, Eminem, Kylie and the people who won *Pop Stars*, but that was only because they were always in the papers. He wasn't really a 'music' person and it was unnecessary, he felt, for Sean to point that out and take the piss. His immediate response was to point out something that Sean might not want to talk about.

'So,' he said, sitting down, 'how's everything going with you and Millie and the . . .' He cupped his hand over his belly to indicate Sean's unborn child.

Sean's eyes swivelled awkwardly towards the kitchen. 'Fine,' he said, 'not bad.'

'Sort it all out, then?'

'Well. Sort of. You know.'

'No – what d'you mean?'

'Well, I'm *dealing* with it.'

Tony thought of Millie's tragically unhappy demeanour and shrugged. 'That's not what Millie says.'

'What Millie says? You mean, Millie's been talking to you about it?'

Tony picked a piece of lettuce off the table-top and fiddled with it. 'Not really – but she said she hadn't seen you for a while.'

'What is this?' said Sean, starting to look a little edgy. 'And why are you phoning Millie all of a sudden, anyway?'

Tony let the piece of lettuce leaf drop on to his table-mat and wiped his hands slowly on his napkin. 'I'm not phoning Millie "all of a sudden",' he began calmly. 'I just decided the flat needed a bit of oomph, remembered that Millie was an interior designer, gave her a ring and she happened to mention that she hadn't seen you for a while. And given the circumstances –' he cupped his stomach again – 'I just thought it was a bit strange. That's all. There's no need to be so defensive.'

It fell silent, save for the sound of Ness and Millie's laughter floating from the kitchen.

'So,' said Tony, 'what's going on?'

Sean bridled a bit and wriggled in his seat. 'Things are just a bit awkward at the moment, that's all.'

Tony threw him a tell-me-more look.

'It's my book. Look – I didn't tell anyone about it at the time, but I've had writer's block for weeks, right. Couldn't write a fucking word. And then I went home last week to do some washing and stuff and something just clicked.' He snapped his fingers. 'It just started to flow. And I realized that it was *Millie* causing the block – it was being at Millie's, away from familiar surroundings. And the bottom line is this: I've got two months to finish this book, and I can't write at Millie's. It's nothing personal.' He turned his hands up in a gesture of futility.

'Well, can't you go round to see her in the evenings, then? When you've finished writing?'

'You don't "finish" writing, Tony. It's not like a job, you know. You don't just close your briefcase at five-thirty and go home. Sometimes I don't even get into the flow until six o'clock. I'm working till gone midnight most nights.'

Both men stopped and looked up when they realized that Millie was back in the room.

'Discussing my absentee boyfriend?' she said, slipping back on to her chair and topping up her glass of wine.

'Yeah,' said Sean, 'I was just trying to explain to Tony about writing, about how it's a bit different to pissing about with Christmas cards all day and then going home at five-thirty.'

'Look,' said Tony, 'this is none of my business – your problem and all that. But now that it's out in the open, Ness –' he gestured towards the kitchen – 'is she allowed to know?'

Sean shrugged. 'Whatever,' he said, 'apparently we're going to be making a big *announcement* at Mum's party anyway . . .'

'I told you I didn't care,' hissed Millie. 'It was just a suggestion, that was all.' She picked up her wine glass and took a big, angry gulp. Sean and Tony both stared at her, but said nothing.

'Everyone ready for their main course?' trilled Ness, bouncing into the dining room with a large knife in her hand.

'I'll give you a hand,' said Millie.

'No, no, no,' said Ness, gesturing at her to stay sitting, 'I'm fine. You relax.'

She left the room and the bright, Ness-inspired smiles fell from their faces.

'So,' said Tony, pouring himself another glass of wine, 'how are you feeling, Millie? How's it going?'

'Oh, it's just delightful,' she said, knocking back more wine. 'I'm exhausted, moody and constantly nauseous. Every morning I wake up, throw up, go to work, throw up, get through the day somehow, come straight home because I'm too knackered to socialize, throw up, wait for a couple of hours for my boyfriend to phone, realize that he's not going to, call him to find out that he's deep in the throes of creative joy and has no intention of coming to see me, hang up, cry for an hour and then go to bed craving a cigarette. Then I wake up the next morning, all alone, throw up, go to work and start the whole process all over again. It's marvellous . . .' She beamed at them, showing off her big white teeth. 'Never been better. Thanks for asking.'

'For fuck's sake, Millie,' snapped Sean, 'I've explained this to you a hundred times. This is just temporary. Once the book's finished things'll get back to normal, I promise . . .'

'Normal? What the fuck is *normal*, Sean? You mean you mooching around the place whinging about me not being as much fun as I used to be? Or maybe you mean staying out all night taking coke with my friends while I'm lying in bed worrying myself sick about you? There is no "normal", Sean. Not until you accept this pregnancy and start dealing with it.'

Sean looked desperately at Tony and then at Millie. 'Look, do we have to talk about this here and now. Can't we talk about this later . . . ?'

'Oh, why bother, Sean? Tony already knows everything, anyway.'

'Knows what?'

'Well, he knows how to treat a pregnant woman, for a start.'

'Pregnant?' Ness stood in the doorway holding a big platter with what appeared to be half a cow with twelve heads of garlic and a Christmas tree on it. 'Who's pregnant?'

Millie raised her eyes to the ceiling and sighed. 'I am,' she said.

'Oh my God!' Ness let the platter drop to the table. 'Oh my God!' She ran around the table and hugged a shell-shocked Millie. 'Oh, that's fantastic! How far gone are you?'

'Nine weeks – nearly ten.'

'Oh my God! Sean – come here!' She dragged him to his feet and squeezed the breath out of him. He smiled grimly. 'That's just the best thing ever. Oh God – the wedding. What are you going to do about the wedding? Shotgun? Or maybe you can wait until your baby's older. Oh, it could be a page boy or a little flower girl. God – a baby – I can't believe it! This calls for some champagne. Tony, that Mumm in the fridge – is it OK to . . . ?'

Tony nodded and Ness ran back into the kitchen. Sean turned back immediately to look at Millie. 'What did you mean by that last comment, exactly?'

'What comment?' said Millie, impatiently.

'Oh, the comment about Tony knowing how to treat a pregnant woman. What was that all about?'

'Nothing,' said Tony, immediately wishing that he hadn't.

'What?' Sean threw him a look.

Millie raised her eyes to the ceiling. 'Look, I just happened to mention to Tony that I was suffering from terrible morning sickness and he very kindly went to Holland & Barrett and bought me all these remedies.'

'Remedies?'

'Yes. Ginger and lemon and things.'

'And . . . ?'

'And he dropped them off at my flat.'

'Tony's been to your flat? You've been to her flat?' He turned and looked at Tony.

The jingle of glasses signalled Ness's return with the champagne. 'There we go,' she said, 'Tony, clear a space, will you? You do the champagne, Tony – I'll serve the food. I can't believe it, you two,' she said, carving the cow, piling it on to people's plates and spooning viscous gravy all over it, 'first you're getting married, now you're pregnant – artichoke, Millie? – and how long have you been together?'

'Three months, nearly,' muttered Millie, draining her glass of wine.

'Amazing,' said Ness. 'And to think – some people can be together for years before they even move in together.' She threw Tony a meaningful but playful look which he chose to ignore. 'So, how long have you known?'

'A couple of weeks,' said Millie.

'Did you know?' she asked Tony, passing plates around the table.

'Yes,' he said, topping up the last glass of champagne, 'Sean told me – last week.'

'And you didn't say anything – you sly old bugger. How did you manage to keep that to yourself?'

'Sworn to secrecy,' he said, passing round the champagne glasses.

'Yes,' said Millie, 'we didn't really want to tell anyone until the first scan.'

'Of course,' said Ness. 'So it's top secret, then?'

'Yes – just for another couple of weeks.'

'God – Bernie is going to be *ecstatic*! Her first grand-child. A toast,' she raised her glass, 'to Sean and Millie – and Millie's bump.'

They all picked up their glasses and clinked them together passionlessly. 'To Millie's bump,' they intoned, 'cheers.'

'OK,' said Ness, settling herself into her seat and tucking her hair behind her ears, 'now – don't be scared of the garlic. I know it looks a lot, but Nigella says that when you cook it for that long, it loses its pungency – so it won't make your breath smell, I promise . . .'

Tony prodded his food with his fork and looked across at Sean and Millie. Ness had engaged Millie in a conversation about pregnancy that Millie had latched on to like a hungry dog with a bone. Sean was chewing resentfully on a piece of meat and staring into the middle distance.

They looked like strangers, he mused, like the result of some disastrous attempt at dinner-party match-making.

They made their way through dinner in a civilized fashion, making conversation about babies and work and family and everything other than what they really wanted to be talking about. Millie finished her cham-pagne and held her glass out when the bottle went round for second helpings. Ness opened a third bottle of wine at some point and then, after an incredibly rich chocolate mousse that nearly blew Tony's mind, she brought out the brandy. Now, every drinker has a weak spot – the drink that they can't resist even when they know they don't need it, the drink that takes them to a place on the pissed ladder that no other drink can – and for Tony it was brandy. It was his favourite drink in the whole world but it always made him a little bit mad – and not mad in a good-times, Tequila kind of a way, but mad in a rankled, bitter-old-man sort of way. And by the time Ness and Millie went into the kitchen to clear up, he'd had three tumblers of the stuff.

Sean glanced tersely across the table at Tony.

'What were you doing at Millie's?' he hissed.

'Christ, Sean – are you still banging on about that?'

'What were you doing?'

'Look,' said Tony, leaning in towards his brother and lowering his voice. 'It was nothing. Millie mentioned that she was feeling really ill, I happened to be in Holland & Barrett, felt sorry for her, bought her some stuff – that's all.'

'But you went round to her place – to *Millie*'s place.'

'Yeah, I know. How else was I going to get her her stuff. I was in town, I was passing, I dropped it off. No big deal.'

'But why didn't you say anything? I don't understand.'

'There was nothing to say, Sean. I bought her some stuff. I dropped it off. At least I was *doing* something.'

'What's that supposed to mean?'

'I mean, she was ill, you were being fucking useless. It didn't take much effort, you know. You could have done it yourself if you'd thought about someone other than yourself for more than a minute . . .' Tony's voice was getting louder and Ness stuck her head around the doorway to see what was going on.

'What are you two getting all yappy about?' she said.

'Nothing,' said Tony, 'nothing. Just brother stuff.'

Ness, who as an only child thought that anything that happened between siblings was somehow enchanted, smiled at them indulgently and went back into the kitchen to talk babies with Millie.

'I can't believe you went to my girlfriend's house and you didn't tell me. Imagine if I went round to see Ness and didn't mention it – wouldn't you think that was weird?'

'No. Not really.'

'Well, I would.'

'Well, I'm sorry, then. Next time I do something nice for someone who you're being a cunt to, I'll remember to let you know.'

Sean's face started to redden. 'Christ,' he said, 'I phoned you up *one time*, the only time in my life I've ever asked your advice about anything, expecting you to be supportive and understanding and instead you've just used it as an excuse to pester my girlfriend and make me look like a toerag.'

'I haven't had to make you look like anything – you've done a bloody good job of that all by yourself. Look, you phoned me for advice and I gave you my advice. And ever since then you've done nothing but ignore it. So stop putting this one on me. You're fucking up single-handedly and you know it.'

'Christ! I can't believe you, sitting there all holier than

thou, all arms-folded, looking at me like I'm a piece of shit. You haven't exactly made a shining success of your own life, have you, Tone? Your own wife ended up shagging another man and you just let her go.'

'Huh!' said Tony, not even attempting to lower his voice now, 'you can talk. Jesus. Just because you wrote some fucking book and all the papers are running round going, "Ooooh, Sean, you're so fucking marvellous", you think you can get away with anything. You think it doesn't matter that for the first twenty-eight years of your life you were a useless slacker who never did anything worthwhile. You're spoilt, that's your fucking problem, spoilt rotten. Never had to work for anything in your life, had it all given to you – council flat, money, dinner at Mum's every night . . .'

'Ha!' Sean got to his feet and started pointing at Tony wildly. '*Me* spoilt?! Me?! That is so fucking funny I think my sides have split. Who gave you the loan for your first business, hmm? And have you paid him back, yet? Er, no – I don't think so. All those cosy little meetings you and Dad used to have about "business". Who the hell ever sat down with me, eh? Who ever asked me what I wanted to do? Who offered *me* money and taught *me* all they knew? All you had to do was sneeze and Mum would get the fucking snot framed and call you a genius. You were always made out to be this fucking *golden* boy who could do no wrong.'

'I've *worked* for everything I've got, Sean. Yes, Dad lent me some money, and no, I haven't paid him back – but I will if it makes you happy. I'll write him out a cheque now, if you want. And if you'd shown even an iota of interest in anything – anything at all – Dad would have given you whatever you wanted. But you didn't. All you were interested in was watching telly with Ned or going out clubbing with him and taking poncey fucking drugs and spending the next day in bed – while I was out earning a living and making something of my life.'

'You call running some sad little card business making something of yourself? Jesus. How low your horizons are, Anthony . . .'

A small purple ball of light erupted in Tony's head at that moment, like a miniature mushroom cloud of pure fury. His vision blurred and an overwhelming emotion flooded his consciousness: hatred. It was an emotion he'd been trying his hardest to avoid acknowledging over the past few weeks but there was no getting away from it now. He hated him. He hated Sean. He did. He hated everything about him, from his stupid fucking book to his ridiculous trendy trainers to the way he was treating his pregnant girlfriend.

'Oh,' he said, drawing himself up to his full height, 'and I suppose you think having one successful book is going to set you up for life, do you? You haven't proved anything yet, Sean, not a thing. It might just be "a sad little card business" but it's a sad little card business that's been around for fifteen years, that's established, that'll pay for me when I'm old and grey. You got fucking lucky, mate – you've got a lot more to prove before you can sit there and tell me you're a success.

And yeah, my marriage might have fallen apart but I worked really hard at making it work – we were together for ten years, and that's a fucking lifetime in this day and age. You - you fuck about for years with a bunch of brain-dead bimbos and then the minute you meet someone decent you fuck it up. I mean, what the hell were you doing proposing to Millie in the first place? Eh? What the hell was that all about?'

'That, Tony, is an *incredibly* interesting question,' said Millie, appearing in the doorway with yet another glass of wine in one hand and the other hand on her hip. 'Yes, Sean,' she said, 'why did you propose to me? Hmm?'

Sean dropped his head on to his fists and took a deep breath. 'Millie,' he said, 'not now. Not here. Please. Can't this wait until we get home?'

'No,' said Millie falling on to her chair and staring straight at Sean. 'No – it can't wait until we get home. I want to have this conversation right now.'

'But this is private, Millie . . .'

'Oh come on,' she said, 'Tony's your brother. He's *family*, Sean – we can talk in front of him. And anyway, you should listen to your big brother – you might be able to learn a bit about life from him.'

'Eh?' Sean looked up at Millie and sneered.

'Yeah – he's a *man*, Sean. Look at him.' She stood up and walked round the table towards Tony. 'Look – he's got broad shoulders.' She grabbed his shoulders and squeezed them. 'He's strong, Sean. He can run a business *and* own his own home *and* drive a car *and* hold down a

303

relationship and *still* find time to think about other people. You could learn a lot from him, you know.'

'Since when did you care about things like cars and flats, Millie? I thought you were supposed to be this cool, easy-going chick with all these socialist ideals about how status and money and property don't matter. But you're not, are you? You're just like every other woman – you just want some man to look after you . . .'

'I do *not* want some man to look after me, Sean. I just want some *man*. That's all. Not a kid who freaks out at the first sign of responsibility. Who thinks that pregnant women have got some kind of lurgy. I mean, has it ever occurred to you that I'm scared, Sean, that maybe I'm as freaked out about having a baby as you are? Just because I'm a woman doesn't mean that I'm pre-programmed to know how to deal with this. I'm terrified, Sean. My identity is being stripped away with every day that passes. You think I *like* being pregnant? You think I like having my body taken over by something?'

'Well then why are you having it, Millie? Why the fuck are you having this fucking baby if you don't fucking want it? Eh?'

'I *do* want this baby, Sean. I want this baby more than anything. All I'm saying is that it's not easy being pregnant and . . . and . . . *I need you to want this baby, too.* That's all . . .'

The room fell absolutely silent and Millie's last words were left hanging in the air like an unanswered doorbell.

Millie stared at Sean beseechingly. Sean stared at the ceiling, drumming his fingertips against the table-top.

Tony stared at his fingernails and tried not to move too much in case Millie took her hands off his shoulders.

'Right,' said Sean, eventually, slamming his hands down on the table and sighing, 'that's it. I've had enough. I'm out of here.' He stood up and pulled his jacket off the back of Tony's sofa.

'What do you mean?'

'I mean, I've had enough of sitting here having my personal life dissected in public and being told I'm not good enough, so I'm going.'

'Well, I'm coming with you, then,' said Millie, taking her hands off Tony's shoulders, much to his disappointment.

'No, Millie, you're not.'

'Yes, I am.'

He threw her an icy glance. 'You. Are. Not.'

'We need to talk, Sean.'

'Yes. You're right. We do need to talk. But not here, not now and not tonight.'

'OK – fuck off, then. Fuck off. I'm going to stay here with Tony. Tony's going to look after me, aren't you, Tony?'

She grabbed his shoulders again and Tony nodded vehemently. 'Yeah,' he said, 'of course.'

Sean stopped in his tracks for a moment and looked at them both. He opened his mouth to say something and then shut it again. 'Whatever,' he said, throwing his hands up in the air in defeat, 'whatever.' He turned and was about to leave the room when he stopped and turned again and stared, not at Millie but at Tony. He stared at him for what felt like about fifteen minutes before finally pointing at him and saying, in a soft voice that sounded drained of anger and full of sadness, 'I thought you were my brother.' He left the room, then, and ten seconds later they heard the front door slam close.

'OK,' said Ness, walking into the room with a trayful of coffee and chocolates. 'Who's for coffee?'

Millie burst into tears.

Brother Merging

'There you go,' said Tony, passing Millie a large cup of peppermint tea and sitting down next to her on the sofa.

'I'm really sorry, Tony.'

'What for?'

'For making you fall out with your brother, for ruining dinner, for being a complete bitch.'

'Oh, don't be stupid. You haven't ruined anything. Tonight was always going to be a bit of a sticky one.'

'Yes, I know, but I shouldn't have brought it to your dinner table. The last thing I wanted to do was drive a wedge between you and Sean. I just lost control tonight. Christ – I can't believe I'm drunk, Tony. Look at me, I'm *drunk*, with a baby in me.'

'Oh, well . . .' said Tony, not really knowing what to say, as getting plastered while pregnant was pretty indefensible in his book, but not wanting to upset her even more. 'I'm sure it'll be fine.'

'Yes, I know it'll be fine. But that's not the point. It's just – it just seems to show a lack of respect, that's all. Poor little thing.' She stroked her belly tenderly. 'Poor tiny, defenceless little thing who's only just growing fingernails and already your mummy and daddy are fighting and rowing and making you drink disgusting things.'

Tony glanced down at Millie's tiny, rounded stomach and felt a deep longing rising inside him. There was a baby in there – a tiny, thumb-sized little baby.

'So, he's got fingernails, has he?' he said looking at the bump in wonder.

'Uh-huh. And little sockets in his gums for teeth to grow in.'

'Wow.'

'And this week, apparently, he's developed little vocal cords – so he can start making noises in there. Imagine that?'

'Amazing,' said Tony, 'can I touch it?'

'Of course,' said Millie, pulling open her cardigan a bit.

Tony put his hand out flat and cupped the little bump that looked more like the result of a big curry and a bit of trapped wind than a pregnancy.

'You won't be able to feel anything, yet,' she said, 'the baby's moving around but it's too small for you to feel.'

'No. But it's just . . . it's amazing, isn't it? A little human being in there. I just want to . . . *connect*. You know?'

He looked up at Millie and smiled and Millie smiled back at him. 'Do you know something,' she said, 'Sean's never once done that. He's never touched our baby.'

'Seriously?' Tony took his hand from Millie's stomach.

'Uh-hm. I don't think he's ever even *looked* at it. Well, not deliberately, anyway. *Christ*. What am I doing? What am I doing, Tony?' She looked at him beseechingly and then let her head fall on to her hands. 'Fuck. I'm going to be a single mother, aren't I? A bitter, haggard, old single mother who gets pissed while she's pregnant. Christ, I'll probably become an alcoholic and neglect it. It'll be taken away by the social services and I'll never see it again. Oh, Jesus, Tony – *what am I going to do?*' She started sobbing again.

'Here, here,' said Tony, picking up one of her hot, clenched little hands and squeezing it gently. 'Things will work out, Millie. Honestly, they will.'

'I mean, a few weeks ago everything in my life was perfect. I'd met the man of my dreams, he proposed to me, I got promoted, everything was going so well. Every day was like a little scene from a film, you know? Like this idyllic golden world that seems out of your reach most of the time, that looks like it's happening to everyone else – except it was happening to *me.* I honestly didn't think that life could possibly be any better. I thought I was the luckiest, most blessed girl in the whole world. And now . . . and now . . . my boyfriend hates me, I'm up the duff, I've got no social life, no fun . . . no waist. And now I feel like my life is like a depressing documentary. You know, like one of those women you see on the TV and you think, "How the hell did you let this happen to you? How could you have been so *stupid*?" I mean, how could I ever have looked at Sean and thought he'd be a good dad – or even a good husband, come to that? Was I that desperate?'

'He doesn't deserve you, Millie,' said Tony, 'he doesn't deserve either of you.'

'He doesn't, does he? I mean, do you think he even

noticed I was drinking tonight? Hmm? Do you think it occurred to him what I was doing? God – maybe he was mentally encouraging me. Hoping I'd have a miscarriage or something . . .'

'Oh come on, Millie – I think that's probably a bit harsh, don't you?'

'No. I don't. You don't know how cold he can be, Tony. I never saw it before. He was always like this excited puppy dog – he was so happy about everything all the time. I couldn't ever have imagined Sean being unhappy. And then I told him I was pregnant and it was like a light switched off somewhere inside him. Like these big, steel doors came down, whoosh –' she demonstrated the doors coming down with her hands – 'and that was the last I saw of the old Sean. Gone. For ever. And I don't know how to get him back, Tony. How do I get him back – hmm? How?'

'I don't know, Millie. I really don't know. Sean's a . . . Sean doesn't know how to share. He never did know how to share. If something was his then no one else could get close to it. And if Mum ever made him give one of his toys to someone to play with, well – he'd disown it. Say he didn't want it any more. Get a new one . . .' Tony shrugged and looked at Millie.

'Are you saying that Sean's sulking because I'm like his toy and now he's having to share me with our baby?'

'I don't know,' he said, 'it's a theory.'

Millie fell silent and stared at the floor for a while. 'Fuck,' she said. 'I think you're right. I think that's it. God, Tony – what would I do without you? It's just like

– being with you – it's like having my very own grown-up version of Sean. I mean, you look like him and sound like him – you even smell a bit like him. But you're emotionally intelligent and he's emotionally spasticated. I wish . . . I wish I could just sort of *merge* the two of you together. Oh God – does that sound funny?'

Tony looked at her, trying to hide the amazement in his eyes. 'Er, no – not really. But, which bit of Sean would you keep in this merging process?'

Millie sighed and thought about it. 'God – I don't know, I really don't know. His . . . his . . . *Nothing*,' she said eventually. 'The way I feel at the moment, there is nothing about Sean I would like to keep.'

'So, this merger – it would just be me, then?' said Tony, laughing nervously.

'Yeah – I suppose it would be.' Millie laughed too.

'Maybe without the, er . . . extra covering, though, eh?' He patted his stomach and laughed again.

'No,' she said, 'I'd keep the covering. I like the covering.'

'You do?'

'Yes. It's cuddly.'

Tony digested the word 'cuddly' for a second, wondering if he liked it or not.

'Remember the other day, Tony – when you came round to my flat?'

He nodded.

'And you said that thing – that thing about how if it all fell apart with Sean, there'd be people to hold me up?'

'Yes.'

311

'Well, I think it might, you know? I really think it might all fall apart. I didn't at the time, when you said it – I thought you were being melodramatic. But now, I'm not so sure. I look at Sean now and I can't see any of the things I fell in love with. They're not there any more. All I see is this stroppy, selfish *boy*. And unless the old Sean comes back . . . I don't think I want to be with him, Tony. And if that happened – if I was all on my own – would you . . . *take an interest*?'

'Take an interest?' said Tony. 'Of course I'd take an interest. I'd do more than take an interest, Millie – I'd do absolutely anything.'

'Would you?'

'Yes. I'd go anywhere, take you anywhere you wanted, do anything and everything for you and the baby. I'd . . . God – money, time, whatever you wanted, whatever you needed. You and the baby are the most important things in the world.'

'Are we – really?'

'Of course you are. More important than anything. I'd do anything for you both – absolutely anything.'

Millie looked straight at Tony and Tony saw her eyes filling with tears. 'God, Tony, if you knew how much I'd been wanting to hear that. To feel like we're special and important.'

'How could anything be more important than you two?'

'Thank you, Tony. You have no idea how much that means to me.'

'I just can't believe that someone as beautiful as you

and as special as you and as *amazing* as you could ever have ended up with someone who doesn't appreciate you. It doesn't make any sense. You should be . . . adored and pampered and looked after and protected. You should be treated like a queen.'

Millie smiled at him and put a hand on his arm. 'Stop it,' she laughed, 'you'll have me believing it in a minute.'

Tony grabbed her hand. 'I want you to believe it, Millie – you're the most beautiful woman in the world.'

'Thank you, Tony,' she said, 'thank you so much.' And then all of a sudden, she threw her arms around him and hugged him. Tony put his arms around her and hugged her back and for a few seconds he stopped breathing.

Ness was upstairs in bed, the room was dimly lit by one lamp in the corner, the David Gray CD was still playing on repeat. Tony was full of brandy and wine. Millie felt warm and strong and smelt of clean hair and rosemary. This felt like a post-date clinch. This felt like . . . *something.* He pulled away from Millie, slowly, until he was eye to eye with her.

There were mascara runs under her eyes. He wiped them away with his thumb. 'You deserve so much more, Millie,' he said.

And she smiled and nodded at him. 'I do,' she said. 'I really do.'

And then, very, very slowly, their lips met and they kissed.

Baby Hangovers

Tony was the one to stop the kiss.

He stopped it after about thirty seconds.

Someone had to, after all.

'This is wrong,' he said. 'We shouldn't be doing this.' And he wasn't just saying it to be a gentleman, he was saying it because he meant it. It *was* wrong. All wrong. Halfway through the kiss, Tony had suddenly realized. This wasn't what their relationship was about any more. It had moved on. In fact, it had moved on from the moment Millie first told him she was pregnant, and he just hadn't noticed.

'I know,' she said, pulling away from him, putting her fingertips to her lips, 'I'm very drunk.'

'Me too,' said Tony.

'It's just,' she began, her hands twisted together in her lap, 'I'm feeling so . . .'

'It's OK,' interrupted Tony, 'I know. We're both confused. We're both pissed. We're both being totally ridiculous.'

Millie nodded vehemently, tucking her hair behind her ear. 'Absolutely,' she said, and then she threw Tony a half-smile. 'God – how the hell did that happen?'

Tony shrugged.

'Who started it? God, was it me? Did I just launch myself at you with my tongue sticking out?'

Tony smiled. 'No,' he said, 'I think it was a two-way effort. You know, fifty-fifty.'

'How embarrassing. Not that I – well, you're a very attractive man, Tony, you really are. But, I have no idea why that just happened. I really don't. It must be my hormones, or something.'

'Mine too,' he said, starting to feel the stirrings of embarrassed laughter somewhere in his stomach.

'God – snogging on the sofa, how juvenile.' She covered her face with her hands and sniggered.

Tony looked at Millie, sitting with a look of numb, semi-amused shock on her face, her cardigan still slightly askew from his passionate fumblings, and an image flashed through his mind, an image of him and Millie snogging on the sofa. And for some reason the image sent him straight over the edge and he laughed out loud. Millie threw him a sideways glance and her own smile increased. Tony looked at her and laughed again. And then they both totally cracked up.

They laughed long and hard for about five minutes, rocking back and forth, clutching their sides, wiping the tears away from under their eyes. They laughed so hard that they couldn't speak and so much that Tony began to feel bruises forming under his ribcage. And they laughed for so long that all the tension from the previous four hours completely dissipated. And when they finally stopped they looked at each other and

Tony knew that he had a new and wonderful friend in his life.

They sat up for a bit longer and chatted about the evening, about the baby and about Sean, and then, when Millie started yawning more than talking, Tony took her upstairs to bed. She let him make a fuss over her as he showed her her bedroom, showed her the en suite shower, brought her toothpaste, a spare toothbrush, gave her a clean T-shirt to wear in bed. She let him sit on the edge of her bed once she was ready and stroke her hair and hold her hand. She was compliant and childlike.

'Oh no,' she said suddenly as she lay there. 'My baby – do you think it's going to have a hangover tomorrow? Like me?'

Tony shrugged.

'Oh my poor, poor baby,' she said, rubbing her belly, 'what have I done to you, you poor little thing?'

Tony brought her more water, then, to minimize her and her baby's hangovers.

'You know, Tony,' she said, as her eyes struggled to remain open and she teetered on the edge of sleep. 'I love being with you. You're so strong and calm and kind. When I'm with you I just feel like everything's going to be all right. You know?'

Tony nodded and smiled and watched her as her eyes slowly closed and her breathing patterns changed, and as he sat there looking at the contours of Millie's face, the way her eyelashes brushed against her skin, the way her mouth puckered up as she breathed in and out, the little whistley noises she made as she slept, he was suddenly overcome by a completely alien emotion.

He felt like a father watching over his little girl.

He felt *paternal*.

That kiss, just now – it had been . . . *nice*. It had been soothing, comforting. But it hadn't set his loins alight. And that, he suddenly realized, was exactly what his relationship with Millie was all about. They were comforting each other. He was making her feel better about the fact that her boyfriend was rejecting her and she was making him feel better about the fact that he'd lost his sense of identity.

It was all a game. The whole thing. It wasn't going to go anywhere. Of course it wasn't. Even if Millie and Sean did split up, did he honestly think he could plough in there and raise his brother's child? It was ludicrous. He didn't want to beat Sean any more. Sean was losing all by himself. The competition was over. His role here, he now realized, wasn't to wrest Millie from Sean. It was to look after Millie until Sean got his act together and took responsibility.

He wasn't the predator.

He wasn't the lover.

He wasn't the winner.

He was the big brother.

After a few minutes, he stood up slowly, switched off the lamp and went to his bedroom.

Ness was awake and reading a book.

'How is she?' she whispered, folding down the corner of her page and putting it on the bedside table.

'Sleeping,' said Tony, unbuckling his belt.

'Poor thing. How awful. The one time you need some harmony in your life and everything's falling apart.'

'Yeah. It's a bastard.'

'You were brilliant with her, Tony,' she said, pulling herself half out of the bed and wrapping an arm around his torso.

He stopped, turned statue-still.

'I can't believe how sweet you've been with her. I was so proud of you tonight, Tony. So proud that you were my boyfriend.'

'Well,' he said tersely, 'she's pregnant. Someone needs to look after her.'

'Come here,' she said, 'come here, my lovely big sensitive man.' She hooked a finger into his belt loop and pulled him gently towards her.

'What?'

'Just come here. I'm feeling all overcome with love. I want a hug.'

'Ness,' he said, pulling away from her, 'I . . .'

'Just come here.'

And then he looked at Ness lying there, naked and full of love, and felt a sudden wave of desire overcome him. Not for Ness but for human contact, for intimacy. She pulled him down on to the bed with her, undressed him, caressed him, and Tony was so drunk and so confused and so full of emotion that he let her. His head was a dark, warm void. His body was a motherboard of feelings and sensations. He kept his eyes closed and lost himself in the moment, lost himself in Ness's body and Ness's embrace. Thoughts flashed in and out of his voided head, like a subliminal slideshow – Millie, Sean, Ness. He had no idea how long it went on for but he'd never before experienced such intensity of emotion during sex. And when he eventually came, he came emotionally as well as physically, and, with tears in his eyes and a look of pure wonder on his face, he shouted out, 'I love you, Ness, I love you so much, love you so much, *love you so much*.' And then he grabbed hold of her and held her tighter than he'd ever held anyone in his life.

And Ness held him after and cried wet tears that seeped through his hair and on to his scalp.

A Love Story in Two Acts

By the time Ned got into work on Thursday morning, he was officially the world's greatest press-pack assembler. He'd folded more than 1,000 folders, photocopied more than 500 press releases and emptied ten Kodak boxes of pictures. Even Hoxton Fin (whose name, apparently, was Marc – although Ned knew this only because he'd heard someone else calling it out across the office) was impressed by Ned's productivity. 'You're making good progress,' he'd said the night before, 'I'm very pleased.' And Ned had felt ridiculously proud and gone home with a little spring in his step.

It was a lovely sunny morning as Ned strode across Soho Square towards his place of work, and as much as he was aware of the fact that he had one of the crappiest jobs in London, he couldn't help feeling a little bit excited about having somewhere to go every day, about being part of the crowd thronging the pavements of the greatest city in the world. It gave him something to focus on and distanced him from his old life. It was good. It was healthy. It was right.

He tapped the security code into the office door and strode through reception, saying good morning to

Fabiola, the lovely Italian receptionist, as he went. He stopped briefly at the coffee machine on the landing and got himself a cup of tea. He poked his head around the press-office door and called out good morning to the few people milling around in there. And then he opened the door to his room and stopped in his tracks.

There was a girl in there.

A gorgeous girl in a pink puff-sleeved blouse and faded old jeans, with a Celtic band tattooed around her upper arm. She had streaky blonde hair that came down to her shoulders with a few strands pinned back, and about eight earrings in each ear, including little silver ones right at the top.

'Nid?'

'Er – yeah.'

'Hi – I'm Bicky.'

'Bicky?'

'Yeah. I'm from the same timp agency as you?'

'You're from Dutch & Dewar?'

'Yeah. Apparently, that guy, er . . . ?'

'Marc.'

'Yeah. That's the one. He wanted someone to give you a hand? So here I am.'

'Cool,' said Ned, rubbing his hands together, 'that's excellent. Has he shown you everything? You know, the folders and the photos . . .'

'Yeah. Uh-huh.'

'And the coffee machine? The toilets?'

'Uh-huh. Yeah.'

'Excellent.' He put down his tea and grinned at Becky.

'So,' she said, 'you've been locked in here all on your own all week?'

'Yup.'

'Jesus. I can't believe they're making us work in here. With *no windows*. On a day like today. It's criminal!'

'I know,' said Ned, so relieved to have someone on his level who he could have a good moan with. 'And it's not as if there isn't enough room for us in there,' he indicated the PR office over the way. 'Have you been in there? It's *vast*.'

'That Marc guy's such a winker,' she said, 'and *what* is going on with his hair? He looks like Sonic the Hidgehog.' She laughed and then stopped herself. 'Shit – listen to me – I've picked up the whinging virus. I sound like a fucking Brit!'

'So,' he said, 'Australia or New Zealand?'

'Australia. Sydney.'

'Oh. Really. Whereabouts in Sydney?'

'Byron Bay.'

'No!' said Ned. 'Seriously?'

'Yeah. Why? Do you know it?'

'Know it,' he said, 'I lived there for three years.'

'In Byron? No way! How long ago was this?'

'Just got back three weeks ago.'

'Wow!' said Becky, putting her hands in her jeans pockets. 'That's amazing.'

And Ned looked at Becky and thought that yes, it was extremely amazing. It was amazing that she was in his cupboard, it was amazing how pretty she was and it was amazing that now there'd be someone for him to talk to all day. And not only that but someone he had so much in common with. As they talked and folded cardboard and drank rotten tea together it turned out that they knew people in common, that they'd been to the same bars and restaurants, had probably been in the same place at the same time on more than one occasion. Becky had been to the Internet café where Ned used to work, Ned had been to a party at Becky's ex-boyfriend's flat.

She was twenty-three years old and she'd been in London for nearly six months and was planning on spending another six months here, then going round Europe for a few weeks before she went home. She was living in a flat share in Wandsworth with four other Aussies and it was really weird for Ned to be having this conversation with someone who was in the same position as he'd been in for the past three years, except on the other side of the world.

At one o'clock they went out for lunch together to buy super-cheap sandwiches from Benjy's, which they took into Soho Square and ate in the sunshine. Becky wore pink sunglasses and sat cross-legged and straight-backed, picking blades of grass and tying them into knots. Ned stretched himself out across the grass and felt its springtime dampness seeping through the denim of his jeans. The sun was hot but tempered by a cool breeze. All around were other people like them, young office workers enjoying their hour of freedom, soaking up the precious rays of sun as if they might preserve the moment for ever.

They talked about music and London and food and football. Becky liked curry, Chinese, pizza and lager, although if someone bought her champagne she wouldn't say no. She went to see a band about once a week (the best thing about living in London was the live music) and supported Chelsea (because they were her local club and all her flatmates supported them, too). She missed her friends and her dog and her mum and dad. They talked about being away from home, about the bittersweetness of having the best time of your life while being so far away from the people who know you and love you the best.

At two o'clock they went back to work and chatted the afternoon away. They took the piss out of Marc, laughed at the photographs of the prepubescent pop star whose career they were assisting and drank hot chocolate from the machine down the corridor. By five o'clock they'd developed a rapport more in keeping with people who'd known each other since they were five, so when they left the building together and it was still sunny and they were still chatting it seemed only right to suggest that they go and get a drink together somewhere.

They went to the Coach and Horses on Greek Street and pulled torn-vinyl-topped stools out on to the pavement, which was heaving with sweaty post-work bodies: couriers, media types and craggy-faced alcoholics. There was a chill in the air as the sun started to sink behind the tall, thin buildings of Soho, but with a pint of lager inside him and a pretty girl by his side Ned was barely aware of the goosebumps on his forearms.

This is it, he thought as he watched Becky walking into the pub to get another round in, this is my perfect sort of night. Unplanned and spontaneous, a mild spring night, cold lager, a lively pub and a gorgeous, funny, sweet-natured girl. This was what being young, free and single in the city was all about. And this was exactly what Gervase must have meant when he'd talked about life's 'pattern'. Ned had been good and good things had come to him. And about bloody time too. He felt the lager gently suffuse through his body, loosening up his limbs and his mind, and he felt himself swell up with pure potential. Summer was just beginning, he was home, he was free from Monica, free from everything. It was all out there, he thought, looking around him at the restaurants, clubs and people, everything he wanted was out there and it was beautiful. He just had to be brave, grab it, have it, look after it.

'There you go, ducks,' said Becky, walking out of the pub and plonking two dewy pints of lager on the table in front of them. Ned smiled at her and she smiled back. She had lovely teeth and her eyes crinkled up when she smiled. This was so nice and normal, he mused, so healthy compared to running away with Mad Monica or fantasizing about his brother's girlfriend. Being with Becky made him feel like a proper human being, not some scrag-end of humanity left out for the bin men, someone who was only fit for weirdoes, psychos and other people's women.

'Cheers,' he said, picking up his pint and clinking it against the side of Becky's. 'Here's to . . . *possibilities.*'

'Absolutely,' said Becky, 'I can't think of a better toast. To possibilities. Cheers.'

Ned looked at Becky and she looked at him. Neither of them looked away. This was it, thought Ned, this was it. New job, new girlfriend. His new life started here.

Bring it on . . .

Ned walked Becky to Tottenham Court Road after the pub closed. It was properly cold now and they walked down Oxford Street close together, their bare arms touching, to keep warm. They were both nicely drunk and in high spirits as they walked, still chatting and laughing and getting on like old mates.

'So,' said Becky, 'which is your favourite Oxford Street?'

'Shit,' said Ned, 'that's a tough one. I think Sydney Oxford Street – it's less tacky. What about you?'

'This Oxford Street – definitely.'

'Why?'

''Cause it's longer. Got more shops on it. And it's in London.'

'So d'you prefer London to Sydney then?'

'I wouldn't say I prefer it. Sydney's such a great place, all my friends are there, the food, the weather – it's a fantastic city – but being in London, it's like being in a bit of history. It's like everywhere you walk, you know that someone important's probably walked on the same paving stone as you. Like this one,' she stopped and pointed at the paving stone she was standing on. 'Anyone could have walked on this – Jimi Hendrix, John Lennon, Laurence Olivier, Princess Di – and for centuries before that, too – kings and queens and discoverers and explorers. And just the sense of recognition here. The red buses, the registration plates, the road signs, the policeman – they're all so familiar, you know, you've seen these things a million times in films and on the TV. That's what I love about London; it's that sense of being in the epicentre of something, not on the periphery. I love it. I love London, I really do.'

She grinned at him and he thought to himself that he wanted to kiss her more than he'd ever wanted to kiss anyone in his life.

'My surname's London, you know,' he said, smiling proudly at her.

'Really?'

'Uh-huh. If you married me you could be Mrs London.'

'Cool,' she laughed. 'Rebecca London – I like that.'

Ned smiled to himself and they carried on walking.

They stopped at the top of the steps down to Tottenham Court Road Tube.

'How are you getting home?' said Becky.

'I'll walk up to Holborn. Get the bus.'

'You're not getting the Tube?'

'Er – no,' he laughed. 'I live in Crystal Palace. There is no Tube. Bus takes me straight to my door.'

'Well, thanks for walking me – that's really sweet of you.'

'It was my pleasure.'

'And see you tomorrow, yeah?'

'Definitely.'

'Have a safe journey,' said Becky. 'N'night.' And then she leant in towards him and at first Ned thought she was going to kiss him on the cheek, so he tried to turn his cheek towards her, and then her face moved a bit and he felt his lips brushing against hers and it felt so good, and he wanted to do it so badly, had wanted to do it all night, that he moved his mouth directly on to hers and started kissing her. It was all so confusing that for a second he didn't even notice her trying to pull her arms from his grip or the fact that she was wriggling like a worm.

By the time he did, it was too late.

'Nid!' she said when she'd finally managed to pull herself free from his embrace. 'What are you doing?'

'Shit, Becky. I don't know. I thought . . . I thought you were trying to kiss me . . .'

'On the cheek, mate – on the cheek!'

'I'm really sorry, Becky. It's just I've been wanting to do that all night and I've had a few drinks and I thought . . . Christ – I'm really sorry. I've really blown it, haven't I?'

'Nid,' she said, resting her hands on his forearms, 'there was nothing to blow.'

'Eh?'

'I mean, I'm sorry if I gave you the wrong impression and everything, but I don't fancy you.'

'You don't?'

'No. I think you're absolutely adorable. You really are a lovely bloke. But – you're not my type.'

'Oh.'

'Yeah. Look. I'm really sorry. I really am. It's nothing personal, honestly. It's just, you're a bit young for me.'

'Young? But I'm four years older than you!'

'Yes. It's not your age – it's you. I like my men a bit more . . . *manly*.'

'You don't think I'm manly?'

'Well, you look manly – well, sort of manly. But it's just the whole living-at-home, temping thing. I'm looking for someone with a bit more of a life going on? You know? Like with their own place, maybe, and a proper job? Does that make me sound shallow?'

'No,' said Ned, bowing his head and staring into the pavement waiting for a large hole to form and take him away from here. 'It's fair enough.'

'God, Nid. I'm so sorry. I really hope it wasn't anything I said or did. I hope I didn't give you the wrong impression.'

'No,' said Ned, wanting just to start walking now and not stop until he'd purged himself of this hideous feeling of humiliation growing inside him like a tumour. 'No. It wasn't your fault. It was me. I . . . er . . . Look, I'm really, really embarrassed, so I'm going to go now. OK?'

Becky nodded and threw him a look of such pity that Ned wanted to be sick.

'Thanks, anyway. Thanks for a lovely evening.'

'You, too, Nid.'

Ned turned and started to walk away, conscious of

the fact that Becky was still standing at the top of the steps, watching him leave.

'Nid.'

He turned around.

'I just wanted to say. You're a really great bloke. One of the nicest I've met since I've been in London. You'll find someone great. I know you will.'

Ned forced a smile and a nod and then turned and walked slowly and heavily towards High Holborn and the number 68 bus stop, cursing Gervase and his fucking 'pattern' all the way.

Tony Has a Good Week

'Ninety-five kilos, Tony. Well done! You've lost two kilos!'

Everyone in the group looked at him proudly and gave him a heartfelt round of applause.

'How much is that in pounds?' he whispered into Jan's ear.

'That's about four and a half pounds.'

'Is that good?'

'It's excellent, Tony – it means you're under fifteen stone. Well done!'

Under fifteen stone, thought Tony, a smile playing on his lips. Fourteen stone something. Fantastic! He took his seat in the circle and smiled around the group. Everyone looked like they were really pleased for him and he felt himself swelling up with pride. He was a winner!

Not that his weightloss had anything to do with following Jan's notes, counting calories or pounding away at the gym. No – his weightloss was due entirely to the emotional maelstrom that was whipping through his life at the moment. After spending so many years in an emotional wilderness, Tony could barely cope with the variety and strength of his feelings since Wednesday night.

The first and most overwhelming emotion had been his hangover the next morning when his alarm had gone off at six-thirty. Quite the most revolting sensation of his life. His tongue had been covered in what felt like a thick layer of garlic-infused brandy and his head felt like a family of oversized beetles with pick-axes had moved in and were slowly chipping away at his brain. The other emotions had had to queue in line waiting for his hangover to dissipate before they could make themselves known. Once he'd showered and had some coffee he was aware of a strange sense of elation. He felt lighter and younger and full of some kind of burning energy.

Ness had come downstairs in his dressing-gown and wrapped him up in a sleepy embrace, then she'd taken the Nurofen from the kitchen cabinet and popped four little capsules out of the blister pack – two for her and two for him – and passed his to him silently with a glass of water. He'd watched her moving around the kitchen, graceful and willowy, her ringleted hair hanging down her back, and had had to control another surge of desire.

Then he'd taken some tea up to Millie and she'd opened her eyes and smiled at him. 'Feel revolting,' she'd croaked, 'want to die.' She'd rubbed her eyes and tugged at her hair and Tony had wanted to pick her up and hold her and make her feel better. He'd had to go, then, leave Ness and Millie in his flat, both rumpled and sore and in a state of semi-undress, and his drive into work had had a sort of surreal quality to it. He couldn't quite believe what had happened the night before.

He'd kissed Millie.

He'd fallen out with Sean.

He'd told Ness he loved her.

And for that brief moment in time, he'd meant it.

The next few days of Tony's life had felt strangely accelerated, like he was on speed or something. He'd gone to work, been super-efficient, joked with his staff, made decisions, forgotten to eat. At the weekend he and Ness had leapt around the place doing chores, shopping, shagging, socializing. He hadn't felt the need to drink very much because he was so high on life. They'd borrowed the dog from Jo on Sunday and walked around Dulwich Common for about four hours and the dog had got tired before him. He felt liberated, he felt young again. The world suddenly seemed like a great big pot of possibilities. He couldn't see any problems, only opportunities.

But the strange thing about the way he was feeling was that although it should have been happiness it wasn't. It was some other kind of emotion entirely. He felt curiously disconnected from everything, vaguely numb. He felt like a character in a film, like everything was scripted and someone else had already decided what was going to happen so he may as well just kick back and relax. Thoughts of the consequences of what was happening in his life would flit through his mind occasionally, but he'd just ignore them, almost like they were the commercial break in between the action.

He phoned Millie three times that weekend, checking up on her, finding out what had happened with her and Sean, reassuring her, *looking after her.* They didn't mention the kiss, but it was there in their conversations, almost like they were both waiting for the other one to say something. But that fact that neither of them did spoke volumes. They both knew what that kiss had really been about and in a way it had cleared the mists and brought them even closer together. Instead they talked about Sean and how he was still in Catford and whether or not Millie was going to leave him and how she was feeling and what was going to happen about the baby. Hugely, vastly, enormously important conversations about life and love and everything in between. But every time he put the phone down he'd almost forget what they'd talked about. Everything he did seemed to exist in a little bubble, independent of everything else. There was no connection between any of the elements of his life, no continuity.

He'd never felt better.

And now this. Fourteen stone something. Everything was tickety-boo. Life was regaining its golden hue.

He beamed around the room and everyone beamed back at him. He felt like he loved everyone, even Kelvin. Tonia gave him an extra special smile and a little wink. He blushed and looked at his shoes.

'So, would you like to talk about your week, Tony?' said Jan. 'Any particular problems? Any triumphs?'

'No,' he said, 'not really. I've just been following the rules. Being a good boy.'

'So you've found it fairly straightforward?'

'Yeah,' he smiled, 'must be beginner's luck.' He laughed and everyone else laughed and Jan turned to the next person. He listened raptly to the stories as they talked about their week. He totted up the combined weightloss as people got on and off the scales and calculated that between the eight of them they'd lost a whopping stone and a half – and that was including the fact that Kelvin had put on three pounds. He was so excited by this achievement that after the session he could barely wait to go to Bubbles with the group. He wanted to talk to people, to be sociable.

He found himself sitting next to Tonia again and this time he reciprocated her flirtatiousness.

'So,' she said, running her taloned fingertips up and down the stem of her glass, 'weightloss seems to agree with you.'

'What do you mean?'

'Well, just that you seem a bit more *animated* than last week.'

'Really?'

'Yes. Last week I couldn't help feeling like you were a bit distracted – had a bit on your mind. But this week, well, you're just dynamic.'

'Dynamic, eh?' he smiled at her. 'Well, I suppose I'm just having a good week.'

'That's good,' she smiled at him. 'Any particular reason?'

He thought about it for a moment and smiled. 'No,' he said, 'just one of those weeks where nothing seems like a problem, I suppose, where life suddenly seems really simple and uncomplicated.'

'God, I could do with some of that,' she laughed. 'What's your secret?'

'I don't know,' he said, thinking, *Telling your brother how you really feel about him, getting off with his girlfriend and then having the best sex of your life straight afterwards with your long-term girlfriend, that sort of thing.* 'Just waking up one morning and not giving a shit any more, I suppose,' he said.

She laughed and looked into his eyes and he laughed and looked into his wine glass. He could have her, he thought, triumphantly, he could have Tonia. She was his. She thought he was fantastic. All he'd have to do was switch on the charm and he could have anything he wanted. If Kylie was to walk in here now he could probably have her, too. And Tamsin Outhwaite. And all the girls in S Club 7. He was invincible.

He didn't want her, though, that was the strange thing. He didn't know what he wanted. There was no room in his seratonin-flooded brain for thinking about what he actually wanted. All he was capable of was doing – not planning, not thinking, just reacting.

He finished his glass of wine and said goodbye to everyone. When he said goodbye to Tonia he gave her an extra meaningful kiss on the cheek, though he wasn't quite sure why. He got into his car and drove home with the roof down, music turned up full volume and singing at the top of his voice, not caring that he looked like a wanker, not even *realizing* that he looked like a wanker.

There seemed to be women everywhere as he drove, hordes of them, all dressed in that summer's-on-its-way style that he loved – glimpses of pale toes and ankles, midriffs and shoulders. Soon it would be officially hot, and legs and backs and entire stomachs would be visible, but in a way Tony preferred the timid revelations of springtime flesh.

Women turned to look at him as he drove, beautiful women, young women. He looked back at them, coolly detached, safe in the knowledge that they were his, he could have them, any one of them. All he'd have to do was stop his car, open the passenger door, let them in.

He parked his car outside his flat and whistled as he made his way through the communal parts, picking up his mail, taking the steps two at a time. Ness was there when he opened the door, sitting on the sofa reading the *Standard*, wearing really quite a nice floral-print dress with puffy sleeves and a low-cut bodice. A bottle of wine was open on the table in front of her.

'Hello, gorgeous,' she grinned, leaping to her feet to greet him.

'I love that dress,' he said holding her at arm's length to admire it. 'It really suits you.'

'Really?' she said, absently-mindedly stroking the skirt. 'You like it?'

'Uh-huh. Makes you look like a lusty young wench.'

She smiled pleasurably at him. 'Well,' she said, 'that's me. Lusty, young and wench-like. Glass of wine?'

He looked at the bottle on the table and shook his head. 'No,' he said, 'I've just had one, actually.'

'Oh yes?' she said. 'Who with?'

'Oh – just after work. You know. It was someone's birthday.'

'Well, you *are* getting sociable in your old age. Come on. Just a glass. We can go and sit on the terrace if you like. It's quite mild out.'

'OK,' he said, looking again at the chilled bottle, 'but just a small one.'

Ness picked up the bottle and Tony followed her through the living room towards the sliding doors at the back that led out on to his terrace. The plastic seats were covered in dead leaves and city dust, which he wiped away with the back of his hand before he sat down. Ness handed him his glass and for a moment he just sat there, enjoying the mild air and the sense of easiness about everything. If only life could always be like this, he thought, if only he could always float around on this super-charged cloud, skimming the surface of everything, seeing it, knowing it, but not having to do anything about it. He stretched his legs, sipped his wine, and sighed contentedly.

And then Ness went and spoilt it all.

'Tony,' she said, moving her chair nearer to his and gripping his thighs affectionately.

'Ye-es.'

'Remember last week, on the way to Rob and Trisha's? Remember what we were talking about?'

Tony felt his cloud lose a bit of speed, start to chafe against the edges of life a bit. He put down his wine glass.

'Well, I was wondering, have you given it any more thought?'

Tony took a deep breath and counted backwards from three. 'Er, no,' he said, eventually, rubbing the back of his neck. 'I haven't really had time. You know.'

'It's just – I don't want to pressurize you or anything, but I had my flat valued last week and guess how much it's worth?'

'I don't know,' said Tony heavily, 'how much is it worth?'

'A hundred and twenty thousand pounds! I've made fifty grand on it, Tony! Fifty thousand pounds. And the agent reckoned that I could get even more than that for it, now that summer's on its way. And I was just thinking what we could do with that money if I moved in here. You could take some time off, a sabbatical, we could go away somewhere for a few weeks, even a few months. I mean, you've worked all your life, Tony – you've never had a break. And I think it would do you some good.'

A sabbatical, thought Tony, time off. What a completely ludicrous idea.

'You could rent this place out, maybe, and the business could run itself for a while, you know it could.'

As if, thought Tony. The place would be on its knees before the plane had left the tarmac.

'And then maybe when we got back we could sell this place, too, get somewhere bigger, you know, with a garden?'

The cloud started grinding painfully against rough edges again.

'Maybe a bit further out, you know, Bromley way.'

And then Tony's lovely soft cloud hit a huge jagged rock and Tony felt himself being thrown bodily from the safe warm place he'd been resting for the past few days. He looked at Ness looking up at him with her big, green eyes, a lacy bra just peeping out of her pretty floral bodice, her blonde hair hanging in tendrils, and realized that his number was up.

Game over.

It was time to take control.

It was the very least that Ness deserved.

'Ness,' he said, 'no.'

'No what?'

'No – I don't want to move in with you.'

Ness's face crumpled. 'But, I thought . . .'

'I know what you thought, Ness. But it's . . . Look, I'm really sorry. But I don't want to spend the rest of my life with you, Ness.' He grabbed her hands where they sat limply on his knees and squeezed them.

Her eyes filled up with tears. 'But – Tony. I don't understand. We've been getting on so well, lately. You've seemed so happy.'

'I know. And I have been. But the thing is, Ness –' he squeezed her hands again and felt tears catching at the back of his throat – 'I'm not right for you. You deserve someone so much better than me. Someone who really loves you . . .'

'But – the other night. You told me you loved me and you were crying, Tony. You were crying. So you *do* really love me . . . you told me . . .'

Tony sighed and looked up at the sky. How the hell was he supposed to explain a moment in his life to Ness when he didn't understand it himself. 'Of course I love you, Ness. *Everyone* loves you. Who *wouldn't* love you? You're inherently loveable. But you're not . . . *the one*. Do you see?'

'So what are you saying, Tony? Are you saying that it's . . . that it's *over*?'

Tony looked at Ness again and felt a physical stabbing pain in his chest. Nothing had felt real for so long. He'd been paralysed by unhappiness and disappointment for such a long time that he'd forgotten what it was like to feel things properly. And then these last few days he'd been propelled headlong to the other end of the spectrum and it was only now that he found himself somewhere in the middle ground, in the place where there was no room for dreams and prevarication, the place where he had to make decisions – even if that meant hurting the kindest person he'd ever known in his life.

'Yes,' he said, 'it's over.'

Ness snatched her hands off his lap and drew herself up straight. 'You bastard!' she said, wrapping her arms around her chest. 'You total bastard! After everything we've been through, all the *shit* I've put up with from you – *Jesus*! I've put up with your moods and your selfishness and your misery. I saw you through the worst time of your life after Jo left. I've been patient and . . . and . . . loving. I've loved you so much. And I've hung on in there when any *sane* woman would have given up. And *now* – now, when I finally seemed to be getting somewhere with you, when you were finally happy and nice and fun to be with – you *dump* me. You even told me you loved me, you bastard. Do you *know* how long I've been waiting to hear that? Do you? Do you have any *idea* how much that meant to me? It was one of the best moments of my life, Tony. I thought . . . I thought *finally* – finally I've broken through the wall you built around yourself after Jo left . . .'

'What wall?'

'Oh come on, Tony – you know what I'm talking about. You were a broken man when I met you. But I could see the real you in there, peeping out at me. And I just wanted to mend your broken little heart, Tony, make everything better. And now you are better and you don't . . . you don't . . . want me . . . any more . . .'

She started sobbing and Tony put out a hand to comfort her. She pushed it away. 'No, Tony,' she said, standing up, pushing her chair back against the wall. 'No. Don't touch me. Don't talk to me. Just leave me. OK?'

She marched across the terrace and into the living room. Tony got up and followed her. 'Where are you going?'

'Home. I'm going home.'

'But, can't we talk?'

'What the fuck is there to talk about, Tony? Eh?' She picked up her denim jacket and her car keys. 'Just let me go. And let me get on with my life. I never, *ever* want to see you again.' She stopped and stared at him, tears running down her face, her hand against her chest. 'You've . . . broken . . . *my heart.*'

They stared at each other for a moment, before Ness turned and slowly walked to the front door and out of Tony's flat.

Tony stood there after she'd gone, listening to the silence echoing in his ears until he heard Ness's Golf starting up in the car park, the security gates creaking open and Ness driving away.

He walked numbly around the flat after she'd left. There were Sainsbury's carrier bags in the kitchen. He peered into them. Two tuna steaks, a bag of rocket, pesto dressing, two low-fat chocolate mousses, a copy of *OK!*, a Lottery ticket. She'd put a frying pan on the hob, washed up the mugs and glasses that had been sitting in his sink this morning.

And now she was gone.

He opened the fridge and pulled out a tub of potato salad and some cold sausages. Then he took them out on to the terrace and ate them while he watched the sun set and finished nearly a whole bottle of wine.

One Door Closes . . .

Ned was actually toying with the idea of having a wank when the doorbell went at nine o'clock that night. He had his hand down his trousers and had been idly fiddling with his foreskin in a half-hearted manner that was more comforting than arousing. Mum and Dad had gone for dinner at Mickey's and Gervase was out somewhere with Bud. He had the whole house to himself and it seemed like a wasted opportunity not to.

His first reaction when he heard the doorbell go, apart from removing his hand from his underpants, was primal fear. Normal people didn't ring on doorbells at nine o'clock at night in London. *Burglars and lunatics* rang on doorbells at nine o'clock at night in London. He caught his breath and then decided it was probably Gervase, probably forgot his keys or something, so made his way warily to the hall and called out a tentative 'Hello' through the closed door.

'Ned – it's me. Ness.'

Ness. Shit. Ned stole a glance at his reflection in the mirror in the hallway. He looked vile. His hair was dirty and he'd had a big zit-squeezing fest earlier in the evening and had a face like a plate of corned beef. 'Ness,' he said, zipping up his trousers, running his fingers through his lank hair and taking off a particularly grim-looking pair of socks, bunching them up and lobbing them into the dining room. 'Hang on. I'm . . . just. Hang on.' He pulled open the door and was greeted by a bedraggled but still decidedly foxy-looking Ness, standing on the door step, wearing a sexy flowery dress, a denim jacket and a strangely stoical expression.

'Is . . . is Bernie here, Ned?' she said in a croaky, controlled voice.

'Er, no. She's not. Sorry. She's out with Dad.'

'Oh,' she sniffed. 'Will she be back soon?'

Ned looked at his watch. 'Half an hour or so. Are you OK?'

'Yes,' she said, 'I'm fine.'

'Do you want to come in – and wait?'

Ness looked around for a moment, looked at her car parked on the road behind her, at her watch, at the hallway behind Ned. 'Yeah,' she said, 'OK then. I'm not disturbing you, am I?'

'No – not at all. I was just, er . . . No – *come in.*'

He took her denim jacket, offered her a drink, sat her down on the sofa.

'So,' he said, bringing her a lager and plonking himself down on the armchair next to her, 'what do you want to watch?' He pulled open *heat* magazine and read out the options.

'I don't mind,' she said, 'whatever.' Her voice caught on the last syllable and Ned looked at her with concern.

'Ness,' he said, 'are you sure you're OK?'

She nodded her head, a stiff, forced little nod. And then she started crying.

Ned leapt off the armchair and sat next to her. 'Ness – shit – what's the matter? Has something happened?'

'Uh-hm,' she said, nodding again, 'Tony just dumped me.'

'*What?!* Shit – you're joking. I mean – *when?*'

'Just now. Literally. I've come straight from his.'

'Fuck,' said Ned. 'Fuck. Ness. I'm really sorry. That's awful. What did he say? Did he give you a reason?'

'Told me I wasn't "the one".' She made quotes in the air with her fingers and laughed wryly.

'The one?' he questioned. 'What the hell is that supposed to mean?'

'I don't know,' she said, 'but the more I think about it, the more I'm starting to wonder if he's been seeing someone else.'

'No.'

'Uh-huh. He's been really chirpy lately, lost loads of weight. Been whistling a lot. Making more of an effort with the way he looks.'

'No,' said Ned, shaking his head vehemently, 'not Tony. Tony wouldn't cheat. Tony's one of the good blokes.'

'Yeah. That's what I always thought. I mean, he's grumpy and bad-tempered, but I always used to let that wash over me because I knew deep down inside he was decent – that he wouldn't hurt me . . .'

'So, that was all he said, was it? Just that you weren't the one?'

'Uh-hm. I'd been talking to him about moving in together . . .'

'Oh well, then . . .' said Ned, slapping his hands off his knees, 'that explains it. You scared him off. That's all. It's like when I was with Carly: we were great together, really great and I never really thought about where our relationship was going – I was just living in the moment, you know what I mean? Didn't really question it. And then one night, out of the blue, she asked me to marry her. And I just freaked. Don't ask me why. I don't know why. It wasn't as if I didn't want to be with her. But there was something about . . .' He strained to find the words to describe an episode of his life he still didn't understand. 'I don't know – it was as if I'd been rolling along for years and years, doing my own thing, and all of a sudden someone else had grabbed the steering wheel off me, taken control of my life. It just terrified me, really.'

'So you went off with that girl from the sports bar?'

'You know about that?'

'Of course I do. Bernie told me. She said it was horrible.'

'It was horrible. It was the worst thing I've ever done.'

'So what is this? Some London-family commitment-phobic gene?'

'No!' said Ned passionately. 'No. Not at all. I'm a reformed commitment-phobe. Dumping Carly – I tell you – it was the biggest mistake I ever made in my life. That's for sure. And I've learnt my lesson. Tony's just *scared*. He's scared. Give him some time. He'll come round.'

'D'you think?'

'Uh-huh. Definitely.'

'Oh, I don't know. I asked him about moving in together a couple of weeks ago and he was really cool about it, said he'd think about it. He didn't look scared then. In fact, if anything he started being nicer to me, more affectionate, giving me compliments. He even . . . he even told me he loved me the other night. Why would he tell me he loved me if he was feeling trapped and scared? Why would he be all super-affectionate?'

Ned sighed and rubbed his hand over his chin. 'I've got no idea, Ness. But I tell you one thing – the guy wants his head testing.'

'What?'

'Well – you – you're . . .' Ned felt his face explode, hot flames of embarrassment licking his cheeks. 'You're *gorgeous.*'

She managed a little smile, then.

'And you're lovely. He must be fucking mad to dump you.'

'Oh, Ned – that's really sweet, but you don't have to try and make me feel better . . .'

'I'm not trying to make you feel better, Ness. I'm just saying – you're gorgeous, you're funny, you're sweet, you're sexy . . . you're . . . you're . . . like the *perfect woman.*' Ned gulped. His face was now so hot that he felt like he was about to spontaneously combust.

Ness threw him a strange look and then started giggling. Uncontrollably. Way too uncontrollably for Ned's liking. It wasn't that funny. It wasn't actually funny at all.

'Oh, Ned,' she said, wiping away a tear with the corner of her crumpled tissue, 'that's so lovely. Will you marry me?'

'Yes,' said Ned. 'Er, I mean, no. Maybe. I . . .' He clamped his jaws shut so that no more ludicrous words would escape.

Ness look at him fondly. 'You've shaved your beard off,' she said.

'Yeah,' said Ned, rubbing his fingertips across his bare chin, 'yeah. It was just getting a bit . . . you know.'

He wanted her to go now. This was just plain embarrassing.

'Much better,' she said, nodding approvingly. 'Can see your lovely face now.'

OK, he thought, maybe he wanted her to stay.

And then he heard the lock go on the front door and the sound of his parents' laughter floating through the house and into the living room. Ness sat upright and looked eagerly at the door.

'Ness!' said Gerry, walking into the room. 'What are you doing here, love?'

She smiled and shrugged.

'Tony just finished with her,' said Ned, helpfully.

'No!'

'Yeah. Just now.'

'Ness. You poor thing. *Bern*. Bern!'

Bernie arrived in the doorway still wearing her coat.

'Ness. What's happened?'

'Tony just finished with her,' said Ned again.

'No!'

'Yeah. Just now.' Maybe he should get signs printed up, he wondered idly.

'But . . . but . . . *why*?'

'I don't know, Bernie,' said Ness, starting to snivel, 'I don't know.'

'Oh, come here, love.' Bernie opened her arms up and Ness fell into them and started sobbing her heart out.

Ned and Gerry looked at each other, left the room and went and sat in the kitchen.

'Well, well, well,' said Gerry, pouring himself a glass of water and sitting down heavily at the kitchen table. 'Oh move over, you dirty great lump, for God's sake.' Goldie looked mournfully at Gerry for a moment before slowly heaving himself a few inches across the floor and then collapsing into another heap. Gerry watched him and tutted. 'I don't think he's got much longer.'

Ned threw him a horrified look. 'Don't say that,' he said.

'Well,' said Gerry, 'look at him.'

They looked at him.

'It's cruel.'

'No it's not,' said Ned, 'he's fine. Look at him. He's happy – he's smiling.'

'Smiling?' said Gerry, shaking his head and pulling a pinch of tobacco out of a pouch. 'He's not smiling, you big tit – he just hasn't got any lips left. They're all worn away. Like his larynx and his corneas and his teeth. Poor bastard.'

'That'll be you one day,' said Ned, indignantly, 'you'll be all worn out and smelly with no lips. Would you like it if we sat around going, *Don't think he's going to last much longer?* Eh? As long as the poor bugger can still wag his tail, he's staying put. Aren't you, mate?' He leant down to pet the corner of Goldie's bottom and he obligingly performed a solitary wag of his almost bald tail. 'See. He's happy.'

'Hmm.' Gerry licked a Rizla.

Neither of them spoke for a moment and Ned wondered what was happening next door. How could Tony have done that to Ness, he wondered. How could he have looked at that sweet, open face, that lovely little flash of lacy bra showing, and dumped her? But then, he remembered, he'd done it, too. He'd done it to Carly.

'So – that's another double room gone to waste, then.'

'Eh?'

'At the Ritz.'

'Dad!'

'Well. They're fucking expensive, those double rooms. If I'd known you boys were all going to end up single you could have shared a room.'

'Look,' said Ned, 'there's still nearly three weeks to go. Don't write me off just yet.'

'Bern'll be so disappointed about Ness not coming now. They're like that–' he twisted his index finger over his first finger. 'It doesn't seem right, somehow.'

'She can still come though, can't she? Just 'cause she's

not going out with Tony any more. She's Mum's friend, too.'

'Yeah,' said Gerry, 'I suppose so. Here,' he said, smiling suddenly, 'she could be your date. What about that, then? You and Ness.' He chortled to himself and lit his cigarette.

'Dad. Stop it.'

'Well – why not? She's young, free and single. So are you. Double bed going spare. Seems a shame to waste it.'

'Dad! That's a bit off. They only split up about five minutes ago, for God's sake.'

'He he he. Wouldn't that be a turn-up for the books, eh?'

'I don't suppose she'll want to come anyway – not with Tony being there and everything. She'll be feeling a bit . . . *delicate*. You know.'

'What – *Ness*? No way. That's girl's got gumption. She's got balls. She'll pick herself up in time. Besides, can you see Ness turning down the offer of free champagne?' He chortled again. 'She'll be there. Mark my words. And I think you should take her. It would be a nice thing to do.'

'Bloody hell, Dad – their relationship isn't even off the morgue slab yet. Give it a rest.'

Gerry chuckled again and Ned grimaced at him.

But deep down inside him there was a little seed growing. A seed that felt like it might grow into a fully fledged crush one day. Or even . . . No. He couldn't think that. It was lunacy. Utter lunacy. But then he

thought of that wink of lacy bra, the tousled hair, the
sparkly green eyes, the brilliant smile, the infectious
laugh.

'How old ... how old is she? Ness?' he said as
nonchalantly as hc could.

'Dunno,' said Gerry, 'twenty-eight. Twenty-nine.'

'Right,' said Ned, 'right. And what, er ... does she do
for a living?'

'She's a lawyer.'

A lawyer. Shit. He'd been hoping Dad would say she
was a shelf-stacker at Tesco's or a manicurist or a
secretary or something. Something he could compete
with on a level playing field. Something that was com-
mensurate with 'twenty-seven-year-old press-pack
assembler living with parents'. But no. She was a fucking
lawyer. With a flat. And a flash little VW Golf.

Fucking typical.

This was it now, he mused, he was at that age. Every
woman he met from here on in was going to be doing
some high-flying fucking job, they were all going to be
like Becky – looking for someone with a 'bit of a life
going on'. He'd have to start lying about his age, put
himself about as a toyboy. Or just go for younger
women. But he didn't like younger women; he liked
women his own age. He had no idea what you'd talk
about with a woman in the early stages of a relationship
if your cultural points of reference were all skew-whiff
and misaligned. And anyway, he'd quite like to settle
down in a couple of years, not be dragged out to night-
clubs and noisy wine bars by some twenty-year-old girl

who'd probably dump him when someone better-looking came along and leave him back at square one. He wanted what Sean had. What Bud had. What Mum and Dad had. But he'd fucked up — big time. He could be married by now, he mused, married to Carly and halfway up a career ladder somewhere.

He sighed and shook this pointless little thought from his head. He needed to heed Gervase's advice from their night in Wood Green, start being a bit more philosophical about life, go with the flow, expect the best. And maybe Ness could see beyond Ned's lack of status, see his potential, or, at the very least, see him as someone nice to take her to Mum and Dad's party.

Dad was right. It would be a nice thing to do. It wouldn't be predatory. It would be old-fashioned — he'd be her escort for the night, her companion. Give her someone to walk in with, make her feel like part of the family and not just Tony's ex, so she wouldn't feel so awkward. Yes, he thought, definitely.

He'd leave a decent amount of time and then he'd ask her to be his date. He'd ask her to be his date, spend a pleasant evening with her and then try to apply a little philosophy to his life.

Getting Dumped in the Rain

'Ned – it's Sean.'

'All right – what you up to?'

'Just finished another chapter, thought I'd pop over – what are you up to tonight?'

'Er, we were going to go and watch Mum sing at the Tavern.'

'We?'

'Yeah, me and Gervase.'

'Oh,' said Sean, feeling slightly put out. 'Right. OK. Don't worry about it, then.'

'No, no. Why don't you come?'

'What – with you and Gervase?'

'Yeah – Gervase is sound, you know.'

'Yeah – he's all right, but, I don't know . . .'

'I know you and Tony aren't that keen on him, but once you get to know him he's a really good bloke. You should come.'

Sean gave it some thought. The idea of going to the pub with Gervase was very odd, especially after what had happened outside the house the other night. But he really wanted to spend some time with Ned and if sharing him with Gervase was the only option, then he was prepared to do that. Besides, it would be good to see Mum singing – it would make her happy. Sean didn't often find opportunities in life to make Mum happy, so it would be worth it just for that.

'OK,' he said, 'yeah. What time?'

'Sevenish.'

'Cool – see you then.'

Half an hour later, Sean was cycling through Crystal Palace towards Beulah Hill in a shockingly heavy downpour of rain. His trousers were splattered with mud, his hair was glued to his forehead and he was wondering why he hadn't just stayed at home and got on with some work. He felt a vibration in his trousers as he pulled up at some traffic lights, and took his mobile out of his pocket.

Millie.

He and Millie hadn't spoken since the night at Tony's. Yes – he was aware of how terrible that was and how he should be feeling about it. But to be honest, he'd enjoyed the breathing space – he'd almost been able to pretend to himself that he didn't have a pregnant girlfriend, that he was an unfettered young man whose only concern was the completion of his latest manuscript. He hadn't spoken to Tony, either, and wasn't sure he particularly wanted to. He had one lasting image of that night and that was the sight of Millie standing with her hands on Tony's shoulders telling him what a 'man' he was. And Tony sitting there with his arms folded looking at Sean as if he was a piece of crap – his own brother.

He'd half-hoped that Tony might phone the following day to apologize or, at the very least, to try and get things back on an even keel. Sean had said some hurtful things to Tony that night, but nothing took away from the fact that Tony was his big brother and he looked up to him and respected him like any younger brother does. He was caught halfway between a nasty sense of superiority and a deep, deep sadness that, despite all his success, despite proving himself ten times over, his big brother still didn't respect him. Sean was on the ascendant – his life had just begun. Tony's life had started and finished years ago. All he had left to look forward to was middle age and an even fatter arse. Tony, Sean had finally come to realize, was jealous.

Well, fuck Tony – and fuck Millie, too. That was Sean's attitude. He knew that this attitude wasn't going to sustain him in the face of reality, but for now it would have to suffice. And it was just about to receive its first test. Talking to Millie. His thumb dithered over his phone for a few seconds, vacillating between the 'accept' and 'reject' buttons, until eventually he bit the bullet and took the call.

'Millie.' He pitched his voice somewhere between 'relaxed' and 'sensitive to their situation'.

'Where are you?' Millie's voice was pitched at 'un-equivocally pissed-off'.

'On my way to Mum's.'

'Oh,' she said, in the manner of one who's just been informed that their flight has been cancelled. There was a long pause. 'Why?'

Sean suddenly realized he was walking through a conversational minefield and mentally waded through the myriad reasons for going to Mum's, trying to find the one that he imagined Millie would find the least provocative. 'I'm going to see Ned,' he said.

'That's nice,' she said tersely, 'I thought you were supposed to be writing.'

'Well, I just finished a chapter and it seemed like a good moment to . . .'

'To spend some time with someone you actually like.'

'Millie . . .'

'Look. I didn't phone you to argue, Sean. I actually phoned to apologize.'

Sean started. That was the last thing he'd been expecting her to say.

'I've been thinking since Wednesday night – *a lot*. We both said horrible things – well, *I* definitely said some horrible things. I was drunk and overemotional and it was wrong of me to compare you to your brother. Very wrong. I know how I'd feel if anyone ever did that with me and Helena. It would really piss me off . . .'

Sean felt a little icy patch inside him start to thaw.

'But we do need to sort this out, Sean. I can't live like this. I have absolutely no idea where I stand with you and I can't handle it. One of the things I thought more than anything over this weekend is that I can live without you. *We* can live without you. In fact, I *wanted* to live without you. In my head it was over – that was why I didn't call. But then I suddenly realized how weird me being pregnant must be for you, how maybe you feel like this is all happening to me and you can't relate to it . . .'

Sean pulled his bike up on to the pavement and listened to Millie with a growing sense of hope and affection. The greatest gift a woman could give a man, he suddenly realized, was to understand him.

'. . . and in a way, I suppose, it's a bit like my attitude towards your book. I have no idea what you're going through – it's something that exists entirely in your mind, like this baby exists entirely in my body. And I resent your book like you resent our baby. It's getting in the way of us. And in a way, we're both pregnant. It's just really bad timing that we're pregnant at the same time. So I was thinking – we need to make an effort to *understand* each other . . .'

Oh God, he thought, she's going to make me wear one of those strap-on bellies.

'It's my first scan next week.'

'Scan?'

'Uh-huh. You know – slimy stuff on belly, little ultrasound thingy, indecipherable image of baby on screen. The most exciting part of the pregnancy process for all happy young expectant parents.'

'What do I . . . do I have to *do* anything?'

'No – you just have to sit there and hold my hand and get all emotional when the nurse points out our child's little fingers and toes. Possibly cry. That sort of thing. Right up your street, really.'

That sounded reasonable enough to Sean.

'OK,' he said, 'just tell me where and when.'

'I've already e-mailed you the details. And in return, to complete this mutual-empathy exercise, I get to read your book.'

Sean's jaw dropped. 'No!' he said, without even thinking of the consequences.

'What?'

'No – no one reads my book. Not until it's finished. No way.'

'Sean – I'm not just anyone. I'm your girlfriend.'

'Look, you can read the proofs. I'll give you the first proofs, I promise. But you can't read it before it's finished. I'm serious.'

'Look, I don't know what this . . . *superstition* is, but this is more important than superstition. This is about us. About getting through this crisis. About understanding each other.'

'But that's exactly it, Millie – that's exactly the problem. You *don't* understand me. If you really understood me you would never ask me to do such a thing. Because there's a big difference between me going and seeing a picture of the inside of your belly and you reading my book. One's physical. The other cerebral. You want to come and watch me have a brain scan, go ahead. That wouldn't bother me. I don't mind you seeing my mind – I just don't want you to see my *thoughts* . . .'

'Right. That's it . . .'

Oh God, thought Sean, here we go.

'Fuck you. Fuck the scan. Fuck your book. Fuck *us*. I've had enough. I've tried. I've tried so hard. I've spent a whole week trying to work out how to save this relationship so that this poor, defenceless little thing growing inside me stands some kind of a chance of having a happy upbringing with *parents* – you know, like you and I both had. But I can see now that I was wasting my time. You're selfish, Sean – selfish to the very core of you. I thought there was hope for you. I thought maybe I'd underestimated you, that maybe somewhere underneath all the me-me-me there was someone who could share and compromise. But Tony was right: you have no idea how to share. You're a nasty little boy who won't share his toys and I don't want a nasty little boy. I want a man. In fact, I don't even want a man. I don't want anyone. I want to be alone. Just me and the baby . . .'

'Millie . . .'

'What?! What, Sean?! I don't want to listen to your shit any more. I always thought I was a good judge of character, but I got it so wrong with you. I really thought you were special. I really thought you were a decent, good human being. But you're not. You're an arsehole. And I'm a fool. Goodbye, Sean.'

And then she hung up.

Sean stood there for a few seconds, gawping at his mobile phone as if it might suddenly offer up a reasonable explanation for what had just happened. Millie had just finished with him. Millie, who'd come into his life and turned it upside down, who'd made him happier than he'd ever thought it was possible to be; Millie, whose beauty was intoxicating, whose body he'd worshipped, who he'd wanted to spend the rest of his life with. Millie of magical Bacchanalian nights at Paradise Paul's, of drug-fuelled parties and country weekends, of twinkling mothball-scented junk shops, shiny truffle-perfumed Italian restaurants and 420-threadcount Egyptian-cotton bedsheets. Millie with the skin and the lips and the hair and the eyes. Millie, who made him feel like his life was one long Hollywood movie. Millie who he'd been so in love with it had almost felt like madness. *That* Millie. She'd dumped him.

And the weirdest thing of all was that Sean didn't care.

He felt nothing. No heartbreak, no guilt, no sadness. Just a numb sort of awareness of his life moving on to another phase. He tucked his phone back into his trouser pocket, remounted his bike, and cycled slowly and circumspectly towards Beulah Hill.

'The Way You Look Tonight'

Ned looked at Sean with concern.

'You all right?'

Sean glanced at Gervase out of the corner of his eye and nodded. 'Yeah, I'm fine. Why?'

'Don't know. You just look a bit edgy, that's all.'

'I'm fine,' he said, and took a large slurp from his lager. Gervase was still staring at him. He'd been looking at him funny ever since they'd arrived at the pub and sat down. If he was looking a 'bit edgy' then it was probably because a bloke with a tattoo of a cobweb on his neck was boring holes into the side of his face with his eyes.

He turned back to look at the stage where Mum was standing under a pair of oscillating pink and blue spotlights singing 'Do You Know The Way To San Jose?'. She looked brilliant and sounded amazing but there was a small part of him deep inside that felt embarrassed watching her singing, like he was twelve years old and being shown-up in front of his mates.

'So, Sean,' said Gervase, his face framed briefly by a perfectly spherical smoke ring he'd just blown out of his mouth, 'how's it hanging?'

'Yeah. Cool,' he said.

'And how's your lovely bride-to-be?'

'She's cool. She's good.'

Gervase squinted at him and nodded inscrutably. 'Good,' he said, 'that's nice.' He nodded again and Sean turned away, but Gervase kept staring at him and didn't stop until Mum had finished singing her song – then he suddenly got to his feet, with his fag still hanging out of his mouth, and started clapping and whistling and cheering.

Sean threw Ned a look and Ned shrugged. 'He always does this,' he whispered.

The applause started to die away and Mum leant into her microphone. 'OK, ladies and gentlemen. This is my favourite song,' she said, 'it was the first dance at my wedding about, ooh, a hundred years ago.' The audience laughed politely. '"The Way You Look Tonight",' she said and a hush came over the whole pub.

Gervase leant in towards Sean and whispered authoritatively into his ear: 'This is the most romantic fucking song ever written. Ever.'

The spotlights stopped moving and darkened to purple and navy and Sean turned in his seat to watch her. And as he listened to the lyrics an unexpected thing happened to him. He started thinking about Millie. Images of her taken from the first two months of their relationship started flashing through his mind – shovelling rocket into her mouth the first time he'd seen her, standing on her huge stucco doorstep in an embroidered silk dressing-gown waiting for him to come back the first time he'd left the flat without her, lying curled up on her big antique bed with her cats, sitting at the bar at Paradise Paul's drinking lager and winking at him across the room, sitting in his parents' living room and petting Goldie, shouting across the rooftops from his balcony the night he proposed to her . . . And then another image came to him: her face that night in his bathroom when she first threw him her curveball — nervous and unsure, but hopeful. Hopeful that Sean was going to be happy about it, embrace the idea, pick her up and spin her around. And instead he'd squashed her flat, like an annoying fly.

And he hadn't seen her smile again since.

He gulped and felt something that felt scarily like tears start to erupt from somewhere deep down inside him. But it was too late to do anything about it. He turned slightly when he felt one escaping and sliding down the bridge of his nose. He wiped it away surreptitiously. And then he saw Gervase looking at him. Gervase threw him a questioning look and Sean turned away again. Mum finished the song and everyone applauded. Gervase leant into Sean again. 'Told you,' he said, 'most romantic fucking song ever written.' He tapped the side of his nose a couple of times and then got to his feet to start cheering over-effusively again.

Sean got up to go to the toilet. All this unwanted attention from Gervase was making him feel claustrophobic and panicky. He strode through the pub, pushed open the toilet door and collapsed against the sink. He stared at himself in the mirror for a while. The overhead lighting was harsh fluorescent and he looked pale and old. There were shadows under his eyes and the glint of the occasional strand of silver in among his dark hair. He turned on the cold tap and ran the icy water over his hands for a while.

'Did I just see some mortar falling out of your wall?' Gervase was standing next to him, addressing his reflection.

Sean jumped, clutched his heart. 'Jesus. Fuck.'

'Sorry, mate. Didn't mean to make you jump. Thought you'd seen me come in.'

'No,' he said, 'I didn't.'

'Sorry about that. Just that, well – I couldn't help but notice that you looked a bit upset out there. A bit cut up. "Way You Look Tonight" can do that to you sometimes. Made me think maybe the wall was starting to crumble.'

'What wall?'

'That wall we discussed the other night. The one you've built up around yourself. Remember?'

'Yeah. I remember. But I've still got no fucking idea what you're talking about, mate. Sorry.'

'Yes you have.'

'I'm sorry?'

'You know what I'm talking about. You didn't last week. But you do now. What's happened? Wanna talk about it?'

'No. I don't.' He pulled some paper towels from the dispenser and started drying his hands roughly.

And then Gervase gently pulled the paper away from

366

him, threw it in the bin and held his hands. Sean immediately got that liquid feeling in his core again, like the steel girders that kept him upright were melting. 'You should talk to someone, you know. It would make you feel better. You're in a bad way.' Gervase gazed into his eyes and Sean felt himself go limp. 'Talk to me, Sean. You need help. I know you can't talk to your family about things like this – I know how families work. You feel you owe it to your family to be chipper. You don't want to worry them. So use me, eh? Talk to me. It won't go any further. I am the very soul of discretion.

'And I don't know what it is,' he said, dropping one of Sean's hands and resting his own against his heart, 'but I'm getting this very strange vibe that I might be of some assistance.'

Sean looked at Gervase, looked into his impossible-to-read eyes and felt his brain suddenly start working in conjunction with his mouth. All the thoughts he'd kept to himself for weeks and weeks started to bubble up through his consciousness and emerge blinking into the light, and then he started talking.

'Millie's just dumped me.'

'What?'

'Yeah – just now, just on the way over. On the phone. She dumped me.'

'Fuck me. What happened?'

And then Sean told him everything, from the first moment he set eyes on her to the night he proposed to her to the curveball and beyond. He told him about how trapped he felt and how scared he was and how she wanted him to let her read his book and how vulnerable that would make him feel, how he didn't understand her and she didn't understand him.

And as he talked, Gervase just listened and nodded. He didn't interrupt with questions, he didn't even make eye-contact with Sean, just let him babble and babble – and it was one of the most liberating experiences of Sean's life. He'd never been one for opening up to people – he liked to keep his thoughts and feelings to himself. It was safer that way. But there was something about Gervase, about his touch and his gaze and his presence, that made Sean feel like he could say anything. And he didn't have any trouble finding the words – he was articulate and eloquent, expressing his emotions and feelings in a way that he could only dream about in his writing.

He stopped talking as suddenly as he'd started and was aware of the resonant silence of the toilets. A tap was dripping loudly and the sound of Mum singing outside was a distant, ghostly echo. Gervase let go of his hand and looked at him.

'You boys . . .' he said, shaking his head slowly from side to side.

'What?'

'Nothing,' he said, 'nothing. Look. Sean. I don't often give advice – well, not specific advice anyway. Usually because I can't really relate to other people's problems – I can just *feel* them, you know. But you – Jees. I don't know what to say to you. I want to say so much. But I don't know where to start. It's just – look, sorry about this, mate.'

'What?'

'This.' Gervase picked up Sean's hand again and suddenly forced it up against his chest. Sean could feel Gervase's ribs, his nipple, the beating of his heart. And then he was overcome by the most intense, excruciating pain he'd ever experienced in his life. Not a physical pain but a sensation like all the sadness and misery in the world coming to rest in his soul, like hearing the worst news you'd ever heard, like losing everyone you love, like *hell*.

Gervase stared into his eyes as he clamped his hand to his chest and Sean desperately tried to extricate himself from Gervase's grasp, but he was paralysed. 'Stop it,' he managed to mutter through his gritted teeth. But Gervase just stared at him. And as he stared at him Sean felt tears again, not puny little soppy-song tears this time, but huge, painful tears that racked his whole body. And then he started sobbing like he hadn't sobbed since he was four years old.

Gervase finally pulled his hand away from his chest and all the pain immediately dissipated, leaving Sean with just a nagging sense of sadness and emptiness.

He fell backwards against the wall and clutched his knees. 'Fuck.'

'Yeah. Sorry about that.' Gervase pulled his Chesterfields out of his jeans pocket and lit one up.

'What the fuck have you done to me?'

'I was giving you an insight, mate.'

'Insight? What the fuck are you talking about?'

'I just gave you a glimpse into my soul.'

369

'Your soul? But that was – that was *hell*.'

'Yup.'

'Jesus.' Sean stood up and stumbled towards the sink, where he splashed his tear-stained face with cold water.

'It wasn't my *whole* soul, though. Don't feel too sorry for me. It was just a little corner of my soul.' He took a big drag on his cigarette and looked at Sean. 'The corner where my son lives.'

'You have a son?' Sean pulled another paper towel from the dispenser and dried his face off.

'Yeah. Charlie. He's sixteen years old.'

'You've lost me, mate. One minute you're talking about me, the next you're . . . you're . . . Jesus Christ, *whatever*, and now you're telling me about your son. What's he got to do with anything?'

'Everything, Sean. Everything. Look. When I was eighteen I met this girl, right. Her name was Kim. She was beautiful. *Exquisite*. Tiny little hands, she had. Sweetest face – like a little angel. She was seventeen. And she *really* loved me, you know. She was the first person I'd ever known in my life who really loved me like that. I was a bit of a Jack the Lad, then. Strutting around, you know, thinking I was the business. She wasn't my only girl – I had a couple of others. I was eighteen, you know? The world was full of beautiful women – I thought I owed it to them to keep myself available.

'Now Kim – she didn't know about the other girls. She was a sensitive little soul; it would have upset her. I think she thought I was all hers. So one day she comes to me and she's smiling and she says she's pregnant. Well, I just fucking flipped out. Just lost it. Could not deal with that – no way. Seen too many of my mates going down that path, tying themselves down with wives and kids, old before their times. So I bailed out. Just walked. Left the area and everything. And then one day, three years later, I was standing outside this launderette in Eltham and I hear this little voice – "Gervase?"– and I look down and there's my little Kim. She's pushing a pram with this kid in it. The cutest-looking kid I have ever seen in my life – jet-black hair, big blue eyes, grinning at me. My son.

' "This is Charlie," she says. "Say hello to Gervase, Charlie." And this little kid who can hardly speak, you know, he's only little, says, "Hello, Giraffe, hello." *Giraffe.*' He chuckled. 'Well, I felt like I'd been kicked in the nuts, you know. I was magnetized by this little kid. *My* kid. But Kim was being, you know – cool. Not like she used to be. Lips all pursed-up, all efficient and busy-busy. Tells me she's got to go. Her *husband*'s waiting for her at home. She's only gone and married someone else. And my kid, this beautiful little kid, is being brought up by another man. *Mick.* What sort of a fucking stupid name is *Mick*? That killed me. So I says, "Look, Kim, any chance I could come and see you, you know? You and the kid?" She purses her lips up even tighter, like this, like a kitten's arse. "No," she says, "it's not fair on the kid. Mick's his dad now. Mick's been his dad since he was six months old. You had your chance." And then she walks off. And I'm left standing there watching my kid being wheeled away down Eltham High Street. And as I'm watching this kid, he turns around in his pram, turns right round and he grins at me – this big, beautiful, shit-eating grin. And he waves. Then they turned the corner. And that was it. The last time I saw him.

'And that pain you felt just now. That's the pain I feel every time I think about that moment. Every time I think about Charlie. It's like there's this big hole in me and it lets in the cold and the rain and the wind. You know.

'I thought I knew myself when I made the decision to ditch Kim – thought I knew what was important, what I wanted. But I knew jack shit. The baby didn't seem real then. All I could see was a problem. I never thought what it actually meant to have a kid, you know – *a fucking kid*. It wasn't real. I thought it was like she had the clap or something – her problem. Nothing to do with me. She had to deal with it. But I was only eighteen. You, though, Sean – I don't want to be harsh, but Jesus Christ, you're thirty years old. You've got fuckloads of money. Get a grip, man. Seriously. I don't want you to feel how I feel, to walk round with this big empty void in you where your kid should be, your kid and your wife. To know that another man is bringing up your child. Because another man *will* bring up your child, mark my words. And you'd deserve it.

'What is it you're waiting for, exactly? Something better? Because if that's what you're waiting for you're going to be sorely disappointed. This is it. Millie. Your kid. Here. Now. Fucking get it together. Fucking go to the fucking scan, fucking let her read your fucking book and then fucking marry her. And stop fucking about. OK?'

Sean and Gervase stood and stared breathlessly at each other for a moment or two. And then the door opened and Ned burst in looking concerned and confused. 'Where've you been?' he said.

'Just here,' said Gervase, sucking calmly on his Chesterfield, 'having a little chat.'

'Christ – I thought something had happened. You've been gone ages. Everything all right?'

Gervase looked across at Sean. 'Everything all right, Sean?' he said.

Sean glanced up at him. 'Yeah,' he said, 'everything's cool.'

'Good,' said Gervase, extinguishing his cigarette under a tap and turning to preen his hair in the mirror. 'Good. Now, let's go back and watch the rest of your mum's set. Yeah?'

Tea and Empathy

Tony's golden reprieve from grinding human misery lasted less than a week. From the second that Ness walked out the door and he heard the electric gates closing behind her, it all came home to roost. All the self-doubt, the apathy, the sense of complete and utter futility. Except this time he recognized it. It had crept up on him so slowly before that he'd never really acknowledged its descent until it was too late. But this time he'd been thrown from the front row of harmony to the dark stalls of shittiness so fast it had knocked all the wind out of him.

Mum hadn't helped. She'd phoned him first thing on Tuesday morning to lambaste him about Ness.

'First Carly,' she'd said, 'now Ness. It's like losing children, Tony. What were you thinking?'

'I don't know, Mum, all right? It just wasn't working out.'

'But that girl *adores* you.'

'Yes, Mum, I know she does. But she adores you, too. And Dad. And cab drivers. And anyone you care to mention. Adoring people is her speciality.'

'I have no idea how you managed to make that sound

like a *fault*, Anthony. Most men would give their left eye for a girl like Ness. Someone that warm and loyal and attractive.'

'I know, Mum, but I'm obviously not most men, am I? Look – I love Ness, very much, I really do. But she wasn't the right girl for me. I'm thirty-five years old. I haven't got time to fuck around. I let it drag on for far longer than I should have, as it is.'

'Oh, Tony. I don't understand. I really don't. I thought you and Ness were going to . . . you know.'

Yes, Tony knew what she meant. She thought they were going to get married and provide her with adorable little ringleted grandchildren.

'Yes, well, we're not, OK? It's not going to happen. I'm really sorry to let you down, but this is my future we're talking about and it's about time I took some sort of control over it.'

'Well, I'm very disappointed, love. I really am. I don't mean to sound selfish, but there you go . . .'

No surprise there, then, Tony had thought. He'd known all along how the maternal cookie would crumble if he and Ness ever split up.

There'd been more phone calls during the week, from Rob, from Trisha, from all his mates, one by one. And not one of them said, 'How are you doing, are you OK?' They all said the same thing: 'Are you *mad*? What the fuck are you playing at? We thought you and Ness were going to be together *for ever*.'

The only person who'd phoned him out of concern had been Ned. Good old Ned – God, he loved that boy, he really did, more so now than ever. Not a word from Sean, of course, and there was no way he didn't know. Tony knew how the familial grapevine worked – Mum would have been on the phone to Sean within seconds, probably asking him to come over and try and talk some sense into him. But Sean was obviously still sulking.

Tony had thought about phoning him, apologizing for the things he'd said the other night, but he just couldn't muster up the enthusiasm to do it. He'd be seeing him soon enough anyway, at Mum's party.

So it had been a bummer of a week – long, empty and lonely. There was no sense of euphoria about having finally cut his ties with Ness, no sense of joy about the future. For some bizarre reason he was only able to feel positive about the future when his life was playing itself out like an episode of *EastEnders*. Maybe he was a drama addict, he mused. The last time he'd felt as euphoric as he'd been last week was when he found out that Jo had been having an affair and they split up. He wished he could find a nice cosy home for himself somewhere in the middle ground between despondency and euphoria – that would be nice, he thought.

On Thursday afternoon he found himself at a meeting in Bond Street and decided to drop in on his dad at Grays. He hadn't been to see his dad at work for ages and felt quite excited at the prospect as he strode up South Molton Street, past trendy shoe shops and glamorous girls in enormous sunglasses eating salads in the sunshine. Dad wouldn't judge or take sides. Dad would just get him a mug of tea and talk about the football.

He walked from the bright spring day outside into the shadowy dusk of Grays antique market and was immediately transported back to his childhood – the smell of old silver, aged paper, musty wood and powdery velvet, the glitter of crystal and gilt, the gleam of high-polished mahogany and rosewood, the glint of brass and antique copper. He strode through the narrow passageways between stands selling faded theatre bills, 100-year-old rocking horses and threadbare teddy bears, militaria, memorabilia, French horns and saxophones, deco glassware, nouveau silverware and crispy-skirted prom dresses.

He recognized a few old faces from his childhood, tweed-jacketed men, hand-knitted-jumpered women who'd been there since before he was born, all with the patinated pallor that comes from sitting indoors in poorly lit rabbit warrens for forty years.

None of them recognized him, though – he'd have been thin the last time they saw him, thin and sharp-suited with an air of purpose about him, not this lost, bumbling soul in too-small chinos and a straining shirt.

Dad was just sealing a roll-up when Tony turned the corner and saw him sitting inside his Aladdin's cave of sparkling silver.

'Hello, son,' he said, leaping nimbly off his stool and giving him a big tobacco-scented hug. 'What brings you here?'

'Just come from a meeting. Had a spare hour. Just thought I'd . . .' And then he stopped when his eye was caught by a figure lurking in the corner.

Gervase.

'All right, Tone,' he said, 'how's it hanging?'

Tony mumbled some sort of response and Gervase sauntered off to get them all some tea.

'What's *he* doing here?' hissed Tony immediately.

'What – Gervase? He's just been doing some deliveries for me. Stopped by for a spot of lunch.'

Tony muttered rancorously under his breath.

'You should give Gervase a chance, you know. I know the outside of him's a bit . . . off-putting. But he's a good bloke inside – a really good bloke.'

'Whatever,' said Tony, 'but I don't like him. He gives me the creeps.'

'Nah,' Gerry shook his head, 'he's a good man. Did you know that Gervase, he's . . .' Gerry put his hands up to his forehead and waggled his fingers.

Tony stared at him, nonplussed. 'He's what?'

Gerry leant closer and whispered in Tony's ear. 'He's psychic.'

'*Psychic?!*' spluttered Tony. 'Don't be ridiculous.'

'No. Honest. He is. He can *sense* things. *Feel* things.'

'What *things*?'

'Well, for example, a couple of months back I was thinking about selling the house . . .'

'The house?! Dad! You can't sell the house!'

'Calm down. Don't panic. It's all right. I changed my mind. But I didn't tell anyone at the time – not your

378

mum, not a soul. It was a financial thing, really. Big house like that in London – worth a fortune now and me and your mum don't need all that space any more, we'll just end up filling it up with more and more crap. So I thought, sell the bugger, cash in, buy a nice flat somewhere. But ever since I first thought about it I started fretting, feeling edgy, not sleeping.

'Then one day, I'm sitting here with Gervase, having a cup of tea, and he suddenly grabs my hands, like this, looks into my eyes and says: "You've got a big decision to make. It's causing you pain. But you don't have to make this decision, do you? No one's putting any pressure on you except yourself." He said, "Whatever it is, it can wait. The time's obviously not right yet. Wait until it feels right." And he was spot on, you know. I'd got myself tied up in all these knots over nothing. So I took his advice and dropped the idea. And I've been as happy as Larry ever since.'

Tony stared at his dad, trying to look cynical and disbelieving but starting to wonder about his own unique experience with Gervase. 'Shit,' he said, 'don't you think that's a bit . . . *spooky*?'

'Well, yeah. I mean, it freaked me out at the time, thought it was plain old *weird*. But, in retrospect, the man was just doing me a favour, you know. Like if he'd seen me struggling with a big chest of drawers or something – he was just giving me a hand.'

Gerry stopped and looked at Tony through a haze of tobacco smoke. 'I asked him to have a word with your mum last night.'

'Oh yeah? What about?'

'Try and calm her down about this, er . . . Ness business. She's taken it quite bad.'

'Yeah,' muttered Tony, 'I know.'

'Don't know if he managed to talk any sense to her or not, but thought it was worth a try. He's a canny bloke, that one. He's got, what is it they call it? *Emotional intelligence*, you know. And she wouldn't listen to me.'

Tony smirked to himself. He knew full well that Dad would have made only the most cursory of efforts to talk to Mum about it. Dad didn't like getting involved in awkward situations.

'So – how are you? You OK?'

Tony shrugged. 'Yeah. I'm all right.'

'Good,' said Gerry, stubbing out his roll-up with nicotine-stained fingertips. 'Good.'

Gervase came back then, clutching a tray with three mugs of tea and three big slabs of Victoria sandwich on it.

'Oh, nice work,' said Gerry, enthusiastically eyeing up the brick-sized slices of cake and rubbing his hands together.

Oh great, thought Tony, looking at the two naturally skinny men who could easily afford to eat extraneous hunks of cake between meals. He thought about Monday evening, about the euphoria he'd felt when Jan had told him he weighed under fifteen stone. He thought about the circle of proud faces and he thought about his lovely French Connection trousers and 'Bryan' wading through the surf in his flowery shorts.

And then he grabbed a plate of cake and ate the whole thing, barely tasting it as it went down.

'Right,' said Gervase a few minutes later, gulping down the last of his tea and slapping his kneecaps. 'I'm out of here.'

Gerry looked at Gervase and then at Tony. 'Actually,' he said, 'I, er . . . I need to pop out myself for a while.'

'Oh,' said Tony with a note of disappointment. He'd just got himself comfortable.

'Yeah. Sorry about that. But tell you what – Gervase, you're off to Battersea now, aren't you?'

'Yeah. Lavender Hill.'

'You don't mind giving Tony a lift back to Clapham do you? It's only five minutes out of your way.'

'No. Not at all.'

'No. Honestly. It'll be fine,' said Tony. 'I can get a cab. Honestly.'

'What do you want to waste money on a cab for? Gervase will take you.'

Gerry threw Tony one of his 'and that's final' glances. 'OK,' he said, compliantly, 'whatever.'

Tony looked round Dad's van in disgust. Old Lottery tickets, bits of packaging, sweet wrappers, lumps of grubby tissue paper, empty bottles. The upholstery was threadbare and tatty, there were wires hanging out of everything and the floor-mats were long gone, leaving just bare metal. Gervase stubbed out a cigarette in an ashtray full of Chesterfields and roll-up stubs and then jammed it shut.

'So, Tony,' said Gervase, 'you've been having a bit of a week, by all accounts.'

'Yeah,' he said, 'you could say that.'

'For what it's worth, Tone, I think you did the right thing.'

Tony threw him a surprised look.

'Yeah – it was obvious she wasn't making you happy. Life's too short. There's no point dragging things out.'

'Exactly!' said Tony, feeling slightly dizzy with the relief of human empathy.

'And she'll be fine, that Ness. Happy-go-lucky girl like that – she'll bounce back in no time. Find someone to make her happy.'

'I know she will. Exactly. That's what I've been trying to explain to everyone. She'll be much better off without me. She was way too good for me.'

'Oh, now, Tone. Don't put yourself down. You're a fine bloke. Ness just wasn't right for you. That's all. Maybe she was too . . . *uncomplicated*?'

'Yeah,' Tony pounced on Gervase's verbalization of exactly what was wrong with Ness. 'Yeah. That's it. I like a bit of conflict in my life, you know, a bit of drama. I need someone to keep me on my toes, stop me from getting my own way and behaving like a spoilt brat. Ness was too *accommodating*, you know? Too easy-going.'

Gervase chuckled. 'Well – takes all sorts, I suppose. Most men could only dream about a girl who was too accommodating.'

'I know. But I'm different. I've got different needs. I've learnt a lot about myself in the past few weeks and one thing I've realized is that I'm spoilt. We all are – all three of us boys – in our own ways. It's not Mum and Dad's fault; they just love us so much, they never questioned our decisions or our lifestyles – as long as we were healthy and close at hand that was all that mattered to them. They never pushed us to do anything we didn't want to do and if I'd ended up with someone like Mum – someone like *Ness* – I'd just have ended up more and more spoilt. I need someone to keep me in check, to tell me when I'm being self-indulgent, someone prepared to wear the trousers. You know?'

Gervase nodded thoughtfully and pulled a stick of gum out of a packet on the dashboard. 'And I see you've knocked the unhealthy obsession on the head.'

'What?'

'The last time we met. You were infatuated with something or other. I told you to knock it on the head. And you have.'

Tony shook his head from side to side in amazement. 'What *is* it with you?' he said. 'Where d'you get this stuff from?'

Gervase shrugged. 'Dunno. My mum, apparently. She had a gift. She died and then *I* had a gift. It was like her inheritance to me. Just as well, really, 'cause she left me fuck all else.' He chuckled again. 'And I tell you what – it's come in fucking handy with you London boys.'

'What – you mean you've seen stuff about my brothers?'

'Yeah,' he said, noncommittally, 'there's stuff going in their lives too. Stuff they'd rather not talk about to the family. So they talk to me. And I help them.'

'What sort of stuff?'

Gervase grinned and shook his head. 'No,' he said. 'Nothing goes any further than me. Ever. So – this obsession – what happened?'

Tony shrugged. 'Just saw the light, I guess. Realized I wanted to be her friend, that I was getting it all confused in my head. Realized it had more to do with someone else than the woman I was interested in. I was just displacing my frustration and jealousy.'

Gervase nodded and folded his gum into his mouth. 'Good,' he said, 'I'm glad. Looks like you really have learnt a lot of stuff these last few weeks.'

Tony nodded. 'Yeah. I've worked out a bit more about what makes me tick. You know.'

Gervase threw him a look. 'You're still not happy, though, are you, Tone?'

Tony gulped and looked at his hands. 'No,' he said in a small voice. 'No. I'm not.'

'You know, Tony – maybe what you need isn't another girl. Yeah? Maybe what you need is another *life*.'

'What – you mean dip my fingertips in acid and change my identity?'

'No, I mean get away for a while. See a bit of the world.'

Tony smiled and shook his head. 'That's exactly what Ness said,' he said, 'but I can't. No way. I've got a business to run . . .'

'But have you, Tone? Have you really? Haven't you got partners? Assistants? People you could delegate to? Or you could sell the business.'

'*Sell it?!*'

'Yeah. Why not? Sell your shares. Become a director – a figurehead, you know? But you wouldn't have to be there every day.'

'Yes, but, my job – my company – it's my *life*.'

'Exactly, Tone. Exactly. What sort of life is that, then? Eh? You've done the graft, now get some pleasure out of it. Seriously, Tone – that's what I'd do if I were you. Sell up and go and have a fucking long holiday somewhere. You've been through a lot these past few years. You deserve it . . .' Gervase nodded decisively and then hit his hand on the horn when a courier on a big crackling bike tried to cut him up at a junction.

Tony looked sideways at Gervase and tried to read his expression. He looked sincere enough, he reckoned; he looked genuine, like he had Tony's best interests at heart. He looked like he cared. Properly. Like people don't tend to care in this day and age.

'Who *are* you?' he found himself saying before he had a chance to stop himself.

'Who – me?' said Gervase. 'I'm just a friend. A friend of the family – that's all.'

He turned to Tony and winked at him and Tony smiled at him briefly before turning to stare out of the window and wonder when the hell Skeletor had turned into the only person in the whole world who really understood him.

A Very Important Appointment

Sean heard the printer fall silent at the other side of the room and pulled the last few pages of text off the rack. He added them to the small pile on his desk and flicked through them, enjoying the feeling of substance. And then he went and sat on his balcony and read through the first 150 pages of his book, trying to see it from Millie's perspective, wondering how she would react to his musings on the condition of unwanted fatherhood, hoping she wouldn't read too much into the chapter when the protagonist goes home with an eighteen-year-old girl, wanting her to find it enlightening and entertaining, not threatening and upsetting.

He looked at his watch. Ten-thirty. Time to leave. He slipped the pages of his book into a plastic folder, dropped it into a Sainsbury's carrier bag, threw on his jacket and then headed for the train station and his eleven-fifteen appointment to meet his unborn child.

Sean watched the nurse rubbing gel over Millie's bare belly and looked at it in amazement. Millie's usually ironing-board-flat stomach was all curved. She had a *bump*. Not a big bump, but a definite, discernible,

Hello Daddy bump. When the hell had that happened?

Sean gulped and smiled at Millie, who responded with a tight upturn of the furthest corners of her mouth. He looked round the room and made mental notes. For his book. Because this had to go in, obviously. He absorbed the atmosphere and the detail and the mood. He breathed in deep to record the smells and traced a fingertip across the gel on the side of Millie's stomach to make a note of the texture.

And then he stopped for just a moment, blanked out the endless chatter of the nurse and the noises from the corridor outside and looked into himself, trying to internally verbalize the way he was feeling, sitting here in an antenatal clinic with a woman who could hardly look him in the eye, about to see the barely formed person who'd ruined his relationship and not knowing what the hell happened next.

He bandied words about in his head:

Scared.

Stupid.

Unknowledgeable.

Pathetic.

Confused.

Angry.

Excited . . .

That last one surprised him, but then he listened to the adrenaline in his ears, the thumping of his heart in his chest, and he knew it was true. He was excited. Impatient. *Hurry up*, he wanted to say to the nurse, switch it on, get it up there, I want to see this thing, this thing that's brought out the very worst in me and turned me into a person I really don't like very much.

Let's have a face-to-face.

A one-to-one.

Let me at 'im.

The nurse switched on a machine that emitted a high-pitched buzz and then brought out a gun-type thing which she proceeded to rub over Millie's glossy stomach while staring at a screen. And as she moved the camera across Millie's stomach, shapes began to appear on the monitor. Monochrome, ghostly almost. Like something from a Fritz Lang film.

The nurse started pointing at the screen, identifying shapes and body parts, and in among the inky blotches and swirls on the screen Sean could make out a kid. It really was. A proper kid. Arms, legs, fingers, toes, eyes, a mouth. Everything. Sean stared at the screen in wonder. This was so sci-fi, so unreal. It even had a face – a kind, gentle face with a hint of a smile. Its left arm was tucked up towards its face and it was . . . was it . . . ?

'See,' said the nurse, pointing out the baby's hand where it met its mouth, 'it's sucking its thumb . . .'

His baby was sucking its thumb.

Like a real baby.

Like Ned used to when he was a kid.

And suddenly a memory came to him from absolutely nowhere – Mum lying in a hospital bed, her blonde hair all messy, wearing a turquoise nylon bed-jacket. Dad standing next to her in a green sweater with a blue shirt underneath, Tony jumping up and down at the foot of the bed and Mum looking down at Sean fondly and saying, 'Do you want to hold him?' He'd been shy at first, hidden behind Dad, shaken his head, but Mum had encouraged him, told him it was fine, so he'd nodded and Mum had passed him this tiny little thing in a yellow blanket. So small, so light, even in Sean's three-year-old arms. He'd pulled back the yellow blanket and peered into the unseeing eyes of his new brother. And then he'd kissed him on the cheek, amazed by the sensation of his lips against such fresh new skin. Mum had taken him back then and put him in his crib and Sean remembered standing over the crib for what felt like hours, just staring at this new person – this amazing new person. He'd known even then that he liked the new baby, that the new baby was going to be his *friend*.

And then it suddenly hit him like a bolt out of the blue that this thing growing inside Millie – it was a little Ned. It was an amazing new person. It was someone who was going to be his *friend*.

It was *his child*.

Sean's breath caught, then, and he squeezed Millie's hand so hard that she winced.

And then he started crying.

Putting On the Ritz

Ned adjusted his bow-tie in the mirror and realized that it was still completely fucked up. He hadn't really thought to check in the hire shop whether they were giving him a ready-made bow-tie or one of these totally stupid do-it-yourself jobs. If he was in a film now, he mused, some slinky fox of a woman in an evening dress would walk in and tie it up for him. As it was, the only other person in the house was Gervase and Ned didn't imagine that he'd be of much assistance. Dad was at work, where he was meeting Mum, and he and Gervase were going to share a cab with Ness, who was on her way over.

He'd finally asked her last week. It had taken all his courage to phone her and he'd kept putting it off, but Dad wouldn't stop nagging him – and then Gervase had got a sniff of what was afoot and put his oar in too.

He'd phoned Tony first, just to check that he didn't have a problem with him asking Ness, and he'd been really cool about it and then Ned had finally got up the nerve to phone Ness and it had been absolutely fine. Not that he'd asked her in a 'Would you do me the great honour' kind of a way. He'd just said, 'Dad says you've got to come and I thought it would be nicer for you if you came with someone so would you like to come with me?' She'd been very gracious on the phone and didn't seem to think that it was at all strange that Tony's kid brother should be phoning her out of the blue to invite her to a party. All she was worried about was potentially upsetting Tony and causing an atmosphere at Bernie's party, which Ned had thought was classically selfless of her and proved yet again what a completely great person she was. And she'd said she was really glad he'd invited her because she'd already bought her dress for the night and it had cost her a fortune.

He pulled the bow-tie open again and started from scratch, ending up with a construction that was almost symmetrical and vaguely bow-like, which he settled for. Fuck it. He wasn't a smooth bow-tie-and-tux kind of guy anyway. He was never going to look sharp no matter how well-tied his bow was, so he may as well go for the slightly-shambolic-but-charming look.

Little Richard was pounding out of Gervase's bed-room and Ned banged his door with his fist.

'Oi – Carl Perkins. The cab's going to be here in five.'

'No problemo,' Gervase shouted through the door, 'I'm on my way.'

Ned leapt down the stairs and checked his reflection again in the hallway mirror, resisting the temptation to start fiddling with his bow-tie. He grabbed Mum and Dad's present from where he'd hidden it in the dining room and quickly scribbled something in a card. And then he heard footsteps on the stairs behind him and turned to see Gervase, carrying an enormous gift wrapped in a silver paper, wearing a lurid blue, ruffle-fronted evening shirt, matching satin bow-tie, baby-blue drapes and electric-blue brothel creepers. Ned stopped and stared for just a second, not at all sure how he was supposed to react to such a vision. 'Fuck me,' he said eventually, 'you look . . . *radical.*'

'Why, thank you very much, Ned. You don't look so bad yourself. That tie, though – it's all wonky.' Gervase came towards him with his arms outstretched and Ned pushed him away. 'No,' he said, 'I've been trying for twenty minutes. This is as good as it's going to get.'

Gervase shrugged and preened his hair in the mirror behind Ned. And then the doorbell went.

Ned suddenly felt a butterfly or two in his stomach and took a deep breath. He opened the door and took another one.

'Ness!' he said, breathlessly. 'You look . . . Jesus – you look *amazing.*'

And she did. She was wearing a black satin strapless dress with a big black-and-white flower on the bodice and a tight skirt to just below her knee. Her hair was up with glittery diamond things in it and blonde curls coming loose around her face. But it was the shoes that did it for Ned – black stilettos with diamond straps and pin-thin four-inch heels. The sort of shoes that made him want to get down on his hands and knees and kiss her ankles, they were that sexy. She was clutching a little black bag and a small gift with a card in a red envelope and she was pure, undiluted essence of fox.

'Thank you,' she said, pulling her skirt up an inch or

two so that she could make her way up the front step, 'nothing to do with me, though. I've got no idea about clothes so I hired a personal shopper for the afternoon.' She eyed Ned up and down with a small smile on her lips. 'My, Ned,' she said, 'you look very handsome.'

Ned blushed and ignored Gervase's finger prodding him in the small of the back.

'Just one thing, though,' she said, putting down her little bag and her gift, 'that bow-tie. It's all wrong. Come here. Let me fix it for you.'

Ned took a step towards her and stopped breathing while she untied his pathetic effort and started again. She smelt of expensive perfume and he wanted to sink his face in the smooth expanse of bare skin between her shoulders and her breasts. He wanted to run his hands up and down the yielding satin that covered her narrow hips, pull the diamond things out of her tousled hair and wrap one of those long smooth legs around his waist. He wanted to cancel the cab, forget the party and have the dirtiest night of his life.

'There you go,' she said, patting his bow-tie and pulling back to appraise it. 'Much better.'

'Thank you,' said Ned, his voice sounding strangely like Lisa Simpson's. 'Thank you very much.'

And then the doorbell rang and their minicab had arrived to take them to the Ritz and as Ned watched Ness swaying down the driveway towards the road in her black satin dress he decided that this could turn out to be the best night of his life.

*

'Hello,' said Sean, putting on his best five-star accent, 'I'm with the London party. There should be a room reserved for me in my father's name?'

He smiled nervously at Millie as the waistcoated receptionist looked up their booking on the computer. 'Ah, yes. There are four rooms reserved.'

'That's right. Has anyone else checked in yet?'

'No, sir – you're the first.'

They registered, turned down the offer of a bellboy for their tiny little overnight bags and headed up a red-carpeted staircase, past pretty *trompe-l'œil* walls and towards their room on the first floor. They didn't speak as they walked, just padded silently down plush corridors. Sean watched Millie in front of him as they walked and smiled to himself. She had a little extra padding around her hips, now, her arms were slightly rounder and her hair, he suddenly noticed, had grown quite long. It had been chin-length when he first met her and now it was beyond her shoulders. She was starting to look very motherly. He noticed Millie shift her overnight bag from one hand to the other and remembered that he was supposed to do something about stuff like that.

'Here,' he said, peeling it away from her, 'let me take that.'

She turned, about to object, but then closed her mouth and smiled at him instead. 'Thank you,' she said.

Sean noticed her cup her stomach with her hand as she turned and walked ahead of him. Cup her baby. Their baby. He felt around inside his jacket and pulled out the photograph again. It was starting to look quite dog-eared now. He'd done nothing but look at it since the nurse had given him a copy last week. He had it up against his computer screen while he wrote.

It amazed him.

Blew his mind.

Totally.

Sean could tell already it was going to be a good baby. He could tell by the placid smile on its face. He'd been a good baby, apparently, and so had Millie. Her mother had told him that last weekend when they'd gone up to Suffolk to break the news. Meeting Millie's parents – now that had been an experience. The private road to their house had taken five minutes to drive up. There was a gravelled carriage driveway and an orchard, a formal garden full of abstract topiary trees and tropical flowers, a drawing room, a reception room, a sitting room, a games room. Mr and Mrs Buckleigh were entirely mad, in the nicest possible way, and were more impressed by the fact that Sean was a published author than Sean was by the size of their estate. Her brother and sister had been there, too, with their respective spouses, children and overexcited animals.

They'd taken in the news as Sean and Millie had hoped they would; couldn't give a stuff about children born out of wedlock or shotgun weddings, just so relieved that their Millie hadn't missed the baby boat and wasn't going to end up eccentric and alone like Mrs Buckleigh's legendary alcoholic sister whose colourful life they'd all worried Millie was going to end up emulating.

They'd oohed and aahed over the scan as well, pointing out barely discernible features and saying things like, 'Looks like he's going to have uncle Nathan's nose, poor bugger', and, 'Look at those ankles – good and sturdy like Helena's.'

And the funny thing about the whole day had been how much a part of it Sean had felt. That was *their* kid they were talking about, their kid who was the centre of attention and it hadn't even *done* anything yet. Everyone was so thrilled with him for providing them with a grandchild, niece, nephew or cousin and Sean had felt proud and involved.

He'd never actively wanted to disassociate himself from Millie and their baby, but Gervase had made him realize that that was exactly where he was heading, that he'd been travelling a path that could potentially take him to a place where he didn't know his own kid – to the place that Gervase had shown him. And he couldn't stomach that.

Things with Millie were still a bit fragile, though. They hadn't resumed their relationship yet – they were taking things slowly. Sean was still deeply involved in his book, but now that they'd completed their 'mutual-empathy exercise' she was more understanding about the fact that he wasn't going to be around for the next few weeks. She was over the worst of the pregnancy anyway, she said. Not so tired, not so sick, not so depressed. She was actually starting to enjoy it, feeling more energized, less needy and pathetic.

At her parents' the previous weekend they'd shared

a bed but hadn't gone any further than a night-time snuggle. They hadn't discussed their wedding plans. Things were aloft. Things were unsettled. Millie was being very cautious, and Sean couldn't blame her. He'd hurt her beyond belief, made her question her love for him, made her question her own judgement. She needed time to be sure she wasn't going to make the same mistake again. And such a dramatic volte-face on the whole baby thing was probably quite hard for her to get her mind round. Not that Sean was any less nervous or unsure about the prospect of having a baby in his life – he didn't know any babies; they were a strange and alien concept. But he was ready to give it a bash now. Definitely. Be involved. Fifty-fifty. Sleepless nights. Dirty nappies. Bring them on . . .

He swiped his key card in the lock of their room and swung the door open.

'Oh. My. God,' said Millie, heading immediately for the window and looking at the view over Hyde Park. 'This is *fantastic*!' She spun away from the window and fell on to the firm mattress. 'I can't believe we're really here! I feel like a big kid!' She bounced off the bed and located the minibar. 'Ah,' she said pulling out a small bottle of champagne and eyeing it fondly, 'time was I'd have drained the minibar within the first five minutes.' She sighed and smiled and was about to put the little bottle back in the fridge when Sean took it from her hand.

'You can have a little glass, can't you?'

She shrugged. 'I don't know,' she said, 'I shouldn't really. I still feel so guilty about that night at Tony's.'

'Just a tiny little glass, then?' he wheedled, pulling the foil off the neck. 'I bet the baby would love a drop of champagne, wouldn't you, my little buddy?' he said, addressing Millie's small bump.

Millie smiled and acquiesced. 'OK, then. Just a little one.'

Sean cracked open the bottle and poured them each a glass. He passed one to Millie and then he raised his and proposed a toast.

'What to?' said Millie.

Sean breathed in. What to?

To us meeting. To you being you. To being one of the one per cent of people failed by a condom. To our baby. To being at the Ritz. To the summer. To life. To success. To love. To Gervase. To Charlie. To making mistakes and learning lessons. To my parents. To your parents. To the little bud of possibilities blossoming inside your beautiful body. To growing up. To being a man. To everything . . .

'To you and the baby,' he said eventually. 'For making me a better me.'

Tony looked at his watch. Fuck. He was running so late. He threw open the door of his accountant's office and stood on the pavement in his tux and dicky-bow, frantically looking out for a cab. He'd just had a meeting with his accountant – at six o'clock on a Saturday night. He'd planned this all so badly, timed it appallingly. But he wanted to get it sorted as soon as possible, it couldn't wait. And his accountant had very kindly agreed to meet him at his office on a Saturday because he was taking his wife out for dinner in the West End anyway.

He ran a hand through his hair and looked around futilely. Not even a car in sight, let alone a cab. Shit. He started walking down Great Portland Street towards Oxford Circus, ignoring the curious gazes of homeward-bound, carrier-bag-laden refugees from Oxford Street. By the time he'd found a cab he'd been walking for nearly ten minutes and had started to sweat quite profusely. It was a muggy evening, overcast but humid, and he was absolutely boiling.

He collapsed into the cab with relief and opened the window wide, enjoying the fresh air against his clammy skin as the cab drove through Soho Square. He stuck a finger into the collar of his rented evening shirt to relieve some of the tightness and then he pulled the paperwork his accountant had just given him from his overnight bag and glanced through it.

It was looking good, he thought, nodding to himself. Feasible. Definitely. He'd had a meeting with his lawyer earlier that week, too, and it looked like everything was going to work out perfectly. All he had to do now was talk to Ned tonight and then he could start the fun bit – making plans for the next stage of his life.

Surprise

'Champagne?'

A tall thin man in black and white casually thrust a tray of champagne at them as they entered the Marie Antoinette Suite where Mum's party was being held. Ned had really wanted to check into his big, flash double bedroom when they arrived but they'd got stuck in traffic at Victoria and Mum and Dad were due to arrive in two minutes so there hadn't been time. Ned grabbed the fullest glass on the tray and looked round the room. Fuck, he thought, Dad really had pushed the boat out with this one. It was a huge high-ceilinged room with ornate plaster mouldings on the walls, a hand-woven carpet underfoot and an enormous brass-and-crystal chandelier hanging from the centre of the ceiling. Candles flickered in enormous candelabra on an oversized marble fireplace and a string quartet played some kind of unidentifiable classical music in the corner.

This was pure class.

Ned recognized relatives and Mum and Dad's colleagues, standing nervously in clutches around the sides of the opulent room, looking awkward in their rented suits and not-quite-grand-enough-for-the-surroundings dresses. He waved stiffly at a few people who were desperately trying to catch his eye, but couldn't face making conversation with anyone until he'd had at least one glass of champagne.

He and Ness and Gervase sauntered to the side of the room and formed their own awkward little cluster, making a big show of putting their gifts on a table. They all looked round the room in awe and felt completely out of place.

'Wow,' said Ness, taking a big sip of her champagne. 'This is so cool. Must have cost a *fortune*.'

Another gliding man arrived at their side bearing a silver tray full of interesting looking nibble-type things.

'What's that?' said Ned pointing at a picture-perfect pink thing with tomatoes on it.

'That is a mosaic of spiced crab and marinated tomato, sir.'

'Yum,' said Ned, picking one up and shoving it into his mouth.

'And what's that?' said Ness, whose eyes were on stalks looking at the canapés.

'That is foie gras parfait melba with black truffle.'

'Oooh,' she said, almost openly salivating and picking one up delicately between her fingertips.

'Sir?' the man inquired of Gervase, stoically unfazed by his attire.

Gervase gave the canapés a cursory glance. 'Er, no thanks, mate,' he said, 'I wouldn't mind a bowl of peanuts, though, if you've got them?'

'Certainly, sir,' said the man, turning to go. Ness grabbed another couple of canapés off the tray before he left.

Ned felt a nudge in his ribs – it was Gervase informing him that Tony had just arrived.

'Ness,' Ned whispered into her diamond-clad ear, 'Tony's here. Are you . . . you know?'

'Mmm,' she said, nodding furiously and shoving another canapé into her mouth. 'I'm fine. Really.'

'Tone!' Gervase bellowed across the room causing everyone to turn and look at him for a second.

Tony turned and waved, walking self-consciously towards them.

Up close he was sweaty and unkempt, his gut bulging slightly out of ill-fitting rented trousers. 'Fucking traffic,' he said, 'lane out on Grosvenor Road. Nightmare. Ness. Hi.' He leant in towards his ex-girlfriend and gave her an affectionate but slightly awkward kiss on the cheek. 'You look great,' he said.

'Thanks, Tony. So do you.'

'Hmph,' laughed Tony, facetiously, obviously aware of the fact that he looked anything but. 'Mum and Dad are on their way. I just saw their car pulling in.'

'Where're Sean and Millie?'

'Fuck knows. Probably stuck on Grosvenor Road.'

But at that precise moment Sean and Millie walked into the room, looking glowing and distinctly post-coital. Sean looked incredibly handsome in his tux and black tie and Millie looked stunning in a red silk Japanese-style dress with a huge red choker and red high heels.

'Very James Bond,' said Ness as they arrived in their corner of the room.

'Where've you two been?' said Ned, eyeing their flushed cheeks and slightly dishevelled hair with amusement.

'Upstairs,' said Sean, knowingly, 'testing out the mattresses. You know?'

Millie threw him a naughty look and Ned couldn't help but glance across at Ness and wonder about the quality of his own mattress. She was talking to Tony and Ned tried to gauge the chemistry between them. Tony was looking edgy and harassed and Ness was looking calm and composed. Their body language didn't seem to imply any latent longing, but it was impossible for Ned to brush away the knowledge that if he hadn't dumped her, Ness would still be Tony's, 100 per cent.

'They're here, they're here!' someone shouted in a loud stage whisper. Someone dimmed the lights and closed the doors and everyone huddled together and whispered excitedly to each other.

'Ladies and gentlemen,' said a silver-haired man with a preposterously English accent, 'I present to you our guests of honour, Mr and Mrs Gerald London.'

The doors opened, then, and the lights went on. Everyone shouted 'Surprise' and Mum and Dad walked in looking dazed and thrilled in their best clothes. Mum's hands went straight to her cheeks and her wide eyes worked their way around the whole room, pointing at people she recognized until her eyes fell upon her three boys standing antisocially in the corner and she burst into tears.

'Oh Gerry!' she kept saying. 'What have you done, you big lummox? What have you done?!' People surrounded them both for a few minutes and Ned and his brothers stood patiently in line until they finally got to throw their arms around their mum and dad and congratulate them.

'Well done, you old farts,' said Ned, squeezing his mum in a bear-hug. 'Forty bloody years.'

'Congratulations,' said Tony, hugging his dad and squeezing his mum's hand.

'Ness!' said Mum, spying her ex-potential-daughter-in-law. 'You're here!' She looked from Ness to Tony for a second, hope shining from her eyes.

'Of course I'm here,' said Ness, 'wouldn't have missed it for the world. And your youngest son very kindly offered to escort me.' She threw Ned a smile and threaded her arm through his and Ned puffed up like a proud pigeon.

'Millie!' she said, throwing her arms around her daughter-in-law-to-be and hugging her. 'You look stunning! Gervase! Oh my goodness – *look at you*! Look at your shirt! What a hoot!'

Dad stood behind Mum, beaming proudly and making polite conversation with Bernie's verbose brother, Uncle Liam. Ned got hijacked by some old bloke from the antiques market who apparently remembered him from when he was three years old and he'd given him a bag of lemon sherbets. Ned smiled politely and wished to God he could remember the lemon-sherbet incident so that they'd have something to talk about. He drank more champagne, ate more canapés, talked to more and more old duffers and was getting to the point when he needed to escape when he felt someone tugging at his elbow.

It was Tony.

'Ned,' he said, 'can I have a word?'

Ned threw him an uncertain look. 'Er, yeah,' he said, 'sure. Is it serious?'

'Yeah. Well. No. It's good. I think. I hope. Look – let's go up to my room and have a chat, yeah?'

Big Brother Is Looking After You

Ned followed his big brother up to the third floor and felt an uneasiness growing inside him as they walked. What was Tony going to say? Was he ill? Were Mum and Dad ill? Or maybe he was going to tell him to back off from Ness because he wanted her back. Maybe he could tell how much Ned wanted her and now he'd changed his mind. Shit. He didn't like the feel of this at all.

Tony let him in to his bedroom and Ned did a quick sweep of the room. Fucking *fantastic*.

'Shit,' he said, 'have we all got rooms like this?'

'Yeah,' said Tony, loosening his tie and sitting down at the desk, 'as far as I know.'

'Cool!' said Ned, perching on the edge of Tony's massive double bed.

'Look,' said Tony, pulling some kind of paperwork out of a bag. 'I'll keep this short. I've got a proposal for you.'

He stopped then and stared at Ned in a way that just increased his feeling of trepidation.

'I'm going away,' he said.

Oh Jesus, thought Ned, Tony's dying! Tony's dying and he's giving me his will.

'Things aren't really working out for me at the moment. I'm a bit lost and I don't know where to turn next. I always thought by the time I got to this age I'd be married, kids on the way, that sort of thing. But it hasn't really worked out like that. So I'm going to get out of the country for a while, do a bit of travelling . . .'

Ned snorted, partly with relief that Tony wasn't dying and partly because the idea of Tony 'doing a bit of travelling' was totally absurd. 'What do you mean, *travelling*?' he asked disdainfully.

'I mean I'm going to get on a plane and go somewhere and spend some time there and then get on another plane and go somewhere else.'

'Yeah, but who with?'

'On my own.' Tony looked at him and Ned saw a small flash of uncertainty in his eyes, a lack of confidence in himself and realized that Tony needed him to be encouraging now, not facetious.

'On your own. Fuck, Tony, that's, well – Jesus. That's cool. That really is. Good on you. But what about the business?'

'Well,' said Tony, crossing his legs slowly, 'that's where you come in.'

'Me?'

'Yeah. Look, I've given this a lot of thought and I've given you a lot of thought. It must be tough doing what you've done – going away, putting your life on hold, coming back and finding everything's changed except you. Mum says you've been temping, that you don't like it that much. And I'm selling London Cards. Selling up and taking up a directorship. I'll still be involved but not hands-on. And I want to make some changes to the business in the next few weeks before I float it. Expand the business a bit, rejuvenate it, bring in some new ideas, some new blood. And there's one area we've never really developed properly at London Cards – fine art. So I thought, how would you like to come into the business, set up a new division?'

'What?!' Ned's head started buzzing slightly. 'Are you serious?'

'Deadly. I was thinking about a new range, say ten designs at a time. You'd have to source them, buy them, design them – there are other people to worry about the minutiae, the marketing, the budgeting, the finance. You'd be my fine-art buyer.'

'Shit.' Ned dropped his head into his hands and ran his fingers through his hair, 'Christ. That's a lot to take in – that's like . . . it's . . .'

'It's a proper job, Ned. With responsibilities and pressure.'

'Yeah. Definitely. I can see that. Fuck. Can I think about it?'

'Of course you can. Are you working on Monday?'

'No.'

'Come into the office. Nine o'clock. We'll talk some more. But I just really wanted to run it by you now – give you a chance to think about it, come up with questions. Absorb the idea.'

'God. Tony. I can't believe this. I thought you thought I was hopeless.'

'Well, you were.'

'Oh *thanks*.'

'No. I'm serious. You were. You both were, you and Sean. But now I look at what Sean's done, what he's achieved, and it just makes me think that you've both got it, you just need to find your niche. Sean's found his niche. And now you need one. You're qualified. You're experienced. You're bright. And I reckon you can be hard-working.'

'Yeah,' Ned nodded, 'definitely.'

'But I'm not being entirely selfless. I'm a control freak, you know that. And it's going to be really hard for me to let go of the business completely – just knowing that there's blood on board, that there's a London, someone with the company name, it'll make a huge difference to me. And to my staff.' He smiled. 'Keep them on their toes. I trust you, Ned. You're my brother and you're family and I know I can rely on you. But it'll be up to you to keep your job going, once I'm gone. I won't be able to pull any strings for you. If you're crap, you'll be sacked, just like anyone else. But you'll be paid a decent salary . . .'

Ned bit his tongue to stop himself from asking *how much* exactly.

'. . . and here's the other thing. My flat. How do you feel about staying there while I'm away?'

'What – seriously?'

'Yeah. Definitely. I don't fancy renting it out to strangers and I don't want it sitting there empty. I know you love it at Mum and Dad's but you're twenty-seven

now, you might want a bit more freedom. And anyway
— I can't have my fine-art buyer going home to his mum
and dad every night, can I?' He grinned. 'So, what d'you
think?'

Ned opened and closed his mouth a few times, trying
to find the right words. 'What do I *think*?' he laughed. 'I
think I'm honoured and surprised and excited and scared
and . . . *God*! I just can't take it in.'

'Just you think about it. Think about all of it and then
let's have a good long chat on Monday. Yeah?'

'Yeah!' said Ned, striding towards Tony and giving
him a big hug. 'Thanks, Tone,' he said, squeezing his
big, fleshy shoulders, 'thank you for thinking about me.
Thank you for having faith in me. I love you, man.'

'I love you, too, Ned,' said Tony, 'you're a good bloke.
The best.'

And then the phone rang.

'That was Sean,' said Tony, putting the phone down.
'We need to get ourselves downstairs — apparently Dad's
about to give a speech.'

Gerry Gets Sentimental

'Well,' began Gerry, looking around the sea of expectant faces nervously and fiddling with a piece of card, 'first of all, let me just say thanks so much to all of you for making the effort to come tonight. I know some of you have travelled a long way. Some of you have even come from east London. And looking around, I can see that Moss Bros have done well out of us tonight, so thanks for that.

'I first set eyes on Bernie here over forty years ago, the spring of 1961. She was sixteen years old and selling baubles in Simpsons of Piccadilly. The minute I set eyes on her I thought, I'm going to marry that girl. Luckily for me, she turned out to be easy. I said I wanted a nice gift for my girl, but didn't know what to get, so I asked her to choose something for me. She picked out a pair of coral earrings. I waited till she wrapped them up and then I gave them to her. Then I asked her out to the pictures and she said yes. And I still don't know to this day whether it was the earrings or my charming personality that clinched the deal; all I know is that we've been together ever since that first date and I've loved every second of my life with her.

'Some people standing here talking about forty years

of being with the same person might say, well, we've had our ups and downs; but not me. We haven't had any downs. When I look at Bernie today I still see that fresh-faced counter assistant at Simpsons, I still see the girl with the yellow hair and the blue eyes who I picked up for our first date on Piccadilly, and I still get the same butterflies in my stomach. Bernie is the centre of my world, my reason for being. She's genuine and talented and down-to-earth. She's kind and loving. She's also fun and lively and makes me laugh every single day. She's never tried to change me or made me feel anything less than a man. I like the person I am when I'm with my wife. There is no one in the world whose company I enjoy more than hers, and the only time I ever feel bad when I'm with Bernie is when I imagine what my life would be like without her in it.

'I don't know what the secret is to our happy marriage – I often think we just got very lucky. But I also think that me and Bern, we have more *fun* than a lot of couples – nothing makes me happier than seeing Bernie smile and I think it's vice versa. A lot of couples forget to have fun, to lark around and to make each other smile. But the most fun we've had in our marriage so far has been bringing up these three.' He pointed at his sons, standing at the front of the crowd. 'From the moment Anthony's little face first came blinking into the light thirty-five years ago, I found a whole new set of reasons to feel like the luckiest man in the world. People these days seem to make such a performance out of kids. They make them just another thing to worry about on their great big lists of things to worry about. But we were never like that with our three. We just enjoyed them. They had their knocks and their bumps and their trips to the emergency wards. They had their scrapes at school and their terrible reports. But we never let that bother us because we knew that we had three good boys and that whatever happened in the future, things would work out for them. As long as we loved them and encouraged them and made their home a nice environment to live in, they'd be fine. And I look at them all now, and I know that we were right.

'I'm so proud of you, boys,' he said, tears brimming in his eyes, 'so proud of everything you've done and everything you've yet to do and I'm so proud of my family. I am the luckiest man in the world – and I owe it all to my beloved Bernie. Bernie–' he turned to address his sobbing wife – 'give us a hug.' Bernie collapsed into Gerry's arms, tears streaming down her cheeks, flushed with pride and happiness, and the room erupted into applause and wolf-whistles.

Sean wiped a tear from his eye. He felt overcome with emotion and euphoric with joy. That was the most fantastic speech he'd ever heard. And, as he listened to the heartfelt applause and watched his parents tenderly hugging in front of everyone they knew and loved, he suddenly knew that it was time. He gave Millie a kiss on the lips and headed towards the front of the crowd.

'Ladies and gentlemen,' he said clanging a spoon against a glass, 'ladies and gentlemen. I have an announcement to make.' The crowd quietened down and turned to look at him. 'First of all, I just wanted to echo everything that Dad's just said about our mother. She is a truly magnificent person and I want to thank her from the bottom of my soul for everything she has done to make us feel like we could do anything we wanted. I would not be in the position I'm in today if it wasn't for my mother's unconditional approval. I would also like to say that I truly hope that there is something in all that astrology business and that my mother's generous and fun-loving personality has something to do with the date on which she was born. Because on December the first, this year, another person is going to be born. And my parents are going to be grandparents. Because me and Millie – *we're pregnant!*'

There was complete silence for a split second, and then Bernie's eyes opened up into wide circles and her hands went up to her cheeks and she opened up her big mouth and screamed like a seven-year-old girl at a Steps concert.

'And if anyone ever deserved to be grandparents, it's these two. I love you both. To Bernie and Gerry,' Sean finished, raising his glass before being accosted by his parents and showered with hugs and kisses.

Sean found Millie's hand and squeezed it. She turned from the conversation she was having with Bernie and Gerry and threw him a smile. And Sean felt himself swell up inside with pride and completeness. Because this was it, he realized, this was love. Love wasn't trendy drinking clubs, unpredictability and nightly sex. It wasn't existing in a vacuum and pretending the outside world didn't really exist. It was him and Millie, growing together, sharing, laughing and having fun together. It was family. It was this.

A couple of hours later, Tony, Sean and Ned found themselves lined up at the urinals, in order of age from left to right, peeing in unison.

They were all very drunk.

'Shit – Sean!' said Ned, zipping up his fly and leaning against the wall. 'I still can't believe it. You're going to be a fucking dad! How long have you known?'

'Six weeks.'

'And you didn't tell me?! You toerag.'

'Sorry, mate,' said Sean, swaying a little bit from side to side, as he zipped himself up. 'Sorry. I was in a bit of denial there for a while. Couldn't quite admit to myself what was happening, let alone tell anyone else.'

'So, you've resigned yourself to it, then?' said Tony, turning to wash his hands.

'Yeah,' said Sean, looking at his feet. 'Well – no. I haven't *resigned* myself to it. I *believe* it. That's the difference. It wasn't real before. Now it is. And it's fucking *great*! Look, Tone,' he said, 'all that stuff the other night. I'm really fucking sorry, all right? You were right. I was wrong. I don't blame you for taking Millie's side . . .'

'What?' said Ned. 'What's going on?'

'. . . and I just said those things because I knew you were right and I couldn't admit it to myself . . .'

'What are you talking about?' said Ned.

'And I just wanted to say – thank you for looking after Millie while I wasn't. I'll never forget it, honest.

And neither will she. You've been a brother to both of us, these past weeks. A real, proper brother. And I haven't appreciated it. And I'm so sorry about everything, Tone, so sorry . . .'

'Me, too, mate,' said Tony. 'I'm sorry, too. I was out of order. I didn't mean those things I said. I was just going through something myself, you know. Feeling insecure and unconfident. I was just jealous of you. But you've done so well and I'm so fucking proud of you, I really am.'

Sean stared at Tony for a moment and Ned saw tears shining in his eyes. 'I fucking love you, Tone. Like really, really,' he patted his heart with his fist, '*love you*.' And then he threw his arms around Tony and squeezed and patted him, and Tony squeezed and patted him back.

'*What?!*' said Ned, starting to feel really left out.

'Nothing!' shouted Sean, jubilantly, 'absolutely fucking nothing! Everything is *perfect*! Come here!' he opened his arms out to invite Ned into the group and for a minute or two the three of them huddled together in a warm, boozy circle of fraternal love.

And then a figure appeared at the toilet door. 'Gervase!' said Ned, grinning at his new friend. 'All right?' grinned Sean and Tony who were still standing with their arms around each other.

'How's it hanging, Gervase?' said Sean, walking towards him and putting an arm around his shoulder.

'Excellent,' said Gervase, rubbing his hands together and looking around the room at the three brothers. 'You boys look happy. Been having a nice time?'

'Rocking,' said Ned.

'Good,' said Gervase, nodding sagely, 'that's nice. So – everyone's happy, then?'

The boys all looked at each other. 'Yeah,' said Ned, 'I reckon. Here. Look. I want to propose a toast. I want to propose a toast to *Gervase*. The most rocking bloke I know and a true friend.'

'Yeah,' said Sean and Tony nodding furiously, much to Ned's surprise. 'To Gervase. Cheers.'

The four men picked up the beer bottles they'd brought in from the bar and clinked them together. Then Sean put his down, looked at Gervase for a minute and suddenly leapt on him and hugged him. 'You're the best, Gervase,' he said, 'you're the total best. I'll never forget what you did for me. Never!'

Ned looked on in wonder. Sean was obviously even more pissed than he looked. Gervase looked pleased but embarrassed and extricated himself gently from Sean's puppy-dog embrace. 'You boys,' he said, looking round at them, 'you're all so fucking lucky, you know that don't you?'

They nodded.

'Sean – you've got Millie and the little one on the way. Tone – you've got your freedom for a while. Ned – you've got your whole future ahead of you and all these people behind you. But most of all, you've got each other. What a gift, eh?' He smiled. 'Brothers – what a gift. Don't ever take it for granted, eh? Appreciate it, every day. Look after each other. Yeah?'

They all nodded enthusiastically and patted each other some more.

'Anyway,' he said, checking his reflection in the mirror. 'I just came up to say that number one, your birds are looking for you.' He looked at Sean and Ned. 'Number two, your Mum and Dad are looking for you. And number three, I'm pushing off, so I'm going to say goodnight.'

'You're *going*?' said Ned, looking at his watch in disbelief.

'Yeah. I'm whacked. And I'm effing hungry, too. Couldn't be doing with those poncey little things on trays. I'm going to KFC.'

'Oh, come on, Gervase. Stay. We'll go up to our rooms. Get some room service or something.'

'No – seriously, boys. I'm off. I need some meat, you know.' He rubbed his stomach. 'But get yourselves back in there, yeah? This isn't just about your mum and dad – it's about you boys, too. You should be with them. Yeah?'

He put his hands in his pockets and looked at them all. Ned looked at his friend standing there in his ludicrous ensemble and felt warmth flooding his body. 'Night, then, Gervase,' he said, putting out his hand to shake his. 'And thanks for everything.'

'Pah de problemme,' said Gervase, shaking all the boys' hands and then heading for the door. 'A pleasure doing business with you.'

And then he passed his hand over the top of his flat-top and left the room, and as the door closed behind him a shiver ran down Ned's spine.

Something Missing

Breakfast the next morning was a delicate, subdued affair involving a full English, tea in silver pots, three different types of toast, four different types of jam, huge linen napkins and not much in the way of conversation. Ned glanced at a pale and sickly-looking Ness across the breakfast table and felt a sense of reassurance and security having her there. He wanted her to always be there. For everything. For ever.

The party had gone on until midnight, then a large group of them had retired to the bar to drink some more. Mum and Dad had managed to stay up till a quite heroic three a.m. and Tony, Sean, Ned and Ness had still been drinking at five in the morning. Nothing had happened between him and Ness last night – they hadn't even really spent any time on their own together – but they had got on incredibly well. They'd made each other laugh all night long and Ness had done a lot of grabbing his arm and squeezing his knee while they talked. At the end of the night, when everyone had started feeling green with tiredness and drunkenness, she'd said she was going to get a cab, but Ned had managed to persuade her to stay by offering her his bed. Not with him in it, of course. He'd shared with Tony and slept with his pillow over his head to block out his voluminous snoring.

'What a night!' said Bernie, getting out of Dad's car outside Beulah Hill later that afternoon. 'What a fantastic night!'

'This is the worst hangover I have ever had,' said a frail-looking Ness, pulling herself painfully from the car and then clinging on to the side of it to steady herself.

'You need a coffee, love,' said Bernie. 'You can't drive home in this state.'

'No,' she said, 'you're right. I'll stop for a while.'

Ned smiled to himself. Gerry unlocked the front door and then suddenly turned around and whipped Bernie off her feet, picking her up and attempting to carry her over the threshold.

'Get off me!' Bernie protested, hitting him with her handbag. 'Put me down, you stupid bastard. What on earth do you think you're doing.'

'Oh shut up, *Granny*,' said Gerry, giving her a big kiss on the cheek.

'Granny,' said Bernie, testing out the word and smiling as Gerry deposited her in the hallway. 'Oh my God – I'm going to be a granny!'

Goldie shuffled into the hallway to greet his absentee family, his expression telling them that he couldn't quite believe that they'd all gone out for the night and had fun without him.

Mum and Ness went into the kitchen to make coffee and Ned looked round the house. Something felt wrong, but he wasn't quite sure what. There was something strange about the atmosphere. Something missing. He wandered through the living room and the dining room and then he went upstairs, already knowing what it was but not quite able to believe it.

The door to Gervase's bedroom was closed. Ned knocked on it. No answer. He knocked again. 'Gervase. Are you there?' Still no answer. He slowly pushed open the door and was confronted by an empty room. And not just empty of Gervase, but empty of Gervase's things. His guitar. His record player. His record collection. His leather jacket. His wardrobe was empty. His shoes were no longer lined up under his full-length mirror. The confederate flag was gone from his window and the picture of Elvis was missing from the wall. His bed had been stripped down to the mattress and the sink in the corner was devoid of his toothbrush and toothpaste.

Gervase was gone.

His friend Gervase.

Gone.

Ned's chin dropped on to his chest. How could he do this? How could he just up sticks and leave them? He was part of the family. He was one of them. He *belonged* here.

He shambled towards his bedroom and opened the door. There was something on his bed. A Robert Gordon album, a proper vinyl album. On top of it was an envelope. Ned sat down heavily on his bed and opened the envelope.

Inside was a card with a picture of Elvis on the front. He opened it up and read:

Ned – nothing personal, mate, but it's time to move on. It's been a true honour hanging out with the Londons these last few months, but I go with the wind, really, and I can feel it changing direction, taking me somewhere new. I've written to your mum and dad separately but this one's for you and your brothers. Your mum's done her best with you and I don't think I've ever met a mum like her, with so much love in her heart. But in trying to love you all to death she did you some disservices – she never taught you about responsibility or how to put other people ahead of yourselves. People are like cakes, Ned – you've got to slice them up and share them round otherwise you'll eat the lot and puke up. Well, not so much you, Ned; you've a kinder heart than your brothers, but you can still be a bit of a flake. I think you boys have all learnt a lot about sharing yourselves these past few weeks – just keep it up, yeah? The more you share, the better you like yourself.

I don't know if we'll meet again – I hope so. You live in London long enough you tend to bump into everyone you know at least once, don't you? So keep your eyes peeled, Ned – you never know!

Live long, live well, love much and keep it real.

Your friend,

Gervase McGregor

E-pilogue

From: Anthony London [SMTP: tonylondon@hotmail.com]
Sent: Tue, 4 Dec 2001 23:14
To: Sean London [SMTP: sean@seanlondon.co.uk]
Subject: My niece

Well you two! You did it! And a girl – about time there was one
of those in the family! Thanks for the picture – am I allowed to
say that she looks like Granddad Seamus when he's pissed? But
then *all* babies look like Granddad Seamus to me! Seriously,
though – I'm sure she'll be a stunner when she's older, like her
mum. How is Millie? She wrote to me last week and said she felt
like she was going to give birth to a walrus. Nine pounds two
ounces – that's fucking big, isn't it? Hope my niece doesn't end
up with my physique, poor little thing. Though you'd probably
not recognize me now – all this sunshine and healthy eating –
I've lost loads of weight. Back to a 36''-waist trouser now!

I'm writing to you from a café in downtown San Francisco. It's
nearly midnight and it's still warm outside. It's fantastic here. I
never thought I'd feel as passionate about another city as I do
about London, but I tell you – this place, it's got everything. You
two should bring little Eva over as soon as you can travel. There's
a spare room in my house and I'm a five-minute walk from the

beach. I'm going to book my flight home when I've finished writing to you. I should be back next Wednesday – just a flying visit, though, I'm afraid. Yeah, you've guessed it, there's business issues. I met up with a guy last week, an illustrator . . . of course we got talking and we're thinking of setting something up – a card business. Well, stick with what you know! I just can't help it; I'm crap at sitting around. I've had my holiday now – it's time to get back to the graft.

Ned's doing really well at London Cards. I keep getting e-mails from my (ex) staff singing his praises. I just hope he's looking after my flat and hasn't turned it into a carbon copy of Mum and Dad's place! And what about him and Ness?! What a turn up for the fucking books! He was really nervous about telling me, as if I was going to get all proprietorial about it and jealous! I could not be happier! I knew they were getting really friendly and spending a lot of time together but I never thought it would turn into anything else. I'm really, really glad for them both – they're both really nice people and they both deserve it.

Mum says the publishers loved the second book and have given you a new contract – that's fantastic. When's it coming out? I'll have to come back for the launch. And send me an advance copy, you fucker! I've got a bit more time these days for sitting around and reading!

Anyway. I'm so happy for you, Sean. So happy about the book and about you and Millie (when are you going to make an honest woman of her?!) and now little Eva too. It's so ironic that you've ended up exactly where I thought I'd be at your age and here I am sitting in an Internet café in San Francisco wearing shorts and flip-flops and behaving like an overgrown student. Life is strange. Good, but very strange.

Love to you all, Sean – to you and Millie and the baby. And congratulations! I can't wait to meet her next week!

Your big brother

Uncle Tony (!)

From: Ned London [SMTP: londonned@londoncards.co.uk]
Sent: Tue, 4 Dec 2001 18:15
To: Tony London [SMTP: tonylondon@hotmail.com]
Subject: Little Eva!

Fuck – can you believe it?! A girl! It's so weird! I went to see her last night for the first time – she was exactly twenty-four hours old! She's a big girl, I tell you. Looks like she's at least a week old! And she looks just like Millie (thank God). You should see Sean – it's incredible – I can't believe he's the same bloke. He just sat there and stared and stared at this kid like it was some kind of miracle. I walked into Millie's flat (God, Tone, you should see her flat – it's amazing) and the three of them were all sitting on the sofa, log fire going in the fireplace, cats everywhere, like some kind of perfect family. Almost felt a bit broody for a minute – just for a minute, mind! Mum went gaga and even Dad got a bit misty-eyed. You'd think this kid was the new messiah or something, the way everyone was behaving!

Life's good for me right now – things with Ness are just getting better and better and we've actually started talking about getting a place – together – fuck! What a year! Don't tell Mum, though – not until we've decided for sure. Mum and Dad are great. The house still feels a bit weird, though, since Gervase went. I still go in to his room every now and then, you know, just to remember him. And of course, it's really weird without

Goldie. Poor old bugger. But he's gone to a better place. And just you wait until you see this new puppy. He's quite big now and he's a total terror. He's chewed half the furniture to pieces and all of Mum's shoes. But he's such a laugh and it's nice for Mum and Dad to have something else to worry about now that I'm not living there any more.

Can't wait to see you next week. I've got so much to tell you – mainly work stuff – but it's just going to be so great having you back for a few days. I've really missed you, Tone. But I think you did the right thing going. I can already tell from your e-mails how much happier you are – maybe you can understand now why I left when I did. Sometimes the time's just right for a change. You have to go with your gut feelings, don't you? And there's no point questioning why some things don't work out – it's all part of the journey and it's where you end up that matters, not how you get there. You sound like you're in a good place, and I certainly am – the best place ever.

Ta-ta for now Uncle Tony – see you next week. And can you bring a bit of that California sunshine with you?!

Love,

Your kid brother

Ned London
Fine Art Buyer
London Cards Ltd